## "COME O[N]  MOVE! MOVE!!"

I0614926

They were heaped up together in tangled clumps, with a few isolated bodies marking men who'd tried to run and been hit before they could get away. Katya saw loose arms and legs, a blood-smeared spill of intestines, and at least one severed head still strapped into its helmet.

Kate shuddered. Damn, *damn!* Infantry against goking warstriders. Unless the infantry had some high-powered support, the contest was always hopeless. Those troops had been wearing combat armor; it might as well have been garlands of flowers. The weapons they'd carried had been chemflamers and satchel charges, thumpers and rocket launchers, all designed to knock out light warstriders. They'd never even gotten a chance to use them.

*There was such an awful lot of blood . . .*

*Other Avon Books in*
*The* **WARSTRIDER** *Series by*
**William H. Keith, Jr.**

WARSTRIDER
WARSTRIDER: REBELLION

Avon Books are available at special quantity discounts for bulk purchases for sales promotions, premiums, fund raising or educational use. Special books, or book excerpts, can also be created to fit specific needs.

For details write or telephone the office of the Director of Special Markets, Avon Books, Dept. FP, 1350 Avenue of the Americas, New York, New York 10019, 1-800-238-0658.

# WARSTRIDER

## JACKERS

WILLIAM H. KEITH, JR.

AVON BOOKS • NEW YORK

If you purchased this book without a cover, you should be aware that this book is stolen property. It was reported as "unsold and destroyed" to the publisher, and neither the author nor the publisher has received any payment for this "stripped book."

WARSTRIDER: JACKERS is an original publication of Avon Books. This work has never before appeared in book form. This work is a novel. Any similarity to actual persons or events is purely coincidental.

AVON BOOKS
A division of
The Hearst Corporation
1350 Avenue of the Americas
New York, New York 10019

Copyright © 1994 by William H. Keith, Jr.
Cover art by Dorian Vallejo
Published by arrangement with the author
Library of Congress Catalog Card Number: 94-94313
ISBN: 0-380-77591-3

All rights reserved, which includes the right to reproduce this book or portions thereof in any form whatsoever except as provided by the U.S. Copyright Law. For information address The Ethan Ellenberg Literary Agency, 548 Broadway, #5-E, New York, New York 10012.

First AvoNova Printing: November 1994

AVONOVA TRADEMARK REG. U.S. PAT. OFF. AND IN OTHER COUNTRIES, MARCA REGISTRADA, HECHO EN U.S.A.

Printed in the U.S.A.

RA   10  9  8  7  6  5  4  3  2  1

# Prologue

It was the celebration of the new year, the first day of the month of *Sho-gatsu*, and the celebrations were in full swing throughout the vast, slow-turning wheel that was Tenno Kyuden, the Palace of Heaven. His Divine Majesty, the Emperor of Man, had left the parties and ceremonials early, however, retiring to his private quarters. Now, he floated alone in space, the stars of the *Shichiju* scattered about him, colored motes in emptiness. That vista of suns adrift against the fog-glowing band of the Milky Way was illusion, of course, a ViReality given form and texture by the AIs that governed the palace, but the Emperor found it a useful one, a way of putting into perspective his own relative unimportance against the sweep and glory of the galactic backdrop.

There were many among his subjects who thought of the Emperor as a god ... though Shiginori Konoye the man was all too aware of his own frailty. In the eighty-fifth year of his reign, which he had called *Fushi*, an era-name meaning Immortality, he was 181 Terran Standard years old. With medical nangineering and the antisenescence meteffectors coursing through his veins, cleaning, rebuilding, and repairing, there was theoretically no limit to the years of additional life he could expect. Expecting, however, was one thing. *Wanting* was something else.

Shiginori Konoye was tired.

With most of his life passing here within the Imperial Court at Tenno Kyuden, the synchorbital Palace of Heaven perched atop the Singapore Sky-el, Shiginori had been raised from childhood in the understanding that government was Imperial Nihon's duty and burden in the great tapestry of the cosmos.

When the West had abandoned space travel five centuries earlier, a Nihon barely recovered from the ravages of war had stepped in, picked up the standard of Man's ascent to space, and carried it on. Within fifty years, the economic strength rising from orbital factories and Lunar mines, not to mention the strategic advantages bestowed by orbital battle stations and laser platforms, had made Nihon the dominant power on the planet, a superpower easily able to assert control over Earth's impoverished, warring nations.

The result had been the Terran Hegemony, fifty-seven nations joined together within the benevolent embrace of the *Teikokuno Heiwa*, the Imperial Peace. And when the K-T drive opened the worlds of other stars to terraforming and exploitation, the colonies of dozens of those nation-states had of course been added to the Hegemony. The Shichiju—the name meant "the Seventy" and was a little out of date for that reason—now embraced seventy-eight inhabited worlds in seventy-two star systems, these motes drifting now just beyond the silken hem of Shiginori's *haori*.

If the rule of Nihon over the Hegemony seemed only right and natural to Shiginori, so, too, did the Hegemony's acceptance of that rule. It was for that reason that the Emperor of Man had been so surprised at the sharp and sudden flame of rebellion.

It was beyond understanding, really. Rising tensions, the appearance of agitators and rioting mobs on worlds as far removed as New America and Rainbow, had preceded the creation of something called the Network, a rebel underground dedicated, it seemed, to tearing the Hegemony asunder. The latest reports suggested that at least five worlds of the Shichiju, and possibly many more, were about to join together in a confederacy, with Network organizers forming the new government. At the same time, riots and protests had exploded at last into open conflict; the first battle of civil war had already been fought, at a world called Eridu some twenty-five light-years from Earth.

*Nairan*—civil war. The very concept was unthinkable in a regime that had ruled in peace for centuries.

The problem, the Emperor thought, lay in the differences between the *Nihonjin*, the Japanese people, and the *gaijin*, the foreigners they governed. Raised with the twin concepts of *Kodo*, the Imperial Way, and *on*, their moral obligation to emperor and parents, the Japanese possessed an inner discipline that foreigners did not.

The stars, the blackness of space itself, dissolved around the Emperor. Startled, he looked around. He'd issued no mental command, and yet the virtual reality projected within his mind had changed. Trees, grass, cobblestone paths, and familiar buildings materialized around him, and he felt again the tug of gravity. He recognized this place, though he'd walked its gardens only a few times, during rare trips back to Earth. This was the shrine of Tsurugaoka at Kamakura, a holy place dedicated to Hachiman, God of War.

Concentrating, he issued orders through his cephlink, attempting to end the simulation, to break linkage, but nothing happened. Taking an unsteady step backward, he felt the rough bark of a gnarled and ancient ginkgo tree press against his spine. The scent of cherry blossoms filled his nostrils.

"What is the meaning of this?" he called. *Someone* must be monitoring this ViRscene, must be listening to his words. Who?

He thought he already knew *why*. . . .

"*Tenno-heika*," a voice said beside him. "Your Imperial Majesty. . . ."

Turning to his left he saw *Gensui* Tadashi Ikeda standing a few meters away in his spotless, Imperial Navy dress whites. The Fleet Admiral bowed deeply, and when he raised his eyes again, his gaze went no higher than the Emperor's throat.

"Ah, *Ikedasan*," the Emperor said slowly. "I would be interested in knowing how you managed to override my personal AI."

"Such things can be accomplished, Your Majesty, when there is great need. As now."

Again, the Emperor tried to disconnect. This scene was *not* real. It was ViRdrama, a dream played out inside his brain by the software of a sophisticated artificial intelligence. His body lay safe in the Palace of Heaven, secure within its duralloy crypt. All he had to do was *wake up*. . . .

But he could not. "What is it you want?"

"I am sure you can guess, Your Majesty. I am most sorry."

"So. Is the condemned man to know the reason for his execution? For his assassination?"

Again, Ikeda bowed. "That is why I am here, Your Majesty."

"Munimori sent you, I suppose."

"*Gensui* Munimori and I drew lots. This honor fell to me, though I am unworthy."

"Indeed." The Emperor waited, expressionless, forcing his assassin to volunteer the information rather than losing face by asking. His expression was that of *shiran kao*, the nonchalant face, revealing nothing.

"I speak for the *Kansei no Otoko*," Ikeda said. "The Men of Completion. They feel that your policies of admitting *gaijin* to the Imperial Navy, to the Imperial Council itself, have done terrible harm to the Empire and are in part responsible for our defeat at Eridu. Worse, you do not comport yourself as . . . as a god should."

The accusation forced a smile from the Emperor, despite his *shiran kao*. The Japanese idea of a "god" was vastly different from that of most Westerners; most Japanese still thought of their parents as "gods" and revered the emperor as a similar god, one slightly higher in the celestial hierarchy.

But a few, the Men of Completion among them, took the idea that the emperor was descended from the Sun Goddess Ameratsu far more seriously.

Did that seriousness actually extend to the murder of the god they claimed to revere?

He took a breath to reply . . . and found his breathing blocked, as though an invisible, silken cord had tightened around his throat. "*Tawakeru na*," he managed to say. "Stop playing the fool!" The cord tightened, the pressure building though it did not bite into his skin. Pain was growing in his chest as well, a burning, crushing pain that arced down his left arm.

*Pain!* Normally, purely physical sensations could not cross the ViReality barrier. That his link was passing them through now was a kind of emergency warning, an indication that his body was in serious danger. He tried to raise his hands, but they dangled useless at his sides. Again he accessed his cephlink, calling for help.

"Your cephlink has been isolated, Your Majesty. I control the AI now, and I have directed it to shut down your breathing and your heart. You will not suffer for long, I promise." Ikeda paused, his image licking its lips. "They will find your body in the palace," he continued. "You will have committed *seppuku*. Your death poem will apologize for your causing civil war and disorder in your realm."

"Who . . . will . . . be emperor? . . ."

"Your nephew and heir, your Majesty. Ichiro Takeda."

"But . . . he's . . . not . . ."

"I very much regret to tell you that Prince Okada, your son and first heir, will also be found dead, by his own hand. Possibly because of grief at the news of your death."

*Iye* . . . Denial flooded the Emperor's mind, a pain worse than the agony in his chest. *No . . . no . . .* Takeda was an empty-headed idiot, a pawn in the hands of Munimori and the other plotters. Evidently, that was what the Men of Completion were counting on.

Then the Tsurugaoka shrine dissolved into darkness, and the Emperor of Man floated once more, adrift in the endless, peaceful night.

# Chapter 1

*To Western sensibilities, the tea ceremony is alien, flat, and lifeless. To Nihonjin, however, each motion, each aspect is charged with subtle meaning, providing aesthetic stimulation, refreshment, and the well-being and security of time-honored ritual. Here, surely, is the soul of Zen, understatement speaking directly to the mind.*

—*Japan: From the Past to Tomorrow*
Frank Harrison
C.E. 2045

All of Earth was in mourning for *Tenno-heika*, the Fushi Emperor, the Emperor of Man. His body had been returned down the Singapore Sky-el, then placed in funeral procession aboard the Imperial hydrofoil yacht *Manaduru* for the voyage across the South China Sea and final cremation according to Shinto rite at the Imperial shrine at Kyoto.

If there was irony that the Fushi Emperor was dead— after all his *nengo*, or era-name, meant Immortality—

7

none cared to comment openly. Even nation-states of the Hegemony that did not accept the godhood of the man occupying the Chrysanthemum Throne recognized that they had lost a friend and advocate, for the twin suicides of Konoye and his only son, his first heir, all but guaranteed that the recent trend toward including non-Japanese in Imperial affairs would quickly cease.

The Fushi Emperor's successor ascended to the Chrysanthemum Throne within the Tenno Kyuden on the fourth day of *Sho-gatsu*, the first month of the Common Era year 2543. Ichiro Takeda had already chosen *Tenrai* for his era-name, a poetic form meaning Heavenly Thunder. There was sharp symbolism in the choice; where the Fushi Emperor had striven for long-lasting stability, for the immortality of Empire and Emperor alike, the Tenrai Emperor would proclaim once again the power of heaven above the Earth and all the widely scattered family of Man. *Tenno-heika Tenrai* would be more god than man, elevated above the affairs of mortals, as befitted his station.

And he would be the warning thunder that would bring the squabbling enemies of the Imperial peace to heel.

The Nihongo word *gensui*, meaning Fleet Admiral, was both rank and title. *Gensui* Yasuhiro Munimori, commander of the Imperial First Fleet and Chief of the Emperor's Personal Military Staff, nodded politely, a restrained formal response to his visitor's bow. Munimori was a large and imposing man, his torso layered with slabs of fat and muscle that reminded *Chujo* Tetsu Kawashima of the man-mountain bulk of a sumo wrestler.

Approaching the Fleet Admiral, Kawashima thought, was much like seeking audience with a mountain, and often as productive. Munimori was a man who set his own course, who told others what he expected of them, and who rarely changed his mind simply because others of lesser rank dared to contradict him. Such contradictions were increasingly rare these days, for with his accession to Imperial Chief of Staff, there were few who could challenge his political position, and fewer still who would.

Vice Admiral Kawashima had been an Imperial Navy officer for nearly forty years, had reached his current position of Fleet Squadron Commander after serving four years as commander of a Fleet Carrier Group. He resented the rapid rise of younger men like Munimori, who'd been a junior *tai-i*, a navy lieutenant, back when Kawashima had been commanding his first ship, and he mistrusted their ambition. Still, with Kawashima now commanding the First Fleet's *Ohka*, or Cherry Blossom Squadron, Munimori was Kawashima's direct superior, and duty, honor, and the ancient demands of bushido all required unquestioning obedience.

"*Konichiwa*, Kawashima*san*," Munimori said, his voice a rumble from somewhere deep within his vast belly. A hand gesture dismissed the genegineered female servant who'd ushered Kawashima through the door. "Welcome to my home."

"*Konichiwa, Gensuisama*. I am most honored."

"Please, come. I have ordered *o-cha* for us."

Kawashima knew that Munimori had orders for him but had no idea what they might be. He'd certainly not been expecting an invitation to the Fleet Admiral's private residence within the Tenno Kyuden wheel. As he glanced about the anteroom, he was struck by the modest and restrained taste of his host, by the decor that a *gaijin* might call Minimalist. The Nihongo word for it was *shibui*, a word that meant the astringent pucker to the mouth caused by just-ripened persimmons. Bare walls, patterned after the quiet beauty of the lattice and paper *shoji* of a traditional house, woven *tatami* on the floors, gentle lighting from no visible source, these were the surroundings of a well-to-do merchant, perhaps, not a *daimyo* of the Empire. The only visible indicators of true wealth were the servants—humans rather than robots, and the women showing the too-perfect beauty of genegineered *ningyo*.

*Munimori must want something exceptional,* Kawashima thought as he followed the big man deeper into the warrens of his private residence. He had never known the Fleet Admiral to show such generosity to anyone save, possibly, to the highest ranking *daimyos* of the Imperial government.

Most of the senior Imperial military officers maintained quarters here within the slowly rotating Palace of Heaven, close by the Chrysanthemum Throne itself. Munimori's residence was located at the one-sixth-G level of the Tenno Kyuden wheel, and the lesser gravity—about what one would experience on the Moon—obviously was to his liking. He moved with an oddly graceful, sliding walk that carried his mass with surprising speed along the smooth, slightly curving floors, and Kawashima had to hurry—carefully for fear of falling and losing face—to keep up. He doubted that the big man would be able to stand in a full gravity.

They stopped in an austerely spartan room—but not the one reserved for the tea ceremony. There were no furnishings at all save a *tatami* on the floor, an antique sword rack, and a peculiar, twisting *inochi-zo* by itself in a small alcove.

"Please wait here," his host commanded, and Kawashima was left alone.

He was drawn at once to the *inochi-zo*, a "life-statue" standing perhaps a third of a meter tall. Like some obscene plant, it grew from a pot of soil, but it appeared to be sculpted of living flesh, an exquisitely delicate homunculus crafted by a genegineer's art. Its overall form was that of a nude man, but the limbs bent and folded about its artistically twisted torso, a part of the body they embraced. Lacking a head, the creature's face had been grafted onto a broadened chest; the mouth gaped in a voiceless, breathless, and eternal scream, while the living eyes followed Kawashima's every move.

He'd heard of such things, of course, but had never seen one, for they were quite rare and extraordinarily expensive. Though each was unique, as befitted a work of art, they reputedly fell into one of two classes, the *tanoshimi-zo*, which lived in continual orgasmic pleasure, and their dark counterparts, the *kurushimi-zo*, for which simply existence was unending agony.

This one, obviously, was in pain. Kawashima stared into those pleading eyes—their irises were pale blue—and shuddered. It seemed as though he was looking into twin wells of bottomless, endless horror.

"I am very proud of that one," Munimori said at his back. Kawashima started. He'd not heard the admiral's return.

"It is . . . most interesting. . . ."

"One of Tsuru's finest masterpieces."

"Ah." Dr. Masanori Tsuru had been one of the greatest of all Nihon's geneshapers, artists who used DNA as canvas and paint to craft living art forms of flesh, blood, and brain. "If this is one of his, my lord, it must be very old."

"Almost ninety years. Still, I'm told it might live for centuries more. I hope so. I find it a most personal statement about Man's eternal suffering beneath the Great Wheel." Paternally, he laid a hand on the thing's hunched and headless shoulders. Kawashima saw the flesh crawl and tremble beneath his touch. "Over ninety percent of this one's genotype is pure human. Its nervous system has been tuned to transmit constant pain, something roughly on a level, I understand, with being burned alive except that the pain never overloads the organism's brain and senses and never dulls. Its brain is fully functional, and according to its papers it was link-educated so that it could, ah, fully appreciate its predicament. That adds so much to the work's meaning, you know. It is not simply a live sculpture, something pretty to look at, but a thinking, knowing soul trapped in a living hell."

Kawashima felt dizzy, and the pale walls of the sparsely furnished room seemed to be closing in around him. *Why?* he wanted to ask, but to demand an explanation for this twisted horror would be to insult his host.

"Can . . . it speak?"

"Oh, no. No lungs, no voice box. The mouth is purely art. I have to provide it with a special nutrient each day, watering it like a plant, or it would lapse into a coma and die. The ears are functional, however. It can hear us and understand what we say. Beautiful, is it not?"

"Remarkable, my lord."

"Actually, I suspect that after ninety years, it must be quite mad. But just look at those eyes. Mad or not, it still *feels*, after all this time! Occasionally I speak to it, promising release for it, one day. I don't know if it believes me or not, but I permit myself the small conceit that it must continue to *hope*, through year after year of unendurable agony. Tell me, *Chujosan*. Do you believe in the transmigration of souls?"

The sudden change of topic left Kawashima off-balance. "I . . . I have never thought about it, *Munimorisama*. I have never considered myself a religious man. I am not sure that I believe in souls."

"So. A practical, pragmatic man, *neh?* Well, I believe. I have seen too much *not* to believe. I sometimes wonder if, by providing the gene-tailored shells of the *inochizo*, we are not providing homes for the spirits of truly wicked men, men being punished for unimaginable sins in past lives." He slapped the bare flesh with a meaty smack, and it writhed soundlessly as his hand lifted. "Perhaps after a small eternity of suffering here, of providing us with spiritual instruction, the way will be clear for this one's final translation to Nirvana. Perhaps some pain here and now will be accepted later with joy, once the Great Wheel's cycle is broken."

Kawashima tried to formulate a polite response and

failed. He felt trapped by those shifting, pain-filled eyes that begged him, soundlessly, for what he could not give, for what Munimori refused to grant. What kind of mind, he wondered, found fulfillment and contemplation in such a sight?

"I have two orders for you, *Chujosan*." Munimori's tone was brusque now, all business. "One for general circulation, the second for you alone."

Stiff-armed, Munimori held out two message disks. Bowing, Kawashima accepted them. Pressing the first against the link circuitry embedded in his left palm, he felt the trickle of data feeding from the disk to his cephlink RAM. As he downloaded a keyword, the message decoded itself, expanding within his mind's eye for his inspection.

The message was short, an Imperial edict under Munimori's seal . . . and from its content, Kawashima was certain that Munimori had been the original author. It was blunt and to the point, calling for the resignation of all naval line officers who were not birth-citizens of *Dai Nihon*, the "Greater Japan" that included territorial enclaves such as the Philippines, Singapore, and the old Pacific Northwest, as well as the original home islands.

Kawashima had been expecting such an order ever since hearing of the Fushi Emperor's death. Many of his *gaijin* officers had already offered their resignations, knowing the mind of the new power behind the Chrysanthemum Throne.

"Will the first order present difficulties, *Chujosan?*"

"There will be no problem, *Munimorisama*. It will be welcome to many of my people."

"Good. Please take the second order, and examine the introduction."

Pressing the second disk to the flesh and circuit wiring of his palm, Kawashima felt the flow of a much longer document downloading into his cephlink RAM. This, he realized, must include fleet orders, complete with individual ship deployments and logistical directives. As he

decoded the document's first level and scanned its pre-
amble, he knew his guess was correct. Ohka Squadron
was being sent to war.

"How accurate is this information?" Kawashima asked,
his eyes closed as he read the words hanging before his
inner eye.

"Completely," the Fleet Admiral replied. "We have
long known of the rebel activities on New America
and have agents in place there, monitoring the political
situation."

Filing the document, Kawashima opened his eyes.
"This is most unexpected, *Munimorisama*. I was expecting orders for Chi Draconis."

Chi Draconis V—Eridu—had recently joined the growing list of Frontier worlds attempting to cut free from the
Terran Hegemony.

Munimori was frowning. "The situation at Eridu is
stable for the moment. The planet's surface and orbital
facilities are still in the hands of rebels, but an Imperial
squadron from Hariti has arrived and taken up orbit. A
truce is in effect, at least for the moment.

"If we content ourselves with simply reacting to rebel
provocations, however," Munimori went on, "then we
place ourselves in a box. It has become clear that 26
Draconis is the political heart of the rebellion. Take that
system, take New America, and the rebel resistance will
crumble."

"Just how substantive is this rebel government we've
been hearing about, my lord? The, um, official line
is that the rebels possess little in the way of internal
organization."

"Though we dislike conferring any hint of legitima-
cy on the rebels by calling them a 'government,'"
Munimori said slowly, "we must be honest with
ourselves and accept that a government is precisely
what they hope to form. A number of representatives from various disaffected colony worlds of the
Shichiju have been gathering on New America for

months now, meeting openly in the planet's capital."

"Meeting, my lord? For what purpose?"

Munimori gave a humorless smile. "Our intelligence suggests that they themselves are not clear on that point. Some of the representatives evidently hope to refashion the Hegemony, possibly remove it from Imperial control, if such a thing is even conceivable. Others wish a complete separation, to create this Confederation of theirs as a separate state." He shook his head. "Obviously, both factions will be in for a shock."

"Yes, *Gensuisama*."

"You will deploy at once with the entire Ohka Squadron, *Chujosan*. The carrier *Donryu*. Five heavy cruisers, eight light cruisers, and twelve destroyers. Eight troop transports with a total complement of over four hundred warstriders. New America has no sky-el, so you will have to use reentry-capable warflyers and military ascraft to seize landing sites for your transports. You will need to go by way of our base at Daikoku to pick up some of your assigned vessels. Detailed plans are included in your orders."

"Your orders will be carried out precisely as written, *Gensuisama*."

"I know, *Chujosan*. I have complete confidence in you. Now, if you would honor me by joining me for tea? . . ."

The room reserved for the tea ceremony was traditional, nine feet square and with a real door rather than a dissolving, nanotech panel, one so low that the celebrants had to go in on hands and knees, a holdover from centuries long past when such a posture spoke of mutual trust and of the leaving of pretense and pomp outside. It was impossible to enter while wearing the traditional two swords, *katana* and *wakazashi*, of the samurai.

Inside, a single scroll hung in its alcove above a simple arrangement of flowers. Through an open panel could be glimpsed the fir trees and moss-covered ground,

the garden and stone water basin, of a scene on Earth.
So perfect was the illusion that Kawashima imagined he
could smell the scent of pine needles behind the subtle
haze of incense . . . and perhaps, he realized, that was
programmed into the scene as well. The ceremony's
hostess, a provocatively lovely *ningyo*, was on her knees
in the garden, simmering water in an iron kettle over
a charcoal fire, each motion one of delicate grace and
economy of movement. Save for the lessened gravity,
it was difficult to remember that this was aboard the
synchorbital Tenno Kyuden, and not in some woods-
shrouded teahouse in Kyoto Prefecture.

The conversation turned now to the formality of the
ritual, outwardly reserved, inwardly relaxed as they com-
mented on the kettles, pots, and bowls, on the scroll and
flower arrangement, on the play of the hostess's hands
as she carried out the ancient motions of preparing tea.

Kawashima felt ashamed, however, and unworthy.
Munimori was extending to him a signal and conspicu-
ous honor, but he found himself unable to leave worldly
concerns and troubles at the teahouse door as custom
required. His thoughts kept turning back to those intensely blue, pain-filled eyes he'd seen in the outer room.

He had no doubt whatsoever that the effect was a calculated one, deliberately staged for his benefit; Munimori
was telling him in a manner much more direct and
meaningful than mere words, that he, Munimori, was
a man of singular power, one who could deliver honor
and great reward with one hand, pain and disgrace with
the other. The hostess knelt before him, beating his cha
to near-froth with a whisk before bowing and offering
him the porcelain cup. Bowing, he received it, but when
he lifted the bitter green liquid to his lips he could scarcely
taste it.

As a good officer, Kawashima had been aware of the
talk spreading through the fleet, talk that had forecast
the first order he'd received, that soon only those native
to Dai Nihon could serve as fleet officers. There were

rumors of worse to come already circulating, rumors to the effect that before long only native-born *Nihonjin* would be allowed to serve in high military or government posts. Those rumors had already caused minor riots and popular demonstrations in Madras, Indonesia, and Anchorage. After all, to be accorded the privilege of Imperial citizenship without the attendant rights and status made the whole concept of Japanese citizenship rather pointless.

For centuries, Nihon had led softly, exercising her control over Earth and her offworld colonies through the instrumentality of the Hegemony, granting her subjects at least the illusion of sovereignty. Now, it seemed, the cloak was being thrown back, and naked force would be the order of the day. Could Nihon rule all of the human diaspora alone? And what of the nonhumans discovered so far, the Xenophobes and DalRiss? If the ways and thoughts of human *gaijin* were strange sometimes, what of those beings, far stranger still?

Kawashima was not confident of the answers to those questions and feared that Munimori and those in his clique were moving too far, too fast, in purging the Empire of *gaijin* influence.

He wondered about the civil war that seemed inevitable now, as Empire and Hegemony squared off against Confederation. The rebels had little in the way of naval power, but they were men and women drawn from the Frontier, the sixty-some worlds beyond the long-settled *Sekaino Shin*, the Core Worlds that included Earth. That meant that they were resourceful and that they were united by a burning anger at the clumsy and wasteful policies of a distant and unsympathetic government. *Hannichi*, they were called, disparagingly, anti-Japanese, as though the word were a synonym for "crazy." But Kawashima had witnessed *hannichi* sentiments firsthand only seven years earlier, during the Metrochicagan Riots. If the Frontier worlds fought as fiercely for their independence as had the people of Metrochicago, Empire and

Hegemony were facing a long and bitter war, one that would kill millions and devastate worlds. There would be little honor in victory over what, after all, was little more than rabble; in defeat—unthinkable!—would be complete humiliation.

Perhaps, Kawashima thought, that was why Munimori had presented him with the warning of the living sculpture. No art form, no expression of a master's will, is without pain. Munimori was telling him that he had the will and the determination to see this filthy conflict through to its inevitable end.

The significance of the tea ceremony was inescapable. Munimori was a steel fist, gloved within the civilized velvet of this ancient ceremony, of Zen simplicity, artistic appreciation, intellectual stimulation, and proper observance of ritual.

And Tetsu Kawashima was an empty vessel, nothing more, one that could do nothing but accept graciously the honor Munimori and the Emperor were handing him. He and his men would be the Empire's spear point against the Frontier rebels.

Politely, he held up his empty cup, commenting, as proper etiquette required, upon its age and delicate beauty. . . .

# Chapter 2

*Basic to all combat is the concept of using an
opponent's strength against him. Victory in any
engagement, whether in a personal test one-on-one
in the martial arts, or in the clash of the mightiest
armies, absolutely depends on this.*

—*Kokorodo: Discipline of Warriors*
Ieyasu Sutsumi
C.E. 2529

The fleet emerged from the blue glory of the godsea,
flashing into normal fourspace in a cascade of neutrinos.
The rebel ships were deep within the target system, so
deep that the enemy almost certainly picked up the quantum flux as space rippled from the K-T translation.

No matter. They would be through the target's outer
defenses scant minutes behind the light-speed wave front
announcing their arrival.

Nano-grown electronic traceries threaded through his
brain linked Captain Devis Cameron with the *Eagle*'s

AI, giving him a clear view of the planet ahead, as though he were dropping through empty space instead of sealed away within a high-tech coffin on the destroyer's command deck. Twin red dwarf suns glowed with ember-sullen light, a double sunrise above an airless, burnt-cinder world of rock and ice.

That star was DM+45° 2505 A and B, an unremarkable M3 double 29.14 light-years from New America, and 21 lights from Sol. Settlers from Rainbow had come here once, several centuries before, and named the place Athena. Too cold and small to be worth the expense of terraforming, it had riches enough—in platinum, iridium, and rare earths—to attract a Frontier mining consortium, the same consortium that had founded Rainbow. Most of the settlers hadn't even been full-human; genegineered workers adapted to cramped quarters and cold, close working conditions were happier, cheaper, and easier to control.

Forty years ago, Athena had been bought out by Imperial Nihon, who'd promptly constructed a major shipbuilding facility in close orbit about the planet. The world's name was changed to Daikoku, god of wealth and happiness—also known as the Great Black One. The orbital station was *Daikokukichi*, Daikoku Base.

Through his cephlink, Dev felt the swift-flowing currents of data from *Eagle*'s passive sensors, the telltale surge of energy indicating that Daikoku's defenses were powering up. Numbers scrolled down the right-hand side of his awareness, listing speeds and angles of approach. Dev absorbed the data, *feeling* it more than reading it, allowing the ship's AI to interact directly with his cephlink, calculating vectors, intercepts, and probabilities. He sensed the tingling wash of low-energy laser light. They were being scanned.

"That's it," Dev announced over the squadron's tactical communications link. "They've got us spotted."

"We're past the abort point now anyway," Captain

Lara Anders, *Eagle*'s senior shipjacker, replied. "We're committed."

Pinpoints of light scattered across Dev's awareness, concentrated like a swarm of luminous gnats about the larger glow of the orbital station, and more were winking to life with every passing second. Each marked the lifepulse of a power plant. Daikoku was waking up.

The Confederation raiders were badly outnumbered.

They usually were. The civil war that was tearing apart the Japanese Empire's puppet Hegemony had been going on for well over a standard year now. More and more worlds of the Frontier had broken away, signing Travis Sinclair's Declaration of Reason in conscious, symbolic mimicry of the signing of a similar Declaration over seven centuries before.

With worlds to draw on, there were plenty of recruits, plenty of the raw materials, plenty of the nanomanufactories needed to transform those raw materials into warstriders and the other weapons of war. What the Frontier Confederation needed more than anything else in the unequal struggle for independence was *ships*.

For centuries, Imperial Nihon had maintained the virtual monopoly on space-based industrial facilities that it had enjoyed since the early twenty-first century. Like most high-tech artifacts, the individual pieces of ships—especially of the starships that allowed travel from world to world within the Shichiju in something less than centuries—were grown in zero-G manufactories and assembled in orbit. Most Confederation worlds maintained their own, homegrown fleets of intrasystem ships and ascraft, and a few like New America could even construct the power taps and K-T drive units necessary for faster-than-light travel.

But *Dai Nihon* still dominated the godsea passages between each of the gulf-isolated specks that was an inhabited world. The Imperial Navy, and in particular the nine Ryu-class dragonships and their battlefleets, were simply unbeatable in any stand-up, one-to-one confrontation. The Frontier Confederation needed more and better starships. To get them, they needed to gamble the handful of FTL-capable ships they already had.

*Eagle* was the Confederation flagship, formerly the Imperial destroyer *Tokitukaze*, captured by Dev during the Battle of Eridu and fresh now from repairs at New America's orbital yards. Spread out behind her were three converted commercial vessels, the hydrogen tanker *Tarazed* and the Commerce-class freighters *Mirach* and *Vindemiatrix*. They were fifth-generation K-T drive ships, three of the very few such vessels in New America's inventory, and all had been radically modified in the Newamie yards during the past six busy months. The freighters had been converted to lightly armed transports, each massing just over 25,000 tons, each carrying four air-space shuttles, five hundred armored troops, and a company of warstriders.

*Tarazed*'s conversion had been more radical. Originally designed to transport cryo-H, the tanker was huge, five enormous spheres strung like beads on a wire between a tiny bridge-hab module and the boxlike bulk of her mammoth drive and power section. Her lead containment sphere had been gutted of cryogenic gear and field generators and rigged with hab modules and a makeshift hangar deck. Airlocks grown through the hull gave access to vacuum; *Tarazed* carried as payload eighty-two warflyers, the equivalent of an Imperial carrier wing aboard one of their big dragonships.

Those three vessels, plus *Eagle*, were all that New America had been able to spare for the Athenan expedition. The rest of their space forces, including those being rushed in from other Confederation systems, were being organized against the probability—no, the *certainty*—of an eventual Imperial attack against the Frontier.

Raids like this one, directed against Imperial shipbuilding facilties across the Shichihju, were an important source of new ships for the nascent rebellion. And possibly, Dev thought as he plunged toward the glittering constellation of lights that marked the Imperial ships and facilities orbiting Daikoku, just possibly such raids would buy the Confederation another desperately needed resource: *time*.

*Chusa* Randin Bradley Lloyd was the senior Hegemonic Guard officer aboard the huge and sprawling orbital complex of habitats and nanofactories called Daikokukichi by the Imperials, but which most of the Hegemony personnel simply referred to as "the Yards." As he floated onto the main control deck and pulled himself hand over hand toward the link pods lining one bulkhead, he thought again about Tanemura and his fat toad of a flunky and bit off a sharp curse.

Lloyd had only two superior officers on the station, both of them Imperials. *Taisa* Tanemura was the base commander, while *Chusa* Kobo was CO of the facility's marine contingent. Under their direction, Lloyd was in charge of all of the base technical facilities, including both the sizable civilian population and the orbital defense lasers.

Senior he might have been, but he'd been having trouble lately applying that seniority in any meaningful fashion. Morale among the *gaijin* both in orbit and on the planet's surface was low, so low that Lloyd had had to seriously consider the threat of mutiny. Discipline among the petty officers and lower-ranking commissioned officers was almost nonexistent. Why work hard, why obey orders, when the Imperials seemed only to care about the color of your skin and the cant of your eyes?

Right now, Lloyd's temper was frayed short by the attitude of his commanding officers, both of whom subscribed to the theory that, in the field at any rate, Hegemony officers were required to defer to *all* Imperial officers, regardless of rank. Two days ago, Lloyd had received a twenty-minute tail-chewing from the arrogant little *shosa* who was Tanemura's *fukkan*, or adjutant, and he was not happy about it. Since a *shosa* was equivalent to an army major or a navy lieutenant commander, one step below Lloyd's naval rank of full commander, he was hardly impressed by the rank alone. *Shosa* Hagiwara was simply a self-important little bastard who thought all *gaijin* foreigners were spies or rebels. Unfortunately, he was a *powerful*, self-important little bastard, and his report carried considerable weight both with Tanemura and with the Hegemony review board back at Singapore Synchorbital.

And Tanemura disliked Lloyd for his religion.

Lloyd's conversion to Mind of God Universalism had pretty much destroyed his Hegemony Guard career. He acknowledged that now, though it didn't make things any easier. A creed holding that all intelligences throughout the universe are evolving toward godhood, that all beings are equal, none better or worse than any other, was almost guaranteed to push the wrong download contacts on the Nihonjin, who tended to be conservative in their acceptance of new philosophies, rigid in their understanding of the barriers between classes, and mistrustful of *any gaijin*, whether it be human, nonhuman, or artificial.

Lloyd could have kept his conversion secret, of course, but that would have betrayed Universalism's Third Directive, that the gospel must be downloaded to every rational creature with the wetware to receive it. Two days after passing his conversion creed to his department head aboard the Guard corvette *Epsilon Lyrae*, he'd found himself transferred to Daikokukichi.

That had been seventeen months ago, almost three times the normal assignment to a hardship duty station. Imperial COs had come and gone, and he remained here, buried and forgotten. He'd been passed over twice for promotion, both of his wives and his husband had severed contract a year ago, and he'd been routinely denied extrasystem leave. He wanted to go home before the tedium killed him.

He wanted to live again.

Life, however, would have to wait. The duty officer had called a class-five alert . . . then almost immediately upgraded it to a class-two.

Who the hell was attacking this 'troid-cluttered garbage pit of a system? Settling himself into the commander's slotseat, Lloyd jacked in his T-sockets and palmed the chair's interface. Instantly, he was hanging in space, the great, black bulk of Athena turning slowly beneath his feet. The two red suns shone bright against the panorama, their red-mottled surfaces cool enough that he could stare into their disks without discomfort. The faces of both suns were heavily blotched with ragged black sunspots, and he could see the rough-textured granulation of their photospheres, the fire-fountain arc of their prominences.

"Whatcha got, Manuel?"

The voice of the duty scanner officer, *Chu-i* Manuel Rodriguez, spoke in his ear. "I'm not sure, Commander. At first I thought an incoming rogue tripped our approach vector alarms. But we've got QPTs out there. One of 'em might be an Amatukaze."

"Where?"

A bright green triangle appeared in his vision, hanging in empty space opposite the planet from the two suns. "Coming in toward our night side," Rodriguez said. "Four separate targets. On their current vector, they'll pass within a few million kilometers."

"AI, enhance," Lloyd ordered.

Four points of light appeared in the triangle, as yet too distant for details to be visible. Data wrote itself next to each in small, neat blocks, giving estimated mass, angle of approach, speed, and course relative to the base. They were definitely ships; their neutrino glow spoke of fusion plants and power taps.

Lloyd pursed virtual lips, giving a low whistle unheard by anyone save himself. One of those babies massed better than eighty thousand tons, and its IR signature matched that of an Amatukaze-class destroyer. The two smaller ones were lesser ships, large patrol vessels, possibly, or corvettes. The fourth could be almost anything, from a transport or tanker of some kind to a frigate.

Imperial ships? Had to be. The Hegemony had nothing like the Amatukazes. But what the hell were they doing sneaking into the system, without IFF or clearance requests, without even running lights or anticollision strobes?

"Tanya! Anything from commo?"

"Negative, sir. We've been hailing on standard Imperial and Hegemony secure frequencies, both radio and laser. No response."

And analyzing that approach vector . . .

"Full power to X-raysers," he ordered. Still unsure of the target's identity, he was taking the standard precautionary steps when dealing with a potentially hostile target. "Track and lock. Stand by to fire."

Then the cloudscreens appeared.

Coming to an immediate decision, Lloyd opened the station's com channel and raised the alert status to one.

"Battle stations! Battle stations!" The voice of Daikokukichi's AI sounded through the link. "We are under attack!"

Randi Lloyd heard the AI voice giving the alarm through his link but managed to push its insistent clamor to the back of his mind. As the targets grew closer, as the base AI assimilated more and more data on power curves and radiation signatures, the ship ID became more certain. And when the cloudscreens appeared in response to his command to power up the X-raysers, he knew that this was an attack. Damn, that largest one *was* an Imperial destroyer . . . but why the hell would it be attacking Daikoku?

Lloyd's first thought was that this was some sort of drill, a test of the combat readiness of his men. The destroyer had snuck past the system's outer defenses and was now preparing to throw a scare into the startled defenders. It would be just like those Imperial bastards to try something dramatic like that. . . .

His second thought, close on the heels of the first, was that these were rebels, ships belonging to the so-called Confederation that was challenging Imperial and Hegemony authority throughout the Shichiju. *That* hardly seemed likely, though. It was widely known throughout Hegemony service that the rebel malcontents were scattered and few, that they had no warships, no leadership, nothing at all to unite them save a vague and hazy opposition to Earth and the Empire. One might as easily believe in space pirates. And surely the authorities would have passed the word down the chain of command if the Confederation had access to Amatukazes!

Xenophobes? Again, hardly likely, though there was still plenty of who-was circulating about Xenophobe war fleets. All of the downloads he'd taken on Xeno updates indicated that they had no fleets, that their spread from system to system had occurred long ago, the result of some kind of weird panspermia rather than anything as high-tech as a starship.

Of the three possibilities that leaped immediately to mind, then, Lloyd decided that the first one was the best. This *had* to be some kind of test. Very well. He would follow the procedure by the book, proving to his superiors that even *gaijin* had their uses; at this point, most of the battle would be fought by high-speed computers in any case, leaving precious little for him to do.

The attacking force had released cloudscreens, in a classic attack deployment. They were certainly going for realism. One question nagged at Lloyd, however. If he had a chance at a shot with one of his X-rayser batteries, should he take it and risk holing an Imperial warship?

The damnable part of all of this was that his operational orders said nothing about possible war games or tests. The base's defensive posture was tested frequently through ViRsimulation, not by live actions with real warships.

The safe play would be to *pretend* that those attacking ships were enemies and fight just as hard he would if he knew them to be Xenophobe warships. They were almost certainly Imperials. The Hegemony, he was pretty sure, didn't have any warships larger than small, Yari-class destroyers or large frigates. If he scorched the armor off a careless Impie ship or two while living up to the spirit of this game, that was their lookout, not his.

Nonetheless, he punched through an urgent summons to both *Taisa* Tanemura and *Chusa* Kobo, calling them to the facility's main control deck. If those bastards wanted the glory of running this godforsaken shipyard, let them have some of the responsibility as well!

"I'm registering multiple QTP start-ups," *Tarazed*'s captain, Jase Curtis, announced over the squadron taclink. "At least four separate sources."

"Roger that," Dev replied, trying to keep his mental voice steady. Most of those stars represented the thin neutrino glare from fusion power plants, but four were significantly brighter and almost certainly marked quantum power taps.

Starships. Capital ships, monsters as big and as powerful as *Eagle* . . . or worse.

"Fifteen seconds until we're in range of primary laser defenses," Captain Anders reported. "They're tracking us on K-band."

Weapons-guidance radar. "Okay, *Tarazed*," Dev ordered. "Time to loose your pups."

From the airlock bays of *Tarazed*'s lead storage sphere, bundles of tiny craft spilled into space. Most were decoys, computer-directed pods with IR and radar characteristics similar to the larger craft hidden among them. The rest were warflyers, DY-64 Raidens and DR-80 Tenrais, most of them, with a few older and much-patched models thrown in as well.

If the principal weapon of land combat was the warstrider, jacked by a cephlinked pilot, the mainstay of close-in space combat, especially for the Confederation and its limited ship assets, was the warflyer. Little more than a warstrider modified for operation in zero-G, it measured a scant few meters in length and massed eighteen to twenty-four tons. Weapons and manipulators were folded into recesses in the armored hull, with fusorpack thrusters and cryo-H tanks mounted in the place of legs. Each was a single-slotter, with one man jacked into the link circuits and with a level-two AI handling the number-intensive functions like targeting and vector computation.

"They're charging their primary lasers."

"Cloudscreens," Dev ordered. "Now!"

Magnetic launchers slung explosive pods ahead of the Confederation ships. Seconds later, EWC-167 nanomunitions packs detonated in swift, silent flashes, loosing swarms of microscopic particles in a silvery, laser-devouring fog. From the framework of the orbital base, an X-ray laser winked on, the beam invisible until its energy was reemitted by the fog as dazzling, violet glare.

Dev watched impassively as the squadron deployed according to plan, sheltering behind cloudscreens as they fell toward the Daikoku base. Fear nipped at the back reaches of his mind. Had he foreseen everything possible? Was this a trap?

He was new to this business of commanding a squadron, and the hardest aspect of the job was knowing that now that the op plan was complete, the assault itself unfolding, there was little more he personally could do . . . but watch, a spectator as Lara Anders spun *Eagle*'s nearly four-hundred-meter bulk end for end, then applied full thrust, braking sharply at 4 Gs.

Now that the battle had begun, he couldn't even boss the other ships in the squadron. Communications between ships during combat was always less than perfect. Radio might be tapped by the enemy, the codes broken by AI decrypto programs and false orders fed into the command net. Lasers offered relatively secure, direct-beam communications, but the beams could be broken by any change of course and speed by either ship, and as the battle continued, more and more of the huge, ghostly cloudscreens drifted through the combat volume, dissolving lasercom feeds into crackling static.

Dev was listening in on the channels assigned to the other three Confederation ships, of course, but what came through was fragmentary, useful only to confirm that the other ships were still in action.

" . . . *ach!* Mirach! *Watch . . . X-rayser . . . up at three . . . niner!*"

" . . . *see it, Tara . . . pla . . . in . . . ling left . . . and high!*"

"*I've got a power build . . . grid . . . eight-three . . . on top of it!*"

He could have fed them orders, but anything he told them would have been as garbled as what he was hearing. Broken and incomplete orders in combat, Dev knew well, were worse than no orders at all.

It would be far worse for the enemy, he thought. Space fleet tactics relied on close, tight formations, working on the theory that ships that moved together could comlink closely enough to fight as a unit, coordinating their movements and their firepower against their opponents one by one. When one side was surprised in dock, however, there was an inevitable delay before they could work clear of their berthing facilities and establish comlink networks. This entire raid had been based on the assumption that the four Confederation ships would enjoy a golden few moments of that most precious of tactical advantages, communications superiority.

The question was, would it be advantage enough?

# Chapter 3

*It is well that war is so terrible. Otherwise we should grow too fond of it.*

—General Robert E. Lee
C.E. 1862

Enhancing a portion of his vision, Dev peered past *Eagle*'s cloudscreen as the paths of the ship and the nanocloud diverged, getting his first good look at the facility that was their target.

Daikokukichi was a roughly cross-shaped assembly of open girders and struts. Fuel and cryo-tanks, storage areas, and hab modules were mounted around the perimeter, while three massive hab modules rotated about the hub on arms to provide spin gravity. Second, third, and fourth levels housed nano storage chambers, pumping stations, and neat arrays of growth vats and molds, the station's fitting and drawing yards; a fifth was devoted to zero-G derricks and gantry arms, to finishing hangars, berthing areas and docks, where finished or near-finished

**31**

ships were moored. Running through the center of the structure was an axis, a long, spindle-shaped central core connecting a power plant module at one end with a control and communications center at the other. The defensive lasers—designed for meteor protection in this rubble-strewn system, but equally effective against marauding starships—were mounted outboard, on raised structures giving them the widest possible zones of clear fire.

Captain Anders was figuratively looking over Dev's shoulder at the same virtual reality display. "Big goker," she said. "Commodore? You think they have close-in reserves, maybe hidden behind the planet?"

Dev almost didn't react to the unfamiliar title. He wasn't used to the strictly honorary and unofficial promotion he'd been given when Travis Sinclair had put him in charge of this mission. The Confederation was still in the process of converting from the Nihongo rank structure employed for the past several centuries by the Hegemony, by resurrecting the system used by Western military forces before the Japanese ascendancy. Dev's formal rank of naval captain, equivalent to an army colonel or the Imperial Hegemony *taisa*, was new and uncomfortable enough, but by a custom old before Man first had left the world of his birth, there could not be two captains aboard one ship. To be called commodore by people who had more experience at command than he did was unsettling.

Ignoring the strangeness, he concentrated on the question. "If they have ships behind the planet, they're powered down right now, or we'd see their neut emissions," he told Lara. "Actually, this place looks a lot quieter than I was expecting."

"Our intel said that there'd be eight or ten capital ships in the Yards," Lara agreed. "Not just four. I wonder where they are?"

The question was a disturbing one. A handful of warships patrolled the outer marches of the Athenan system, but it would be hours yet before they knew anything was amiss, so vast were the distances within even such a pocket-sized star system as this. During the final moments of their approach the attackers had picked up four different energy sources that might be warships powering up, but there could well be others lurking nearby. In fact, the Impies *should* be keeping a small squadron close at hand for just such surprises as this, either docked at the shipyard itself or in near orbit. Where were they? *What* were they? If the Impie squadron included another destroyer or something larger, this raid would be one of the shortest and most inglorious on record.

"Well, those ships in the docks are operational," he told her. "Or they will be when they get their pods manned. But tell your scan personnel to keep their eyes open and their links clear. I don't want anyone surprising us. And tell them to watch for nukes."

The greatest danger at this stage of the attack was that the enemy would toss a nuclear warhead at the warflyers. Cloudscreens couldn't stop missiles or hard radiation, and a nuke could be detonated beyond the range of point defense lasers and still do a hell of a lot of damage to a ship.

That possibility, fortunately, was a remote one. According to intelligence, Daikokukichi possessed both Imperial and Hegemony personnel. Long-standing policy restricted nuclear weapons to Imperial forces alone. Hegemony officers were not trusted with them, and even the Nihonjin skippers of any Imperial ships present would need release authorization from much farther up the chain of command before they could turn scourging blasts of nuclear fire against the swarms of attackers.

Still, it wouldn't do to get complacent. Policy could have changed since Dev had last read an Imperial Fleet directive, or the Imperial officer in command of

Daikokukichi could be an unstable son of a bitch who nuked first and got authorization later.

"Commodore!" Lara warned. Colored lines highlighted parts of his view, indicating four separate points within the shipyards. A red diamond flashed insistently, indicating a ship rising above the clutter of gantries and open, duralloy-strut frameworks. "Imperial frigate boosting clear of the Yards! Range nine-five-zero-zero, boosting at point five. . . ."

"Got it," Dev snapped back. "Hit him before he fogs our lasers."

Data cascaded through *Eagle*'s sensors; the target was broadcasting standard Imperial IFF, which included ident and stats. According to the warbook readout unfolding in Dev's vision, the moving ship was *Senden*, Flashing Lightning, accelerating clear of the orbital docks and repair gantries on white-blazing drives. Since she was listed in the datanet—the newly constructed warships had not yet been named or given net IDs—either she must have been docked at Daikokukichi for repairs or else she was part of the Imperial garrison force here. An Inaduma-class frigate, she was over 100 meters long, massed 1,800 tons, and carried a crew of 210. Though no match for the much larger and more powerful *Eagle*, she could still cause a hell of a lot of grief for the destroyer at close range. Possibly, *Senden*'s skipper was simply trying to win free of the Yards before he was attacked, but Dev couldn't take that risk.

Lasers flicked from *Eagle*'s starboard bow mounts, invisible bolts that turned duralloy sun-bright at their caress. Metal vapor puffed into space, briefly and silently illuminated by starcore energies.

"She's launching," a voice on *Eagle*'s tactical net reported. More colored graphics winked on in Dev's vision, highlighting a cloud of stars curving out from the frigate under 60-G boost. "Missiles incoming!"

"Tracking," another voice said, calm despite the stress of the moment. "AI targeting lock. We'll take them with the PDLs."

PDLs—Point Defense Lasers—were batteries of one hundred–megawatt coherent light weapons deployed in clusters about the warship's outer hull, arranged to give maximum coverage from every side and angle of approach. Too weak to penetrate a starship's armor, indeed, too weak to make much of an impression on any hardened target through the light haze of antilaser fogs that quickly filled the battle volume, they were hot enough to burn through a missile's relatively thin outer skin in milliseconds. One by one, then in groups of two and three and five at an instant, the incoming missiles flared white-hot within Dev's virtual reality panorama.

Space combat was primarily a war of maneuver. With nano-based cloudscreens to block incoming laser fire, with banks of AI-directed lasers to take out enemy missiles in lightning, close-in point defense bursts, ships had to draw fairly close before they could do serious damage to one another. Exotic beam weapons, like kaon cannons, CPGs, and electron guns, could usually be dispersed by manipulating hull magnetic fields; the most effective weapons were long-range Starhawks that could be remotely jacked by human pilots all the way to the target.

At point-blank range, then, the ship that could outmaneuver an opponent—ducking in and out around drifting cloudscreens, loosing clouds of missiles from precisely calculated points, pulling the unexpected maneuver, finding blind spots on an opponent's hull—was the ship that would score the kill.

Four Starhawks left *Eagle*'s forward missile bays with a jarring thump that rang through the destroyer's hull. Guided by jackers aboard the Confederation ship, they twisted past *Eagle*'s dissipating cloudscreen, locked onto the accelerating frigate, and went to full throttle up. Lasers winked from *Senden*'s port side. Two of the Starhawks vanished in white-hot balls of plasma, followed an instant later by a third.

The fourth, already locked onto a collision course, was detonated by its jacker before the frigate's PDLs could find it.

Lloyd was directing the base's defenses, calling laser batteries on line and ordering all ships to launch, a headlong scramble to get clear of the vulnerable Yard docks before the attackers could get a solid target lock on them and melt them down into slag. *Senden* was clear, accelerating toward the hostiles now at 5 Gs. Her sisters, *Shiden* and *Raimei*, were nearly ready to launch; power cables and umbilicals were being freed now. A fourth Imperial ship, the Yari-class destroyer *Asagiri*, was bringing its fusion plant on-line and would be ready in minutes.

With stunned horror, Lloyd realized that this was not, *could* not be a drill. The attackers had fired their lasers, scoring several solid hits to the *Senden*'s hull while she was still working clear of the docks. *Senden* had replied with a missile barrage, and the volley had been returned. The base's radar and AI analysis painted the detonation of that last Starhawk warhead as a blue-white spray of tiny sparks, fireworks against the night.

The Starhawk's warhead was canister, a modern twist on an ancient artillery weapon. After boosting a full ten seconds at 50 Gs, the thousand or so depleted uranium ball bearings packed inside the warhead were whipping along at nearly five kilometers per second, a deadly spray of ultradense shrapnel following the same path that the Starhawk had been taking at the moment of detonation.

The warhead was twenty-five kilometers from *Senden* when it exploded, spraying the load of ball bearings toward the target in a diffuse, slowly expanding cloud. Point Defense Lasers flicked and snapped, directed by the frigate's sophisticated, AI-linked radar tracking system, but there were simply too many targets, and too little time. In five seconds, *Senden* was able to decelerate enough that perhaps half the incoming slugs missed, flashing silently past her bow, while her laser defenses took out perhaps four hundred of those that were left.

Approximately one hundred depleted uranium bearings slammed into *Senden*'s armored hull in a shattering demonstration of $F=ma$. Laser turrets were swept away in the storm; sensors were smashed; the port-side drive venturi crumpled like paper; whole sections of duralloy armor peeled up like shingles beneath a hurricane. At the same instant, hits rang through Daikokukichi's main control center, an insane hail of shot that had missed the smaller target. Red warning flags flashed up in Lloyd's mind as an AI voice intoned the damage: *pressure loss in sections eighty-one through eighty-eight; damage to secondary base IR sensor suite; minor damage to laser batteries seven, nine, and eleven . . .*

He was beginning to respond when, with a chilling abruptness, the scene of battle surrounding him was wiped away. There was a burst of static . . . and then he was lying in his slot on the control deck, blinking up at a gray ceiling covered by painted-over cables and power conduits.

"What the goking hell . . ."

At first he thought the base link network had gone down . . . a serious failure and one that should never have happened, so many redundancies were built into the system. But the constellation of green and amber lights flickering and shifting across a readout console close by his head showed the system to be functioning normally. He brought his palm implant down again against the sweat-slick coolness of the interface. There was a burst of static, an unfolding view of ships and orbital base and the looming bulge of Daikoku . . .

. . . and then he was bumped off again, hard.

"You are relieved, *Chusasan*," an electronic voice said in his ear. "We will take it from here."

Lloyd recognized Tanemura's dry and matter-of-fact phrasing. So, that was it. Tanemura had come on-line and booted him off. Elsewhere on the control deck, Lloyd saw other men and women, all *gaijin*, rising from their link couches with looks ranging from bewilderment to anger. The Nihonjin had kicked every non-Japanese off the net, had decided to fight the battle themselves without *gaijin* help!

Their very evident lack of trust burned in Lloyd's gut like a hot coal.

Even now, after so much had happened, it seemed strange to be on *this* side of Hegemony targeting radars and lasers. Just a couple of years ago, he'd been a loyal soldier of the Hegemony, a warstrider, and well on his way to a command of his own. By being the first human to establish peaceful contact with the alien Xenophobes, Dev had been made a hero of the Empire despite his *gaijin* status. As a *koman*, an Imperial military advisor, he'd been sent to Eridu, Chi Draconis V, to help suppress the rising tide of anti-Imperial, anti-Hegemony discontent there. He'd cast his lot with the rebels, however, when his warstrider unit had been ordered to destroy one of the colonists' domed cities.

There were some deeds for which orders—even orders backed by threat of court-martial or of summary execution—were simply not enough. He'd mutinied, refusing his orders, and had been arrested and interrogated by Imperial agents as a result. Katya had gotten him out.

Katya Alessandro. He missed her, missed her more than he'd expected to. He would have liked it if she could have accompanied him on this mission, but she was back on New America, busily trying to hammer together something like a decent warstrider force out of raw recruits and Hegemony expatriates. Once she'd been his commanding officer, but that seemed like ages ago, back when they'd both been warstriders in a Hegemony unit, fighting the Xenophobes on Loki, then venturing with the First Imperial Expeditionary Force into the true Frontier beyond human-inhabited space.

That had been when Dev had finally made meaningful contact with a Xeno. As a result, he'd received the Imperial Star and been made an Imperial *koman*. Katya had rejected the Empire, returning to her native New America to work with the Confederation government, and with Travis Sinclair.

She'd made the right choice, and Dev had made the wrong one. He knew that now. A government system as corrupt as the present Imperial/Hegemony stewardship of Terra could not be reformed from within. Maybe reform would have done some good once, but the rot had gone too deep, the people in power now had too much vested interest in maintaining that power, at any cost. Human governments had followed the same pattern time after time after bloody time in the past, reaching the point where only revolution could cleanse the slate and let people start anew.

With little choice in the matter, then, Dev had joined the rebels and participated in the Battle of Eridu, leading the assault team to capture the *Tokitukaze* at the planet's synchorbital station while Confederation warstriders and native Eriduan militias had held off the Imperial Marines at Raeder's Hill. They'd fought the Imperials to a standstill, partly because Dev and his raiders had dropped the captured Imperial destroyer into an orbit that took her across the battlefield. A salvo from the destroyer's shipboard laser batteries had been more than enough to break that final Imperial attack.

Dev had no regrets about joining the rebellion . . . not really, though he'd frequently questioned the rebellion's chances for any outcome in this war short of complete annihilation. It was just that he still wondered sometimes what he was, and why.

*Senden*, demolished by the shotgun blast from the teleoperated Starhawk, appeared to be adrift now, powerless, her weapons down. Smaller ships accelerated out from Daikokukichi, only to be met by searing laser bursts from the hard-accelerating warflyers. The enemy's defenses appeared uncertain, almost hesitant. Had the surprise been that complete?

A familiar, pulse-throbbing excitement surged behind the flutter and scroll of data cascading through Dev's awareness. The sensation was an alluring one, enough so to bring with it a twinge of guilt. Sometimes, Dev wondered if he hadn't begun enjoying war too much. It was at times like this, jacked into the AI of a ship going into combat, that he began to feel more than human, somehow, almost as though he were addicted to the surge of power, to the exultation thrilling through his being, and the feeling of invulnerability.

Full linkage often had that effect on him, especially in a tight meld with a good AI either aboard ship or within the towering, durasheathed embrace of a warstrider. In some people, the feeling arising out of such a union could be one of godlike power, a conviction that nothing was impossible as the linker wielded unthinkable energies through the medium of thought alone. Taken to extremes, that feeling could be classified as a psychotechnic disorder, TM, or technomegalomania, and it had grounded plenty of striderjacks and shipjackers in the past.

Gently, Dev disentangled himself from the pulsing, triumphant joy of electronic battle. "Communications," he snapped. "Order all units to converge on the station. Keep repeating until they acknowledge."

"Affirmative, Commodore."

*Concentrate on the fighting*, he told himself. *The warflyers are getting close now*. The enemy's fire was increasing again in volume. Possibly, their fire control had just been briefly knocked off-line.

Damn, casualties were going to run high on this one. Dev just hoped the catch would be worth the butcher's bill.

# Chapter 4

*Where warstriders are the descendents of twentieth century tanks, for all that they move over rough terrain on articulated legs rather than treads, warflyers trace their lineage back to the combat aircraft of the same era. Similar to conventional warstriders overall, they are equipped with fusorpacks and thrusters that give them a measure of maneuverability in zero-G conditions.*

*Scorned by the pilots of conventional space fighters, they are considered undergunned, over-armored chimeras, composites neither fish nor fowl designed to do all things, consequentially doing nothing well.*

*—Armored Combat: A Modern Military Overview*
Heisaku Ariyoshi
C.E. 2523

Long before his arrival at New America, Dev had downloaded to his personal RAM the complete text of Ariyoshi's exhaustive study of armored warfare, a work already well on its way to becoming a classic of military history. He knew that Ariyoshi, together with most modern Imperial tacticians, still considered the warflyer to be something of a makeshift and make-do weapon, even though it had been in existence now for well over three centuries.

It *had* been a makeshift weapon, once. They'd started off as workpods adapted to the needs of warfare not long after the first combat use of warstriders; originally conceived as manned constructors designed to haul building materials and manipulate large, free-floating structures during work on space stations, synchorbital facilities, and other large, zero-G projects, they had considerable endurance, but all of the grace and maneuverability of a small asteroid. Even now they weren't much more than jacked-up workpods fitted with missile batteries and lasers and run by a low-will onboard AI. They were so small that, as with warstriders, their jacker-pilots thought of themselves as *wearing* the things rather than riding them, and a large number of flyers could be carried aboard even a moderate-sized ascraft. Their greatest disadvantage was still their low thrust-to-mass ratio, which was rarely more than 4 Gs or so. That made them *slow* in combat, and they had nothing like the high-G maneuverability of a true space fighter.

That meant that in any kind of stand-up fight, in orbit or in deep space, they were going to take heavy casualties.

Casualties were very much on Dev's mind as *Tarazed*'s wing of warflyers dispersed, each pursuing a separate, parabolic path toward the orbital facility expanding in the ViRsimulated view ahead. Nine out of ten were decoys, piloted by low-level AIs too simple to understand their own deaths. The remaining tenth were better armored, yes, but vulnerable still to even a light caress of a 100-MW point defense laser.

What hurt was that most were piloted by *children* . . .

well, by men and women younger than Dev's twenty-seven standard years. He wondered if all revolutions were fueled by the idealistic fervor of children. Realistically, Dev knew that he could scarcely be considered old.

He just felt that way sometimes.

They'd started calling him *Lucky Rol*, and that was the name painted on the blunt prow of his DR-80 warflyer.

Tall, flamboyantly blond, with ice blue eyes, Torolf Bondevik was Lokan-Scandinavian, born and raised in Midgard in the shadow of the Bifrost Towerdown. He'd become a warstrider during the fighting with the Xenos there, joining Alessandro's Assassins and participating in the Alyan Expedition of 2541. He'd stayed with the unit when it opted to join the Confederation forces and had gone to Eridu to support the Rebel Network's rising there against Hegemony and Empire.

He'd been with the jackers who'd boarded an ascraft at Babel in a desperate bid to seize an Imperial destroyer docked at Babel Synchorbital. During the attack on the berthed warship, he'd remote-jacked a warflyer from the ascraft, his mind riding the craft into a barrage of laser fire until it was destroyed.

Torolf had been unharmed, of course. With the remote link broken, he'd simply awakened back aboard the ascraft, but he'd later joked with the other rebels about having been fried by a gigawatt laser during his approach. The tag "Lucky Rol" had naturally followed.

He hoped the name held true today, because he wasn't jacking remote this time. He was tucked into the coffin-sized jackslot aboard the stubby DR-80, with nothing between him and the Imperial base's laser batteries but a few centimeters of durasheath armor.

"Red Squadron!" he called over his tactical link. "This

is Red Leader. I'm going to try for that array of struts and cross supports near the cryo-H tanks at two-five-zero."

"Rog . . . that, Red Leader. Red Two, Red Three . . . with you!"

"Copy, Red . . . dron . . . on our way!"

The replies, blasted by ECM static and interrupted by his own movements and those of his fellow flyers, were fragmentary. Coordination at this point was nearly impossible; all he could manage was a ragged "this way!" and a hope that enough of his people saw what he was doing to follow.

A beam flashed, a dazzling green thread that seemed to miss him by meters, then brushed a decoy a kilometer to his rear, dissolving it in a soundless flash. The graphics had a feeling of unreality to them, like the cartoon images of a training ViRsim; the warflyer's AI was painting in the beams to help him pick his approach.

Not that *seeing* the beams was any great help. How do you step out of the way of something that announces its arrival with the same gigawatt flash of light that turns the toughest armor to a flare of exploding plasma?

Still, the display did help him spot active laser batteries, in particular a bank of squat, staggered turrets arrayed stepwise along a parapet of open struts overlooking the main shipyard. Colored indicators flickered across his vision, each color, each shape bearing additional information. Two of those batteries had just bathed him in radar illumination, tracking him, locking on; their turrets were swinging toward him now, their charge coils building toward release . . .

*Now!* Decelerating savagely, he backed down on a stream of white-hot plasma, careless of where that seething cone of tortured atomic nuclei washed across the framework of the orbital base. A ship's plasma drive, even one as relatively small as that rigged to a warflyer's hull, could be a deadly if short-range weapon, but the base's crew were the enemy, weren't they? Parts of the open structure glowed red hot in his exhaust as he spent delta-V like water. Maneuvering thrusters fired, and he thumped into a girder hard enough to momentarily blur his visual feed.

"I'm down!" he called over the tactical link, though "down" was strictly a term of convenience in zero-G. Panels opened in his black hull, like a flower's petals unfolding. Jointed arms unlimbered, telescoping clear of the warflyer's body. Two clamped to the girder with nano-hardened fingers, gripping fast, halting the flyer's clumsy rebound and sideways drift; a third trailed the power cable for a bulky, 250-MW laser.

Their radar lock on his flyer broken, the laser turrets on the parapet rotated, weapons elevating to track other, incoming targets. More decoys flared and vanished . . . as did two DR-80s with flesh-and-blood jackers aboard. Bondevik sensed their screams an instant before contact was broken.

Another warflyer pod struck home, fifty meters to his left. *Passion Flyer* was the name painted on its armored prow just below a garish image of a nude, seductively posed woman. Sublieutenant Enrique St. John was New American, fresh out of recruit training and just assigned as Torolf's wingman.

"Whee-oh! What a ride!" St. John called, jubilant. His DY-64 Raiden was longer and bulkier than Torolf's Tenrai, massing a good twenty-four tons. The arms were heavier, the blunt snout of an electron cannon more threatening than the '80's laser.

"Rocky!" Torolf called. "Cover me, at two-five-zero!"

"You got it, toke!"

Levering past the duralloy struts and beams, *Passion Flyer* released a cloud of dumb missiles, then loosed a bolt from the electron gun. Lightning arced, violet-white and jagged, as it grounded from one of the laser turrets.

Torolf was moving in the same instant, propelling himself across the gantry framework with smooth, powerful articulations of his multiply jointed arms. Targeting sensors detected an energy flux building, his AI threw a red targeting reticle over a power feed juncture . . .

*Fire!*

Metal vaporized in white heat; a pressure hull breached, spilling atmosphere in a silver cloud of swiftly crystallizing air and moisture. Something dark tumbled after, a body, possibly, rapidly swallowed by the night. Torolf shifted targets, firing again, and all the while he kept his flyer moving toward the lasers, now some two kilometers distant. It occurred to him how silly the machine must look, skittering leg-over-leg across the gantrywork like some outlandish, metallic spider.

Other warflyers landed, grappling with the gantry framework, swaying themselves across gaps in the structure on jointed arms, or firing harpoons trailing buckythread cables and reeling themselves across on hard-driven winches. A few tumbled past, helpless or dead, some with hulls still glowing white-hot and softened to featureless lumps.

The Confederation had adopted the Imperial system for deploying fighters and warflyers: two ships to an element, two elements to a flight, three flights to the squadron. Six squadrons, seventy-two ships in all, plus another ten as spares, recon vehicles, and worker drones. He was skipper of Red Squadron, twelve paired Raiden and Tenrai warflyers so newly organized they hadn't even had time yet to choose a unit name. How many of them had been lost already, Torolf wondered. Three? Four? No time to think about that, no time to think about anything except knocking out those batteries.

A laser bolt seared close, brushing a squat, gray sphere embedded in the framework like a fly in a spider's web. Metal sparkled, turned to vapor . . . followed close by a jet that looked like steam, which was actually slush hydrogen boiling free into space. Who'd fired? It didn't matter. The vapor cloud, briefly opaque, offered cover.

Torolf focused a coded thought, triggering his boosters. The kick sent him soaring low across the station's framework, plunging into shadow as he moved behind the rapidly expanding cloud. Emerging into red-hued sunlight once more, he found himself with a better vantage point. The laser turrets were clearly visible from here, lined up as neatly as ViRsim targets in a newbie recruit's shooting gallery.

Anchoring himself, Torolf locked on to the nearest turret and opened fire. A tiny sun flared at the breach of one of the two mounted lasers; chunks of metal and freezing air wafted into space, along with the slow, end-for-end tumble of a 10cm laser's barrel. He shifted his aim to the next turret, then the next . . .

"Lieutenant!" St. John's voice was shrill, near ragged panic. "To your left!"

He was already reacting when the bolt hit, moving left and rotating his flyer's torso. Red alerts flashed across his vision, warning of energy overload, of charged particles washing across the smooth surface of the warflyer, channeled by the network of fine, superconducting threads embedded in the armor.

Lightning arced. Three of his sensors went dead, leaving him blind to port, but he'd turned far enough to see the enemy warflyer, angling toward him across the station's framework like a knobby, black-shelled crab.

He didn't recognize the model, though it looked a bit like a spacegoing version of the Daimyo warstrider, powerful and heavily armored. Torolf snapped off a laser shot even as he was casting free from his anchor point. One of his arms came free, still clinging to metal, its struts melted through by the overload from other's proton cannon. Damn. That black hull seemed to *drink* laser light. . . .

At his mental command, another arm dropped from a ventral hatch, an arm bearing a bulky cylinder perforated on one end with four-centimeter holes that flashed and spat rippling flame. Recoil acted like a rocket, accelerating Torolf's DR-80 backward and giving it a slight tumble; the projectiles, M-490 4cm rockets with deplur penetrater warheads, slashed through the enemy warflyer's armor shell like fléchettes through flesh, plunging deep, then detonating with sharp, rapid-fire explosions that sent chunks of duralloy spinning through space.

Swiftly, Torolf reached out with his remaining grasping arm, snagging a crossbeam and arresting his tumble. His laser was up and locked in, ready for another shot, but the enemy was dead, a black hulk trailing wires and interior plumbing like entrails as it fell away into blackness.

A shadow passed over him and he shifted to his dorsal sensors.

*Eagle* was there, slowing on forward maneuvering jets. In every direction, other Confed warflyers were either under thrust or moving along the Daikoku base's framework, making their way toward a central, domed tower crowned by antenna arrays that must house the facility's control center. The defensive laser fire seemed to have fallen off.

Cautiously, he released his handhold and boosted forward.

Randi Lloyd bit off a curse, then pushed off from a bulkhead, sailing across the control deck to an EC panel. "Randi!" *Sho-i* Cynthia Collins said, pleading in her voice. She was struggling to unsnap herself from her link couch. "What's going on?"

"We're under attack, damn it," he snapped back in reply. "And the *sheseiji* won't let us fight!"

A babble of voices reached after him but he ignored them, as he ignored the distant shrilling of a pressure alarm elsewhere in the station. Bumping to a halt at the environment control panel, he dropped his palm on the interface and phased the overhead dome to transparency. He wasn't sure what he expected to see; the attackers had been too distant to make out with the naked eye when he'd been linked seconds before. But as he floated up into the dome, he could see suns and the curved horizon of Daikoku, the complex sprawl of the Yards, and the leapfrogging motion of advancing warflyers.

And ships. There was *Senden*, still close to the station, drifting free now, a lifeless hulk. Another ship, the Amatukaze-class he'd IDed on his original scan, loomed overhead like a great, black cloud, slowly eclipsing first one of the red suns, and then the other. The ship was staggeringly huge this close up, almost four times longer than the battered *Senden*, far bulkier, and massing over forty-five times as much in sheer gross tonnage. Paired anticollision lights flashed, marking off the bulk of star-swallowing blackness, shaped like a fat cigar embraced by streamlined fairings and cupolas. He found himself staring up into the wicked, crystalline eyes of gigawatt lasers and felt his heart hammering inside his chest. There was no way the Yards could possibly resist such firepower at point-blank range.

A flash caught his attention—its brilliance stepped down by the dome's optics to protect human vision—and he turned in time to see the last of Daikokukichi's defensive laser batteries tumbling into space.

Still palming the interface, Lloyd requested more data. *Shiden* and *Raimei* and *Asagiri* . . . where were they?

Colored symbols flickered across the dome, almost as stark and clear as if they were part of a projection within his own brain. *Shiden* was under boost . . . but away from Daikoku on a parabolic path that would take her out through the planetoid belts. *Raimei* and *Asagiri* were still in their berths, both powering down in token of surrender. Evidently, their captains shared Lloyd's appraisal of the tactical situation.

The battle, mercifully brief, was already over.

*And it serves the bastards right!* The thought, fierce and unrelenting, caught him by surprise. Just where did he stand in this unexpected fight?

Randi Lloyd was from Earth, from Metrochicago in the North American Hegemony Protectorate. He'd been in space back in '36, the year of the Metrochicagan Riots, but when he'd heard about them at his next planetfall, he'd assumed, as had the rest of the Earth-born crew, that rabble-rousers and troublemakers had broken the peace, had provoked the slaughter of civilians as a means of making a political point. He'd not learned that his sister was numbered among the dead until he returned to Earth almost a full year later.

So many months robbed his loss of urgency, if it could not ease shock and grief. Who was to blame? Who *could* be blamed for what was officially a miscalculation—a junior Guard officer had panicked as the mob spilled out of Grant Park and advanced onto the Michigan Moving Way, and summoned Imperial reinforcements. The crime had not been so much in the shooting—the mob was breaking the peace, after all, and had been warned to disperse—but in the way they'd kept on firing after the crowd had begun to scatter. Was the system to blame, Lloyd had wondered, or a handful of poorly trained Imperial peaceforcers caught up in the moment's bloodlust?

Lloyd had decided to blame the individuals, if only because there was nothing within the vast and impersonal bureaucracy of Earth's Hegemony and the Nihonjin Empire for him to point a finger at and say, "*There!* That is evil, and must be changed."

He'd shipped out aboard a merchant ship as quickly as he could, putting distance between himself and Earth; several years later, given a chance at converting his merchantman's second officer's stripes to a *shosa*'s commission in the Hegemonic Guard, he'd grabbed at the opportunity, passed the tests and officer's training, and been assigned to a ship, the Guard corvette *Epsilon Lyrae*.

Two years and one promotion later, he'd ended up . . . here, on a shipbuilding yard on the backside of nowhere, booted off-line by officious Imperials, watching unknown forces swoop down on his station.

Still at a level-one link, he felt something happening. Querying the base AI, he learned that Tanemura was busily purging data files. Reluctantly, he drew his hand away, breaking the link. His eyes met Cynthia Collins's. "What is it?" she asked. "Who's attacking us?"

"Must be rebels," he replied, grinning wryly as he said it. Damn, either the rebels had picked up one hell of a lot of delta-V, lately, or the government had been lying to them all about how good the rebels were. They'd snuck on Daikoku out of nowhere, launched a sharp, short, professional attack, and crippled the station in the space of seconds.

Through the dome, the destroyer loomed above the station, terrifying in its size, its scale made evident as a second ship passed slowly between the destroyer and the Yards. The newcomer looked like a K-T drive freighter, considerably modified; there were laser turrets attached to its long, square-angled body, but they had the look of improvisation about them . . . as well as haste.

Thrusters flared briefly, outshone by the pulse of anticollision strobes. The freighter was drawing closer to the control center's external lock.

Lloyd squared his shoulders. "I guess we'd better square away to receive visitors."

As if to prove his words, a hollow clang sounded from the main airlock beneath the control deck.

# Chapter 5

*In all the military works it is written: To train
samurai to be loyal, separate them when young,
or treat them according to their character. But
it is no use to train them according to any fixed
plan. They must be educated by benevolence. If
the superior loves benevolence, then the inferior
will love his duty.*

—Tokugawa Ieyasu
early seventeenth century

Resistance had ceased throughout the Daikoku orbital
base, a victory more sudden and more complete than
Dev could possibly have hoped for. With *Vindemiatrix*
docked directly with the station's main airlock, New
American troops were storming aboard, armed with
laser rifles and slug pistols and wearing combat armor
instead of their accustomed warstriders.

Dev remained aboard *Eagle*, surveying the prize
through electronic senses. Though he was linked to the

tactical channel being used by the boarding party, his attention was on the take. Eighteen warships, including three Yari-class destroyers. He felt a thrill there. His father had been put in command of an Imperial Yari destroyer, the *Hatakaze*, the ship with which he'd saved the refugees over Lung Chi.

They'd done it! *He'd* done it, and with only four casualties out of his strike force, and seven warflyers damaged.

It was too bad, he thought, that there wasn't some way to take over this entire facility. New America and a few other worlds in the Confederation had shipyards, but they weren't as large or as well equipped as this one.

In theory, it would one day be possible to *grow* an entire starship, complete right down to the brightwork and the loaded AI programming, by turning appropriately instructed nano loose on a lump of asteroidal iron and assorted, raw trace elements. In practice, the sheer size and complexity of even a small starship required each vessel to be grown in sections, which were extracted from the nanovats and assembled like enormous three-dimensional puzzles by swarms of remotes, workpods and constructors, or even genegineered workers. The assembled hulls were then repeatedly bathed in a nano flux that added their durasheathing, layer upon layer of diamond, monomolecular duralloy, and ceramics, together with the microscopic superconducting grid that afforded protection from charged particle radiation in space. Finally, highly specialized nano flowed through the ship's interior nervous system, programming AI components, plating out and completing electrical connections, and hardwiring the control circuitry. Weapons, except for the largest and most massive systems like spinal mount PPCs that were part of a ship's overall design, were added later, dropped into hardpoints and wired into the control network by specially programmed nano.

From the embrace of his slot aboard *Eagle*, Dev surveyed the assault force's prize with growing excitement.

Through the crisscross of girders, Dev could make out long, black ships moored between gantries and docking access tubes on the facility's third level, eighteen military vessels of various types, ranging in size from cutters and corvettes to three small destroyers. All appeared to be brand-new, their gleaming, durasheath hulls night-hued, unmarred by dust impacts or wear. They hadn't even been painted yet with unit markings or the insignia of Imperium or Hegemony. More ships were visible in the fitting and drawing yards close by, still resting in their nanovat cradles or newly emerged from their armoring flux and awaiting only the finishing details of drive controls or weapons or AI installations to make them fully operational.

All that most of those ships needed were crews and full loads of cryo-H in their tanks. Several more— a close inspection would tell them how many—were ready save for weapons. Even unarmed, they would be valuable additions to the Confederation fleet, and something could be done about arming them back at New America.

As for the rest, Dev studied each with a small pang of regret. They included the monster frame of a half-assembled Kako-class cruiser and two Naka-class light cruisers, as well as twelve smaller vessels; if only they could be made operational!

Unfortunately, there was no time. Imperial or Hegemony ships could arrive at any moment, and it was critical that Dev both get the captured ships back to New America and preserve the original members of his squadron. All he could do was order the destruction of the unfinished ships.

After the shipyard was secured. According to the boarding party, most of the base's complement of Imperial Marines were either on the ground or still in their barracks, a duralloy cylinder attached to the control center by a long access way, already sealed off as though they were expecting a siege. A handful

of marines in the station proper resisted; the firefight—
the fire*fights*, actually, since the skirmishing was widely
scattered and completely uncoordinated—were over in
minutes.

"We've got 'em," Lieutenant Gary Langley reported
over the net. "Control center secure!"

"On my way." Dev broke contact.

Minutes later, he made his way through the zero-G
tangle of corridors toward the orbital base's control section. With him were several members of his shipboard
staff, including Simone Dagousset, a Confed computer
expert with his command team. Bodies floated there,
broken and bloody, though mercifully few. More of
the Imperials had chosen to surrender than to fight, it
seemed.

A door dissolved open, and he pulled himself hand
over hand onto the main control deck, a large, circular
room cluttered with electronic consoles, the gray bulk of
a dozen full-linkage couches, a projection dome over all
set to view surrounding space. *Eagle* hung there beyond
the fragile barrier, a most convincing inducement to
surrender.

Langley met him. He carried an unholstered blast pistol, and there was a blackened, half-melted slash across
his armored plastron. "This was the control crew, sir,"
he said. "The Nihonjin were linked when we came in.
The others weren't."

"Thank you, Lieutenant."

"Uh, if you'll excuse me? Some of my boys are busy
with the Impie Marines."

"Go ahead, Gary. I've got the watch."

The prisoners watched him narrowly as he moved
closer. They'd segregated themselves into two groups,
Nihonjin and *gaijin*, beneath the guns of the Confederation troops who'd burst in here moments ago. The
Japanese—there were five of them, all men—looked
sullen and resentful. The *gaijin*, four men and three
women of various skin shades and ancestries, seemed

less monolithic in their emotions, which ranged from fear through confused uncertainty to outright hostility. All wore bodysuits of utilitarian gray; moments earlier, they must have been linked through the station's AI to its defense and communications systems. They clung, like Dev and the others, to handholds in deck or bulkheads to keep from drifting. Giving the others scarcely a glance, Dev centered his attention on the oldest-looking Japanese, assuming that he would be the one in charge. He appeared to be in his fifties, with a long, creased face.

"*Konichiwa, Shikikansan,*" Dev said formally. By addressing him as commander—the word meaning position rather than the rank—Dev hoped to put the proceedings on a less-than-hostile footing. "I am *Taisa* Cameron, of the Confederation Navy." How strange that sounded in his own ears!

The Nihonjin officer did not sneer, not quite. "You seem somewhat young for such high rank." His English, if stiffly precise and formal, was perfect.

A bulldog-faced Japanese at his side snickered and said something low. Dev caught the word *shiro*—an epithet meaning, roughly, "white boy." *Kuso!* He had no credibility with these people at all. No *kao.* . . .

Heat brushed his cheeks. "Sergeant Fillmore?" He turned to the armored noncom Langley had left in charge of the Confed troops. "Find a place for these people. I want to have a peek at their datanet."

"Yes, sir," she replied. She holstered her handgun and rasped out an order to part of her squad.

"You will get nothing, *kaizoku,*" the bulldog snapped. The *Nihongo* word meant pirate. "You're too late! The storage banks have been purged."

"He's right, I'm afraid," another voice said from the second group of prisoners, which was positioned now at Dev's back. "They were busy killing its memory when your people barged in. My God, Dev . . . Cameron is it? Is that really you?"

Dev tugged on the handhold he was clinging to and rotated his body. It couldn't be—

"Lloyd?" He had to search for a first name, so much had happened in intervening years. His cephlink helped. "*Randi* Lloyd?"

Randi Lloyd had been First Helm on the freighter *Mintaka*, years ago when Dev had first signed aboard that ship. He'd taken Dev under his wing, a raw newbie with his sockets still slick with sterile shipping fluid, showing him the feeds on his first shipboard slot, junior cargo officer. He'd left not long after, reportedly to join the Hegemonic Guard. Dev had admired him; his own decision to join the Guard had come at least in part from Lloyd.

"You know this guy?" Sergeant Fillmore asked.

"I certainly do." Dev gestured. "Simone? Check out the computer."

"Yes, sir."

"Small galaxy, eh?" Lloyd said as Dev drew nearer. "When did you turn pirate, son?"

Older than Dev by fifteen years, his face was seamed and he was showing some gray at his temples. He'd aged a lot since the day Dev had last seen him. No wonder he'd not picked him out immediately.

"Who says I did?" Dev replied, smiling, more to hide his own uncertainty than anything else. "I'm fighting for the Confederation now. Maybe you've heard of us?"

He'd not seen Randi Lloyd for years now. He still felt as though he were the junior apprentice, and Lloyd the teacher, and had to suppress the urge to add the word "sir."

"Aye, I've heard," Lloyd said. He didn't return Dev's smile. "I never figured you to throw in with a bunch of losers like that, though. You know, don't you, that they've got the proverbial snowball's chance on Moloch?"

"You will all be utterly destroyed," the base commander added from the other side of the compartment.

"Well, I'm not here to debate it with you," Dev replied. "With either of you. What's the word, Simone?"

Dagousset had just pulled her hand clear of a terminal interface. She shook her head, short red hair bouncing with the movement in zero-G. "I don't think they actually deleted anything," she said. "More like they locked it away under a password, with a false front to make us think we've come up dry."

"Really?"

"I don't *know*. Just a feeling, the way things're organized in there."

Simone Dagousset was the sharpest mind with a computer net Dev knew. Sometimes he thought she was more than half computer herself. "Okay, Simone. Thanks."

"I can whittle away at that password if you want."

He nodded. "Do it."

Lloyd raised his eyebrows. "What is it you're looking for, Dev?"

"Actually, all we're here for is a few of your new ships out there. But we're always interested in having a peek at the opposition's computer files. You never know what you might learn about prowords, general orders, fleet movements, that sort of thing."

"Fleet movements?" Lloyd said casually. "Like the one we had through here a week ago?"

"*Damare-yo!*" the Japanese commander shouted, lunging toward Lloyd. "Shut up!"

A struggle broke out with the Japanese prisoners. Fillmore kicked off a bulkhead, intercepting the commander with a shoulder block across his knees that sent both of them tumbling out of control. Other Confed troops closed in, blocking off the captives.

"*Uragiri-mono! Kono yogore!*" The bulldog-faced man struggled in the grasp of two of Dev's men, his face flushed with rage. "Traitor! Filthy bastard!"

"Get them the hell out of here!" Dev shouted above the confusion. The Confeds hustled the Japanese prisoners out of the room, and there was silence once more.

"I don't think you scored many points with your boss just then," Dev said. "You want to tell me what that was all about?"

Lloyd exchanged glances with the other *gaijin*. One of the women shook her head. "Randi, I don't think—"

"Damn it," one of the men snarled. "We swore oaths of allegiance!"

"You think we owe those bastards anything?" Lloyd replied, bitterness in his words.

"Jamis," Dev said, signaling one of the remaining Confed troops. "Take these people someplace else. Not with the Imperials. See that they're made comfortable."

"Right, sir."

"The rest of you wait outside, please."

In a moment, Dev and Lloyd were alone—except for Simone, who had jacked herself into one of the link couches and was now in the room only physically. Mentally, she was deep within the AI program running the base.

The Hegemony officer looked him up and down. " '*Taisa*,' eh?" He chuckled.

"It's not something I'm real comfortable with yet, okay?"

"Oh, I wasn't criticizing. Every navy has its own ways of doing things."

"You wanted to tell me something?"

"You arrived here from New America, right?"

Caution stayed Dev's tongue. "No. What makes you say that?"

"I was a merchant spacer quite a while, remember." He nodded toward the dome, to where part of the *Vindemiatrix* was visible at the base docking port. "I know a Newamie long-haul design when I see her."

"We get our ships from all over," Dev said, a little stiffly.

"I don't doubt it. Including, I gather, Hegemony automated shipyards."

"When we have to. What's your point, sir?" The honorific slipped out, unbidden.

"Tanemura didn't want me spilling the feed, Dev. We had a major fleet movement through here eight days ago. All Imperials, no Hegemony ships at all. They called it the Cherry Blossom Squadron, and it was under the command of an Admiral Kawashima. A tough old bird, I've heard. One dragonship, the *Donryu*. Thirteen cruisers, five of 'em big sons of bitches, Kako- and Atago-class. Ten destroyers, four of 'em Amatukazes, like your big boy out there. Eight transport *marus*, big ones."

"Good God," Dev said. "That's a major invasion force."

"On target. They pulled in here to pick up two new-grown destroyers and to take on a full load of slush-H. I was linked into the commnet just before they boosted clear, and I heard Kawashima talking to Tanemura."

"Tanemura's your boss here? The one with the long face?"

"That's him. One of 'em, anyway. I heard him wish Kawashima *gambatte kudasai* at New America."

"Good luck," Dev translated. The news left him numb. An invasion force of that size had passed through the Athenan system over a week ago, headed for New America? And the presence of eight troop transports suggested that when they got there, they planned to stay.

"You . . . you have proof of this?"

The other man shrugged. "It's all in the datanet. There should be a complete set of IFF codes in there, signal protocols, ViRcom frequencies, everything."

"I don't suppose you have the net's access password."

"Um . . . try *fugaku*."

Dev considered his old shipmate. The word, a poetic form for Mount Fuji, in Japan, *could* be a code unleashing some sort of dump order in the AI's memory. He didn't think so, though. Lloyd looked sincere . . . and angry, and Dev could feel an inward bond with the man, a warrior's *yujo*. Besides, surely the system's Japanese masters would have already initiated a dump, if they'd had it set up that way.

Lloyd must have noticed Dev's hesitation. "That was the keyword for most of the secure fleet traffic stuff. If there's a higher security access, I don't know it. They kicked the lot of us *gaijin* off-line and took over just as you made your move out there. I imagine they put up security blocks once they figured nothing we could do could stop you."

Dev looked hard at the man. "Why?"

"Eh? Why what?"

"Why do you want to help? We *are* enemies, aren't we?"

"I . . . guess we were. But all we've heard about you officially is that you exist. Terrorists, guerrillas, that sort of thing." He shrugged, the motion setting him slowly rotating until he reached out and snagged the edge of a console to steady himself. "I never dreamed you had any kind of military muscle behind you!"

Dev glanced at the overhead dome, at the warships stationed close by the base. "I don't know if you could call that muscle. The Empire's a lot bigger than we are."

This was the question Dev had been confronting within himself. What had made Lloyd betray Hegemony and Empire with scarcely a moment's thought? Not the appearance of a single, battered destroyer and a few made-over transports, surely!

Lloyd scowled, then looked away. "Dev, things have changed a lot since we were shipmates. *I've* changed a lot."

"Hegemony service'll do that to you."

"This was more. I'm C of MGU now."

"Huh?"

"Mind of God Universalist. I converted a year and a half ago."

Dev blinked. Not a religious person himself, he'd known plenty of people who were, and he tried to keep, if not an open mind, then an accepting one. But there were far too many sects, cults, and competing beliefs across the Shichiju to ever keep track of them all.

"Sorry. I don't know that one."

Lloyd smiled. "I'd be glad to download to you, of course. Now's hardly the time or place. Basically, we believe all Mind is part of God, that God is nothing less than the sum total of all Mind everywhere and everywhen, from the Creation to the end of time. It's like we're each of us subroutines in a universal AI. We—"

"As you say, Commander, this isn't the place. How'd all that get you in trouble?"

"I downloaded to my department head."

"An Imperial?"

Lloyd nodded. "An *annaisha*. Not too smart, huh?"

"Well, I suppose even one of God's subroutines can make a mistake." *Annaisha*, "guides," were Imperial officers serving with the Hegemony Guard. Some served openly, as military liaisons, but others, reportedly, were plants, Hegemony officers who reported secretly to an Imperial control on morale and loyalty within their Hegemony unit.

From what Lloyd had just told him of his beliefs, Dev could understand why he'd been posted out here. The Imperials preferred belief structures that supported the status quo, not wild and unsettling philosophies stressing equality or the divine nature of all intelligent beings. That sort of thing could give *gaijin* the wrong sorts of ideas.

"But you still haven't answered my question," Dev went on. "Why should you want to help us? What you just did could get you shot, you know. Or psychoreconstructed, at the very least."

"And it would be worth it, Dev. To keep them from burying us."

"Who, the Universalists?"

"Good Mind of God!" Randi said. "Yes, us. *And* the Church of Christ of the Cosmos. *And* the Disciples of

Deseret. The Baptists. The Greens. The Back-to-the-Soilers. *Everybody*, Dev, who doesn't think the way they do! That's what Empire and Hegemony are all about. And that's what you and your friends are fighting against, isn't it?"

Dev understood perfectly what Lloyd was saying. He'd heard much the same from General Sinclair, back on Eridu.

*We hold that the differences between mutually alien, albeit human, cultures render impossible a thorough understanding of the needs, necessities, aspirations, goals, and dreams of those disparate worlds by any government body. . . .*

Those words, downloaded from Dev's RAM, hit him with a sudden and unexpected power, as though he'd never really read them before. Human culture was diverse, but the stronger any government was, the less it could tolerate diversity. Freedom of speech, freedom of religion, freedom of thought . . . all were at heart antipathetic to any government big enough and strong enough to believe that *it* knew what was best for its citizens.

"That's what they're fighting for," Dev agreed slowly. "But with twenty-some Imperial warships on their way to New America, I'm afraid the fight may be about over." It seemed pointless for Dev to deny his interest in the world any longer.

"Then you *did* come from New America! We'd heard who-was, rumors, that the rebels were holding some sort of big meeting out there." He scowled. "Dev, the Imperials are going to take that system down, and they're going to do it hard. If I were you, I'd avoid it. It's not going to be a real healthy place to be."

*Katya*! Fear writhed within, fear for Katya, fear for other friends and people he knew who'd stayed behind. How to warn them? *Kuso*, there was no way, even if he could lay his hands on a fast courier. With a week's head start, the Imperial squadron would get there long before he would.

Making his way to a nearby console, he brought his hand down on an interface. "Simone?"

"I'm here, Captain," the computer tech's voice replied in his head. "There's a lot of data here, but it's going to take a while to run through the possible access codes. And . . . I'm pretty sure there's a 'three-times-and-you're-out' watchdog. We could lose it all if I don't hit the right—"

"Try *fugaku*."

There was the briefest of pauses. "That did it! We're in!" Dev felt the flow of data unleashed by the password.

Not that access to all of the secret codes and IFF frequencies in the Shichiju could help now. There was no repealing the laws of physics—not even the seemingly magic laws of the K-T plenum.

New America was about to be hit by an overwhelming force, and there wasn't one damned thing Dev could do about it.

# Chapter 6

*The country must have a large, efficient army, one
capable of meeting the enemy abroad, or they must
expect to meet him at home.*

—The Duke of Wellington
C.E. 1811

It was still midmorning when Katya Alessandro emerged
from the maglev station in the heart of Jefferson, took
her bearings from a public infolink broadcast, and started
across Franklin Park. The golden light of 26 Draconis A
had just cleared the Ironhead Mountains to the east of the
city and seemed pinned between the mountains and the
gilt-edged scimitar of Columbia, New America's large,
close natural satellite, suspended overhead.

In fact, it would be midmorning for another several
hours yet. With a day lasting just over eighty-three
standard hours, schedules on New America had little in
common with cycles of day or night. This was Katya's
favorite work cycle time to be up and about, however,

and she'd decided to take advantage of it today, riding the maglev shuttle from the starport into the city rather than one of the more convenient—and faster—point-to-point public magflitters.

As she stepped onto the Park's moving way, a cloud of bright-winged morninglories exploded from an amberbrush, chirruping raucously as though to welcome her . . . or to laugh at her surprise.

Surprising, too, was how *good* it felt to be home once more, finally, despite the lingering pain.

She'd been back to New America only one other time in the past eight years, and then briefly. It had been almost four months now since she'd returned to New America this time, though Katya had been working so hard for those months that she'd had little time for sightseeing or looking up family or old acquaintances. That, she thought, was probably just as well.

She'd never expected to return to the world of her birth at all. Katya had never been so happy as the day she'd finally won free of her parents' farm outside of Nowakiyev and set off on her own. Her decision to mortgage eight years of expected future earnings in order to purchase her three-socket implants, her downloaded education at Jefferson, her determination to go into space, each had one by one snipped the ties binding her to her old home outside New America's Ukrainian colony. Her subsequent decision to enter Hegemony military service, followed not long afterward by her wholehearted defection to the rebel cause, had completed the break.

New America was a rich and diverse world, one shared by three separate colonial populations. Largest and most powerful was the North American colony, also and confusingly called New America, with its capital at Jefferson, but the south-hemisphere Cantonese and Ukrainian colonies together accounted for nearly half of the world's population of some five hundred million. The American colony was one of the Frontier's loudest proponents of independence from the Hegemony; the Cantonese were just as strongly loyalist. The Ukrainians, as they often were on political issues, were still stubbornly and loudly divided.

As divided as was Katya's own family. Her father had been from Jefferson originally, but he'd never shared the New American ideals of self-government. The Hegemony had heavily subsidized his *nowagreebi* farm, after all, and his Ukrainian wife was adamantly opposed to what she called the anarchy of revolution.

Katya didn't like to remember her father's last message to her, four years ago, the one advising her not to send another ViRcom download, because they upset her mother so.

The hell with them both. . . .

Jefferson was both planetary capital and the provisional capital of the entirety of the new Confederation, and its spaceport, on the Dickson Peninsula twenty-five kilometers south of the city, was the world's principal link with the rest of the Shichiju. Jefferson was thriving, far busier now than it had been eight years earlier. Though not so modern as some of the Imperial cities she'd seen on Earth, Pulau Kodama, say, or Tokyo itself, Jefferson had the bustle and energy of a city far larger than its population of almost one million suggested. There were no arcologies here, but gleaming, old-fashioned skyscrapers and office domes rising among sprawling parks choked by the native green-gold vegetation. The faintly out-of-date atmosphere was belied, however, by the thronging crowds flowing along the walkways beneath and between those buildings, and by the magflitters and other skycraft warbling overhead.

The city's people were a cosmopolitan lot. Some wore the traditional kilts of the New American Outback, but most looked as though they'd be at home in any major Hegemony city, people in pastel skinsuits or coveralls or worker's garb, businessmen in formal wear and shoulder cloaks, soldiers in uniform—both the brown of the Confederation and the gray of the Hegemony, interestingly enough—and even a scattering of the more exotic dress of other Frontier worlds. Not all within the crowd were full-human, either. Many of the figures in worker's clothing were genies, thick-shouldered, long-armed dockworkers, many of them, or the small, lithe, silver-furred forms of techies.

Katya noticed a pair of warstriders—a couple of aging RLN-90 Scoutstriders with Confederation insignia on their pauldrons—standing guard in the park's central plaza. Peacekeepers. When news of the Emperor's death had reached New America, it had touched that world's different populations in markedly different ways. There had been mourning; there'd been rioting. Calls to completely sever the Frontier's links with the Empire had alternated with calls for reason, for caution, for reconciliation. Things had been quiet for the past couple of months now, but the Confederation Command Authority continued to keep a few striders on alert status, patrolling the city's public gathering areas, just in case.

With a fine sense of irony, the towering, blue-green Sony Building looming high above Franklin Park had been taken over shortly after its former corporate owners had departed, its offices and central AI shifted from the business of an interstellar corporation to that of running a brand-new government. It was still called the Sony Building, in fact, but the corporate logo that had adorned the peak of the eighty-story building for nearly a century had been taken down. In its place glowing, holographic letters floated before the building's facade: FIRST PEOPLE'S CONFEDERATION CONGRESS.

Delegates from Frontier worlds across the Shichiju had been meeting here for months now, trying to hammer out a new government . . . or even just a common set of goals. For her part, Katya had had little time for politics since her unexpected promotion to colonel and assignment to the new-formed 1st Confederation Rangers. Even when she'd joined General Sinclair's personal staff in addition to her other duties, she'd steered clear of the political debates raging now in the Confederation's capital. Sinclair was the politician, she'd reasoned, and the man to deal with the fragmenting ideologies of fifty different cultures on a dozen separate worlds.

That had been changing, lately. For the past month Katya had been dividing her time almost evenly between the old militia barracks near the capital's spaceport and the Delegates' Hall in Jefferson. Her position on Sinclair's staff gave her freedom to come and go pretty much as she pleased even when Congress was in session. It was a fascinating position to be in, giving her as it did a chance to watch an infant government in the making. At the spaceport, meanwhile, she was her old, apolitical self, busily organizing and training the warstrider unit recently designated as the 1st Confederation Rangers.

Technically, the 1st Rangers were commanded by Colonel Jacob R. Weiss, a New American who'd formerly been CO of the 1st New American Minutemen. Weiss was an excellent administrator and a fair organizer, but—as with most of the Confederation's senior military people—he lacked experience in combat. For that reason, Katya was Weiss's 2IC, his second-in-command, normally a position held by a lieutenant colonel. Sinclair had told her privately that when the Rangers went into combat, Weiss would receive a promotion, and she would take over the unit officially instead of merely in fact.

She was more than happy *not* to be in official command, for running a regiment was as new for her as jacking a warstrider in combat would have been for Colonel Weiss. The challenge was overwhelming at times. Most of Katya's command experience had been topjacking a company, three or maybe four platoons of eight warstriders each, no more than thirty-two machines and—with the support, admin, and maintenance personnel attached to the company—a total of perhaps 150 people. The Rangers were a full regiment—three battalions, each of five companies, for a total of 480 warstriders and a total roster carrying twenty-five hundred names.

At least, those were the numbers on the Rangers' TO&E. Glowing in the black recesses of some adminjacker's linked mind they looked damned impressive, but Katya knew just how misleading the figures were. So far, the 1st Confederation Rangers mustered exactly 148 warstriders, half of them obsolescent relics, plus 867 men and women, of whom only 115 had three sockets, with the physical ability to jack a strider in the first place. Of those, seventy-eight had actually jacked a warstrider into combat.

Those seventy-eight, though, had seen plenty of action. Most were veterans of Raeder's Hill, on Eridu. Some were from her old 2nd New American unit, and had experience fighting Xenos on Loki or with the 1st Imperial Expeditionary Force. Good people, all of them, shoulder-companions well disciplined and steady. They would provide the core of this new regiment, this new idea that Sinclair so wanted her to begin.

A purely *Confederation* army.

"You're aware, aren't you," he'd asked her one morning recently, during a break in the debates on the floor of Congress, "that none of what we're doing here is new?"

She'd just told him how much she admired his drawing organization out of vacuum, order out of the chaos that was the rabble of people, cultures, and causes that made up the Frontier.

"You've told me the original Americans went through something very like this . . . when? Six hundred years ago?"

"Seven hundred sixty-seven years, to be precise. At the very dawning of the First Industrial Revolution. The ancestors of the New Americans managed a revolution of their own, and against odds as great as those we face now. The scale was not so grand, perhaps, but the ideas, the causes, the hopes, they were much the same. One people—actually a collection of diverse and insular cultures, farmers, merchants, seafarers, scholars, frontiersmen, and God knows what else—seeking to express their own ideas of individuality and personal freedom while under the rule of what had once been their motherland. The mother had become tyrant, you see, and wanted to keep a firm hand on them. They'd grown, however. Living on the frontier had changed them, enlarged their spirits. As living on the Frontier has enlarged us. And the mother, like the Empire, could not afford to let them simply turn and go their away."

Sinclair shifted in his seat, rubbing at his graying beard. "One of the biggest challenges those early Americans faced," he continued, "was getting such a diverse group—thirteen separate and quite individual colonies—to work together. Each was jealous of the others ... as Varuna or Nowakiyev are of New America, say. Many had particular grievances with one another over issues like trade or slavery, very much like Liberty and Rainbow."

"Slavery? Slavery's been outlawed for centuries."

"What about the genies?"

The words had been soft, with no hint of reproach, but Katya's face had burned ... with embarrassment? Or shame? She'd never thought of the issue in quite that way before. For that matter, she'd rarely thought about genies, though she'd seen them countless times in Jefferson's walkways and parks. On most worlds, and for the most part, they were a tiny minority, kept comfortably out of sight.

"In any case," Sinclair had gone on, "a regiment of Rhode Island militia didn't want to find itself marching into battle with a bunch of Marylanders and New Yorkers, say. And they wanted a good, steady Rhode Islander in command, not some damned Virginian."

The names meant nothing to Katya, though she guessed they were the colonies Sinclair had mentioned. "I thought they were all Americans?"

Sinclair smiled. "That idea hadn't quite taken hold yet, you see. A man was a Rhode Islander, or a Virginian or a Pennsylvanian first, an American second. 'America' was just too big a concept. Sort of like our Shichiju. Can you really picture the scope and sheer damned *size* of an empire comprised of seventy-eight worlds? When one world alone is such a universe of diverse peoples and cultures and history and wonder as New America, say, or old Mother Earth?"

"I've never really thought about it that way, General."

"So those first American generals had to invent an American army. It took an act of Congress and it damn near took an act of God, but they created what they called the Continental Army and it became their elite, led by the best officers they had, supported in the field by all of the individual state militias."

"And it won the Americans' war for independence?"

Sinclair gave her a wry smile. "Actually, they got the *kuso* kicked out of them time after time, and what the British regulars didn't do to them, winter and disease and an almost total lack of supplies did. Katya, I tell you it's a damned miracle New America wasn't named New Britain. It was a damned close-run thing."

"*Kuso!*" It was almost a wail. "What hope have we, then?"

"Ah, but they *did* win, remember. Eventually. Through perseverance. Through learning from their mistakes . . . and by making fewer mistakes than did their enemy.

"And always remember, Katya, that the past is never repeated exactly. Its patterns might repeat, but never the particulars, never the details. You and your 1st Confederation Rangers, you might be our analogue to that first Continental Army. But with an understanding of our own technology and strengths and abilities that those early Americans never had, we've got a chance, a fairly *good* chance, to beat the Imperials before they really take notice of us and decide to step on us like bugs. Hell, all we need do is convince them that it's easier and cheaper to let us go without a fight. In the long run, you see, that's how *all* revolutions succeed." His eyes had gone vacant for a second then, as he consulted some inner data. "Blast. You've let me ramble, girl. We should be getting back to the floor. I have a weakness for history, Katya. You shouldn't have let me run on so!"

But Katya routinely downloaded to her personal RAM all of Sinclair's "ramblings," as he called them. Often she played them back in the quiet of her quarters during off-duty hours, and lately she'd begun editing, organizing, and cataloguing them into a history, of sorts. Sinclair's intense, almost archaic love of the peoples and issues and events of past times helped weave a framework against which Katya could hang the events she saw unfolding around her now.

As she stepped off the slidewalk and bounded up the steps of the Sony Building, she found herself remembering again that particular conversation and wishing that Dev were here so she could download it to his RAM and discuss it with him afterward.

If only Dev could hear some of this! It might well give him the perspective he needed to understand the *rightness* of the Confederation's cause. They'd often disagreed in the past over what the Confederation was trying to do, over whether or not it was worth the cost.

She suppressed a small, inward shudder that mingled both hope and fear. Dev must be on his way back from the Daikoku shipyards by now. Was he still alive? Never mind the success or failure of his mission, *was he still alive?*

She found she very much wanted to see him again despite all that had happened to drive them apart, and the power of that wanting caught her by surprise.

Katya palmed the ID reader at the entrance to the Congressional Hall. Tired and feeling thoroughly dirty, she'd just come straight from a twenty-hour session with a new shipment of warstriders. They'd belonged originally to Nowakiyev, fifteen machines donated by that colony's militia nearly a year ago and kept in storage since then on the outskirts of Port Jefferson, the spaceport outside of the planet's capital. They were ancient pieces, some of them; the most modern was a hulking KR-9 Manta manufactured at Earth's Toshiba Orbital in 2531, twelve years ago and already bordering on obsolete.

The oldest? Ah, that would have to be the pair of T-90 Gunwalkers. They'd come off the assembly lines a full century and a half ago, and what a record they had! They'd served in the Osiran uprising, and later in the colonial militia on Shiva. The Shivans had sold them both to Nowakiyev in 2501, when news of the first Xeno incursions on An-Nur II had created war panic and invasion hysteria across the Frontier.

The Ukrainians had contributed those fifteen striders to the then Greater New American Defense Force, a unit long since disbanded. Now, thanks to the political strains between New America Colony and the other two settlements on the world, there were unexpected problems. Spare parts needed to get those machines on-line were not to be had. Katya also needed nanopattern technicals, the complex data bases that described a piece of equipment virtually molecule by molecule, allowing repair and service nano to be programmed to carry out their assigned operations on that particular machine.

Sinclair had more pull than most with the disparate elements of the New American delegation. Perhaps he could help.

She arrived in the Hall, as she usually did these days, in the middle of a firestorm of debate. For the past month or so, discussion had centered on the issue of genies, on whether or not they could be—or should be—accorded the rights of full humans. That fight had waxed hot, with Liberty and Rainbow taking opposite poles on the issue and attempting to batter the rest of

the delegations, by words if not by force, into choosing
one side or the other.

Ten days ago that issue had been tabled. There were
signs of growing strains within the fragile Confederation. The Emancipator Party of Liberty had demanded
an addition to the Declaration, one proclaiming those
supporting genie slavery to be "outlaw states, unworthy
to sit with civilized men." In reply, the Rainbow delegation had threatened to walk out if genies were allowed to
vote or given representation in Congress. Sinclair and the
other moderates had hoped to give both sides some time
to cool off and consider their positions . . . and options.

What followed, though, had exploded even hotter, a
nova's flare of recriminations and ill-feeling. Why was
it, colonies like Nowakiyev and Canton and Deseret
wanted to know, that the hotheads of sister colonies
like Liberty insisted on complete dissolution of all ties
with the mother empire? The Reconciliationists, as they
were coming to be known, wanted to effect a repair of
relations between the various Frontier worlds and the
rest of the Hegemony. Surely, reform could be won
through negotiation, while the only result of war would
be the absolute and total destruction of everything Man
had built on the Frontier.

Palming her ID into a final security station interface,
she waited for the door to dissolve. Duane Lassiter's 3-D
image dominated the central display in the amphitheater
beyond. A delegate from the Frontier world of Eostre, he
spoke Inglic; a wholehearted Reconciliationist, he spoke
with desperate, articulate passion.

"Do you actually believe," he was saying as Katya
entered the Hall, "that a mere handful of systems can
survive on their own, with no trade with the Hegemony?
Cut off, isolated from the rest of humanity . . . for mark
me, such would be the fate of worlds who turned against
their brethren.

"Worse, would war with the Hegemony pit New
Americans against Cantonese and Ukrainians in a bloody

civil war, brother against brother, father against son? The fratricide of civil war, I tell you, has always been the bloodiest, bitterest, and most genocidal war of all. . . ."

Katya tuned out the speech as she descended the walkway to the seating area of the New American delegation. She'd heard that speech, or variations on its themes, time after time in the past month, and each time the words conjured images of her parents, and the rift between them and herself.

The Reconciliationists made a powerful point: it would be better to live in peace with Empire and Hegemony. The only trouble was, who was going to get the Empire to agree to those terms? "The Emperor has declared us to be in rebellion," Sinclair had announced during one memorable reply to a recent Reconciliationist speech. "Perhaps it is time that we did as well!"

But still, the talking, the wrangling went on.

She slipped into the seat next to Sinclair.

"Katya!" he said, half turning. "It's been a while. I thought we'd lost you!"

She blinked back tiredness. "If you do, General, it's because I've gone sound asleep in one of my striders. Switched off and powered-down. Can we talk?"

"Now?"

"Any time in the next couple of hours."

"That might be a good idea," he said, his brow furrowing with concern. "Go up to my office and take a nap. You look done-in, lass. Tsuked out."

She managed a smile. *Tsukarasu* was the Nihongo for tired, "tsuked out" a recent and popular bit of derivative Frontier slang.

"*Shinda*-tsuked," she said, adding the Nihongo word for "dead." She held up her hands, stained so black from silicarb and lubegel that the interwoven wires of her embedded interface seemed to gleam against her left palm with a light of their own. "I may never be clean again. But anyway, I can't really afford the nap. Thanks just the same. Actually, I could download what

I need to your desk system, or maybe talk it over with your analogue."

Sinclair's analogue was a computer program duplicating enough of his memory and personality to serve as a stand-in and personal secretary during routine ViRcommunications and conferencing. Under most circumstances, it was impossible to tell an analogue from the human himself.

"Hell, Katya, you don't want to talk to him. He's got delusions of grandeur, complete technomegalomania. C'mon. We'll talk now . . . but only if you'll promise me to get some sleep. I can't afford to lose you, you know."

"General, with all due respect, you don't know what you're asking. I—" She stopped. The Hall had just gone very quiet. A military officer was now in quiet, urgent conference with the speaker. The silence lengthened, then dissolved in a gradually expanding ripple of low-voiced murmurs. *Something* was happening. But what?

"Fellow delegates," Lassiter said after a long moment had passed. "I, uh, I've just been given rather disturbing news. A large, a—uh—a *very* large Imperial war fleet has just been sighted dropping out of K-T space on the boundaries of our system. Initial reports are fragmentary at best, but the word is that elements of the local militia space forces challenged the fleet and were swept aside. The fleet is now en route to New America and is expected to arrive within twenty to thirty hours.

"It seems the Imperials are responding to the challenge, gentle people. They've come to debate the question of independence with us in person."

"*Kuso!*" Katya groaned. "And just when you'd about convinced me to take that nap. . . ."

# Chapter 7

*In pre-spaceflight days, air superiority was the
watchword for the massive military contests on
the ground in Europe and the Middle East, even
those where heavy armor was the deciding tactical arm. Dai Nihon's conquest of space gave
a new dimension to the tactical balance: space
superiority. Today, it is axiomatic that control of
a planet's surface can only be achieved through
control of circumambient space.*

—*Armored Combat: A Modern Military Overview*
Heisaku Ariyoshi
C.E. 2523

*Donryu* meant Storm Dragon, and she was flagship of
Kawashima's Ohka Squadron. Nine hundred meters
long, massing nearly two million tons, she was a *Dai
Nihon* dragonship, one of only nine such vessels in the
entire Shichiju. Though she was as swift within the K-T
plenum as her smaller consorts, in normal space she had

a maximum acceleration of less than half a G and a combat maneuverability that led her crew to call her *o-yuseisan*, "honored planet," or, in a more bantering tone, *Shiri-omo*, "Heavy Ass." Indeed, her core shielding had begun service as a small, nano-shaped planetoid, and her crew of six thousand was larger than the population of some outpost worlds.

In combat, however, she was not expected to maneuver. Her vast size reflected the massiveness of her Quantum Power Tap; she could generate a harmonically tuned singularity pair massive enough to leak $10^{13}$ joules through her skyscraper-sized converters—some ten thousand gigawatts per second—most of which was required simply to move her ponderous bulk through space. More than enough energy was left over, however, to power her batteries of charged particle and neutron guns, and the exhaust of her plasma drive alone could theoretically sterilize a planet. Her primary long-range weapon, however, was the carrier wing of *sentoki*, the sleek, highly maneuverable air-space interceptors popularly called space fighters.

There was nothing, *nothing* throughout the Shichiju to match these Ryu-class carriers. They'd been conceived and constructed during the first four decades of the twenty-sixth century, when the Imperium recognized that the Xenophobes posed a serious threat to humankind but still believed that the alien foe must possess some sort of powerful space fleet in order to spread the Xeno infestations from world to world. That theory had been disproved by the Alyan Expedition, of course, but the *Ryus* remained a visible symbol of Imperial power, prowess, and invincibility . . . and the ultimate threat to any challenge of Imperial authority.

There would be no further challenge of that authority, not after 26 Draconis was brought back into the Hegemony's fold.

Jefferson was dissolving into chaos. Though the government's first impulse had been to withhold from the public the news that an Imperial fleet was in-system, word had leaked out within minutes through a hundred separate sources. Now, mobs of people filled the parks and walkways between Jefferson's archaic glass towers, like brightly colored rivers lapping between blue and silver cliffs. A giant towered above them; a five-story display screen raised along the side of the Weiler Building overlooking Franklin Park was replaying Duane Lassiter's announcement of the fleet's arrival. As Katya crossed the park, the image of the Eostran delegate seemed to be speaking directly to her, even though she couldn't hear the words. For that, you needed a newslink feed pressed against your palm interface, or, if you had T-sockets, a ViRcom plugged in and tuned to the appropriate channel. Half of the city's population, Katya estimated, must be 'faced in by now, as the world's news services downloaded megabytes of news, sound, picture, and virtual reality, to the panicky crowds.

Katya was amused, in a sour way, that the news services, which had taken surprisingly little interest in the proceedings in the Hall of Congress during the past weeks, had been out in force since Lassiter's announcement. Reporters and sensors for all the major ViRnews downloaders had invaded the former Sony Building, seeking sensory downloads from anyone who'd had anything to do with the proceedings in the Hall of Congress, but most especially with General Sinclair.

He'd told Katya what he wanted her to do—she'd had troubles of her own getting past the media's sensorecorders—then slipped out with a small retinue through the building's sublevel flitter parking garage. His destination was the command center in the mountains to the northwest; Katya would complete her assignment here for him, then join her unit at Port Jefferson.

Overhead, an incoming ascraft scratched a white contrail across the sky. They were already starting to abandon New America's orbital station—the military personnel assigned there, at any rate. There were far too many civilians aboard to evacuate them all before the Japanese fleet arrived. The only hope was to abandon the station to them without a fight and hope the Imperial authorities simply occupied it rather than choosing to make some sort of example of its several thousand inhabitants.

No, Highport's population should be safe enough. If the Imperials wanted to create an object lesson, they would find the educational material for that lesson here, on the ground.

The giant was still silently gesturing at her, but she escaped his scrutiny when she descended an escalator into a fabricrete cavern, an entrance to Jefferson's subsurface maglev network. She didn't follow the holographic arrows or the nervous crowds of people toward the train boarding tubes, however, but turned instead down a side passageway. After threading her way through a tangle of bare tunnels dripping with condensation, she palmed an ID access interface that took her past two New American militia guards in combat armor and through a massive door marked "Authorized Personnel Only."

The underground complex was one of several Confederation strong points in the city. "Good afternoon, Colonel." A final checkpoint blocked her way, three men in armor, one with a bulky squad support plasma gun.

"Hello, Captain Adyebo," Katya said, offering her hand for another interface. As a security AI probed her personal RAM through her palm circuitry, a life-size holo of her own head and shoulders materialized in the air, slowly turning.

"So, what's the word?" Katya asked. "Am I me?"

Adyebo's teeth flashed white against his dark face as he accessed her ID. "Looks like, Colonel. What can we do for you?"

"I just need to check on Fred," she said. "Then I'll be making arrangements to move him."

"Very good. I'd hate to think of the Impies getting hold of him." The nano of the door blurred to transparency, then dispersed. "Go on through."

Inside an otherwise empty storeroom, an egg-shaped travel pod rested in a cradle, illuminated by overhead fluorescents. Approaching the pod, Katya reached out with her left hand, palming a small touchplate in the slick, nangineered metal. With a thought, relayed through her cephlink and the circuitry in her hand, she transmitted a code to the simpleminded electronics of the egg. Part of that golden surface rippled like water, then dilated open.

Black motion glistened within, catching the overhead lights with shimmering, prismatic glistenings, like rainbows on a puddle of oil. With a mingling of awe and fear, Katya stared into the writhing substance of what had been, until very recently, Mankind's deadly and implacable enemy.

*Xenophobes.*

"Not Xenophobes," Katya reminded herself aloud. Xenophobe, of course, was a human name for an entity that had no label for itself other than a concept that seemed to translate as "Self." Now that peaceful communications had finally been established with at least two of the strange, corporate beings, a new name had been coined for them to avoid the biases of fear and bloodstained mistrust that still clung to the old.

"Naga," the name of a race of wise, benevolent, and nonviolent serpent deities in Hindu mythology, seemed apt. Xenophobe war machines were huge, serpentine bioconstructs, classified by type and named after poisonous Terran reptiles. Hostile colonies were still called Xenos, but with this Naga's help, perhaps the Confederation would be able to win more of the vast, dark beings into an alliance unlike any before known to Man.

It would be a while before she could easily think of these things as anything other than "Xenophobes," however. Mastering an unsteady queasiness at the sight, Katya leaned against the cool, nangineered slickness of the travel pod next to the opening and peered inside.

The . . . creature? creatures? . . . within moved with a liquid, slithering sound. The travel pod contained only a tiny fragment of the Eridu Naga, about one ton of the original creature's mass, budded from the parent and brought here to New America, months ago. Because the bud contained patterns of data stored by the parent, Confederation xenobiologists had suggested that it might be possible to use this fragment to communicate with other, still-hostile Xenophobes.

It was an exciting idea, one with great promise.

Assuming "Fred," as his human attendants called him, didn't fall into Imperial hands in the meantime.

Despite his nickname, Katya still couldn't look at the entity without a twinge of revulsion. Each individual unit, or *cell* looked like nothing so much as a lump of tar or grease adrift in a black and viscous liquid, slug-shaped, the size of a man's head and massing perhaps a kilogram or so. Filaments twisted within the liquid, joining each cell to its neighbors in an alien analogue of human neurons and dendrites. Individually, the Xeno units were no more intelligent than the electronics in Katya's cephlink, responding to outside stimuli with all the insight and rationality of a flatworm. Together, however, they formed a colony creature with an intelligence that was almost certainly far greater than human.

Any uncertainty in that classification was due not to doubt about the being's intelligence, but to its sheer *difference*. Xenos didn't think like humans. With group-memories spanning millennia, possessing a bewildering array of alien senses but lacking both sight and hearing, and with a worldview of the universe literally inside-out from the human perspective, Xenophobes' awareness of their surroundings simply could not be defined in human terms.

Without even a common means of perceiving the universe around them, it was small wonder humans and Xenos had blundered into a war that had lasted some forty-four years now. They'd been found on several planets colonized by man, subterranean organisms, thermovores drinking the heat of a world's core, dwelling in caverns and passageways eaten out of solid rock. Over the course of hundreds of centuries, they multiplied in those caverns, spreading out, seeping through the joints and crevices between strata, reproducing until each colony was a single titanic organism massing as much as a small moon, a vast network threaded through much of the planet's crust.

If the things had just remained underground there would have been no conflict with humans, but eventually pieces of these planetary organisms had risen from their chthonic bastions, drawn by the vast concentrations of pure metals and artificial materials that made up human cities. Several colony worlds—An-Nur II, Lung Chi, Herakles—had eventually been evacuated, abandoned to the Xeno scourge.

For four decades, humans had been fighting back, with cephlink-piloted warstriders, with orbital laser banks and HEMILCOM battle stations, and eventually with nuclear depth charges sent burrowing into the Xenophobes' subsurface lairs along channels of magnetically deformed rock. On a few infested worlds, on Loki and on alien, far-distant Alya A-VI, the Xenophobes had been obliterated, and the cities were being rebuilt.

Only now, after contact with the alien DalRiss of Alya A and B, was it possible to communicate with the things.

A DalRiss comel was waiting for her in a cylinder mounted beside the travel pod. Rolling up her left sleeve, Katya thumbed the cylinder open. Wet, glistening gelatin was revealed within, and she carefully pushed her hand and bare forearm into the amorphous mass. Sensing her body warmth, the comel molded itself to her skin. Its touch was cold and surprisingly dry. Like the Naga, the comel was a thermovore, feeding on Katya's body heat.

The Xenos, with their direct cell-to-cell networking, possessed nothing like a human language, and communication had been possible only through an intermediate agency, the sheath of translucent, alien tissue now covering Katya's left hand and forearm like a rubber glove.

She flexed her fingers within the creature's velvet embrace. The *comel* was a living construct grown and programmed through the biological wizardry of yet another nonhuman intelligence, the DalRiss of distant Alya. Exactly how they managed that still seemed little short of magic, so far as human biologists could determine, but the DalRiss had been in constant contact— and warfare—with the Xenophobes infesting their two worlds for tens of thousands of years. Evidently, they'd learned a great deal about the enemy which they were as yet unable to communicate to humans.

"Okay, Fred," she said. "Talk to me, fella."

Slowly, Katya reached her comel-sheathed hand into the sphere, plunging through the layer of translucent jelly and touching one of the pulsing black masses within. . . .

*Wonder . . . and dazzling excitement. Only recently sundered from the dark warmth and comfort of the vaster Self,* >>self<< *was not yet fully adjusted to the sharply narrowed vistas of memory and thought, or to the intense loneliness that isolated it now. Despite its loneliness,* >>self<< *trembled in the keen joy of revelation. . . .*

Reeling, Katya pulled back, her comel hand pulling free of the Naga's embrace with a sucking sound. It took a moment for the spartan gray of the storeroom to reassert itself on her senses. The intense cascade of emotion and strangely twisted imagery from the Naga had been overpowering.

She'd come here frequently throughout the past months, trying to better understand Fred, trying to better understand the enigmatic Naga view of the universe. Katya had already learned that Nagas could not get bored . . . a good thing, she'd decided, for a being that, if her understanding of the visions transmitted through the comel was accurate, was essentially immortal. A Naga's sense of time appeared to be measured not by artificial demarcations like seconds but by the passage of events.

*That's another way they're inside-out from us*, she thought. *For us, subjective time passes slowly when nothing's going on, fast when everything's happening at once. So far as Fred here is concerned, it's only been a few moments since I talked to him last, and that was weeks ago.*

Figuring that one out had been more hunch than brain work, a flash of inspiration that Sinclair had wryly called woman's intuition. Now, if she could just figure out what Fred thought about the prospect of meeting a Naga that was *not* its original Self. . . .

Each Naga, evidently, had considerable difficulty understanding the concept of other intelligences . . . even of other Nagas. A planetary Naga was a literally Self-absorbed creature, its awareness limited to what was Self and what was not. Scouts—fragments such as Fred—yearned for reabsorption into the greater Self, to be Self instead of the sharply delimited and shrunken >>self<<, but even that experience couldn't wholly prepare a Naga World Mind for the shock of meeting *another* being like itself.

The Nagas, it was now known, once they'd converted much of the crust of a planet to their own purposes, entered a reproductive phase, hurling spore pods by the billions into space on intensely powerful magnetic fluxes. Most of those pods were lost in vastness, but a scant few, guided by biologically programmed instincts homing on heat and magnetic fields, reached the worlds

of other stars after millions of years of dreamless sleep
adrift. Touching down, they tunneled into virgin crust
and began the cycle anew.

But from the weirdly inverted Naga point of view,
it wasn't that way at all. The universe was a Void
surrounded by endless depths of rock; so far as the
Nagas themselves were concerned, their voyages across
interstellar space were mere excursions from one wall of
a rock-walled gulf to another . . . and the eventless ages
separating launch from planetfall and rebirth literally no
time at all.

Bracing herself, she reached in once more with her
comel-clad hand. . . .

*Excitement. Shells of the not-Selfs-that-know move
within the Void.*

Katya furrowed her brow as she leaned closer, trying
to decipher the torrent of alien thoughts.

*Enemy . . . the enemy? The enemy . . . is coming, and
>>self<< must be protected. . . .*

She concentrated on key thoughts. Soon, the Naga
would be taken into the Void once more—*Wonder!
Soaring, dizzying emptiness stretching out forever on
every side!*—and transported to another world—*What is
"world?"*—where it would be allowed to rejoin a Self
that would have no knowledge of humans.

*Where is . . . not-Self-that-knows-called-Dev?*

Pressing back frustration, Katya tried to concentrate.
Fred, a tiny fraction of its Eriduan "parent," possessed
limited intelligence. Talking with it was like trying
to talk with a small and ofttimes single-mindedly
stubborn child.

Focusing her thoughts, she tried to explain that Dev
was someplace else, another world.

*What is world?*
*Where is Dev?*
*What is love?*

That last startled her, and she pulled back again.
God, what had Fred managed to pick up from the

currents whipping back and forth across the surface of her brain?

*Where is Dev?*

*What is love-Dev?*

Damn! She liked Dev . . . but didn't love him. True, she was worried about him, about the fate of the mission to Athena, but . . .

"Oh, it's just you. Where's the general?"

Katya whirled at the sound of the voice, her arm pulling free from the Naga with a wet slurp. "Gok, Pol! What the hell are *you* doing here?"

Pol Danver was one of Sinclair's senior aides, a chubby, self-important man who, Katya sensed, resented her presence, her violation of his territory.

"I have the same clearance you do," he said. "Listen, I can't find Travis." He emphasized the first name, as though proving a point. "Someone said he was down here with you."

"Hardly. He's on his way to Henry," she told him, naming a town northwest of Jefferson, in a valley high amid the rugged, wooded vastness of the Silverside Cascades.

"Huh. The who-was is we're pulling out."

"We are. The general said to carry out Plan Kappa, then get the hell out. His words, Pol."

Danver looked stubborn. "I'll need authorization for that, Colonel. You understand I can't simply take *your* word for it."

"It's already downloaded," she snapped back, pointing at a computer access panel on the wall. Danver had been grating on her since she'd come here, and she was in no mood to coddle him. "Palm it for yourself."

The aide hesitated, opened his mouth as though to say something more, then whirled, touched a contact, and stepped through the dissolving door.

Danver, Katya thought, was a jouleech. The word, originally coined to describe a Maian powervore that attached itself to sources of electrical or thermal energy, had come to mean people like Danver who thrived on being close to the centers of political power. His use of Sinclair's first name, for instance, was little more than a means of shouting *I'm important*.

It was a kind of flattery, she supposed, to be disliked by such a man. Within the rather informal structure of New American politics, Travis Sinclair was not in fact anything more than one of the several dozen delegates representing the North American colony on the planet. In the real world, however, and beyond the posturings and public imagings of Congress, Sinclair was one of a small handful of men and women who were almost single-handedly responsible for creating the Confederation. As chief architect of the Declaration of Reason, Sinclair, more than any other man, could be considered the spirit, the motivating force behind the entire rebellion.

It was only natural that such power should attract people like Danver.

Composing herself, Katya removed the comel and replaced it in its container. She wasn't sure what she'd managed to communicate to Fred, but at least it was anticipating another voyage through space. Danver was gone by the time she left the chamber.

In Franklin Park, Lassiter's giant image still gestured and mouthed silent platitudes. It looked as though the ViRnews services were playing part of his address to Congress, from the moments just before news of the Imperial's arrival had reached him. God, Katya thought . . . was the ViRnews media actually downloading that to the public? That was exactly the sort of defeatist propaganda the Imperials would love to see disseminated throughout New America.

What would be next, she wondered, a call for surrender?

Her task here done, she left. Returning to the Sony Building, she completed the transfer of essential computer records to Henry. Five hours later, after battling through the crowds clogging the city, she rejoined her unit at Port Jefferson.

Twenty-eight hours after dropping out of the K-T plenum, the first elements of Ohka Squadron entered close orbit around New America. Eighteen hours after that, *Donryu* made orbit as well, close-escorted by her retinue of cruisers and transports.

By that time, the destroyers *Hatakaze* and *Yakaze* had already docked with the station, and their complements of black-armored Imperial Marines had stormed aboard. There'd been no resistance. All local militia and Confederation troops had withdrawn hours before, escaping in small ships that were now scattering through the system, or riding ascraft down to New America's surface, where several sizable armored units were beginning to congregate.

The marines had orders to secure the station and maintain control but to leave the civilian population alone. Except for a few, inevitable incidents—the initial report downloaded to Kawashima from the station commander included mention of eight dead civilians, forty-five reports of theft or looting, twelve rapes, and one marine murdered by one of his victims—those orders had been carried out precisely. Kawashima was well aware that his presence here was to be one of *controlled* power.

There was no denying that he wielded terrible power over the 26 Draconis System and its inhabitants. A massive bombardment from orbit, or simply turning *Donryu*'s searing plasma drives toward the planet from a hundred kilometers up, could exterminate every trace of life on New America. But such a brute-force approach would be counterproductive. New America was one of the Hegemony's richest and most productive worlds; more, it was a rarity within the Shichiju, a world that had not required terraforming for humans to live unaided on its surface. If Kawashima captured it by reducing it to a radioactive desert, he would have lost . . . and in the losing been completely disgraced.

He would employ terror tactics where necessary, certainly, but he would employ them selectively, and with extreme precision. New America's Highport would become his orbital base of operations, though, for now at least, he would remain in his headquarters aboard *Donryu*, parked a few kilometers beyond the station.

The next step was as obvious as it was necessary.

Kawashima would have to capture Port Jefferson.

# Chapter 8

*A warstrider's chief strength lies neither in its armor nor its weaponry, but in its flexibility. With legs instead of tracks, wheels, or jets, with a sealed hull and self-contained life-support system that permit operations in environments ranging from corrosively poisonous to hard vacuum, the warstrider can go almost literally anywhere. Warstriders have climbed mountains and penetrated forests inaccessible to tracked vehicles, have waded swamps, have even operated in the depths of the sea, though their mobility is necessarily limited in such environments.*

—*Armored Combat: A Modern Military Overview*
Heisaku Ariyoshi
C.E. 2523

Katya was receiving very little data from the outside world, had been virtually isolated for the past four hours. Her hull sensors were sending in a steady flow of information on pressure, temperature, and the like, but the data were unchanging, confirmation merely that though hell was rampaging across Port Jefferson's fabricrete apron, the seas just off the stony beaches of Cape Dickson were quiet.

Her only feed from the world above came through a tiny sensor packet bobbing on the surface of the water five meters above her head, connected to her RS-64D Warlord by a slender fiber-optic cable. The sensor pack was too small to give her more than low-res visual and access to the combat radio frequencies, and it increased her feeling of smothered isolation. Old dreads—of darkness, of being buried alive—stirred uneasily just below the fringes of her conscious thoughts.

Sometimes she wished she had an Imperial Marine's mastery of *Kokorodo*, the Way of the Mind. She'd been exposed to the discipline, of course, during her training for the Hegemony Guard, enough to allow her to focus her thoughts on mnemonic codes. Nothing she'd learned, however, would take away the raw, nerve-grating fear . . . especially in the long wait before a battle.

Four hours earlier she'd taken command of thirty-six warstriders, one quarter of the 1st Confederation Rangers' entire complement, and under the sky-screening cover of billowing smoke clouds had waded into the steep-bottomed, high-tide waters off Cape Dickson. There, the striders had released their sensor packets and hunkered down to wait. The waters, if calm, were murky, heavy with silt backwashed from the surf along the beach. Tides on New America, prodigious with huge Columbia in the sky, were nonetheless ponderously slow. World danced with moon here in a lockstep two-to-three ratio—a pair of 5.2-standard-day orbits of Columbia to three of New America's eighty-three-hour days. At low tide, Cape Dickson rose above kilometer upon empty kilometer of wet, weed-choked tidal flat; at high tide, the surf lapped nearly to the perimeter of the port. Luck had begun the Imperial assault before the tide was in full ebb. Had the invaders delayed their attack by so much as another couple of orbits of their fleet, Katya's plan might not have worked.

That fear, at least, was ended now. The fighters had appeared, and eighty minutes later the first of the striderpods had streaked in out of the west, shedding foil chaff and decoys, arrowing in toward the port on flickering white tails of plasma.

Thank God that the last of the shuttles bearing key members of the Confederation government—and Fred, still secure in his travel pod—had rendezvoused hours ago with the *Transluxus*, a big, fifth-generation K-T drive passenger liner owned and operated by the pro-rebellion Highstar lines. Most of the independence-minded delegates ought to be safely on their way to Mu Herculis by now, escorted by a precious few of New America's interstellar ships.

General Sinclair and the senior military leaders, however, had remained on the colony world. New America was too vital to Confederation interests, as a base, as a symbol of resistance, as a *world*, simply to surrender it to the Imperium without a fight.

A victory here, at the spaceport, before the Imperial assault forces achieved a firm beachhead, might be enough to delay the enemy's attack indefinitely, as at Eridu.

It had better. It was all they had to work with now.

"Ready," she transmitted, the coded signal flashed to the other bobbing sensor packs in the sea around her. Her plan called for close coordination and precisely calculated timing. The counterattack would go nowhere if it was launched in spluttering fits and starts, a few warstriders emerging from the sea at a time. Peering from her vantage point, bobbing on the waves a hundred

meters from shore, she waited until she was certain the
Imperial assault wave had grounded.

It was time. "Forward!"

Through her tenuous link with the surface, she could
see very little of the shore a hundred meters ahead, so
shrouded was it in billowing clouds of smoke. She fixed
her gaze on one particular part of the beach, flexed her
powerful legs, and started moving.

"Take it, Ken," she told Sublieutenant Ken Maubry,
her number-two in the three-slot Warlord. Number-
three was her weapons tech, Warrant Officer Francine
DelRey.

"Yes, sir," Maubry replied, and control of the Warlord
passed smoothly to him. Maubry was a raw newbie,
newly recruited from some town in the Newamie outback. Francine had been Hegemony Guard for four
years before she'd elected to join the rebels . . . and
an enlisted trooper, a "crunchie," in the New American
militia for three years before that. Katya was counting
on Francine's steel-nerved steadiness handling the strider's weapons so that she, Katya, could concentrate on
running the counterattack.

Though Ken was jacking the machine toward the
beach, she could still feel through the Warlord's sensors.
The ground was steep beneath her massively flanged
feet, a mix of course-grained sand and stones smoothed
to pebbles by the tides. Progress was painfully slow as
the nearly sixty-ton machine dragged its massive shell
through the water. She could feel the tide's ebb-flow
current on her skin, clutching at her, dragging at her
with each step forward like a cold and sluggish wind.

Then the Warlord's upper works broke the surface,
exposing submerged sensors as water cascaded down
the machine's curved flanks, and Katya's awareness was
once again flooded by light and motion and noise. She
reeled in the sensor pack with a thought, then pulled
down a quick scan of the entire panorama. The coastline
ahead was shrouded in smoke and the more ominous,

drifting gray patches of ground-hugging fog that marked
nano-disassembler clouds. Flashes, like muted lightning,
flared and stabbed through the mist, accompanied by
thunderous rumbles, but so far there was no direct sign
of the enemy.

Progress was faster now as the Warlord's torso cleared
the water. The machine plowed ahead, trailing a churning wake. Movement flashed, high and to the left; the
Warlord's upper torso canted and turned, weapons tracking . . . then discharging in twin bolts of blue light from
the arm-mounted proton CPGs. Locked in the flashing
embrace of a targeting cursor within Katya's ViRdisplay,
a Ko-125 Akuma flared sun-brilliant for an instant, then
disintegrated, smoke-streaming fragments descending on
the sea like a fiery rain.

"Never mind the ascraft," Katya warned Francine.
"Save it for the heavies ashore."

"Sure, Katya," the weapons officer replied. "That bird
was radar-locking us, though."

"Nice shooting. But if you have to bird-shoot, use the
hivel. I want full-power on the main weapons when we
wade ashore."

"Yes, sir."

Gouts of water rose to either side; steam boiled away
as lasers grazed the surface. To left and right, a ragged
line stretching for a kilometer in either direction, the
rest of Katya's reserve heavy company splashed out of
water that now broke and curled about the warstriders'
feet. Wading out of the surf and onto the steeply sloping
beach, they entered the wet intertidal zone that had
been submerged a few hours earlier, but which now
was open and exposed. Rocks cracked and popped
beneath the great weight of her RS-64's feet; a stray
shell whined lonesomely overhead. Battle fog swirled
about the advancing machines, cloaking them as their
surface nano shifted from water-dark to smoke gray.

Movement . . . nano-shrouded, but large and heavy.
The Warlord's CPGs barked again; steam exploded

from a tumble-down of water-smoothed boulders. A laser flashed in return, an emerald sparkle in the fog-heavy air. Katya felt the beam hit. Pain was not transmitted through the link, of course, but the sensation was one of being lightly punched, a solid thump against her side.

*Fire!* She willed the return volley, though she didn't verbalize the order. Francine returned fire with left-right-left hammerblows from the CPGs, a salvo of rockets from the Warlord's ventral Mark III weapons pod.

The target, revealed now as a KR-86 Tachi, was half the Warlord's bulk, lightly armored, built for speed rather than endurance. Explosions savaged its side and dorsal surfaces, gouged holes through layered duralloy, smashed the left leg motivator assemblies in a fine spray of broken parts. Another CPG struck home, a bolt of blue-white light that melted through the machine's left side. Oily smoke boiled from the crater, where wires and circuitry glowed red-hot. The Tachi twisted right, shuddered, and fell, right leg twitching spastically with the final nerve discharges of its dying pilot.

The AI in Katya's Warlord keened warning: an unidentified strider to the rear. Maubry spun in time to catch another Tachi rising from the water, twenty meters offshore. Evidently, some of the incoming assault striders had undershot or overshot the narrow cape that was their target and come down in the sea. Francine hit with a twin laser–CPG blast that sent great clouds of steam boiling into the sky and ripped the right arm from its joint. The Tachi swung fast, trying to bring its electron cannon to bear, but Francine completed the destruction with a long burst from the hivel cannon, slamming fifty rounds through the Tachi's armor and punching it back beneath the rolling tumble of the surf.

"Watch yourselves!" Katya warned over her company's tactical channel. "We've got some with us in the water!"

To her right, another Warlord, jacked by Captain Vic

Hagan and his crew, lumbered onto the sand, water
streaming from its armor. Nanoflage blurred its outlines
and color, save for a bright patch of nose art—a shaggy
blond caveman shouldering a club beneath the legend
*Mission Link*. Hagan's strider had just smashed a third
Tachi at the water's edge.

"Hey, Boss!" Hagan's voice rasped across the tactical
lasercom channel. "Easy pickings!" Katya's command
Warlord was *The Boss*, though no nose art accompanied
the name.

"These guys were stragglers," she replied. "It'll be
tougher with the guys already ashore."

The rest of her ambush company was emerging all
along the beach. She'd placed her most experienced
people and her only two heavies—the Warlords jacked
by herself and by Vic—near the center, the greener
striderjacks on the flanks. If this counterpunch had
any hope of success, it would be with an all-out,
strength-in-the-center punch. "Come on, Rangers!" she
called over the tactical link circuit, urging her people
forward. "Move! Move!"

Pacing Hagan's *Mission Link*, her Warlord stilted up
the last few meters of beach. An RLN-90 Scoutstrider,
a Confederation machine, lay in a shattered heap of
barely recognizable fragments at the top of the beach,
still burning. Farther in, on the unyielding surface of the
fabricrete apron, her optics picked up the fallen hulk of
a Newamie Militia Manta and, close by, the bodies and
body fragments of an infantry squad, cut down by heavy
autofire.

They were heaped up together in tangled clumps, with
a few isolated bodies marking men who'd tried to run
and been hit before they could get away. Katya saw
loose arms and legs, a blood-smeared spill of intestines, and at least one severed head still strapped into
its helmet.

Katya shuddered . . . or rather, she felt the icy mental shiver that would have accompanied such a purely

physical response, even though her body was now out of the circuit in its padded slot. As often as she'd seen such things, she could never get used to them.

Damn, *damn*! Infantry against goking warstriders. Unless the infantry had some high-powered support, the contest was always hopeless. Those troops had been wearing combat armor; it might as well have been garlands of flowers. The weapons they'd carried had been chemflamers and satchel charges, thumpers and rocket launchers, all designed to knock out light warstriders; they'd never even gotten a chance to use them.

There was such an awful lot of blood. . . .

Dev Cameron, Katya remembered, had pioneered joint infantry-strider close combat tactics on Loki. They'd worked well enough against Xenos, but Katya still had her doubts about the place of infantry in strider-to-strider combat. Infantry, even civilian mobs, had faced striders on Eridu . . . but casualties had been heavy in what had been acts of sheer desperation.

Well, so, too, was this. With so few recruits available with the three sockets necessary for jacking a warstrider or other large, full-linkage combat machine, the only option open to the Confederation was to find ways to employ infantry—lightly armed and armored foot soldiers—against enemy warstriders.

It was no wonder, though, that striderjacks referred to infantry as "crunchies," supposedly because that was the sound they made when stepped on by a strider.

"Stay . . . stay with me, Vic," she told Hagan. "Stick close."

"You got it, Boss."

Passing the tangled bodies, the two Warlords angled toward the main spaceport buildings. The entire line, according to plan, switched on their radars. That illuminated themselves as well as any targets, of course, but they had to *see*. Katya's AI processed the returns, showing massive shapes moving eighteen hundred meters ahead, and they weren't showing the flashing white star the Confederation AIs were using to flag friendly IFF signals.

"Take them long-range," she told the others. Her tiny command was heavily outnumbered; they would accomplish more by sniping at the enemy than getting into knife-fighting range, at least to start with. Later, perhaps, as the assault developed further . . .

There was no time to think about later, only now. Francine bracketed a ghostly, slow-moving radar target and loosed one of the Warlord's Striker missiles, which slid off the RS-64's aft-mounted Y-rack with a hiss like tearing paper. To left and right, other missiles arrowed into the murk, which suddenly began to flash and strobe with brilliant, internal lightnings. The Confederation line advanced, still firing, tracking and firing and firing again. Something exploded beyond the low-lying cloud, sending up a fireball visible even through the gloom. So thick was the smoke now that Katya found it hard to remember that it was, in fact, afternoon, that outside the battle area the sky was clear and the sun was brightly shining. *Fire!*

Then the first Imperial volley slammed a reply into the advancing Ranger line, rocking the warstriders with thundering explosions. Two of Katya's striders went down, limbs thrashing; a third, a Ghostrider, was badly damaged, the duralloy peeled back from its dorsal hull like the ragged edge of some terrible, deep-slashed wound. Her own Warlord, under the faster-than-human reflexes of its AI, knocked down two incoming rockets a split second before they hit, whipsawing them from the sky with bursts of deplur slugs from the hivel mount.

*Damn!* How many of the enemy machines were there? During their planning for this engagement, Katya and the members of Sinclair's combat staff had estimated that the Imperials would allot at least two companies of assault striders to the capture of the spaceport, and more likely a full battalion. The volume of highly accurate rocket fire thundering in from dead ahead had convinced Katya that she was facing a battalion, possibly more.

"Keep firing!" she ordered, as Francine launched the last of their Striker missiles. Now it was unguided rockets . . . until they were close enough to the enemy that they could engage him with beam weapons.

Thunder rolled low overhead, passing west to east, an ascraft of some kind, though bigger and more powerful than the air-space interceptors they'd seen so far. Katya ignored it. Damn it, though, it would have helped if they could have held onto air superiority here, instead of just surrendering it to the Imperials.

"Let me take it," she told Maubry, issuing the mental code that shifted control of the big Warlord from his cephlinkage to her own. Her reflexes, her linked control, were better than his, faster and more automatic.

Mostly, though, she had to be *doing* something. The Warlord lurched toward the enemy line, a bipedal carnosaur with mincing gait. A pair of Tachis confronted her and she exchanged salvos, shrugging off a pair of rockets that slammed against her armor, then burning the legs off one of her opponents as Hagan lumbered up to engage the other.

"Nano count!" Maubry warned, his voice sharp. "Point three-one, and rising!"

Those warheads had packed nano-disassemblers instead of conventional explosives; the stuff was deadly, programmed to attach to any artificial material within reach—like duralloy—and begin taking it apart molecule by molecule. The point number was a measure of concentration in the air. The higher the number, the faster a strider's armor was dissolving.

Alert flags were already flashing in her field of view. "I see it! Francine! Pop the AND!"

Point three-nine, now . . . and thicker to the right. She moved left, as Francine triggered the Warlord's hull-mounted AND canisters. A fog of anti–nano-D shrouded the warstrider, nano hunting nano in a deadly, invisible, and ultrahigh-speed battle in the air around the machine.

Then the battlesmoke parted in front of her just as three Tachis sprinted forward, their nanoflaged hulls shimmering between fog gray and dappled where a sudden shaft of sunlight touched their flanks. An explosion just in front of the Warlord staggered her, opening a pit in the fabricrete pavement and pelting her with gravel.

She felt her footing give way, struggled to regain her balance. An electron bolt caught *The Boss* in the left flank, arcing through control circuits and power feeds, jolting her with all the force of a lightning bolt. There was a searing blast and a howling noise, both abruptly chopped short as her sensor feeds failed.

All sensation vanished, and she toppled forward. . . .

*Someday, military commanders will be able to cut
through the fog of war to see both the dispositions
of their forces and those of the enemy, to fully
direct the course of battle. On that day, military
science will become worthy of the name, a true
science, instead of the fuzzy, half-blind guesswork
it is now.*

—General Saiji Hatanaka
After his rout of Manchurian forces
at T'ungchou, near Beijing
C.E. 2212

Battle management for the Confederation defenders was
in the hands of General Mathan Grier, a big, bluff man
with craggy features and a fanatic's absolute dedication
to the Confederation cause.

Born on Liberty to wealthy parents, he'd been sent
to Earth to attend school, first MIT and then, after his
acceptance by a Hegemony Guard educational program,

the Osaka Military Academy. His Hegemony military career had been long, if undistinguished. His only combat experience had been against Xenos—as a *sho-i*, a sublieutenant, on Herakles in 2515, then again as *taisa* in command of a regiment on Lung Chi twenty-two years later.

His disaffection for Hegemony and Empire had followed, as he watched the government laying the blame for the Lung Chi disaster with the *gaijin* in Imperial service, then later as Imperial troops were dispatched to Liberty to quell the rioting there. He'd resigned his commission immediately after the Commons Massacre of '38, returning to Liberty to take command of a militia regiment. Six months later, the Confederation's General Darwin Smith had offered him a place on the Confederation Military Command staff.

Grier was a competent enough officer, if not a particularly imaginative one. His elevation to the CONMILCOM Battle Staff was at least partly political—a means of answering Liberty's fears that New America was set upon dominating the new Confederation—and he knew it, but his fervent belief in independence transcended politics. As a commander, he was both conservative and cautious. Watching the battle for Port Jefferson unfolding in ViReality, he knew that his key concern there was not so much *winning* as it was *not* losing.

Linked into the CONMILCOM Battle Direction Center's AI, his body was in a secure bunker half a kilometer beneath the rugged, bunker-studded slopes of Stone Mountain overlooking the town of Henry. In his mind's eye, however, he was hovering above Port Jefferson, looking down on the battle.

The display was precisely like those of the war games he'd played at the Academy. Sensors scattered about the battle area, including small remote flyers, relayed a steady stream of data back to the BDC's AI— energy discharges, radiation signatures, radar returns, visual images, RF leakage, even the sounds of moving warstriders—all fed through an enhancement program, matched against a comprehensive data base, and displayed as a three-dimensional map surface crawling with centimeter-high, red and blue holo-images of warstriders. Smaller, slower moving flecks of blue marked Confederation ground troops, tagged by their armor IDs and comm channels.

The mapping wasn't perfect. Their speed and their nanoflage-stealth characteristics made warstriders surprisingly hard to locate precisely on a battlefield, and what he was perceiving was actually the AI's best guess as to dispositions and identities; large portions of the field were blanked out, uncomfortable zones from which no data was available and where *anything* could be hiding. Not even Artificial Intelligences or cephlinks could completely penetrate the age-old fog of war.

Still, the command system gave him a measure of control over the battlefield that Napoleon or Patton or even Hatanaka had never enjoyed, or even dreamed of. By visually tagging any one strider's image, he could get a complete readout of all available data, its type, its vector, and full pilot data for Confederation machines; with a thought, he could open a comm channel to any of the strider commanders, if necessary, though such communications were generally reserved for Colonel Weiss, the senior officer on the field.

Grier knew well the dangers of micromanagement from the rear.

From his unique vantage point, however, he could sense the flow, the pacing of the battle, from the circular expanse of Port Jefferson to the clustered glass towers of Jefferson itself. He'd watched the Imperial assault troops land, watched patches of the terrain stained red, showing areas of Imperial control. Weiss's 1st Rangers and battalions of local militia were moving to cut off the incursion. Their main defensive line had been thrown up along the northern outskirts of Port Jefferson, in the sprawling manufacturing center and spaceport strip known as Braxton.

He'd seen Colonel Alessandro's dramatic emergence from the sea off the coast, a single line of over thirty striders sweeping across the fabricrete apron and neatly trapping over a hundred of the Imperial Tachis near the spaceport's main buildings.

But Grier, trained in Imperial military theory, could not shake certain of its basic preconceptions. A weaker force could not drive or pen a stronger one; at least a three-to-one advantage was necessary for attack; internal lines of communication and movement were superior to LOCs around the outside of a circle; infantry could not stand in the field against warstriders.

The Confederation forces, though they possessed larger and more powerful striders, only roughly matched the attackers in numbers. The Japanese commander surrounded at Port Jefferson could move in any direction and find only a single, slender line of Confederation machines blocking his path. Breaking that line would be easy, and the first step toward annihilating the defenders piecemeal.

Worse, at least two Imperial assault companies had come down on the mainland, scattered across a broad area of towns, ridges, and farmland between the spaceport and the capital; the Newamie militia under General Kruger was giving a good account of itself so far, but inevitably the invading warstriders would pull their scattered forces together and begin pushing the defenders back, isolating Cape Dickson from the mainland. When that happened, the 1st Rangers still at the spaceport would be trapped, cut off from the rest of the Confederation defenses. Grier could *see* the trap unfolding, could see it . . . and know just what he had to do to stop it.

Grier had considered calling in Travis Sinclair, Darwin Smith, or one of the other senior Confederation leaders, but immediately discarded the idea. Grier had become comfortable with the idea of himself as savior of the New American forces; Sinclair had approved his deployment and his battle plan. He would show these New Americans what a man from Liberty with a *real* military education could do!

"Colonel Weiss," he called, searching for the tagged holographic image of the Rangers' CO. "Colonel Weiss! Come in!"

There was no reply, and Grier wondered if Weiss had been killed. Who was Weiss's 2IC? Downloading the Rangers' command structure, he frowned. Alessandro? Technically the woman was a colonel, but Grier scarcely regarded that. Until last month she'd never topjacked anything bigger than a company, and he frankly doubted her ability to handle anything so complex as a regiment now.

*Chikusho!* Where the gok was Weiss?

As he studied the neatly ordered arrays of colored figures on the map, he was briefly tempted to let things go a while longer. The ambush by Alessandro's forces certainly appeared to be driving the Imperials, knocking them off-balance and sending them reeling back.

But no, the danger was simply too great. The blank spaces on the map were spreading across large areas of the spaceport and the terrain between Cape Dickson and the capital. That meant remote sensors were being knocked down or were succumbing to the corrosive effects of nano agents hanging over the battlefield. If he waited much longer, he would lose control of the situation entirely, and the Rangers, the only specifically Confederation force on the planet, could be lost.

He wouldn't risk it. Saving the army, in Grier's opinion, was far more important than winning the battle.

"Colonel Weiss! This is General Grier, CONMIL-COM! Come in!"

"This . . . this is Weiss." The voice was ragged with strain. "I'm . . . kind of busy right now, General."

Zooming in closer from his gods'-eye point of view, Grier could see Weiss's machine now, a command-rigged Warlord highlighted by a flashing star. The machines with him were crouched behind a hastily nano-fabricated barricade protecting the industrial facilities and manufacturing plants of Braxton. The defensive line was solid at the moment, sealing off Cape Dickson, but pressure from the assault force had been mounting steadily for several minutes. A steady flow of infantry was already streaming back off the spaceport and through Braxton, in full retreat from the clash of titans behind them.

"Weiss, listen to me! The spaceport is lost, and you're in danger of being cut off. Open your link for a tactical download."

"Link open."

With a thought, Grier sent a summary of the mapboard simulation funneling through Colonel Weiss's link. The data showed clearly what Weiss could not see for himself, that the broad peninsula he was defending was in danger of being cut off by the Imperials between him and Jefferson.

"I . . . see it, General," Weiss flashed back after a moment. "What do you recommend?"

"Fall back to Monroe." Monroe was a large town, a suburb of Jefferson on the mainland squarely between the capital and Port Jefferson. "Consolidate your line with General Kruger. I'm dispatching the reserves to back him up."

"Order acknowledged," Weiss replied. "We're falling back."

"Colonel Alessandro," Grier called. "Do you copy?"

Again, silence. This was what Grier disliked most about topjacking a large unit. Individual commanders tended to be independent, too caught up in battlelust, with no time to spare for the senior officers overseeing the battle from behind the lines. Katya Alessandro, from what he knew of her, was no exception.

"Colonel Alessandro! This is CONMILCOM! Respond!"

"CONMILCOM, this is Captain Hagan," a man's voice replied. "The Colonel's down, and I think her comm's out."

"Understood. Who is senior officer in the detachment, Hagan?"

"Uh, I guess I am, sir."

"The order is break contact and retreat. Rally with Colonel Weiss at Monroe."

"Uh, CONMILCOM, that isn't possible just now. We've got—"

"Don't tell me what is possible, damn it! You're in danger of being cut off and surrounded! Now get your people and machines out of there, Captain! Now!"

Sometimes, Grier thought, you just had to know how to deal with these stubborn junior officers. They tended to see only their narrow slice of a battle and forget that there were much larger things at stake. He noted with satisfaction that Weiss's warstriders were already falling back through the manufacturing complex, abandoning their jury-rigged barricade. Hagan's thirty-some striders were isolated far around the enemy flank but appeared to be breaking off all along the line. Good. If the Imperials gave them half a chance, they should be able to get clear, swing around the Imperial flank, and easily reach the rendezvous at Monroe.

A brilliant maneuver, he concluded, requiring only immediate obedience on the part of his officers.

Almost imperceptibly on the map, the pace of the retreat was increasing.

"*Chikusho*, Captain!" Sublieutenant Witter's protest mingled anger and hurt. "We were winning! Why are we retreating now?"

"I guess they know something we don't know," Vic Hagan told his pilot, already coding the general message to the rest of the unit ordering them to break off and retreat.

He was worried, though. Confederation and Imperial forces were by now so intermingled there was no front line, and breaking contact with the enemy at this point was a hell of a lot easier ordered than done.

Besides, Katya was down ... her position overrun moments before by a pack of swift-moving Tachis. He could see her machine, inert on the fabricrete a hundred meters away, but with no telemetry from her Warlord he couldn't tell if she was alive or dead.

"We can't just leave the Boss in there," Sergeant Toland, his number three, said.

"Agreed. Witter, take us in closer. Sarge, give me the lasers. You take the rest. I want those Tachis down!"

"Now you're talking, Captain. Let's get the gokin' *sheseiji!*"

But Vic was more concerned for Katya.

One of the two Tachis had stopped meters from the fallen strider, was stooping, bringing a heavy laser to bear on the wreckage. Hagan cut loose with the twin, fifty-megawatt lasers mounted like an insect's pincers to left and right of the Warlord's fuselage. The bolts seared into the Tachi's side; Hagan thrilled to see the machine twist and snap back, looking for all the world like some huge, two-legged beast that had just been sharply stung.

The second Tachi took a step forward and opened fire.

Katya was not sure whether or not she'd been unconscious. When her linkage with *The Boss*'s AI was broken, she'd awakened inside the narrow, padded coffin of the machine's center linkslot, with no light at all save that from a tiny constellation of green and amber marking the slot's manual controls. Claustrophobia encircled her. Her breathing came in short, hard gasps as she slapped her palm across the interface, trying to relink.

Nothing. The Warlord was dead.

She knew how lucky she'd been. That surge of power from the Tachi's electron gun could have fried her brain. Fortunately, the link safeties had worked as advertised; the Warlord's AI had cut her out of the circuit even as it died.

Had the others aboard come through too? Using the auxiliary interface, she opened an intercom line. "Francine! Ken! Are you there?"

"God, what happened?" Maubry asked.

"Okay, Skipper," DelRey said. "I'm in the dark, but okay."

"All systems are off-line," she told them. "Time to odie, gang."

Odie, soldier's slang from the Nihongo word for "dance," meant to get the hell out, fast. Swiftly, she unhooked the wires and feed tubes that connected her with the Warlord's now-dead life-support system from her bodysuit receivers, then removed breather helmet and gloves from a side compartment. New America might be one of those rare worlds in the Shichiju where humans could walk and breathe unaided, but the modern battlefield was deadly to anyone foolish enough to enter it unprotected. Poisonous fumes from wrecked striders, volatile gases from binary explosives, and, most deadly, unseen mists of nano-D guaranteed that unprotected humans would be dead in minutes.

She made a final check through the interface—good, local concentrations of nano-D were low—then broke contact and sealed her gloves. She typed a code into the panel manually, then braced herself as the outer hatch slid open.

As always when she stepped in person onto a battle-field, she was surprised by how dark and murky the air actually was. When she was linked, her AI provided an enhanced view of the world around her; like most jackers she tended to forget just how much a strider relied on superhuman sensors, on fog-piercing radar and infrared, and on the combat-loaded AI's educated guesswork.

It was like stepping into a heavy, silver fog. Her Warlord lay nose-down on a broken rubble of shattered fabricrete, one leg folded beneath the hull, the other extended behind it like a broken trail of steel struts and wreckage. The other two slots, set to either side of hers on the dorsal hull, were open, and their occupants were scrambling out, like her attired in gray bodysuits and transparent life-support helmets. Francine DelRey cradled a PCR-28, the high-velocity combat rifle she'd brought with her from her days in the infantry. Maubry and Katya both wore megajoule hand lasers holstered on their hips.

Toys against warstriders, useless. Katya sensed motion close by and looked up.

Looming out of the fog, the Tachi stood only a bit more than twice as tall as a man but was bulkier, twenty tons or so precariously balanced on slender legs angled sharply back at the knees. Its hull rippled through shades of gray as its nanoflage responded to changing light. The legs and gait gave it the menacing look of some huge and dangerous bird as it stilted over cracked pavement and loose rubble . . . or of a carnivorous, bipedal dinosaur.

Only the hazy outlines of the thing were visible through the drifting smoke. Katya raised her hand, warning the others in her crew to silence. The audio sensors on a strider were quite good, as were its visual and motion sensors. Damn, it ought to see them already.

Ah! That was why. The Imperial strider was busy with something else, a Confed strider lurking unseen somewhere in the murk. Black smoke was curling from a gash in its side, and its stubby weapons packs were tracking something in the mist to Katya's right. There was a flash and a sound like swarming bees, and Katya was left blinking purple afterimages from her eyes. A moment later, a triplet of explosions cracked off the strider's ventral hull, sending a patter of shrapnel across the ground. With dawning horror, Katya realized that the three of them were in danger of being caught in the open between two warstriders in combat. The only thing worse from a crunchie's point of view was having a warstrider actually chasing you.

Urgently, she signaled the others. *This way! Fast!*

They ran as a CPG bolt caught the Tachi in the side, ripping it open, gutting the machine and spilling its internal assemblies in smoking fragments across the pavement. The three kept running, picking their way across blocks of broken fabricrete. . . .

. . . and stopped. A second Tachi was there, lurching forward out of the smoke just ten meters away, each footstep a clash of metal on stone, the monster close enough that Katya could see the surface nano rippling back from an ominous bulge mounted on its flank. The black muzzle of an AP pod gaped at her like a questing eye.

"Down!" Katya screamed. "Cover!"

The 40mm cannon mounted in the Tachi's antipersonnel pod barked as she dove for the nonexistent shelter of the mangled pavement.

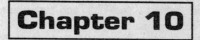

# Chapter 10

*Time is everything; five minutes make the differ-
ence between victory and defeat.*

—Admiral Lord Nelson
ca. C.E. 1805

The weapon was called *sempu*, "whirlwind," and it
was built into the hull of some warstriders as a
close-range antipersonnel measure. Often it was set
to fire automatically and indiscriminately, when any
moving target came within range. A 40mm shell disintegrated as it cleared the weapon's muzzle, loosing
an expanding cloud of lead pellets like a shotgun blast.
The pellets were strung together by tangled meters of
monofilament, threads no thicker than a single molecule
and far stronger than steel. Dispersing in a filmy, high-
velocity cloud, the stuff sliced through everything in its
path, vegetation, light armor, muscle, bone, all with
equal ease.

Lying facedown in the pavement rubble, Katya felt

the ripping wind of the horror's passing half a meter above her back. An instant later, a CPG blast struck the Tachi like a lightning bolt, dazzling her even through tight-shut eyelids, ripping the strider's dorsal armor apart in a splatter of molten duralloy. It took another step, then crashed forward, and the concussion jolted Katya through the ground.

There was a long moment of relative silence; the roar and thud and crackle of battle still thundered all around her, but it was quiet here. Then she heard a stifled sob over her helmet's speakers, and something that might have been a groan.

Shakily, she rolled over, looking back. Francine, blood-splattered but not obviously hurt, was lying on her side, staring with shock-gilt blankness at a nearby tangle of steaming, neatly diced flesh and viscera. The *sempu* blast must have caught Ken Maubry full-on as he dove for cover. The left side of his head from nose to ear lay unmarked on the ground, the unwinking eye staring at Katya with something that might have been accusation.

"Come on, Francine," she said, rising to her knees.

"He . . . he . . ."

"We can't help him." *That* was obvious. "Let's move!"

Francine tried to sit up and her left arm dropped from her body in a sudden gush of blood. The weapons tech just sat there, staring stupidly at the limb, severed just below her elbow, where it lay on the ground in front of her.

*Damn!* A loop of the *sempu* cloud must have snicked through her arm, and she hadn't even felt it. Shock was numbing her now, could kill her if Katya didn't move fast.

Moving to Francine's side, she gentled the woman to the ground, then used a length of bloody flexcloth— she thought it must be a strip sliced from Maubry's bodysuit—to tie off the stump.

She was giving Francine an injection of emergency medical nano from her belt first aid kit when the hum and creak of a moving strider close behind her made her turn and look up.

Relief flooded through her. It was *Mission Link*, the Warlord's hull torn and scratched in places, but undamaged. The big machine's blunt fuselage dipped toward her, a parody of a bow, and the central bulge of the commander's module opened up. Vic Hagan sat up in the slot and waved. "Katya! Katya, you all right?"

She waved back. "I'm okay! Francine's hurt."

"We have to odie, Boss. They're pullin' us out."

He slid out of the open slot, clambered to the ground, and hurried across to Katya and Francine. Together, they half carried half dragged the woman back to the motionless Warlord. The medical nano was already taking effect, sealing off the bloody stump and easing her into a painless haze. If they could get her back to a med center, nanosomatic engineers would take care of the rest, right down to growing her a new arm.

*If* they could get her back. According to Vic, the Confederation forces were already in full retreat from Cape Dickson and the spaceport.

"*Kuso!*" she swore. "Who gave a nullheaded order like that?"

"It was right from the top," Vic replied. "General Grier. At least he was the one who told me."

Katya shook her head. "But we were winning, damn it!"

"That's what Witter said. I dunno, Boss. I just work here." Carefully supporting the almost unconscious Francine, they scrambled up the Warlord's flank, then squeezed into the riderslot together. Warstriders weren't designed with passengers in mind; the commander's module was coffin-sized, large enough for one person lying down . . . or possibly two if they were very friendly.

Or for three squeezed in and sitting upright with the
hatch open. Katya clung to a handhold on the hull
as Vic barked an order and the machine straightened
upright again. He spoke again, his words picked up by
the strider's external audio sensors, and the warstrider
pivoted sharply, then swept forward with long-legged,
ground-eating strides.

Odd. When she was linked, Katya was never aware
of this lurching, swaying motion as the machine paced
across open ground. She hoped she wasn't going to
disgrace herself by being sick inside her helmet.

Vic had his glove off, his palm pressed against the
command module's interface, an expression of studied
concentration on his face as he stayed in communication
with the strider's pilot.

"Okay," he said, opening his eyes and pulling his hand
off the contact. "Bad news, I'm afraid. Witter says a lot
of our people got hit while they were trying to disengage.
The line's falling apart."

Katya could picture it. Of all tactical maneuvers, the
hardest are those carried out in the face of the enemy,
especially if they require a force already engaged to
break off the action. When the force trying to withdraw
is composed primarily of newbies and raw recruits, the
maneuver is almost certain to disintegrate into a confused, every-man-for-himself rout.

This was not the way it was supposed to work, Katya
thought. The plan had called for her ambush force to
punch the invaders off the north end of the spaceport,
sweeping across the apron like the swinging of a gate,
then joining up with the rest of the 1st Rangers in the
spaceport strip. If the Imperial assault unit could be
driven into a tight enough pocket, its numbers sharply
reduced, it would be trapped against the sea, unable to
maneuver, unable to do anything but surrender or be
destroyed.

The order to retreat with the maneuver still only half-
completed had turned the situation completely upside

down. Katya's striders were streaming off toward the east and southeast now, desperately vulnerable to a sudden counterpunch from the hard-pressed Imperials.

"I'm going to have some words with Grier when I see him again," she promised.

*If I get out of this alive.*

"What the hell were you thinking of!" Sinclair demanded. Held up in a meeting at the new government headquarters under Stone Mountain, Sinclair had arrived on-line only moments ago, to find the battle already begun . . . and already lost. Floating above the sprawl and color of the virtual reality battlefield, he could see the Imperial striders emerging from the pocket into which they'd been jammed, rushing forward in fireteams of two and four machines, slicing into the disorganized rabble that was the Confederation retreat.

Grier bristled. "What do you mean? *Kuso*, Travis, Alessandro's wing was dangling way out in the open, completely exposed! If I hadn't given the order to retreat, she'd have been cut off and destroyed!" He pointed, a sweep of a virtual arm. "And these Imperial landings on the mainland! All they have to do is move here, and our entire army on the cape is trapped!"

Sinclair studied the flow of red and blue for a moment. "Your timing, General," he said slowly, "is off. Another twenty minutes, and Katya would have had the lid welded shut!"

"I saved the army!"

"I think, General, that you don't fully understand what is at stake here. If we simply hold on, if we simply survive, we lose."

"But—"

"We needed that spaceport, General! To get our people out. Our only hope was to bloody the Imperials badly enough to make them pull back and maybe reconsider a second landing. Now . . . I don't know."

"We . . . we could order our people back into the attack." Grier sounded contrite now. "The Imperials aren't well organized yet. We could still throw them off the spaceport and into the sea."

"No. Look there, and there. They've already taken the offensive back. And our people are too disorganized to stop them now. It's going to take hours to form them up again. We've already lost it."

Minutes more passed, and the retreat continued all along the line. In the air above the spaceport, a tiny, golden beetle flitted across the battlefield, moving west to east. It was followed closely by a second . . . then a third.

Sinclair knew instantly what those glittering objects were without having to tap the AI's data base. Ascraft— big transport ascraft, Stormwinds and Typhoons—dropping down from orbit, circling the battle-torn spaceport and settling to the apron on blasts of fusion-heated plasma. Focusing closely on one, he saw new warstriders unfolding from the riderslots in their bellies.

Other ascraft were coming out of the west in waves.

"That's it," he said slowly. "The heavies are coming down. All we can do now is save what we have."

These, he was sure, were the Imperial heavy striders, the second assault wave consisting of powerful Daimyos and Katanas and Samurais. Too massive to pod-drop from orbit, they had to ride down aboard ascraft, landing at a spaceport already secured by advance forces. No doubt the enemy commander's plan had called originally for seizing the spaceport so that the heavies could land, then throwing the newcomers against Jefferson itself.

Obviously, the enemy had altered that plan; as long as they could find a place to touch down, the heavies could be used as effectively as reinforcements at the spaceport as anywhere else.

And they were coming down squarely in the rear of Colonel Alessandro's forces, trapping them between themselves and the surviving Tachis.

Sinclair blamed himself. He might pride himself on his ability to choose good people, but, though Grier was not a bad officer, he'd been a poor choice for this particular slot. He'd been the weak link in the chain, and Sinclair should have been here, helping to manage the battle.

"Okay, General," he said gently. "Let's see what we can salvage out of this mess."

*Donryu* remained in orbit about New America, close beside the planet's space station. Though her weapons personnel were all linked in, her most powerful laser and CPG batteries ready to fire, she did not participate in the fighting for Port Jefferson. For one thing, since she was in low orbit, her actual time over a given target was measured in minutes, an extremely brief period of time for sensor scans to be updated, then evaluated by AI terrain and military specialists in order to single out worthwhile targets. More important, the landing forces were everywhere closely engaged with the rebels, both on the spaceport apron and on the mainland outside of the capital. Nowhere could the orbiting forces target rebel warstriders or equipment without risking hitting their own people, and Tetsu Kawashima, like every good military commander, was well aware of the dangers posed by so-called friendly fire.

Better to remain patient, keeping *Donryu* and her consorts here in command of local space, and leaving the fighting on the surface to the men trained to do it. Ozawa and Mishima, Kawashima's two assault commanders, were the best there were for this sort of combat. The heavy assault striders under Takeo Fuchi would be touching down by now as well, and Fuchi was a veteran of Lung Chi, Loki, and Alya A-VI.

It was always chancy, launching an invasion from space against any world. Even with complete control of local space, orbiting spacecraft could scan and track only a fraction of what was going on in and beneath a planet's atmosphere. Too, they were operating against an entire *world*, with a population of tens of millions, a surface area composed of hundreds of millions of square kilometers of ocean, woods, mountains, and rugged outback terrain. There were too many hiding places, too many villages, settlements, remote encampments for space or ground forces to control everything. The best the invaders could hope for was to seize and hold certain key positions—factories and manufacturing centers, the spaceport and airfields large enough to serve as ports, the capital.

Fortunately, that was all that was really necessary. With those in Imperial hands, resistance might continue in more remote areas, but it would be isolated and scattered, and it would be the Empire that controlled the planet's production and economy. Complete victory was only a matter of time, *if* the invaders moved with deliberation, calculation, and overwhelming force.

Kawashima knew well that it was still possible to lose what he had already gained here, through carelessness, through haste, through ill-preparedness.

He was determined to make no such amateur's mistakes.

"Vic! Watch it! Hang on!"

The Warlord dipped and spun as heavy caliber rounds snap-snap-snapped overhead. Vic, still sitting in the open command module with Katya and her unconscious weapons tech, leaned forward against Katya's back, pressing her forward into the slot. "Hide your eyes!" he snapped, and an instant later, the Warlord's left CPG discharged with a crackling blast of blue-white energy and the acrid stink of ozone. The fog lit up, though Vic could see neither the target nor the effect of the shot. Above and behind him, the Warlord's rotary cannon suddenly spun and shrieked, the racket tearing at his ears for an agony of seconds.

"Okay, Captain," Witter's voice said, speaking in his mind. Somehow, despite the commotion, Hagan had managed to keep his palm implant against the interface. "We got him."

"What was it?"

"Another Tachi. We fried him, don't worry. You guys okay up there?"

He leaned back, letting Katya straighten up again. In front of her, Francine DelRey was still slumped back into her lap. Turning, Katya met his eyes and nodded, her short, dark hair bobbing inside her transplex helmet.

"We're okay, Witter," Hagan said. "Keep moving."

"I'm getting targets all over the place, Captain. Movement and heat. Negative on IFF. Y'know, I think we're surrounded."

"Keep working east. There's got to be a way out, even if we have to wade through the sea to find it."

"Yes, sir."

Katya eased herself back, pressing against him. "Captain?" she said over his headset. "Helmets off."

He hesitated. In the past few minutes they'd had to take several detours to avoid low-lying patches of nano-D, and removing their helmets could be deadly. Still, they were on the fringe of the battle here. The smoke was thinning, enough so that the sun was sending dusty shafts of yellow light slanting down through the overcast, and there'd been no nano warnings for some time now. The warstrider swayed gently beneath them as it continued pacing off the meters. Reaching up, he unsnapped his helmet release and pulled it off, as she did the same with hers.

"Just for a moment, Vic," she said, turning in the slot so that she could look back at him. "I didn't want your crew eavesdropping."

"Sure. What's on your mind?"

"I want you to drop me off. Here. Right now."

His throat tightened, and he shook his head, an almost convulsive denial. "Negative! No way!"

"Captain Hagan, use your head! You can't fight this machine with the damned hatch open. The first time an Impie takes a shot at you, he'll fry you, me, Francine, and half your control circuits. You have to button up if you're to have a chance of getting out of here."

"But—"

"Shut up and listen. There's room in there for you and Francine. I know. I shared a ride that way once. It'll be tight, but you can link while she rides on a PLSS. The portable life-support system'll keep her alive until you can get her back to a med center."

"What about you? Damn it, Katya, I can't just drop you off here, a million klicks behind enemy lines!"

"We're not a million klicks behind enemy lines. It's more like five or six, okay? And there's plenty of cover. That's the strip district up there, and beyond that, Braxton and the port manufacturing center. I'll be able to lie low, move quiet, and slip through the lines when it gets dark."

"That'll be hours, yet!" His heart was hammering in his chest. Damn it, she couldn't ask this of him!

He knew he was more than half in love with this woman, that he had been for a long time. He'd served with her for six years, ever since the days of the old 2nd New American Minutemen, and then later on Loki, on Alya B-V, and Eridu. His had always been a kind of love from afar; she was his commanding officer, and though neither Hegemony nor Confederation regulations forbade such a relationship, it was never a good idea for the grunts to become romantically involved with their commanding officers.

Too, he'd been well aware of her close relationship with Devis Cameron. He'd deliberately kept his distance then, sensing Katya's interest in Cameron, and knowing the dangers of lovers' triangles in any mixed military unit.

Of course, he'd also been aware of the fact that Katya and Cameron had become more distant again, starting with an argument they'd had on Earth just before the Eridu mission. Ever since, he'd been wondering whether that meant he actually now had a chance with her.

Except that he *knew* Katya, knew that she was a professional and that she didn't like mixing that profession with close, personal entanglements, especially now, after her breach with Cameron. Hagan rather suspected that she'd broken some self-imposed rule by getting involved with the guy in the first place, and that she now regretted it.

And Vic Hagan, for all of his years in the militia, the Hegemony Guard, and now in the Confederation Army, was shy, at least when it came to women. Hell, he'd not even been able to ask Katya to recjack with him, though he'd had plenty of opportunity aboard the *Eagle* and here on New America. He was afraid that she would think he was just looking for entertainment, a jackin' Jill for a quick plug-in. As a result, much of his RJ downtime was spent in erotic simulations with AI personas that looked and sounded and smelled very much like Katya Alessandro.

And now the real Katya was wedged into the open slot with him, practically in his arms . . . and she was telling him to drop her off, to save himself and the others while she wandered around the battlefield on foot.

"Damn it, Katya, you don't know what you're asking!"

Reaching up, she touched his lips with one gloved forefinger. "I think I do. *Vic.*"

The way she stressed his name sent a shiver through him. Did she know what he felt for her? How could she? He'd never said a word. . . .

"Vic, if I stay, the next time we run into an Impie strider the three of us get fried, and maybe your crew as well. Do you want that? I'm not going to abandon Francine."

"Look, we can put you in one of the other slots. If you snuggled up with Witter or Sergeant Toland—"

"*No!*" The negative was so sharp, so urgent, it startled him to silence. "No," she said again, more gently. "Damn it, Vic, just follow your orders, okay?"

"I don't understand. This is a three-slotter. We could make it, all of us. . . ."

She sighed. "Maybe I don't either. I . . . I don't like being shut in, Vic. I don't think I could take it!"

"But you're a striderjack, for God's sake!" By definition, that required her to shut herself up in darkened, narrow cubbyholes. "Look, we can jack you to *Mission Link* and I'll be the passenger."

She shook her head. "It would take too long to reprogram your AI to accept my patterns, and we should keep moving, anyway. Vic, if you'll just—"

The explosion tore into the ground meters away, sending great clods of earth and gravel hurtling into the air.

"Captain!" The voice came from his helmet phones, tinny and distant with the helmet beside him. "We got two bandits, comin' in on our six! They were hiding behind that building!"

He resisted the urge to look. What Witter could see through the strider's optics would still be invisible to him. The warstrider lurched hard to the left, pivoting, its weapons coming up. Battle fog swirled past, impenetrable.

"Come on, Katya! Squeeze in with—"

"No!" Reaching up, she gave him a quick, hard kiss on the mouth. For an instant, he felt her warmth . . . and then she was gone, grabbing the PCR-28, rolling over the side of the Warlord's fuselage and dropping three meters to the ground.

"Katya!"

"Go, Vic!" Scrambling to her feet, she waved him on. "Go!"

Another high explosive shell snapped overhead, as the Warlord reared back on angled legs, then loosed three quick CPG bolts at the unseen attackers. Hagan dropped back into the slot, pulling Francine down on top of his legs and stomach. He fumbled with the console, unable to find the right button . . . and then the module hatch sealed shut, plunging the two of them into crowded darkness. One-handed, he managed to reach various cables and feeds, plugging them into her bodysuit. It was a tight squeeze, and he had to wiggle back and forth to make the connections, but the life-support feeds would keep her alive and out of shock. That done, he jacked three plugs home into his sockets, two temporal, one cervical, and palmed the interface.

With a crackle of light, sight and sound were restored. He was again a warstrider, his vision piercing the encircling fog. Two . . . no, three Tachis were moving in, range two hundred meters and closing fast. The Warlord was tracking them, weapons ready. Another shell whizzed in, detonating with a ringing crack against the Warlord's upper hull. Katya had been right. If the module had been open when that shell had hit . . .

Where was Katya? He extended his scan left and right, searching. There . . . darting away swiftly past the warehouse wall, heading in the direction of the spaceport strip.

*What the hell was that all about*? he wondered.

"What was that, Captain?"

He'd not been aware that he'd put his thoughts out over the link. "Nothing, Ken."

"Where's the Boss off to? She won't last ten—"

"Never mind that! That Tachi on the right. We're gonna take him! Lewis!"

"Sir!"

"Target! Bring him down!"

"Yes, *sir!*"

He watched Katya vanish into the rubble of a fallen building. He felt sick.

# Chapter 11

*Historically, of course, economic access was the great divider of society. There were the rich, upper classes which didn't need to work and could devote their time to recreation or to the management of their society; the middle classes which used their skills and their limited economic access to acquire the means of joining the upper classes; and the lower classes, condemned by their lack of economic, educational, and political access, by and large, to remaining where they were.*

*Early developers of cephlinkage hardware were confident that the old rules of power and class distinctions had been broken at last, that direct, electronic linkage to global information nets would at long last provide economic and educational access for all, abolishing forever class distinctions.*

*Of course, we now know that they were com-
pletely wrong.*

—*The Rise of Technic Man*

Fujiwara Naramoro
C.E. 2535

*What's wrong with me? Why couldn't I go with him?*
Katya leaned back against a cracked and smoke-
stained wall, gloves and helmet off, the combat rifle
cradled in her lap. It was growing dark at last, the long,
long New American day dragging to an end with the
sun's slow drop below the horizon. It was a true night,
too, with both Columbia and the bloody pinpoint of 26
Draconis B already long since set. Through a shattered
wall and ceiling on the other side of the room, the
sky glowed an angry orange-red, reflecting the light of
burning buildings. The crump and thud of far-off gunfire
proved that the battle continued.

She'd found this building—a bar called *The Newamie's
Down*—hours earlier, while it was still light, choosing it
partly because it was a large building, offering plenty
of hiding places, but mostly because she thought she
might find food and water there. Though her warstrider
umbilicals kept her blood chemistry balanced and kept
her from becoming dehydrated while she was linked,
they did nothing for her physical hunger. She'd not
eaten for nearly fifteen hours, since she'd been back
at the 1st Rangers' Port Jefferson headquarters, and her
stomach was growling.

So she'd devoted several hours to exploring *The
Newamie's Down*, using its sanitary facilities, prowling
the mealprep area in search of food, helping herself
to a glass and some water from a still-working sink
behind the bar. Finally she'd settled down here to wait,
in the bar opposite the tall, arched entrance to the main
dining area.

Obviously, the place had taken a direct hit sometime during the fighting that had raged back and forth across this part of Cape Dickson that morning. Tables and chairs had been swept to one side of both the bar and the restaurant in smashed tangles of plastic and carbonweave, and the area behind the bar was awash in broken glass, mingled with pooled liquor and those bottles that had miraculously escaped intact. The mealprep area proved useless; the building's power was out, and she hadn't been able to open any of the storage lockers or vats where food cultures were grown.

She'd finally found several packs of soy crackers and settled for those and water as dinner. It was ironic; there was a bewildering variety of alcoholic drinks available in those bottles that had somehow survived the battle without being broken, but Katya didn't drink liquor, wine, or beer. She'd tried one or the other a time or two, of course, back in her shipjacking days, but she didn't care for the taste of the vile stuff, nor did she like the loss of control or the false values it created.

The alcohol did tell her something about this place, and this neighborhood, though, as did the Level 1 comm banks in the building's foyer and the lack of full-link ViRcom pods or sim modules. This was definitely a lower-class neighborhood, and Katya was glad that patrons of this place were gone.

The people who came here would have Level 1 hardware, no more, and many might even be nullheads, kept at the very bottom of the economic and educational ladder by being unable to interact with technic society at all. Level 1 hardware—distributed free by the state—consisted of a palm interface and a single T-socket, sufficient to download ID and credit information, to interact with computers and AIs, and to receive low-res input from public entertainment channels.

Two temporal sockets and extended cephlinkage hardware allowed high-level access, including full ViRcommunications and sims. With double T-sockets you could jack in on a bewildering variety of recjack programs, from mild euphoric stimulation to elaborate, interactive ViRdramas to virtual sex. And a third socket in the base of the neck provided neural feedback, allowing high-level jacking of remotes or direct-link machines, like warstriders.

People with two- or three-socket implants rarely drank alcohol. Cerebroactive chemicals, especially depressants, could drastically affect cephlinkage control, and that was not only bad, it was stupid. Too, linkers didn't need them as diversion or anaesthetic, not when there was such a broad range of diversions to enjoy with a clear head and clean circuits. Oh, Katya had heard of brainburners and current norkers, of course. Who hadn't? Those were the isolated exceptions, though. You needed *discipline* to handle nano-grown hardware woven into your personal wetware, and since zapping your pleasure center for an unending orgasm was nothing more than a very pleasurable way to commit suicide, undisciplined linkers were rather neatly deselected out of the net, a high-tech version of survival of the fittest.

Every once in a long while, though, Katya wished she could let herself get drunk. It might be nice to lose control, if just for a little while, and maybe dull some of the sharp edges to the self-recrimination that always seemed to be circling out in the shadows that hedged in around the borders of her mind.

Her hands tightened on the ribbed foregrip of her rifle. *What's wrong with me?* she asked herself again, then shook her head. *Delete that. You know why you couldn't go with Vic. The question is why you can't lick this. Damn it, girl, you're as habit-hobbled as a brainburned twitchie. And you'll be about as useful as one, too, if you don't get your wetware jacked under control!*

She'd carried this, this quirk of hers for a long time, ever since her starship days back before she'd joined the Hegemony Guard, in fact. She'd been jacking a ship, the *Kaibutsu Maru*, when a failure in the ship's AI interface while she was linked had left her in sensory deprivation for a period of hours—a small eternity in subjective time.

Katya never talked about it, didn't even like to admit it to herself, but to this day she had trouble with near or total darkness. The smothering, claustrophobic feelings darkness raised in her made her acutely uncomfortable in any closed-in space, and jacking into a ship's navsim was now all but impossible for her.

She'd wrestled with the thing for a long time, now, long enough to begin thinking of it as her "beast," as though it were an annoying and sometimes demanding pet. Vic was right. It didn't make sense for her to dislike shut-in spaces, not when she had to shut herself into one every time she strapped on a warstrider. But in one way it *was* logical. As a striderjack, she could grit her teeth as she lay down in the war machine's slot and felt the hatch seal shut over her, could bear the second or two of smothering closeness until her hand touched the interface and the darkness vanished, replaced by the limitless panorama of her AI's sensory feed to her brain.

Linked in, the warstrider serving as her body, its sensors more sensitive and more discerning by far than her own eyes and ears, she was no longer crippled by her beast. It was her *mind* that was claustrophobic, she often told herself, not her body; it didn't matter that her body was shut up, blind and catatonic, so long as she had a feed from the outside world, so long as her real self was jacked in, free and unrestrained. For some few individuals, linking with a warstrider was a kind of recreational drug, inducing a technomegalomania that robbed them of judgment and rational discernment as efficiently as alcohol. For Katya, linking to a strider was a drug of an entirely different kind, providing, if not a cure, then at least a temporary healing that banished the darkness that always seemed to be pressing in around the borders of her mind.

What Katya couldn't understand, though, was why she hadn't been able to overcome the beast a long time ago. On Alya B-V she'd forced herself to descend a pitch-black well plunging far beneath the surface of a dead and alien city, confronting the nightmare that was never far beneath the surface of her mind. On Eridu she'd experienced far worse; swallowed by a Xenophobe traveler, she'd been carried to a cavern so far underground she'd been convinced that she would never see the world's sun again. Surely, if anything could get her over her irrational fears, those experiences should have done it.

But they hadn't, and she was beginning to think the beast would always be with her, would be as inseparably a part of her as the interface circuitry woven into the palm of her left hand. When Vic had suggested it, the mere thought of squeezing into the close, dark coffin of a linkslot, of riding there unlinked, unable to see out, able only to feel the warstrider's rocking gait and hear the wheeze and whine of its drivers, had filled her with a dread colder and more personally threatening than any mere fear of death in battle.

She tried to tell herself that it was more than her own weakness that had made her order Vic to leave her behind. There'd been no time after *Mission Link* had materialized out of the smoke to stow both Francine and herself safely away in separate slots.

But a good five minutes had passed between the time Vic appeared and the attack next to the warehouse. *Face it*, she told herself, hoping for amusement in the thought and finding bitterness instead. *You're norking goked-up in the head.*

Outside, the sounds of heavy shelling and rocket fire rose to a crescendo. She could feel the hard, diaplas floor vibrating beneath her feet and buttocks with the concussions, and the loudest shocks were preceded by a flicker through the window, like summer's lightning. Someone was doing some heavy-duty bombardment, and fairly close by from the sound of it. Was she hearing the Imperial warstriders? Or were the Impies potshotting the

Confederation lines from orbit? She supposed it didn't matter. One way or the other, she was going to have her work cut out for her sneaking back through the lines tonight.

She checked her cephlink's time readout; it was well past forty-two hours, late enough that she could probably make her move pretty soon now. Gripping Francine's rifle, she stood up, then reached for her helmet and gloves, which were lying on the floor beside her.

A sound from the next room, beyond the dark and open archway leading to the restaurant area, made her start. The rifle came up, her finger on the trigger. No time to hide . . . no place to seek cover. . . . "Who's there?"

What had she heard? It had sounded like the scuff of a boot on the floor, but she couldn't be sure. Heart pounding, she edged toward the doorway.

A gasp—she was sure it had been a gasp, sure it had been a *human* sound—came from the darkness beyond the archway, and then she heard the clatter of someone stumbling over one of the pieces of wrecked and over-turned furniture. The sound actually emboldened her a bit; no Imperial Marine, no adept of *Kokorodo* would have made so much noise trying to watch her from hiding—and he damn sure wouldn't have tripped over a table while trying to run away. Rifle at the ready, Katya leaped to the wall next to the open archway, braced herself with a quick breath, then rolled around into the next room.

Enough light spilled in from the room at her back for her to see dim shapes among the shadows. She didn't have enhanced eyes, but her cephlink included software that processed visual input somewhat more efficiently than her natural wetware. As her eyes adjusted to the dark, her linkware took over, sharpening contrasts and enriching her natural night vision to bring some defini-tion to the shapes. The dining area of *The Newamie's Down* had been fairly luxurious for what she thought of as a lower-class food- and booze-joint. Those were holo screens curved along the far walls that must once have projected views of the city or other, less realistic illusions, though they were dead and empty now. Eating booths lined the walls of the circular room, while tumbled-over chairs and tables were scattered about the center. She'd already searched the place carefully, but there were several entrances. Slowly, she scanned the wreckage, looking for movement, for anything out of place. . . .

*There!* Golden eyes, large and luminous in the gloom, blinked back at her from behind a table . . . then, with a flash of movement, something man-sized bounded toward the left, toward the door leading to the mealprep areas. The building's automatic doors were out, along with everything else requiring grid electricity, but these were partly open, wide enough at least for the . . . whatever it was to scrabble through.

Katya stood still for a long moment, rifle still raised. What had she just seen? Not a human, certainly. Not with *those* eyes, though they could have been artificial implants. It had certainly not been an animal. Though New America boasted its own native ecology, evolution—at least on land—had not progressed nearly as far here as it had on Earth. Land-dwelling animal life tended to be small, airy, and airborne, like morninglories, or sluggish, like treewalkers, and nothing on this world had evolved anything like eyes. Plenty of Earth species had been imported, of course, but mostly as pets, since bioengineering allowed the creation of food animals that neither moved nor sensed the world around them in any save the most vague and imbecilic ways.

Those eyes had blinked back at her with intelligence and with purpose. She was pretty sure she'd just seen a genie.

But what kind?

"Hello!" she called, still facing the door to the mealprep area. "Come out! I won't hurt you!" There was no reply, save something that might have been a soft stirring beyond the half-closed door. "Please! I'm a friend!"

"That remains to be seen, don't it?" a voice, male, but high-pitched, almost a child's, answered from the dark. "You came with the stilters."

Stilters. Warstriders?

"My name is Katya. I'm from right here on New America. Who are you?"

"You're Newamie?"

Katya jumped. That voice, female this time, had come from just behind her.

She whirled, staring. The speaker was a woman, a delicate, extraordinarily lovely woman with fine-boned features and large dark eyes. Her hair was mingled gold and silver and hung to her waist; she wore sandals and a wisp of translucent, holographic smoke that did almost nothing to conceal her anatomy.

She also held a Colt-Mitsubishi 4mm FMP-60, a very real and nonholographic fléchette autopistol, centered squarely between Katya's breasts.

Carefully, Katya lowered the muzzle of her rifle until it was no longer pointed at the woman. "I, I'm Newamie, yes," she said. She jerked her head toward a wall, indicating the rumble of battle audible beyond. "I'm with the Confederation military forces out there."

"Confed, Impie," the male voice said, emerging from the wall behind her. "None of that means much, do it?"

"I'd say it does," she replied. "The Impies are invading our world. I was trying to stop them."

"All by yourself, girl? Heh! Must be more t'you than meets the eye."

Slowly, she turned to face the man. He was small, shorter than she was, with long, slender arms, short legs, and a hairless head that gave him a childlike look despite the crow's-feet and worry lines. His eyes were large and golden, almost catlike, though the irises were round rather than slit. He wore an orange worksuit with the emblem of Dow-Mitsubishi Nanochemical on the sleeve, and he, too, held a pistol in his hand, a Japanese Type 36 with suppressor hood and integral laser sight-tracker beneath the barrel.

"I'm Tharby," he said. He gestured with the pistol. "I haven't quite got the hang of this thing, but I'm pretty sure all I need to do is put the red light where I want it and pull the trigger. Why don't you give Sonya your gun?"

The woman stepped closer, hand out. Briefly, the thought flitted through Katya's mind that Sonya had just made a serious tactical mistake; she was too close to Katya and had moved partway between Tharby and her captive, a rank newbie's blunder. A sudden thrust-and-spin, and Katya would have the woman pinned from behind, using her as a shield as she cut Tharby in half with a burst from her PCR.

No. These were genies and they were New Americans. Better to learn about them, about what they wanted, than to kill them out of hand. Clicking on the safety, she handed her rifle to the woman, then stood there, staring at the man, her hands raised.

"Aw, gok it," a third voice rumbled. "Kill 'er an' let's gokin' get outta here."

The ruby-glowing tip of the tracker flashed brilliant in Katya's eyes as the pistol's aim shifted slightly, and she imagined the blood red target spot wavering unfelt against the skin of her forehead.

"I'm with ya, mannie," Tharby said, and Katya watched those golden eyes harden.

# Chapter 12

*Where then lies the difference, if a thinking, know-
ing, feeling creature was created by nature, by
man, or by God? Surely it cannot be the creator
that sets the creature's true worth.*

—*Intellectus*
Juan Delacruz
C.E. 2215

"Don't shoot!" Katya cried. "Please! I'm on your
side!"

"*Our* side?" Tharby grimaced . . . or had that been a
smile? Katya was finding it difficult to read his facial
expressions. There were subtle differences in the mus-
culature of his face from that of full humans. "Yer with
the army, right? Armies an' killin'. Yer all the gokin'
same, an' we don't have no use fer any of you. Right,
mannies?"

That last had been addressed to the others in the room.
Katya could see them with her enhanced vision, man and

manlike shapes emerging from hiding behind toppled furniture and from various doors. Some, like the woman with the FMP-60, looked completely human but had the exquisite, elfin loveliness of *ningyo*, of genegineered sexual toygirls. The rest were males, low-level workers, she thought, from the nearby nanofactories and spaceport warehouse complex. Most were A-techies, bald and spindly armed but still fairly close to human, like Tharby. A few, though, had somotypes considerably altered from that expressed by the original human DNA; there was one blunt-faced, hairless, naked giant, muscled for heavy labor and lacking any sign of external genitalia, and several were crossmuted B-techies, with body fur like spun silver and fingers and brains tailored to trace and repair damaged electronic circuits.

*Mannies.* At first, she'd thought it was someone's name. Now she remembered that speech-capable genies referred to themselves as mannies when they were with each other. The word, she understood, had come from *gene-manipulated*.

"You don't want to kill me," she said, trying hard to keep her voice level, calm, and matter-of-fact. "I'm not your enemy. And I might be able to help you."

"Eh?" Tharby's golden eyes narrowed. "How?"

Genies were bred with very specific limits to their intelligence—there was no sense, after all, in bestowing genius on something that would spend its entire life tracing circuits or loading specialized cargo into spacecraft holds. The brightest were likely to be the female *ningyos*, since some of their clients liked sex partners that could carry on a decent conversation, but even they wouldn't be able to follow complex or convoluted arguments.

Best to keep it simple and to the point.

"The Impies are attacking Port Jefferson," she told them. "They're attacking everyone here. Me. You. Everyone who lives here. We have to work together, to join forces against the Impies, if we're to save ourselves."

She watched the group digesting that, trying to assess how well she was getting through. Some few carried firearms or clubs. Most were unarmed, their facial expressions, what she could read of them, tight and grim. Several began discussing the problem among themselves as the others listened in. Katya was beginning to identify the leaders of the group: Tharby and several workers who might have been his brothers; Sonya and several of the other toygirls. How could she reach them? *Convince* them?

One large laborer shook his bald head. "Ah! No talk. Let's do 'er an' odie." Crowding forward, he reached out and brought a powerful hand down on Katya's shoulder, the grip tightening painfully.

Dropping her arm and turning, Katya seized the offending hand, snapping it back until the wrist popped. "Ow!" the owner yelled. "Watch 'er!" Then her heel came down on his instep, hard, then snapped up against a knee. No matter how it might be designed, apparently, knees were weak points in any biped. The worker bellowed, and dropped to the floor, all further interest in grappling with Katya gone as he clutched his leg. The rest milled about, uncertain and confused.

"We're not enemies!" she shouted, facing the ring of weapons and hard faces. "We're on the same side!"

"You ain't one o' us!" a toygirl snapped back, scornful. "You're a gokin' holder!"

"Damn it, I'm not!" She pivoted, balanced for a fight, praying that she could talk her way out of this. She would never be able to hold her own against so many, even if they were untrained and clumsy.

"Okay," Tharby said at last. "We listen, humie. But not long." He gestured toward the dead projection wall. "Stilters're out there, an' they might come back."

"Dak *hurt*!" the laborer on the floor said, still rubbing his injured knee.

"I'll hurt you more if ya try t'do somethin' like that without me sayin' so."

Yes, Katya decided, Tharby was definitely one of the leaders here. He would be the one she would have to reach.

"Are you all here . . . by yourselves?" she asked. "I mean, aren't there any full humans about?"

"Y'mean th' holders?" A warehouse worker grinned, slapping a massive club against his open palm. His voice was thick and raspy, as though his vocal cords weren't fully formed, but the words carried the full force of his sneer. "They's runned, ain't they?"

"Eh. Jus' her left, then," said another who could have been twin to the first . . . and perhaps he was. Successful genie models were often created sterile, with reproduction handled in vitro through cloning, and the embryos implanted in gene-tailored host mothers. Even those that could engage in sex were more often cloned than not, simply to guarantee the preservation of desired physical traits. The sameness of the faces surrounding her contributed powerfully to their doll-like, almost stylized look, that of mannequins, identical save for details of hair, dress, or rare facial blemish.

Katya zeroed in on Tharby, on the Dow-Mitsubishi logo on his jumpsuit. "You!" she demanded. "Who did you work for?"

The genie jerked a thumb over his shoulder, in the direction of the big manufacturing plant outside the spaceport. "Chemical nanoplant, o' course. Jefferson Nanochem, Contract Number 897364." He recited the information in a mechanical staccato, as though it had been drilled into him over the course of years.

"Right. And they're owned by who?"

"Uh . . . Dow-Mitsubishi." He sounded less confident now.

"And where are they?"

He shook his head. "Don't know."

"Earth," she answered for him. "Tokyo, on Earth. So the people who hold your contract answer to Tokyo. Right?"

"I guess so. . . ."

"Don't let 'er gok yer head, Tharby," another genie said. "Th' guys what holds our contracts is Newamies. Like *her*!"

"If they work for an Earth corp," she said evenly, "you can bet they work for Nihon. Tokyo controls just about all of the business in the Hegemony, one way or another. That means they hold Jefferson Nanochem's contracts, just like Jefferson Nanochem holds yours."

"Aw, full humies ain't under contract," a silver-haired *ningyo* said. Others added their opinions, many of them more like animal grunts than speech. Many low-range genie models, Katya knew, were designed without vocal cords. For the simplest workers, it was necessary only that they understand orders, not speak themselves.

How much of all of this, she wondered, were they understanding?

"They are if they're linked to Nihon for yen and promotions," Katya replied. "Do you know what yen are?"

"Uh, like work credits," the *ningyo* said. She caught her lower lip between small, perfect teeth. "Only 'lectronic. Yeah?"

"Yeah. Your holder can't do a thing unless Nihon pays him. Exactly like your contract. That's why the Confederation is fighting the Hegemony. We want to hold our *own* contracts!"

"How . . . how could you help us?"

Katya wasn't sure of the answer to that one herself. Genies, after all, were bred not only for low IQs and specialized work, but for docility as well. What kind of warriors would they make?

Still, *these* genies had obviously turned some kind of corner. Carrying weapons, threatening a full human, talking about leaving their workplaces for other cities . . .

they certainly were not acting like typical genies. *Watch yourself, girl,* Katya told herself. *Just like with humans, these guys are individuals. There's no such thing as "typical."*

"I'm not sure," she admitted after a moment. "I might be able to teach you how to fight, how to defend yourselves. If you help me get back to my own people, we should be able to find work for you. Work that you . . . that you'd enjoy."

There was a long silence at that. Katya could sense the crowd's uneasiness, could smell it in the hot, close air of the place. The silence went on so long she wondered if she'd said the wrong thing.

This was a dark and normally well-hidden aspect of New American life that Katya had never examined, had rarely even been aware of. New America's Hegemonic charter specifically outlawed slavery, but genegineered "constructs"—they were never referred to legally as "human" or as "people," of course—did not share the rights of their creators. Katya remembered well the ongoing debate between Rainbow and Liberty over whether or not genetic constructs should be considered the same as full humans and given full-human rights.

That particular political question had never been resolved. On the one hand, freedom parties insisted that intelligence and self-awareness themselves defined what could be legally called human, even though those terms were subject to some pretty fuzzy interpretation sometimes. How intelligent did a creature have to be to qualify, especially when no one could even agree on a good definition of what intelligence was?

Katya was struck by an amused revelation. Neurologists and somatic engineers understood the mechanics of the nervous system well enough to grow cephlinks that interacted directly with human thought processes, allowing the downloading of information, even of sensory data like sight and sound, directly to the brain. Yet they *still* couldn't precisely define "intelligence," or even measure it on any kind of absolute scale.

Even the slowest genies were almost certainly more intelligent in more different ways than unmodified Terran chimpanzees, and chimps were smart enough to devise tools, plan future actions, and use symbolic language; the smartest genies were brighter—in the sense of knowing more, reasoning better, speaking more clearly—than any dull-witted adult human or, say, a four-year-old human child. Tharby, for instance, to judge by his speech, was probably only a little below the full-human mean on the intelligence scale. Where could one possibly draw any kind of line?

On the other side of the argument were those cultures and economies that required cheap genie labor, or at least claimed to, and insisted that they were bred for happiness doing what they'd been created to do. That argument—and the moral issues of exploiting intelligent genetic constructs—could be as murky and as circular as any question about the nature of intelligence. Even in a society where energy was essentially free, and where most manufacturing was carried out in nanotechnic plants, there were still plenty of jobs suited for specialized laborers. Nanopart assembly, repairing complex or non-standard circuitry, quality control, running dumbloaders, providing nonvirtual sexual entertainment for people who couldn't or didn't use ViRsexual recreation, those were all tasks too demanding or nonprogrammable to be carried out by robots, too dull-minded to be efficiently or economically handled by socketed workers.

Genies liked their work; they'd been *designed* to like it. Genies were cheap, easy to make, cheap to maintain. They weren't *owned*, not in a legal sense, so they couldn't be called slaves, but their contracts were bought and sold by genetic labor brokers, so it amounted to much the same thing. They didn't have the implants in hand or brain to enable them to interact with human datanets, including, of course, financial linkages, so they couldn't be paid in yen or planetary currencies. Instead, they received "labor credits" for room and board, clothing, and other needs, all provided by the humans who held their contracts, their "holders."

Katya wondered how such a disparate band as this one had gotten together in the first place. Where were their holders? Fled, she supposed, when the first Impie fighters started booming down through the skies above Port Jefferson.

Finally, Tharby sighed. "Take 'er out back," he said. "Let's *show* 'er."

She thought they meant to kill her, but she was escorted out of *The Newamie's Down* with an almost ceremonial courtesy, taken around the corner of the building through a narrow back alley that opened onto a wider street.

Katya had not been on this side of the building when she'd entered it, hours before, and she was unprepared for the horror she saw there, a nightmare that came upon her so suddenly she gasped and nearly fell.

There'd been a slaughter here, right in the middle of the street, dozens of people cut down by the obscenely neat, random slices of repeated *sempu* blasts. There were so many pieces of arms and legs and torsos, so many severed heads and recognizable fragments of heads, so many unraveling tangles of internal organs and other chunks that were simply unrecognizable save as raw, blood-soaked meat that Katya could not even begin to guess how many people had been killed here. The blood had pooled in the low-lying parts of the street, ankle-deep or deeper.

People? She checked herself. That vacant-eyed, long-haired head lying in the street a few meters away could be Sonya's identical twin. These were *genies*, slaughtered en masse. Hell, they must have been packed together in a group, a mob, when the *sempu* started flying.

"That's what they did to us," Tharby said. "That's why we ain't goin' back. Never. *Never*."

Katya opened her mouth to say something, anything . . . and the sudden hot lurch in her stomach caught her completely off guard. Turning away from her escorts, she leaned heavily against a wall, emptying her stomach in a racking succession of deep, explosive heaves.

No mere battlefield horror had ever affected her this way. Indeed, years ago, during her recruit training, some of her official downloading had been designed specifically to harden her against the raw stuff of nightmares that was a modern battlefield, scenes exactly like this, wet with crimson gore, and she'd seen the reality plenty of times since.

But nothing could have prepared her for the sheer, mass-murder horror that she saw in front of her now.

"They was hidin' in that warehouse over there," Tharby said behind her. "I saw it. Lots of us did. A stilter came up outside, right over there, ordered 'em t'come out, hands up. They did. It was a full human that was givin' them the order, right? They had t'obey. They came out, an' then th' stilter started shootin' that tangled thread stuff that'll snick off a finger if'n you ain't careful. Chopped 'em to bits, then flamed the warehouse, just t'make sure they was all dead."

"What . . . what kind of stilter?"

Tharby snorted. "Don't know th' name. They's all pretty much the same, right?" He thought about it a moment. "I guess it was one o' the smaller ones, though. An' different from the ones I seen around here late, like."

Imperial, then. But she'd known that. Confed or militia striders wouldn't turn *sempu* on civilians. She didn't even think they carried *sempu* in their military inventory.

Katya wondered why they'd done it. Possibly the enemy striderjack had panicked at seeing such a large mob emerging from the building. Or maybe he had orders to spread terror among the area's inhabitants, or to keep large numbers of civilians from wandering around behind the Nihon lines.

Or maybe he'd simply assumed, as so many people did, that genies were biological robots of some kind, near-mindless and of no particular worth save to their owners. *Sempu* was a cheap way of killing a lot of unarmored or lightly armored people all at once.

"This," she said, her words tasting sour, "is part of what we're fighting against. The Impies've declared war against all of us, you and me. And maybe, maybe I can help you."

"We fightin' our own wars now," Dak said, menace in his voice. "Don't need help from humies. We *fight!*"

"Against warstriders? Stilters? I don't think so." She nodded toward the length of pipe another laborer held in his hands, a crude club. "Think you'd fare any better than *they* did, attacking a warstrider with that?"

"Then what are we supposed to do?" a toygirl wailed. "They'll come an' kill us!"

"You *could* learn to fight," Katya said softly. "And with weapons that'll give you half a chance. But you'll have to decide whose side you're on first."

"We don't need your Con, Confudration," a warehouse loader said. "Way I hear it, th' Chinese an' the Ukies ain't even in this war. We could go there, t' Canton or Nowa-K." He looked around at the others near him, as though searching for support. "This war is between th' Nihons and th' Newamies, right?"

"Yeah. Ain't got nothin' to do with us," a girl added.

"It does if you expect to get out of here alive," Katya replied. "The Impies have their, their stilters everywhere. Hear them? That rumbling noise is them bombarding Jefferson, from the sound of it. You'll have to pass their lines, and I don't think they'll just let you walk through." She gestured at the pitiful scramble of blood-soaked genie body parts. "No more than they let *them* go."

A discussion started among several of the genies and quickly grew to argument status. Tharby was really getting into it with another techie who looked exactly like him.

The sight was amusing . . . and instructive. Katya had seen her share of poorly written ViRdramas, both narratives and interactives, which had introduced cloned genies at one point or another in the tale. It never failed to amaze her how many people thought in this day and age that clones were copies of one another in mind as well as body, robots as interchangeable as circuit blocks.

Sheer nonsense, of course. Clones many genies might be, but that meant simply that they possessed identical DNA within the nuclei of their cells, not identical thoughts, goals, or ideas. Each was born as an infant just like a full-human child, raised in a crèche, and schooled individually—though without cephlinks, of course, they couldn't receive downloads and their education was for that reason sharply limited.

But they *were* individuals, with all the disagreement and confusion that entailed. The debate shaping up now was between a group urging that the genies slip out of the city and head south, for either Canton or Nowakiyev, and another group urging them to stay, to listen to what Katya had to say, even to help the Confederation against the *real* enemy that had slaughtered their mannies in the street. Eventually, the argument soon drifted back inside *The Newamie's Down*, where several genies stood guard over Katya while the rest took their debate into another room.

Katya was tired . . . and hungry too, she realized now. She'd had nothing but soy crackers in the last fifteen-plus hours . . . and lost most of that being sick outside. She was also thirsty, longing to wash the unpleasant taste from her throat. Her captors brought her water but refused to let her forage for more food. Tharby, or someone just like him, told her to sit where she'd been sitting most of that afternoon, and they refused to let her move from the spot.

Otherwise, they seemed to ignore her, listening instead to the conversation continuing in the next room. Genies came and went, joining in the debate, or leaving it. The only time any of them said anything to her was when, nearly two hours after the start of the conference, several toygirls appeared with some male workers in tow, leading them to clear spots on the floor on the other side of the room. One *ningyo*—was it Sonya?—walked up to Katya, struck a pose, and touched some hidden control at her waist. Her smoke-film holoclothing winked off, leaving her naked save for a belly chain with a small pouch holding personal belongings and the electronics that had holoprojected her clothing. The delicate triangle of her pubic hair was the same silky gold and silver that adorned her head.

"You want to play?" the toygirl had asked, smiling down at her.

"Uh . . . no. No, thank you." She turned her head away. Noisily, across the room, the other toygirls began coupling enthusiastically with the male genies, or with each other. Katya hadn't realized that male constructs enjoyed sex, those that were capable of it, as much as humans. Why had that particular set of behaviors been left in them, she wondered, when artificial methods were necessary to maintain pure genetic lines?

"How 'bout you, Tharby?"

"No, Glora. Not just now."

"Later, then." She turned and walked toward the group orgy. Katya kept her eyes averted. She didn't think of herself as a prude, but she'd been raised within a relatively conservative culture on New America, one that accepted appropriate social nudity, but which strongly disapproved of public sex. Well aware that different cultures viewed such activity in different ways, she was still shocked to encounter those differences in an unexpected setting. Shaken, her gaze met Tharby's.

"Don't condemn 'em," the genie told her. More intelligent than most of his companions, with a better vocabulary, he seemed better versed in the way full humans thought than the others were. "It's th' way they're made. Th' way *you* made 'em, y'know? They need sex, like you 'n' me need water."

"No," she said. "I *didn't* know. And I had nothing to do with making them that way."

"No?" He didn't sound convinced.

"Anyway, I don't condemn it. I'm just not, not used to it, is all."

"Yeah. Like we ain't used t' bein' allowed t' be havin' guns, or babies o' our own, or, or th' right t' quit 'n' go elsewhere if we don't like th' way things are, huh?"

"I thought you genies liked your work."

" 'Cause we was made t' like it, right? Well, there's work, an' there's work, an' th' way I heard it explained, DNA can give you an, an *aptitude*, like, but it can't make hell into heaven, y'know? Even a tailor-made dreamslot can be bad with th' wrong guy ridin' you. An' anyway, things's changed, ain't they? Likin' what we do don't mean we gotta like gettin' butchered like a brainless meatbeast."

His gaze made her uncomfortable, and she decided to change the subject. "What's going to happen to me if they decide not to stay?"

"Beats me." He shrugged philosophically. "Pro'ly kill ya, I guess, so's y'can't tell the Impies where we're goin'."

"But . . . I'm full-human!"

He looked away, shifting uncomfortably. "Maybe . . . maybe some of 'em think it's easier t'kill humies now. After what happened outside."

And he would say nothing more to her throughout the rest of that long night's watch.

# Chapter 13

*Humanity has a tendency, written into its monkey's genes, to find inferiority in difference. Family names, color of skin, religious belief, political ideology, place of origin, sex, sanitary practices, social status, language, education, intelligence, technological prowess, athletic ability, and—most damning of all, perhaps—failure to abide by the social wisdom of the dominant culture, all these and more have been used throughout history to set one group above another, to establish a pecking order of haves and have-nots, to prove what is thought at the time to be self-evident, that one tribe is superior to another.*

—*Man and His Works*
Karl Gunther Fielding
C.E. 2488

Two hours later, the conference was still going on, rising sometimes to the pitch and intensity of all-out argument.

Tharby left Katya after a while, his place taken by a dockworker who regarded her with sullen disapproval. She thought it might be Dak, the laborer she'd taken down earlier, but she didn't want to ask.

This, she decided, would be her best chance to get away, while most of the genies were either coupling on the floor or arguing in the next room, with only this one to watch her. She *thought* that Tharby might be on her side, that he didn't want to have any part of killing her. Some glimmer of . . . had it been compassion? . . . had lurked behind those golden eyes as he'd said the words, but she was still having trouble reading what they were really thinking. Once, a thick, gravel voice had risen from the eating area. "Aw, gok! Kill 'er an' be done with it!" Was that the same one who'd said almost the same words when she'd first been captured? Or another one?

No matter. Some of the genies, at least, were serious about killing her despite their conditioning. Seeing their fellow mannies cut down like that must have been a devastating shock.

The argument dragged on, and Katya's senses, her awareness of her surroundings, became hyperacute. The genie conditioning to obedience might have been trashed, but they still didn't know what to do with their newfound freedom. They still couldn't decide things for themselves, didn't know how to abide by a vote or to delegate authority. They might never decide anything . . . until one of them took matters into his own hands or a warstrider came smashing through the front wall.

She had to get away. Now.

Dak, if that was his name, was armed with her own PCR. Did he know how to use it? She remembered switching on the weapon's safety when she'd handed it over to Sonya. Katya doubted that any of them knew much about firearms. The idea of arming genies was repellent to most people.

More than once in the past few centuries, geneticists and military research combines had explored an old, old idea. If you could tinker with the human genome to create humanoid constructs that were docile, focused on a particular job, loyal, and clever at certain tasks, wouldn't it be possible to breed a genetically tailored warrior, a creature clever with weapons and at combat craft, fearless, obedient even to suicidal orders, and ruthlessly savage in battle?

The answer should have been yes and the thing had been tried often, but with less than total success. The greatest technical difficulty lay in what to do with the creatures during periods of extended peace. The alternatives appeared to be mass euthanasia—extremely risky when dealing with an entire army composed of tens of thousands of deliberately bred killers—or to watch them go insane from boredom. They *liked* to kill—that being part and parcel of their tailored genetic makeup—and no responsible government leader was prepared to suggest that they be used in paramilitary police or riot units.

The geneticists never had been able to gene-manipulate creatures that had both a drive to survive on the battlefield, and the sense of altruistic self-sacrifice and common decency that would make them quietly suicide when the war was over. In any case, it took a minimum of twelve years to raise a genie warrior from an embryo, too long, in most cases, to be of any use in a new war. The idea had never caught on, at least so far as Katya was aware.

But, even more than the fact that the attempts to breed DNA-manipulated warriors had so far failed, it was public reaction to the *idea* of such creatures that had blocked further work in the field. There were countless rumors of secret projects and conspiracies, of armies of artificial warriors kept in suspended animation, of gene-tailored spies and assassins walking in the midst of humanity unobserved. Katya had heard plenty of such stories herself. ViRdramas and documentaries showcasing warrior genies had managed to convince the public not only that gene-tailored soldiers were a bad idea, but that using *any* genie in the military would somehow lead to disaster.

The idea of actually arming one was unthinkable to most people, at least to those, like Katya, who'd had few dealings with them. Whether or not it was a bad idea in itself, though, the fact remained that few genies ever had the chance to use a weapon of any kind. She'd seen a few handguns among this bunch, probably scrounged from the effects of full humans who'd fled and left their genies to fend for themselves.

But how much had they managed to practice with them?

She stood up. Dak stiffened, the PCR swinging to cover her. "Sit down," he told her.

"I just want a drink of water." She nodded toward the bar. "There's a sink back there that works."

He eyed her uncertainly. "Tharby said fer you t'stay put."

"He didn't mean for you to make me die of thirst!" Hands on hips, she glared down at him. Damn it, genies were bred for loyalty and obedience! Had the deaths of their comrades wiped out every trace of respect for humans? "You want to go ask him?"

Dak stared up at her for a moment, then sagged, looking away. "Go ahead, then. No tricks."

"Of course not!" Turning, she walked toward the bar, a course that took her right past *The Newamie's Down*'s front door. She could feel Dak's eyes on her back, felt the muzzle of the rifle tracking her.

*Now!*

Lunging suddenly to the side, she dove headfirst out the door, landing on the walkway outside, rolling, coming to her feet already running. "Aw, *kuso*!" exploded from behind. "Gokin' gun don't *work*!"

Running as hard as she could, Katya dashed down the street, took one turn left, then another to the right. She needed to get well clear of the area before heading *that* way . . . north, away from the spaceport and back toward the Newamie lines. Caution quickly slowed her pace. She'd heard no sounds of pursuit, and running wild like that there was no telling what unpleasantness she might stumble into, unseeing. There were streetlights here, each with its own battery pack so some still worked, casting stark pools of illumination that deepened the shadows around. Slowing to a rapid walk, she stuck to the shadows, wishing that she had a warstrider's senses now instead of the only marginally enhanced seeing and hearing of her cephlink.

Nevertheless, she heard them first, and before they saw her. A metallic clank from ahead brought her to an adrenaline-charged halt. Dropping to her belly, she edged her way to the end of the building at her side, then peeked around the corner.

It was an Imperial patrol, and they were checking every building on the street ahead with the meticulous care of professionals as they moved slowly in her direction. A warstrider, a night black Mitsubishi Samurai, stood squarely in the middle of the avenue, as heavily armed and armored foot marines moved from building to building. Man-made lightning flickered to the north, followed by low thunder. By shellfire and streetlamp, Katya estimated thirty men at least, a platoon charged with rooting out those who'd remained behind when the Confederation forces had withdrawn. Farther down the street, masked by shadows, the lumbering bulk of a Zo APW waited, massive and patient. The four-legged armored personnel walker could carry fifty troops or so in its cavernous belly, verifying Katya's guess of a platoon-strength search.

A shout from one of the buildings. Soldiers emerged, prodding three civilians, two men and a woman, ahead with rough caresses from gun butts and muzzles. The sign on the building's front indicated that it was a travel agency, but that meant nothing. Those three must have simply found it a convenient place to shelter from the storm. Troops, faceless in their black armor, lined them up in the street. Orders were barked, too far for Katya to understand. One of the men struggled as a marine grabbed his arm.

They scuffled, and then the struggle was ended by a piercing crack; the man collapsed, rag-doll limp, onto the pavement. More orders . . . and the two remaining prisoners began stripping off their clothes with desperate haste. Soldiers roughly searched prisoners and clothing, then, both bare-handed and with palm-sized circuitry detectors. Katya understood. A deadly weapon could be designed to be insignificantly small and cunningly hidden beneath skin or within a body cavity. Apparently, the searchers found nothing. A final command, and the prisoners were led, naked and with wrists bound behind their backs, down the street toward the waiting Zo.

At a range of some fifty meters, Katya could not tell whether the prisoners were genies or full humans.

With that realization came another. Did it matter?

She decided that it didn't. At the rate the search party was moving, it would reach *The Newamie's Down* in an hour or less. She'd seen no indication of sentries posted by the genies, not even the commonsense of a lookout on some convenient rooftop. When the Imperials reached them, all of the genies there would be slaughtered . . . or led away like those two captives to uncertain fates in an Imperial internment center.

Katya knew that she could easily avoid that patrol. Knowing where it was, what direction it was moving on, gave her a tremendous advantage. She could circle around behind, cut across to another street, and be on her way north in minutes. She owed the genies nothing. . . .

But she couldn't do it. The whole question of whether genies could be considered human had become meaningless for Katya as soon as she'd met them. If not as intelligent as most people, they spoke, they reasoned, they discussed. Some had treated her with hostility. Others had shown kindness . . . or at least a willingness to listen, which was more than could be said for some full humans she'd known. For some reason, she was reminded of Pol Danver.

Besides, she felt an almost parental responsibility for them. She'd seen how they'd been hurt—abandoned by their creators, then slaughtered by an enemy they didn't even understand.

She couldn't simply leave the survivors to be killed.

Grimly, quietly, Katya began retracing her steps.

The events of the next few hours proved to be anticlimax. She'd walked back in the front door of *The Newamie's Down* without even being challenged, to find the argument still going full blast. Genies, she decided, were chokies, as long in the tongue as any member of the Confederation Congress. Was *that* built into their genes, she wondered, to keep them from working together, or was it a trait left over from those strands of human DNA in their cells that remained untampered-with?

She'd walked in, steel coil–tight, ready to break and run if she were attacked. The genies' reaction, though, was almost comical. Tharby had gaped at her, as astonished at seeing her as he might have been at the repeal of some law of physics. Dak had blustered, threatening her with the still-safed combat rifle, while the others had simply stared. She'd stared both of them down.

"I came back to warn you," she'd told them. "There are Impies four blocks from here, coming this way. They're searching every building and rounding up everyone they find. There's a stilter with them, a big one."

That news had ended all debate with the decisiveness of a gunshot. The majority of the genies by that time had already decided that their best bet lay in fleeing Port Jefferson, then making their way south to Nowakiyev.

They scattered, some through the building's front door, the rest through other exits. Dak went with them, still clutching the "broken" rifle.

Ten, however, including both Tharby and the *ningyo* Sonya, had decided to follow Katya to Newamie lines. There was no mention of the earlier threat to kill her; perhaps her warning had changed their minds about "holders." Perhaps they felt gratitude.

Or perhaps it was simply that they retained a few shreds of inborn loyalty.

Exfiltration from behind Imperial lines had not been as difficult as Katya had expected, even with ten civilians in tow. The invaders had still been less than organized at the time, fighting in small, tight groups rather than along a broad front with troops and combat machines arrayed with any kind of depth. Twice, the little party had taken cover in burnt-out shells of buildings as Imperial warstriders and marines stalked along the night-blackened streets outside, but the most dangerous encounter occurred when they were stopped by a nervous New American sentry.

They'd been lucky that the kid had actually challenged them instead of shooting first and checking their IDs later. He'd been young and inexperienced, armed with a bulky Mark XIV plasma rifle longer than he was tall, a clumsy weapon without its steady mount harness, but one that still could have wiped out the refugee party with a single burst as effectively as a blast from an Imperial *sempu*.

Playing it safe, Katya had "surrendered" to the kid, who was not at all sure that she was not Japanese, then downloaded her ID and current orders to the New American intelligence officer who'd eventually shown up to interrogate her.

Five hours later, she'd been on her way to Stone Mountain.

The rebel forces still clung to Jefferson, but CON-MILCOM headquarters had been moved far to the northwest, to an underground bunker complex under Stone Mountain. The place had originally been tunneled out as an armory, a storehouse for Hegemony military supplies and equipment. With New America's secession from the Hegemony, it had been seized and enlarged, until it served now as the new meeting place for the Confederation's government-in-exile.

Travel by air was not safe with so many Imperial ascraft in the sky. Katya had made the trip by groundcar along little-used roads, and four times her driver had pulled off the road, sheltering beneath the feathery sway of New American trees as a flight of Imperial fighters screeched overhead.

She'd been debriefed by Travis Sinclair himself, along with several other senior officers from CONMILCOM. To her considerable surprise, Grant Morton had been there as well. She'd thought the president of the Confederation Congress had escaped with the other pro-independence delegates aboard the *Transluxus*.

Word of her escape—and her refugee charges—had circulated swiftly through the Confederation camp, attracting considerable interest among the government's higher-ups still on New America. The genies' reception in the Newamie lines, however, had turned out to be less than enthusiastic.

"It might not have been a smart idea bringing them across the lines, my dear," General Dmitrin Kruger had told her, shaking his bald head. The others watched her, impassive. A viewall in the back was set to monitor Jefferson's city center. Much of the capital was already in flames as Imperial forces pounded it from a distance. The Sony Building showed black gaps among glass windows, and Franklin Park had lost most of its trees. Katya thought of the morninglories there and wanted to weep.

"Indeed," General Grier said, nodding. "They're going to be more trouble than they're worth."

"But they *want* to fight!" she cried. Okay, so the genies weren't trained. That didn't mean they *couldn't* be trained. Damn it, why were these men so close-minded?

"Yes?" Grier demanded. "And how much use would these, these constructs be against warstriders?"

"That's beside the point!" Katya replied. She'd not forgotten that Grier had ordered a retreat before she'd completed her maneuver at Port Jefferson, but she tried to rein in her anger. "This is their world too! Surely they have the right to help defend it! To help fight for their own freedom!"

Grant Morton cleared his throat, and the other men in the room looked to him. Though no longer a military officer, he retained a keen interest in things military. Like Sinclair, he'd resigned his commission in the Hegemony Guard when his home district had elected him to Congress, but, unlike him, he'd not accepted a new commission in the Confederation armed forces. From what Katya had seen of his military ideas, that was just as well. He seemed to be something of a dilettante.

"Perhaps so, ah, Colonel," Morton said, "though there're some who'd tell you that if they don't have the rights of humans, they don't have the responsibilities either . . . like fighting for a freedom that they can neither understand nor ever hope to attain."

"Why you bigoted, hypocritical—" Katya began, temper flared.

Sinclair interrupted her with an upraised hand. "Gently, Katya. No one here thinks that the genies shouldn't have a say in this."

"We are neither hypocrites nor bigots," Morton told her bluntly. "We are simply practical men, doing our best in difficult times."

"Exactly," Kruger added. "There are, um, thorny political considerations in the question. . . ."

"Rainbow, you mean." She'd heard plenty in the past few months about Rainbow, and its bitter feud with the Emancipator Party of Liberty and elsewhere. "Damn it, General! These are *people*!"

"Again, my dear," Kruger had said, "not everyone would agree with you. In any case, remember that they were designed to be, um, less than brilliant, shall we say, and that they have no cybernetic prostheses. How useful to our cause could they possibly be?"

Katya had scowled her reply. Kruger tended to treat her with condescension, Morton as a nonentity.

"A word with you, Colonel," Sinclair had said, standing up. "If I may? I think we're about done here."

"Of course, General," Morton said, dismissing them. "Colonel. Thank you for coming."

They'd excused themselves. Minutes later, when they were alone in Sinclair's office, the general had turned on her. "That, Katya, was a very poor display of judgment!"

The words were like a physical blow. If she didn't care for Kruger, Grier, or the rest, she *did* respect Sinclair.

"I understand the way New Americans think," he told her. "After all, I'm one myself. We have within us a certain egalitarian spirit brought here by our ancestors from Earth, from North America, in fact. It expresses itself as a distinct lack of awe for anyone who is supposed to outrank us.

"But damn it, Colonel, you don't talk back to generals, and you *damn* sure don't call the president of Congress a bigot!"

"I'm . . . I'm sorry, sir," she said. "I was out of line. I know that."

"Sorry doesn't link." Sinclair had gone on to give Katya the richest chewing-out she'd had since she'd been a hojie, a raw recruit just entering basic training. He'd not raised his voice, he'd kept his cultured and good-natured poise, and he told her that he understood that she'd been through a lot in the past day or so, but he'd reminded her in no uncertain terms that certain military standards of discipline and professionalism had to be set . . . and kept.

"I cannot have officers in my command," he told her, "who can't muster the personal discipline to keep their mouths shut, when necessary, or who dive in blind and unthinking when only cold, hard-headed reason will serve."

And just when Katya had been convinced that Sinclair was about to bust her all the way back down to lieutenant, he'd grinned at her. "So, Colonel Alessandro, do you have any ideas as to how we can use these recruits of yours?"

"Uh . . . sir?"

"Lecture over. Your penance, Katya, will be to come up with some way that we can use these people." She'd blinked at him and he'd laughed. "Well, that is what you wanted, isn't it?"

It was, and she'd given a lot of thought to the problem during her walk back to the Newamie lines. Still shaken by the dressing-down he'd given her, she began to explain her idea.

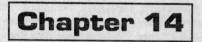

# Chapter 14

*We hold that the vast distances sundering world
from world and system from system serve to insu-
late the worlds of Mankind's diaspora from one
another and from Earth, and that government
cannot adequately bridge so vast a gap of time,
space, and culture;*

*We hold that the differences between mutually
alien, albeit human cultures render impossible a
thorough understanding of the needs, necessities,
aspirations, goals, and dreams of those disparate
worlds by any central government. . . .*

*Further, we hold that human culture, economy,
and aspirations are too varied to administer,
regulate, or restrict by any means, but should
be free, allowing each to thrive or fail on its own
merits.*

—*The Declaration of Reason*
Travis Ewell Sinclair
C.E. 2542

The New American raiding force had departed from Daikokukichi within twenty hours of their victory there. Dev had been in a hurry to leave. Now they were into the last few hours before breakout, and Dev was linked into *Eagle*'s control system, watching the blue currents of the K-T plenum break past him, feeling their buffet against his ViRsimulated being.

"Dev?" Lara Anders broke into dark and circular thoughts. "Coming up on the final countdown. What's the word?"

Dev considered, then gave the linked analogue to a heavy shrug. "We'll have to play it like we planned it, Lara. Nothing cute, like at Athena. We just drop in like we have every right to be there."

"I'm afraid I agree." He could feel her worry. "But we're running against damned long odds. I'd feel safer with the rest of the squadron at my back."

"Which wouldn't extend our survival time by more than a few minutes, right? This way, at least, we've got a chance. Instead of firepower, we'll be counting on the hidebound blindness of Imperial bureaucracy. Given that, I'd say our chances are really pretty good."

"Oh, we won't have any trouble at all getting in," Lara told him. "It's the getaway that's scaring me."

*And me*, he thought, but that was not a thought to put out over the link.

Thirty-three days earlier, *Eagle* had left Daikoku and the rest of the Confederation fleet. The raiders had not destroyed the orbital shipyard or the planetary base, though Dev had been tempted, and his orders from Sinclair had at least given him that option. If the Daikoku Yards were destroyed, Dev had reasoned, the Imperials might well not rebuild them, relying instead on their shipyards within the Sol system, bases that would be extremely difficult to get at. By leaving most of the station intact, it was at least possible that the rebels would be able to help themselves to its bounty again, sometime in the future.

They *had* grabbed every ship that could fly, however, and as many military consumables—missiles, shells, nano-D—as they could find and load. Those newgrown ships that were not yet operable, including the incomplete shell of the Kako-class cruiser, had been destroyed by timed charges releasing clouds of nano-disassemblers within their hulls, which stripped them down into crumbling, bare-metal skeletons in a matter of hours. The nanovats, too, had been contaminated by specially designed nano, viral self-replicators that entered the shipyard's nanotechnic control modules and corrupted their programming. When the Imperials tried to start them up again, they would find the vats growing garbage instead of starship parts; the Yard's entire maintenance and assembly facility would have to be zero-purged and reprogrammed before it could be brought on-line again, a process that might take a year or more.

The facility crew and marines, disarmed, had been marooned on the planet. There was an old mining habitat called Atlas some thousand kilometers west of the planet's surface facility at Carlson, left over from the planet's pre-Imperial days and abandoned when it became unproductive. As Dev's people were busily stripping the shipyards, ascraft from the *Mirach* and *Vindemiatrix* had ferried the prisoners down to Atlas and left them there, first making certain there was food, water, and air enough in the hab domes to last them until the next Hegemony ships came by and picked up the SOS from their emergency beacon.

The personnel at Carlson itself were left alone; Dev had planned to take that facility as well, which was why he'd brought the warstriders aboard *Mirach* and *Vindemiatrix* in the first place, but they were no threat where they were, and if they ventured into orbit aboard their own ascraft, the Confederation ships could easily blast them long before they could approach the station.

With that implied threat hanging literally over their heads, the Imperials and the *gaijin* mining crews at Carlson had obviously decided to sit it out on the surface, and Dev had given orders that they be ignored. He couldn't afford the trouble—or the casualties—of storming their base, and there was no military reason to do so.

All Japanese personnel on the orbital facility were taken to Atlas after routine questioning. The *gaijin* personnel, however, were given a choice—stranding with their Japanese masters, or a slot with the rebels. Randi Lloyd, the Hegemony *shosa* in charge of Guard personnel at Daikoku's orbital shipyards, and thirty-two other new Confederation recruits had accepted Dev's offer.

Dev had been disappointed that the number hadn't been higher, but Randi had explained that the rebel cause was still unknown to most people in the Hegemony. The government hardly went out of its way to publish the Confederation's side of things, and for most people within the Hegemony Guard, the rebels were nothing more than a ragged band of discredited malcontents, political agitators, and terrorists . . . if, indeed, they existed at all.

That belief extended to the Imperials as well. People who assumed they were fighting rabble often got careless, and carelessness led to mistakes.

Which, of course, they were counting on . . . that, and the AI codes and security protocols lifted from Daikokukichi's computer. Lloyd's help, Lloyd's *treason*, might well prove to be the difference between success and failure.

The return journey from Athena to 26 Draconis had seemed to drag on forever, day following day in a slow-crawling procession. Dev had passed that time by spending nearly every waking hour linked in with *Eagle*'s AI; when he wasn't actively participating in jacking the vessel home, he was running simulations, elaborate ViRdramas of what they *might* find when they dropped out of K-T space on the borders of the 26 Draconis system, given the size and strength of the Imperial force that had called at Daikokukichi.

Basically, the possibilities as Dev had worked them out boiled down to just two: either the Imperials had been able to move swiftly and decisively enough that they'd been able to seize Jefferson—and with it most of the Confederation government—within a few hours or days of their first landing; or the fighting would still be going on when *Eagle* arrived. The chances of the Confed forces blocking the Imperium's local space superiority were so slim that *Eagle*'s AI wouldn't even assign them a probability. Imperial forces *would* land; there was no way to stop that. The only question was whether or not they could crack the Confederation defenses and break all resistance on the planet within one week of those landings.

Of the two, *Eagle*'s AI gave a slightly higher probability—one of sixty-one percent, in fact—to a longer, more protracted fight. Engineering the invasion of an entire world with a population of half a billion people was a complex problem in both strategy and logistics. Unless the Nihon admiral in charge had been extraordinarily lucky, or the defenders had been extraordinarily clumsy, by D+7 the Imperials would control New America's major cities and spaceports, including, of course, Jefferson itself, but enough of the Confederation armed forces and local militias would have been able to escape intact that they could almost certainly continue the fight, even if they were forced to become little more than guerrilla units scattered about in the New American Outback.

In fact, the world of New America was especially well suited to guerrilla warfare. Its native, human-compatible ecology would allow the defenders to live off the land; cities, farms, and settlements were not all enclosed within sealed and vulnerable domes, as on

Eridu. The rugged, usually mountainous, often heavily forested terrain would shield the defenders both from warstrider patrols and, to a lesser extent, from orbital scans. Though Imperial victory was virtually certain in the long run, New America's defenders could keep the fight going for years, so long as they had the willingness, the *heart* to do so.

That—the question of heart—was more than anything else what worried Dev as *Eagle* swam through the blue glory of the godsea toward far 26 Draconis. He remembered the political divisions within the Confederation Congress before he'd left, and wondered if the rebel government might not simply cave in when confronted by the full, crushing weight of Imperial space and ground forces. It was one thing to proclaim the benefits of full independence when the Emperor's battlefleet was forty-eight light-years distant, quite another to proclaim them when that fleet was in orbit, its assault forces pounding on the doors to the Sony Building itself. All it would take would be a majority vote by the more timorous members of Congress, one agreeing to accept Imperial terms, and *Eagle* might arrive to find the Confederation government dissolved, its army disbanded, and the promise of Sinclair's Declaration of Reason only a fading memory.

Dev was surprised to realize just how much he *didn't* want that to happen. He still felt ambivalent about the Confederation's chances for victory in the long run, but he'd learned something important from Randi Lloyd, from his decision to betray Empire and Hegemony.

With seventy-eight populated worlds to choose from, with the promise of unnumbered more worlds yet to be discovered and explored beyond the boundaries of the Shichiju, with the technology to create space habitats and orbital colonies entirely independent of the presence of Earthlike worlds, the Cosmos ought to be big enough for everyone, big enough for every group and culture and faction that had its own rules for living and its own goals to reach for.

*Ought* to be. But Nihon and Earth's Hegemony together were committed to controlling each offshoot of Humankind's diaspora the way a parent Naga controlled its fragment >>selves<<. To maintain that control they needed to maintain conformity. Oddball sects and factions like the Disciples, the Randites, the Greenies, or the Church of Mind of God Universalists needed to be suppressed, or at least actively discouraged from spreading messages of personal freedom or of individuality or of resistance to governmental authority; Japanese thought, in management and in government, stressed the concept of *sodan*, or group consultation, whereby a consensus could be reached for which no individual need take full responsibility. Consensus and conformity were the keystones of Imperial rule, individuality its greatest enemy. From the government's point of view, for its very survival, individuality *had* to be suppressed everywhere within the Hegemony simply to keep the assembly of human worlds and cultures from splintering into countless, squabbling fragments.

Dev suspected that such had been the case for authoritarian regimes throughout Earth's history; the disintegration of the Soviet Empire during the closing years of the twentieth century, the collapse of the Chinese state a half century later were obvious cases in point. That most such empires had originally been established—like the Hegemony—to keep the peace and protect their citizens tended to be forgotten in the trail of government-sponsored horrors aimed at promoting conformity of thought.

Sinclair had had much to say about individual liberties, Dev remembered. He'd downloaded Sinclair's Declaration of Reason into his personal RAM, but over the course of the past few months he'd played it back so many times that the words had long since been burned into his organic memory as well. Much of that document, explaining why the Frontier worlds had to sever themselves from Imperium and Hegemony, was devoted to a single theme. No government, it stated, could unite the brawling, clashing, vibrantly discordant variety of human culture without mashing it all into a grim, gray sameness . . . and it shouldn't be allowed to try. Was that a principle worth fighting for, no matter how long the odds?

Dev now knew that it was. Randi Lloyd's decision to help the Confederation force at Daikokukichi had impressed him with just how very much there was at stake in this struggle. *If anything stops the Shichiju from becoming a boring sameness on every world it possesses*, Sinclair had told him and Katya once, privately, *it's the hodgepodge of wonderfully varied human cultures on every planet we've set foot on. Hell, they're what keep things lively!*

And Dev was convinced now that Sinclair was right. The odds were still damned long. . . .

*Yoroshii.* He was in this thing now, and the hell with the long odds. The Confederation had no chance at all if he and all the other jigging chokies caught in the middle of this fight didn't link in and download everything they had to the Cause. Even the Empire would have to admit sooner or later that no government, no matter how sprawling or massive or powerful, could be maintained for long against the active resistance of its citizens. The Shichiju was too large for any one government to control; when enough worlds realized that and demanded independence, *something* was going to give.

In the meantime, the New American raiding force had taken a big step to throw some mass behind the Confederation's demands. A pity, Dev thought, that there hadn't been a way to loose the Confederation's brand-new navy against the Imperials at 26 Draconis. *That* would have shaken Imperial complacency!

It would also have been suicide. Though Dev had played through hundreds of tactical simulations to check his initial feeling, he'd been certain from the beginning that the new Confederation fleet could not seriously challenge Ohka Squadron. Hell, that dragonship alone might prove too much for one destroyer and twenty-odd frigates, corvettes, patrol boats, and assorted small stuff . . . and it didn't help at all that most of Dev's people were little better than newbie recruits. Most had jacked ships before, but few had been in combat. Too, they'd been stretched damned thin among the captured vessels; some of the officers and crew on the smaller ships would be standing watch-and-watch all the way to their destination.

If he couldn't challenge the Imperial squadron at New America in battle, then, he would have to find another way to get past them. Before leaving Daikoku, he'd assembled his battle staff and the commanding officers of his force in *Eagle*'s conference lounge for a marathon planning session, discussing alternatives.

Most had recommended that the raiding force return to New America and challenge the Imperials. Understandable. The majority of them were New Americans; it was their homes and families and friends that *Donryu* was threatening, and the need to go back and do something, *anything*, was an almost palpable presence in the compartment.

In the end, though, Dev had exercised his command authority and overidden the majority's recommendation; there would be no attempt by the raiding force to engage *Donryu* or her escorts at New America, not when such an attempt would mean almost certain destruction. Instead, he'd left the captured fleet, as well as *Mirach*, *Tarazed*, and *Vindemiatrix*, at Daikoku, all under the command of Jase Curtis, *Tarazed*'s CO.

He'd given Curtis explicit orders for what they were to do next. *Eagle* alone would making the passage from Athena to New America, her crew made up entirely of volunteers drawn from the entire squadron. Also aboard were a dozen transport ascraft, some shuttled over from the *Tarazed*, others picked up new from the Daikoku Yards.

Randi Lloyd, now a commander in the Confederation navy thanks to a field commission conferred on him by Dev, had elected to join *Eagle*'s crew, along with the other *gaijin* former Guardsmen. The rest had been left on Daikoku with the Imperials. For *Eagle*'s new crew, the five-week journey had been a constant round of preparation and simulation. Dev had an idea about how *Eagle* might run the Imperial blockade at New America, but it required every one of those thirty-three days for *Eagle*'s crew, working with her AI, to get everything right and ready.

Dev wondered again about the Confederation fleet, *Tarazed*, *Mirach*, *Vindemiatrix*, and all of the captured ships as well. He'd taken a terrific gamble with them.

Almost as large a gamble as he was taking now with the *Eagle*.

"One minute to breakout." That was the voice of *Eagle*'s AI. Dev could sense the cascade of data flowing through the ship's network. With a pseudovelocity of a light-year per day, overshooting the meticulously calculated instant of breakout by one second could lead to an error of over 110 million kilometers. Only a ship's AI could calculate to that order of precision. Older ships frequently needed to make several K-T space transitions, creeping up on the target through a set of successively tighter calculations.

"All hands," Dev broadcast. "Get ready. Remember, we're supposed to be Imperials. Don't shoot unless I give the word." He measured the flow of data through the navsystem. "Thirty seconds."

Then it was time. *Breakout.*

They dropped out of K-T space on the mark, ten AUs out from 26 Draconis A, with red dwarf B a tiny ruddy disk hanging in space to the left. There were ships . . . *lots* of ships, and all were broadcasting Imperial IFF on the fleet frequencies.

"Start squawking," Dev said. Lara gave an order, and *Eagle* began broadcasting IFF of its own.

The code had been part of the package handed over by Lloyd back at Daikokukichi, recorded when Ohka Squadron had docked at the Yards. With luck, fleet units in-system would register *Eagle* as another Imperial destroyer, arriving late, or as reinforcements from Earth.

It would take some minutes for the burst of neutrinos marking *Eagle*'s arrival, traveling at the speed of light, to reach Imperial ships sunward. Under Lara's steady guidance, the destroyer accelerated sharply, then fell toward New America, visible in the navsim display as one bright star among many.

Minutes passed . . . slow-dragging. Certainly, the Imperials knew by now of *Eagle*'s arrival. Dev and the others waited, listening, wondering what the response would be.

"D983, D983," a voice called over the ship-to-ship audio. The number referred to *Eagle*'s borrowed identification code. "This is Imperial picket *Tosshin*. We have received your IFF code transmission. Please confirm your ID visually. Over."

So. They weren't going to take the IFF's word for it. Smart . . . and unfortunate, though Dev had been expecting a challenge. The stakes had just gone up a notch.

"Transmitting vessel at zero-five-eight, ascension two-zero," *Eagle*'s AI said, as a targeting diamond marked the corvette's position ahead and warbook data scrolled across Dev's vision. The picket was a small vessel, a Hari-class corvette of 800 tons, with a twenty-five-man crew. No match for a destroyer, its orders would be to challenge intruders and report to the Imperial's in-system headquarters.

"Range, fourteen point four million kilometers," the AI continued after a brief pause. "Time delay at that range, forty-eight seconds."

"That's it," Dev told the human components of *Eagle*'s linked network. "Let 'er rip!"

One of *Eagle*'s watch officers gave the actual command, loosing a ViRcom laser transmission stored in *Eagle*'s memory. Traveling at the speed of light, it would reach the Imperial corvette in less than fifty seconds.

Then, in fifty seconds more, allowing for the time delay of any return broadcast, *Eagle*'s anxiously waiting crew would know how effective their preparations had been.

# Chapter 15

*In the days before cephlinks and virtual reality,
of course, EW—Electronic Warfare—was restricted to mean those tactics employed by opposing
forces to learn about the enemy's dispositions by
listening in on his radio and radar transmissions,
while simultaneously baffling his attempts to do
the same through jamming and various types of
electronic countermeasures.*

*With ViRcommunications, of course, the game
became far more complicated, and deadly.*

—*Man and the Stars: A History of Technology*
Ieyasu Sutsumi
C.E. 2531

When Dev and Katya had lifted off from Eridu in an
ascraft months before, they'd been pursued by Imperial
warships, by Amatukaze-class destroyers identical to the
*Eagle*, in fact. As with all ship-to-ship communications,
the ViRcom exchanges between Dev and *Arasi*'s captain

had been recorded, both by Dev's own cephlink and by the ascraft's lasercom circuits. By downloading those records to *Eagle*'s link network, the destroyer's AI had been able to create a computer analogue of the captain of the Imperial destroyer *Arasi*.

*This is* Taisa *Yasuo Ihara*, the computer-generated image had said, mimicking perfectly the real Ihara's gruff manner and harsh-slurred Nihongo. *Captain of the Imperial destroyer* Arasi. *I require direct passage to Ohka Squadron's operational area. Over.*

The time lag, as *Eagle*'s lasercom transmission had crept across intervening space to the waiting corvette, then again as the corvette's lasered reply crawled back, had seemed interminable. Randi Lloyd had provided all of the current Imperial codes and passwords stored at Daikokukichi, as well as every scrap of electronic data he'd been able to record when Ohka Squadron had stopped at his base, but there was always the possibility that Ohka possessed some secret recognition code that Lloyd had not intercepted, or that a *real* messenger from Munimori would have some private access word agreed upon back on Earth. Of particular concern was whether *Arasi* and Captain Ihara were still at Eridu, as seemed likely, or whether in the past few months they'd been reassigned to Ohka.

It would be suspicious, to say the least, if a destroyer claiming to be the *Arasi* dropped out of K-T space with a secret communiqué for Kawashima . . . and the real *Arasi* was already parked in orbit a few kilometers off *Donryu*'s starboard side.

"We have a return laser," *Eagle*'s communications officer reported over the link. "They've acknowledged!"

"Play it."

A scene formed in Dev's mind as he accepted the transmission downlink. Giving a mental command, Dev took on a new ViRcomm persona . . . that of *Taisa*

Ihara on *Arasi*'s bridge, as reconstructed by *Eagle*'s AI. According to ViRcomm protocol, the setting for any exchange was aboard the ship belonging to the higher-ranking officer; juniors always reported to their senior's bridge, never the other way around. Dev's persona was seated on a thronelike and purely imaginary seat, surrounded by the bulky jack modules for the bridge crew. Before him stood the persona of a Japanese naval officer in an immaculate dress uniform.

"*Yoku irasshaimashita, Taisasan!*" the man said, smiling and bowing low. "Welcome, sir! I am *Chusa* Shioya, of the Imperial corvette *Tosshin*. Your transmission acknowledged! Please transmit special clearance codes and ID. Over."

Shioya's Nihongo was precise and polite, with no hint of a challenge behind the words.

"*Ah, Chusasan!*" he said, allowing the computer to shape words in Ihara's cold, rough growl. They sounded strange in his mind's ears. "I am here on the express special orders of *Gensui* Yasuhiro Munimori, Commander of the First Fleet and Senior Admiral of the Imperial Military Staff. My business is with *Chujo* Kawashima, and it is classified *kimitsu*." He paused, to give the words a dramatic emphasis. "There is no need for you to know more. You will tell no one that I am here. Over."

Shioya did not react to the words immediately, of course. The image remained statue still, as though frozen in time, as Dev's reply headed back across the light-seconds.

This was the most critical part of the deception. If Shioya demanded code authentication that Dev could not give, the mission was over. There'd be nothing more to do but turn and flee for K-T space, abandoning Sinclair and Katya and the rest to New America's invaders.

But discipline within the Imperial fleet, as Dev knew well, was imposed from the top down by successive hierarchies of power. A corvette's commander would make a special report to Kawashima only if he'd been specifically ordered to do so; in the absence of such orders, if "Captain Ihara" ordered him to tell no one, invoking the authority of Munimori himself, well, there was a good chance that he would let them pass.

The word *kimitsu*—the military classification equivalent to "top secret"—would carry a great deal of mass with Shioya as well. No Imperial naval officer, especially one as junior as a commander, would willingly risk tangling with the TJK, the Imperial intelligence service. A single word from a *Teikokuno Johokyoku* official could ruin almost any military officer's career.

Shioya's image had been waiting patiently throughout the time necessary for the communications lasers to carry Dev's answer back to the *Tosshin* at the laggardly speed of light, then for Shioya's reply to return. Suddenly, the image stirred, then bowed.

"*Hai, Taisasan!* As you command! You are clear to shape course for the inner system. This is Imperial picket *Tosshin*, out!"

The transmission ended, fading to black.

Dev sagged within the linkage, relief flooding through him as *Arasi*'s bridge faded away and was replaced by the more familiar view of stars and black-velvet space. They weren't out of the radiation belt yet, not by seven hundred rads, but they'd taken the first, vital step . . . and managed to carry it off.

*Eagle* continued accelerating in-system.

The LaG-42 Ghostrider entered the forest clearing and stopped, the wide-band scanners mounted in its chin turret sweeping left and right with quick, urgent flicks, its nanoflage rippling to a pale, dappled pattern of greens and yellows as the sunlight struck it.

At twenty-five and a half tons, a Ghostrider was less than half the mass of a Warlord and had only two slots for jackers, positioned side by side along the top of its long, blunt fuselage. It had less muscle, too; its primary weapons were two Kv-70 weapons packs mounted above and to either side of the hull, plus a hundred-megawatt laser jutting from its chin turret in an improbable and unintended piece of phallic imagery.

Smaller and less powerful offensively the LaG-42 might be, but Katya preferred jacking the Ghost to the Warlord. It was faster, more nimble, and felt more responsive to her guiding thoughts. When she was jacking a Warlord, Katya walked; when she wore a Ghostrider, however, she *danced*, and the machine's bright feedback played across her cortex receptors like a song.

She took a moment to absorb the play of light and shadow of the forest. New America's native trees were slender below, feathery above. Their movement in even the slightest wind set light to glittering on the wiry tangle of forest undergrowth. Nearby, a swarm of sundancers—smaller, distant cousins to morninglories—bounced and jittered on a shaft of sunlight.

*Come on, come on*, Katya thought to herself. *Where are they?*

Movement stirred the fronds at the clearing's far edge. Katya tensed as readouts indicated approaching life-forms, man-sized and man-warm. Was it?

It was. The patrol filed into the clearing, looking less than military as they milled about in an uncertain clump, ten meters from the Ghostrider's guns.

"Keep her hot, Chet," she told her Number Two. Sub-lieutenant Chet Martin was another newbie, painfully young and enough like Ken Maubry in looks and speech and attitudes to have been the dead jacker's brother.

*Cannon fodder*, she thought bitterly as she broke linkage, then unsealed her slot. Daylight flooded her narrow pilot's module. *Worse*. Sempu *fodder*.

Scrambling from the open slot, she worked her way to the ground on handholds strategically placed down the inside of the strider's leg. She'd been thinking along such lines ever since her return to friendly lines, grim, unworthy thoughts, she supposed, for someone who was supposed to be fighting for liberty and justice and all of the other fine words in Sinclair's Declaration.

Why were revolutions won—or lost—on the blood of children?

The people waiting for her in the clearing were children too, of a different sort. The genie who called himself Tharby was there, with fifteen of his mannies, twelve males, three *ningyo* women.

Two, she noticed, were missing.

"Hello, Tharby," she said. "Welcome back."

The former nanochemical techie didn't even know how to salute yet. Instead, he bobbed his head, the movement clumsy in his broad, flaring helmet. "Hey, Colonel," he said. "We're back."

"So I see. How far did you get?"

The genie leader shifted his Pk-30 laser carbine uncertainly from hand to hand. " 'Bout twenty klicks. There's Impies there. Lots of 'em. Couldn't go no further."

"Good! That's what we wanted you to find out. How many Impies? Where are they?" When he hesitated, she said, "Show me." Stooping, she began sketching out a rough map of the Gaither Valley approaches to Stone Mountain, using a stick to scratch the lines into soft, bare dirt.

The genies had still not been accepted by the Confederation command, at least not completely. Sinclair's authorization had cleared some of the red tape, securing uniforms, light infantry armor, and weapons for them, but she found she still had to be careful not to mention what—or who—the equipment was for to officious supply officers or suspicious bureaucrats. Prejudice against arming genies was not to be found solely among civilians. Military personnel had started off as civilians, after all, and they dragged their prejudices along with them when they joined the service.

The genies stayed in a special camp outside of Stone Mountain, more or less sequestered from other troops.

Even so, there'd been trouble. Three days ago, one of the *ningyo* women had been grabbed by several drunken militia troops and raped. The soldiers responsible were in the brig under the mountain now, awaiting trial. Ever since, there'd been grumbling among the enlisted men to the effect that the prisoners had done nothing wrong. After all, that was what *ningyo* were for, wasn't it?

Officially, the genies were now the Port Jefferson Scouts, a special unit attached to the 1st Confederation Rangers and directly under Katya's personal command. CONMILCOM had balked at authorizing the unit . . . and then, just one of New America's long days after Katya's return to friendly lines, Jefferson had fallen to the invaders. Everywhere, it seemed, Confederation and militia forces were in full retreat. The 1st Confederation Rangers had drawn up in a semicircle blocking the enemy's advance northwest out of Jefferson, sitting astride a line of rugged, heavily forested ridges and controlling access through a series of broad valleys.

With the Imperials maintaining almost total control of the skies, without even satellites to provide data on Japanese troop movements or ship landings, there was now a truly desperate need for scouts, men and women who could slip close to enemy positions in small groups, record what they saw, and return the information to Stone Mountain. Several Confederation infantry platoons were being converted to this sort of mission, ditching their heavy weapons and assault gear in favor of light armor, nanoflage, and laser carbines.

And Congress had authorized the recruitment of genies.

Katya had been working with them now for only a little over a week. Starting with the ten who'd followed her out of Port Jefferson, she'd added twelve more who'd escaped from the capital, heard that genies were in training at Stone Mountain, and made their way through the wilderness to join them. Technically, the Scouts were just beginning recruit training . . . except that there was no time to do a decent job. If they were to become soldiers, they had to do it *now*, learning the hard way, in combat.

Which made Katya feel no better about what she'd done. It was bad enough throwing trained infantry at warstriders. Hurling untrained newbies—and genies at that—onto a modern battlefield was little short of murder.

For that reason, her training sessions with them so far had actually concentrated on keeping them out of battle. She'd noticed during their passage across the lines that they moved silently, with a grace and an efficiency that Katya herself, with all her experience, was hard-pressed to match. Genies might be a bit slow to catch on, but they were not clumsy. And while few had ever been outside of an urban environment, they seemed to have no trouble adapting to moving about in the woods. They didn't appear to have a typical city dweller's prejudices about forests or rough terrain.

So far as their tailored behaviors went, Katya had seen few differences between Tharby and the other genies and ordinary humans. If any vestige of their "docile" or "obedient" natures remained, it had been blasted by their experiences outside of Port Jefferson the night after the invaders landed. They seemed more than willing to try anything asked of them, and in some ways they seemed as adaptable as their human counterparts.

Which made sense, Katya admitted. They still had human DNA in their cells, even if it had been tinkered with. If they could just be trained to watch and listen, to sneak up on enemy positions, or stay motionless in a camouflaged listening post for hours at a time, then report back what they'd observed, they would make great scouts.

So far, they'd done well. Though they carried weapons and she'd shown them how to use them, they'd not yet been in a firefight, and she'd impressed on them the need to fade back into the forest if they came under fire.

Her map of Stone Mountain and the Gaither Valley complete, she handed the stick to Tharby. "Where did you run into Impies?" she asked. "Twenty klicks, you said?"

Tharby's brow furrowed as he studied the scratches in the dirt. Map reading was not an intuitive skill for him. It involved a use of symbology that, while not beyond the brighter genies, was not second nature to them, either. "This is valley?" he asked at last, pointing to two slashes leading down the side of the mountain.

"That's right."

"This is maglev?" He drew a line winding past the southwestern face of the mountain. Katya's eyebrows raised. He *did* understand the symbology. "Yes! Good!"

"Here," he said, marking a spot on the lower end of the valley. "Near maglev where it passes bottom of valley."

"Okay," Katya said, concentrating in turn. This procedure would have been a hell of a lot easier if she could have shared a ViRcom holomap with Tharby, getting him to mark positions in color and 3-D . . . but the genies didn't have cephlinks and wouldn't have known what to do with them if they had.

"And what did you see? Warstriders?"

"Warstriders," Tharby said, nodding. "Four. And soldiers on foot, with guns. And . . . and something else."

"What?"

This was the hardest part of dealing with the genies, getting them to accurately identify what they saw. Four warstriders . . . were they Tachis or Daimyos? Details like that could make a difference. And what was this "something else" that Tharby claimed they'd seen?

The genie was drawing in the dirt again. "Never seen this before," he told her. "Like warstrider, sort of, but no legs. Big."

"No legs? How did it move? Did it fly?"

"No. Wheels . . . and, and something going around th' wheels."

"Tracks?"

He shrugged, but sketched a line of circles, representing wheels, and enclosed them in what could be treads.

"Buildings on top," he continued, still sketching. The drawing was so crude Katya could hardly fit the pieces together into a whole, but Tharby's words raised fresh dread in her. She thought she knew now what he'd seen.

"Guns here . . . and here," Tharby continued. "It . . . it saw Rita and Gove. Killed them. We faded back into woods, like you told us. Soldiers in armor followed us, but we lost 'em."

A few words, but Katya could picture it easily. A sensor sweep had detected the genies where they lurked in the brush. Antipersonnel weapons—machine guns, light lasers, or *sempu*—had opened up. Death . . . panic . . . and the crash of the enemy thrashing through the woods in pursuit.

"You said this thing was big. How big?"

"Uh . . . maybe as long as from here to . . . to those trees."

Eighty meters, near enough. Even allowing for exaggeration . . .

"Tharby. Don't tell me you saw a siege crawler!"

"Don't know 'bout siege crawlers," Tharby said. He gestured at the child's drawing proudly. "But it looked like *this*!"

Siege crawlers—massive, mobile fortresses as long as a city block, riding on multiple sets of tracks and massing two thousand tons or more. If the Imperials had siege crawlers on New America, they must be planning for a major push right up the Gaither Valley. Nothing in the Newamie arsenal could stop one of those. Not much could, in fact, except for nukes, and the Imperials had been very careful to maintain a monopoly on nuclear weapons. Possibly a massed warstrider assault . . .

She glanced up at the sky, empty for the moment. There'd been an awful lot of shuttling back and forth to and from orbit by the Imperials, lately. If they'd brought down a crawler, that explained some of the activity. Crawlers were so large they were ferried to and from a planet's surface in pieces, and assembled in place.

"You did wonderfully, Tharby," she told him. "I'm sorry about the two people you lost."

Tharby shrugged. "War means killing," he said simply. "We understand that."

In that moment, Katya could no longer think of the genie as dull-witted or a child.

# Chapter 16

*You tell me I can't stand up to monstrous Ajax?*
*I tell you I never cringe at war and thundering*
  *horses!*
*But the will of Zeus will always overpower the will*
  *of men,*
*and tears away his triumph, all in a lightning*
  *flash,*
*and at other times he will spur a man to battle.*
*Come on, my friend, stand by me, watch me work!*
*See if I prove a coward dawn to dusk—your*
  *claim—*
*or I stop some Argive, blazing in all his power,*
*from fighting on to shield Patroclus' corpse!*

—Hector, in *The Iliad*
Homer
ca. 800 B.C.E.

Space surrounding New America seemed crowded with
ships. True, even a vessel as large as a Ryu dragonship

was tiny to vanishing insignificance compared to the volume of space through which it orbited, but the IFF and communications code signals flashing across Dev's visual download gave the impression of ships, big and little, jostling one another for slots in low planetary orbit.

*Donryu* and the five largest cruisers were clustered in a tight, defensive group alongside Highport, orbiting some three hundred kilometers up. Most of the light stuff, corvettes like the *Tosshin*, and a few frigates, had been dispersed across a defensive, three-dimensional perimeter some forty AUs out. Complete coverage of such a vast area was impossible, of course, but they could keep watch for the neutrino bursts marking incoming starships, and they could report anomalies to *Donryu*.

The rest of Ohka Squadron, the light cruisers and destroyers, had scattered about New America in separate, world-hugging orbits. That was standard Imperial fleet procedure, and Dev had counted on that when he'd worked out *Eagle*'s possible approach vectors. He'd timed the destroyer's approach for a period when the planet was hidden behind the cratered, slow-moving bulk of Columbia, masking her. Then, as *Eagle* emerged from behind the moon, skimming scant kilometers above dust gray maria and the silver flash of airless, dust-rounded mountain peaks, Highport and *Donryu* were just slipping down behind the horizon of New America.

"Nice timing, Commodore," Lara had told him, admiration audible in her mental voice. "That was easy feed slick!"

"The AI showed me how to do it," Dev told her. "All I did was follow directions."

"Yes, but you thought of it in the first place."

Perhaps, but Dev would have been happier with the congratulations coming later. Each step, each minute took *Eagle* deeper into Ohka Squadron's operational area, a mouse challenging a pride of lions.

Yet, *Eagle*'s solitude and her daring were her chief weapons now, those and her AI's simulations of a Japanese ship captain's link persona. Even with full watch kept by the Imperial pickets, one ship, traveling silently, was all but lost in emptiness, so vast is space.

With a final hard-driving, 6-G burst of deceleration, *Eagle* slipped into low orbit around the planet a few hours after skimming Columbia's mountains, safely shielded from *Donryu* by the planet itself.

"Incoming laser communication," *Eagle*'s comm officer warned. "We're being hailed by the *Yubari*. Naka-class light cruiser. *Taisa* Mitsuru Hasegawa, commanding."

"I'll take it," Dev said, opening his mind to the ViRcom transmission.

Again, he stood on a ship's bridge. This time, since *Taisa* Hasegawa was senior to *Taisa* Ihara in the size and importance of his command, Ihara's image was summoned to the bridge of the *Yubari*. Too, Hasegawa was older than *Arasi*'s captain. Dev couldn't estimate his age closely but judged that he was certainly in his fifties. Protocol demanded that Ihara/Dev defer to Hasegawa.

"IFF code D983, this is *Taisa* Hasegawa, of the Imperial light cruiser *Yubari*."

This time there was no time lag during which Dev could gather his thoughts. *Yubari* was only a few tens of thousands of kilometers distant.

Dev bowed deeply. This situation called more for tact than for bluster. "*Konichiwa*, *Taisasan*. *Taisa* Ihara, Imperial destroyer *Arasi*. How can I be of service?"

"Just welcoming you on station, *Taisasan*." Hasegawa's manner was correct, but friendly. "And looking for news. Did you just arrive from Earth?"

Dev considered before answering. He'd expected to

be quizzed by curious Imperials about his origin. Some Imperials here would know *Arasi* had last been stationed at Chi Draconis. Eridu to Earth was twenty-five and a quarter lights, Earth to New America almost forty-nine, for a travel time of something like seventy-four days at the minimum . . . plus a couple of weeks at least for in-system maneuvers and servicing. The real *Arasi* could have made that roundabout hop in the intervening months, but it was much safer to say that she'd made the run straight to 26 Draconis from Eridu, a hop of just over thirty-six lights. It was unlikely that any of the ships in Ohka Squadron had been to Eridu recently enough to see that lie.

"We came from Eridu, *Taisasan*," he told Hasegawa. "A courier from Earth rendezvoused with us there, with special orders."

"Ah. And the news from Eridu? Of the landings there?"

The news chilled, a prickling of worry at the back of Dev's mind. Had the Imperials broken the Eridu truce at last? It made sense, certainly; if they were ready to confront the Confederation head-on by invading their most important world, there was nothing to stop them from snatching Eridu back from the local rebels and restoring the Imperial Peace.

Unfortunately, Hasegawa knew more about the Imperial plans than Dev did. Had Ohka Squadron already received word, by fast courier or by the arrival of ships—such as the *real Arasi*—that the landings on Eridu had already begun? Or was Hasegawa simply alluding to information acquired on Earth about a landing that was *supposed* to take place at a certain date, and he was now asking about what Ihara ought to know?

A wrong answer could ruin everything.

"The operation is proceeding according to schedule," Dev said simply, and ambiguously. "*Arasi* would not have been released to come here were it otherwise, *neh?*"

"*Itarimae-yo!*" Hasegawa replied, nodding. "Of course!"

"What is the situation here?"

"All goes well. The initial landings were made with surprisingly light casualties and succeeded in capturing the *kaizoku* spaceport and landing zones near their capital. We captured the capital itself not long after that. Since then, the rebels have been fighting a guerrilla war from bases in the mountains. From what I've been told, the ground forces expect to capture their military headquarters within the next few days."

"*Yatta!*" Dev said. "That's great!"

And he meant it. He was not too late! This told him nothing about whether the Confederation government survived . . . or Katya was still alive, but there was still a chance!

"Would you care to exchange downloads, *Taisasan?*"

"I am very sorry," Dev replied. That was one courtesy he could not afford to engage in . . . a direct sharing of RAM data between the two ship captains. While Dev would have loved to get a download from Hasegawa—on Imperial deployments in-system, for example, or on the current military schedule—*Yubari*'s captain would need only a glimpse into Dev's personal RAM to see through this entire charade. "I cannot."

"Eh?" Hasegawa's eyes narrowed. "Is there some problem?"

It was not impolite, exactly, to refuse a sharing of RAM, since that sharing could be extremely personal. Still, it was an honor for a lower-ranking person to have the request from someone above him, and in the military, especially, such a request was rarely refused.

Unless the person refusing had something to hide.

Dev bowed. "*Taisasan*, I would be honored to share memories with you. Unfortunately, time is pressing. I have . . . a small problem to attend to, aboard *Arasi*. Perhaps we could exchange data later."

"Of course," Hasegawa said, bowing in reply. "You must have much to attend to, having just entered orbit."

It was a polite dismissal.

"Thank you, *Taisasan*. I look forward to talking with you more fully later."

He broke the ViRcom link and awoke weightless in a bridge link module aboard the *Eagle*. Sweat clung to his forehead. A single bead drifted off the tip of his nose, a tiny, gleaming sphere adrift like a miniature planet. He didn't think Hasegawa was suspicious; more likely, the older man was simply hungry for news. That bespoke much of the organization within Ohka Squadron—and of rumors and stories passed from captain to captain, but little effort at the top of the pyramid to tell them what was really going on.

It made *Eagle*'s deception somewhat easier.

Reentering the ship's linkage network, he alerted Lara and the rest of the bridge officers that it was time to proceed with the plan.

Hours later, Dev was jacked into another slot, bucking a VK-180 Skywind down from orbit. The big ascraft was brand-new, one of the ships lifted from the Daikoku Shipyard, so new that its hull, though nanocoated for radar and visual stealth, had not yet been painted with group or unit markings. As Dev watched the flow of piloting data scrolling past his mind's-eye view of the reentry fireball, green diamonds marked the probable locations of the seven other ascraft. Other diamonds marked possible contacts. During reentry, all data from outside the fireball was suspect. Ionization trails stretched out for kilometers astern through night side darkness, glowing a vivid green-gold. Then the craft thumped into thicker sky, the fireball fading away as the ascraft's speed dropped below Mach 7.

Moonlight—far brighter here than beneath a full moon on Earth—turned clouds ahead and below to streaks and swirls of molten silver. To port and starboard, the other seven ascraft maintained their formation. It was a lonely feeling, for each ascraft carried but a single crewman, its pilot. No transmissions passed between them, not when the Imperials were certain to be monitoring all such. Aboard *Eagle*, before launch, Dev had carefully briefed the other pilots on Imperial flight formations and techniques. Their descent toward New America now was nearly flight-academy perfect, a drill for Imperial pilots.

Far below, contrails scratched ivory lines ruler-straight above the clouds. Imperials, those, almost certainly. Would they challenge the intruders, or assume that they were what they seemed to be and let them pass?

Dev shifted his attention to an inset mental view of the ground, a map graphic updated continually by radar and low-wattage laser scans. According to the display, the ascraft were over the Forrestal Sea, with Stone Mountain to the southeast, less than five thousand kilometers ahead.

They had to be at Stone Mountain. The old Hegemony arsenal there was the best defensive position on the planet, and he knew that the government had had contingency plans for moving there should Jefferson fall. There would be plenty of room in the old underground bunkers and warehouses for a government-in-exile, sheltered beneath meters of hard granite. He kept watching the inset display; as the cloud deck broke up beneath the ascraft's belly, low-power laser scans began returning high-definition imagery of the ground and matching it with what the ascraft had stored on New American terrain. Excellent. On course . . . on time. A coastline, then a village—scattered buildings, some outlying farms—flashed by thirty kilometers below.

"Ascraft flight, IFF D369, this is Sorataka Flight *Kondoru*." The words, clipped and precise, sounded in Dev's mind. Shifting his gaze, Dev could see the Se-280s, four of them, sleek and deadly and taking up positions above and behind the larger, slower ascraft. "Please identify yourself."

"*Kondoru*, this is ascraft flight *Tozan*." The flight identifier, a poetic form meaning "Eastern Mountain," had been agreed upon by Dev and the other pilots only hours earlier. "Transmitting code."

Again, the code had been drawn from the signals protocols Lloyd had revealed at Daikoku. Had any of them been changed?

"*Tozan, Kondoru*. What is your mission, over?"

"Reinforcements for Special Assault Group One. We should have advance clearance from *Gensui* Munimori."

There was danger here, a danger that grew deeper as the silence stretched out. "Special Assault Group One" was fiction, as was the advance clearance. By speaking of them as though the Se-280 squadron ought to know about them, however, Dev was placing the responsibility of checking squarely with the squadron's skipper. He could radio his headquarters for verification . . . and either lose face because he didn't have the proper information, or, worse, make his commander lose face because *he* didn't have the proper information.

Or he could assume that the ascraft were what they appeared to be . . . a flight of Imperial ascraft carrying reinforcements to the battle at Stone Mountain.

Hell, what *else* could they be? Throwing in Munimori's name merely provided an extra bit of incentive. Few squadron commanders would dare call headquarters for verification!

"*Tozan*, this is *Kondoru*. You are cleared for your approach. Be careful in Grid 57 slash 10. There's been heavy fighting there all night."

"Affirmative, *Kondoru*. Thank you."

Together, the four Se-280s stood on their stubby, dihedral wings and arced sharply toward the south. In seconds, the night swallowed even the flare of their exhausts.

At an altitude now of less than ten kilometers, Dev thought he could see the battle ahead. Mountains wrinkled and puckered in the darkness, backlit by the silent flare of explosions. They were past the Nihonjin outriders protecting the battle zone itself. Now all they needed to do was make contact with the Confederation forces . . .

. . . without getting shot out of the sky as Japanese.

Ragnarok—the final battle of the gods—had come to New America. The approaches to Stone Mountain, particularly the broad, gently curving glacial excavation called Gaither Valley, was lit by the near constant strobings of pulse lasers and rocket fire, by the savage detonations of long-range artillery, and by whiplashing swarms of rockets arrowing through the sky on trails of golden light.

Once a town called Anversen had stood here, a farming community on the main road to Stone Mountain. After an earlier Imperial air bombardment little remained but the shattered shells of buildings, jagged black walls upthrust against the dazzling flash and flare of battle. Smoke—both the battle haze of antilaser aerosols and the thicker, darker pillars rising from burning vehicles and buildings—hung heavy across the battlefield, as depressions in the ground filled with the deadly white sheen of nano-D.

The DYN-12 Kyodaina siege crawler had already left a trail through half the ruin of the town, a path not so much of destruction as of complete and utter annihilation. Walls struck by that duralloy behemoth were toppled effortlessly, then ground beneath three-meter tracks that reduced stone blocks and pavement to rubble and mashed the remnants into a pulp of churned earth and gravel. Designed as much for the terror it instilled as for power, the crawler moved slowly, a few kilometers per hour, and it chose its path forward with care. Unlike warstriders, a crawler was restricted to certain types of terrain, to ground solid enough to support its titan's weight, and open enough to admit its breadth.

Very little could stand against it, however. So large a vehicle could carry tons of onboard munitions, anti–nano-D, and the power to charge and fire lasers and particle cannons worthy of a small spaceship. Multiple fusion plants yielded energy and to spare to move wheels four meters across, bearing the weight of meter-thick durasheath armor, slabs of duralloy interspersed with layers of polyceramics, woven diamond monofilament, and superconducting mesh.

Jacked into the long line of onboard control modules, *Tai-i* Hideki Ozawa, formerly of Blue Company, First Battalion of the *Zugaikotsu* Regiment, had decided that he definitely preferred warstriders to this crawling monster of a fortress. It was so *slow*. No matter if this behemoth packed a thousand times the firepower of a single warstrider, he'd much rather be jacking a quick-stepping Tachi.

Ozawa's duty as assault company CO had come to a sudden end at the rebel spaceport, when a Starhawk missile had screamed in from the south, its detonation ripping his Tachi's left leg from its joint and touching off his remaining rockets. He'd punched out, ejecting just as the shattered warstrider had crumpled to the ground and exploded; a week later, with more combat striderjacks available than working machines to pilot, *Shosa* Yoshitomi had assigned him to the crew detailed to assemble the massive pieces of the siege crawler as they were brought down one by one from orbit. When it had come time to tell off a crew for the beast, Ozawa had immediately volunteered.

He'd seen the beginning of this campaign. Now he wanted to see the end of it. The rebel forces

so far had revealed an almost laughable disorgani-
zation—contriving at one point a brilliant ambush
of his new-landed assault force, then throwing it
all away moments later by a hasty and ill-advised
retreat. Ozawa still couldn't believe his luck; his
force had been trapped and in danger of being utterly crushed when the rebel attack had simply fall-
en apart.

In the past few weeks, the rebel capital had fallen
and several more attacks had been beaten off. As
the crawler had grumbled north out of Jefferson, a
furious enemy attack had destroyed several of the
crawler's supporting warstriders and even managed
to put a Starhawk into the monster's upper deck,
but they'd been completely unable even to slow the
Kyodaina's march. One more good push ought to do
it.

But the damned crawler was so *slow.* . . .

Outwardly, the crawler was much as the genie patrol
had described it—flat, broad lower hull supported by
six sets of treads, two to either side set one ahead of
the other, two more grumbling along within a cavernous
well down the center of its belly; and on top, curve-sided
domes, barbettes, turrets, and guntowers, the firepower
of a small starship grinding up the valley toward Stone
Mountain.

Katya watched, her Ghostrider crouched in the sheltering rubble of a half-collapsed building as the land-
crawling leviathan passed her position, a scant fifty
meters to the north. She could sense the ground trembling as the monster rumbled passed, noted plaster dust
spilling from the walls around her in time to the thing's
earthquaking rumble.

Gods, it was big! The massive, sprocketed wheels
half-glimpsed beneath the port-side armor skirts each
were taller than her warstrider. Scanner dishes and the
muzzles of weapons pivoted this way and that, seeking

targets, and Katya knew a piercing fear, sharp as any dread of night or closeness, as she wondered if the small army of Imperial Marines linked into the behemoth's AI system saw her now.

Unlikely, that. The ambush platoon had been carefully planted here, beneath the covering screens of antisensor aerosols, and crouched now at near total power-down, with only life-support and AI-link network systems on-line. Four enemy striders had already stalked past in close formation and seen nothing. Too, the Imperial crawl-jackers would be concentrating on their target kilometers ahead, the outer ring of the Stone Mountain static defenses, rather than searching for rebels gone to ground.

Her trained eye spotted weakness against the strength, however. It had taken damage during the past hours of combat—a guntower on the starboard side reduced to scrap by a trio of Striker missiles; a gaping, jagged-edge cavern where a Starhawk had nearly scored a kill.

"Christ of the Cosmos!" Sublieutenant Martin called, the words jerked from his thoughts. "We can't attack that thing! We gotta get out of here!"

"Steady, Chet!" Katya snapped back over the Ghostrider's link intercom.

"It's no good! It's no good!" She could sense him fumbling with the mental codes that would release his link.

Sharply, she took full control of the link network, blocking Martin's shutdown, electronically pinning him in place. "Negative, Sublieutenant!" she said. "You can do it or you can come along for the ride, but you're staying right where you are!"

"We . . . we . . ."

Thunder cracked and rolled outside the Ghostrider's hull, as treads ground stone to sand.

"We can do it, damn it! We can take that monster! But we have to stay together, do you understand?" When silence answered her, Katya nudged the volume of her mental voice up a notch. "*Are you linked?*"

The old recruit training gimmick knifed through Martin's panic. "Uh . . . linked, sir!"

"What was that?"

"LINKED, SIR!"

"Okay! Now you take the chin laser, right? I'm going to be busy!"

"Yes, sir."

"Iceworld, Chet! We can *do* this."

*Now if you could just believe that yourself. . . .*

"So! Are you linked, Sub?"

"Linked!" Hesitation. "I . . . I'm sorry, Colonel. . . ."

"Deleted and forgotten. Just pull yourself together. Let's not let the Impies think they're up against an undisciplined rabble!"

"I won't let you down, sir."

"I know you won't."

Courage, Katya knew, was nothing more than the willingness to press ahead despite the terror that turned knees weak, mouths dry, and stomachs to twisting emptiness. Her own fear was as sharp as Martin's but was held under more rigid control.

Still, there had to come that moment, scant seconds away, now, when she would have to give the order and step out from under cover. Worse, still, she would give the order that would assure the deaths of members of this platoon, people she knew and had fought with.

She thought she understood Dev now, his vacillation when it came to wholeheartedly supporting the rebellion. Where was the value in bravery, in sacrifice, in attacks that were little short of suicide, when nothing useful could be accomplished? All the courage in the Shichiju would count for nothing if, minutes from now, her eight warstriders were blazing, hull-torn hulks, and the Imperial crawler was continuing its ponderous advance up the Gaither Valley.

Yet something *had* to be tried. Do nothing, and failure was certain. The Confederation would be crushed.

Pushing the darkness back in her mind, Katya braced to give the order.

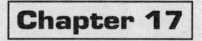

# Chapter 17

*Section I: TANK HUNTING.*

*THE ADVANTAGES ARE WITH THE HUNT-
ER. The big game sometimes hunted . . . are tanks.
Like any other kind of big game hunting, the
advantages are with the hunter; he almost always
is the winner; but there is enough danger to keep
the hunter on his toes. With courage and determination [he] can use his weapons to hunt down and
destroy 80,000 pounds of fighting steel.*

—Basic Field Manual
Engineer Soldier's Handbook
FM21-105, Chapter 7, Section 1
mid-twentieth century

A warstrider close-assault was the Confederation's sole
remaining chance to stop the crawler short of Stone
Mountain, a last-ditch effort before it reached the fortress's static defenses. Hours before, a powerful mine
hidden in the monster's path had been detected by the

Impies and detonated harmlessly. Then a defensive line of Ranger and militia warstriders behind a fabricrete barricade had been swept aside, the wall smashed through.

A savage strider-to-strider battle at the wall had stopped most of the Imperial striders escorting the crawler, but the tracked combat machine's armor had proven too thick for the rebel weapons. It had continued its relentless advance up the valley, alone now save for intermittent strikes by covering ascraft and a light support force of three Tachis and a Katana. Intelligence reports told of more Imperial warstriders massing a few kilometers to the southeast, pushing forward in the crawler's wake. They would be the enemy's final assault force, meant to overrun the Confederation compound once the crawler had breached its inner perimeter.

And then . . . hope! Unexpected and vanishingly slender the hope might be, yet remote-jacked surveillance drones had spotted damage to the crawler's hull after the fight at the breach. Hits had scored after all, weaknesses been revealed. An ambush plan had been worked up, hastily planned, more hastily laid. The town of Anversen offered the last place along the crawler's expected route where a strider close-assault team could be hidden with a chance of reaching the crawler's side.

The ambush plan called for crippling the monster, if possible, by disabling its driver wheel with planted packs of high explosive, or by adding to the destruction amidships already wreaked by Starhawk and Strikers.

"Okay, team," Katya broadcast over the tactical net. "Full power! Let's do it! *Now!*"

She urged the Ghostrider forward, smashing through the sheltering face of a flame-scorched wall in an explosion of rubble and dust. The crawler, alerted, perhaps, by her radio emissions, bathed her emerging machine in radar and laser illumination, as point defense weapons pivoted swiftly to track and bring her down.

Katya triggered her Kv-70 weapons packs, hurling a salvo of M-490 rockets at nearly point-blank range. They struck dead on target in stuttering, flare-streaked bursts, their warheads alternating high explosives with charges of duralloy-devouring nano-D. Martin fired the hundred-megawatt chin laser in a ripple of quick-pulsed bursts, taking out a line of point defense lasers and hivel cannons on the monster's flank, then triggered a smoke screen of antilaser aerosols. White fog blanketed Katya's view, thinning as she sent the Ghostrider forward with ground-eating sweeps of its long legs.

To left and right, seven other warstriders in her ad hoc assault platoon emerged from cover as well, hammering away at the behemoth with everything from laser and CPG fire to high-speed deplur rounds from shrieking rotary cannons. Missiles scratched and flashed through the sky, slamming home in thunderous detonations. The night was filled with white flame and violence.

As Katya raced forward, her Ghostrider's long legs scissoring through the smoke, she had a clear shot at the lead driver wheel and concentrated her fire on that. The damaged section of the crawler's hull was a good fifty meters farther back along that curving, black cliff, and high enough up on the thing's broad and thickly armored deck that she would not have a clear shot at it.

Tucked in close behind the Ghostrider's chin turret was a McEverett Pack, a tubular, plastic satchel filled with one hundred kilos of C-30 plastic explosives and a fusion detonator with time and pressure triggers. An arm with gripper manipulators had been plugged into the Ghostrider's number-three auxiliary link-interfaced hardpoint. As Katya moved, she mentally shifted link control for her left arm from the strider's left-side weapons pack to the remote arm, passing the weapons pod to Chet's control. With a shrill whine of servomotors, the arm unfolded, dangling heavily between the strider's legs and dragging the heavy pack with it.

Together, she and Chet kept up their barrage against the crawler. Shots struck home, flashing and cracking with savage detonations, but to little outward effect. The wheel and its bearings were heavily shielded, the track itself composed of nanowoven diacarb fifteen centimeters thick. Even as her first shots slammed into armor, point defense lasers mounted in teardrop barbettes above the skirt swiveled to take the Ghostrider under fire.

Katya pushed harder as hundred-megawatt bursts of coherent light snapped into the Ghost's starboard hull, melting armor in glittering puffs of vapor. Warning flags flashed in her mind: power loss . . . damage to the right weapons pack . . . damage to the right motivator array . . .

At least the McEverett Pack was still okay. Touch that with a laser and there'd be little left of the Ghostrider save scrap.

*Closer!* She had to get closer! If the big main guns were able to depress far enough to track her, she and the other seven striders were already dead. "Closer everyone!" she yelled over the tactical link channel. "Get in closer!"

"I'm with you!" Captain Phillad Jobrey's Scoutstrider stilted past her on the right, its CA-5000 high-velocity auto cannon slamming rounds, two a second, squarely into the target. Pawlovski's Ghostrider, forty meters away, crumbled in a fusillade of close-up bursts, writhing as lightning played across its hull. Then the other strider's explosives pack detonated, the blast filling the air with hurtling chunks of hot metal, the concussion jolting Katya and nearly making her stumble.

The crawler's skirts and track were like a sheer cliff now, just ahead. Lightning grated against her eyes, painful even as her strider's AI stepped down the illumination to safe levels, and a volcano's thunder pealed. For a horrible instant she thought she'd been hit. Then she realized that she'd witnessed the muzzle discharge of the crawler's main gun, a particle cannon as powerful as those mounted by a light cruiser. Its target, a Confederation gun emplacement on the face of Stone Mountain fifteen kilometers away vanished in a dazzling pulse of pure light and the forked, blue-white stab of grounding charge.

The last of her right-side M-490 rockets slammed into the crawler's driver wheel from a range of fifteen meters, still without effect. Enough nano-D must be clinging to that armor by now to eat a hole through a dragonship's hull, but clouds of anti-nano were already boiling down the vehicle's curved side like dry ice fog, neutralizing the corrosive vapor before it had more than pitted the duralloy's surface.

All she had now was her chin turret laser, and its hundred-megawatt bursts would no more than scratch the surface of the thing. Snapping an order to Martin to keep firing, she tried to move closer. If she could just get close enough to plant the McEverett charge in the port-side tread. . . .

Ozawa watched the rebel close-assault waver with an inward nod of satisfaction. Again, the rebels had been unable to properly coordinate their attack. So few striders offered little threat to the crawler and would be easy targets for the supporting Imperial warstriders outside and for the crawler's own guns.

There was a likely target, a LaG-42 Ghostrider sprinting into his watch area. He swung the targeting cursor for his big, two hundred-megawatt laser onto the target. Lock! He triggered the weapon. . . .

A laser bolt slashed into the Ghostrider's upper hull as Katya lunged forward. Smoke erupted from a red-hot crater. Warning flags danced at the borders of her vision. Fire erupted from the Ghostrider's left shoulder assembly; Chet engaged the fire control dispensers, bathing the strider's upper works in an icy fog.

Damage? Some armor lost, but nothing serious ... yet. Another such hit would boil through the strider's internal circuits like a railgun bolt through tissue.

She was still lugging the McEverett Pack, but she wouldn't be able to use it unless she could get all the way up to the crawler's side. The volume of laser fire from the huge vehicle was frightful; twenty meters to go. ...

By the flaring light of rapid-fire explosions, she saw truth. They were *never* going to wade through fire this heavy. Close-assaulting a crawler required a regiment of warstriders, not a single, ragged platoon.

Yet to retreat was unthinkable. Safety was in the hulking lee of the giant; to move back was to move into the target lock of heavy lasers and the buzz saw caress of hivel rotaries.

"Colonel!" Jobrey called. "We've got Imperial ascraft, coming in at three-zero-zero!"

From the other side of this slow-moving duralloy mountain. Craning a hull sensor, she searched the night sky.

There! They dropped out of heaven like black, stub-winged bats, illuminated from beneath by the crawler's searchlights. Katya groaned as she saw them ... three ... no, four ascraft, a Typhoon and three Skywinds. Each could hold a number of warstriders, or a bellyfull of armored infantry. If this was the crawler's infantry support, moved up to close with its attackers, then the battle was nearly over. The close-assault force was down to five machines. They couldn't face the crawler and a company of Imperial striders as well. ...

Tracers and laser beams snapped toward the newcomers, but Katya's orders snapped louder. "Never mind them! Kill the crawler, damn it! We've got to kill the crawler!"

If they could ... before the reinforcements landed.

\* \* \*

Ozawa cursed as he saw the LaG-42 stagger, then continue moving. The enemy machine was so close that hitting the damned thing was almost impossible, a tight deflection shot against a swiftly moving target.

One last chance. The Ghostrider was moving more slowly now, clearly damaged, and Ozawa's cursor slid onto the machine's torso and flashed red, the signal for a target lock.

The rebels really were a pathetic lot. Even if they managed to get too close for the crawler's point defense weapons, the aircraft hovering overhead would pick them off easily. He began forming the command to fire. . . .

The jolt was unexpected, an earthquake shuddering up through the siege crawler's treads, unfelt by the men in link but noticeable as the landscape outside shuddered. An instant later, power failed with a burst of static, and Ozawa was kicked off-line . . .

. . . to awaken an instant later in a searing, flaming hell, his legs already withering away in the blast furnace heat of molten metal spilling into the jacker compartment. Hideki Ozawa had time for a single shriek of agony before he died, still wondering what had gone wrong.

The lead ascraft balanced in on shrill-hissing jets of superheated plasma, hovering fifty meters above and behind the crawler. The laser bolts that seared into the giant ground combat machine's back numbed the senses, numbed the *mind*, so startling, so completely unexpected were they. The other flyers were joining in, lancing shot after shot into the already damaged sections of the crawler's armor, striking and striking and striking as explosions lit up the sky.

Smoke was boiling from the old Starhawk wound, now, and an interior explosion sent bits of burning metal hurtling high into the air. Point defense lasers swiveled, bearing on this new and devastating threat from above. In an exchange too quick to follow, hundreds of laser bolts crisscrossed through the dark. Laser turrets flared white-hot and melted; one ascraft circled toward the south, wing holed and smoke pouring from a savaged engine, but now the defense lasers had ceased firing, their control systems knocked off-line. The ascraft hovered lower, their belly turrets scant meters above their targets as they continued to fire.

"God!" Jobrey called over the Confederation net, awe turning his voice ragged. "Colonel, who *are* those people?"

"Never mind! never mind! Just plant the goking charges!"

Delight leaped and thrilled in Katya's thoughts . . . and excitement. "That," she said, "has *got* to be Devis Cameron! No one else I know would take on a siege crawler with transports!"

To her left, Lauber's aging Calliopede exploded, red flames licking up into the night. "*Colonel!*" Chet yelled over the link. "*Check your nine!*"

As quickly as it had come, delight and excitement were gone, replaced by the battle-keen awareness of danger. Movement, silhouetted against the burning night. Warstriders, Imperial warstriders, were racing toward her from the left. The crawler's support force had been spread out farther ahead but was reacting now to the rebel close-assault with a thundering charge. As the skeleton of Lauber's Calliopede crumbled in the flames, a pair of Tachis opened fire on Katya's Ghostrider, their twin, 88mm lasers in a flat dorsal turret lancing through the smoke- and dust-laden air.

A KR-9 Manta, Gerris Fitzhugh's machine, staggered beneath the touch of diamond-hard laser light. His left weapons pod detonated, a reserve of chemflamer fuel ignited. The wreckage flared, then burned like a torch. Katya saw none of the crew eject.

Then the Tachis were on her. Concentrating fire from her chin laser on the closest one, she saw it stagger, its dorsal turret flaming. Rockets slammed in from somewhere, toppling the machine as she shifted her targeting to the second Tachi.

Explosions flashed like lightning, and their thunder was an endless, keening roar. Something hit her Ghostrider hard, square in the torso, and the ready light for her laser winked out.

She was completely unarmed now, save for the McEverett Pack, and the surviving Tachi was blocking her path.

From behind a tumbled-down wall, Tharby rose, the satchel charge clutched in one hand. "Let's *go!*"

The genies weren't supposed to be here, weren't supposed to be anywhere within ten kilometers of the fighting, but when he'd heard that the Colonel had volunteered to try to take down the moving, armored mountain he and the others had seen in the valley, Tharby had known that, once again, the genies were going to demonstrate their newfound capability for disobedience. The Port Jefferson Scouts had slipped out of their encampment shortly after Colonel Alessandro had departed, hours before. They'd trailed her at a safe distance, then found hiding places of their own in the ruins. Tharby knew in principle what those huge McEverett Packs were supposed to do, since he and some of the other techies had helped assemble them. It had been simple to put together smaller packs of HE, massing thirty kilos apiece and easily genie-portable.

The initial flash and thunder as the ambush erupted had caught all of the genies by surprise, and several had scurried away into the night. More had fled with the approach of the ascraft, or with the attack of the Imperial stilters seconds later.

Tharby and four other techies had held on, however, eyes narrowed to yellow slits against the glare, hands

cupped over ears as peal followed deafening peal. No
one, genie or full human, could survive unprotected in
that hell of fire and noise, but Tharby was determined
to wait for his chance. . . .

Then he'd seen the Colonel's machine engage one of
the stilters and knock it down. There was a whirlwind
exchange of fire. Flame roared; the Colonel's machine
had been hit, and hit hard.

"Now!" he yelled, leaping forward. "Take th' bastards!"

Their original idea had been to attack the siege
crawler, but watching the monster lumber forward out
of the night, Tharby was realist enough to know that his
paltry, thirty-kilo charges were not going to even scratch
that massive armor. But another target had presented
itself . . . the small strider squaring off now against the
Colonel's bigger machine.

The five genies bounded across the open. . . .

The laser ready light winked on as Katya willed a
bypass circuit to life. Ignoring warnings of coolant leaks
and overheating, Katya triggered the chin laser, spearing
the Tachi in front of her with white light. The nano
aerosols and anti-laser fogs were heavy here, drinking
the energy like a sponge, but at point-blank range she
was bound to do some damage.

The Tachi staggered, a section of its left torso glowing
like a red-hot coal, but it didn't fall. Katya took a step
closer. . . .

Movement caught her attention, stayed the thought
that was about to launch another bolt of coherent
light. Were those *crunchies* swarming over the Tachi's
feet?

The Tachi seemed to detect this new threat at the same
moment, its angular torso bobbing in an almost comical
parody of a bird doing a double take at its own feet.
A point defense machine gun mounted in a ball turret
pivoted. . . .

*   *   *

A gun on the Tachi spoke and Nomet was torn open from throat to crotch, the splatter of his blood as black as ink in the dim light. Tharby leaped onto the stilter's broad, flanged foot as gunfire shrieked. Close beside him, Kanned threw up his long arms and went down in a bloody, thrashing tangle, but Tharby managed to cling to the monster's leg with one hand as he jammed his satchel charge into an unarmored gap in the thing's foot just where it joined the massive upright of the leg.

Kanned was sprawled motionless on the ground now, but Yodi and Leddun were on the strider's other foot, ramming their charges home. Overhead, the machine gun spoke again . . . then exploded as the Colonel's Ghostrider lanced it with a dazzling beam of light. The flash was blinding, and nail-sized chunks of metal pinged and bounced off Tharby's body armor. Then the Tachi's leg started to come up, and he just had time to yank the arming string before the foot snapped forward, whipping him off like a dog shaken from the back of an angry bear. Leddun screamed, his body writhing in a halo of white flame.

An instant later the charges went off with a triple thunderclap of sound. With a shriek that was almost human, the Imperial strider twisted wildly, fighting for balance, then toppled to the side. . . .

*Now was her chance!* Katya urged the Ghostrider forward as the second Tachi fell, still startled by the boldness of the assault she'd just witnessed. Three of the five genies were down, the others bolting for cover, but they'd blown one foot clean off the Tachi and badly mangled the other.

No time to wonder. Ten more strides and the LaG-42 was alongside the crawler, badly hurt, but still advancing with all the relentlessly unstoppable power of an incoming tide on New America. Smoothly, concentrating on moving her hardpoint arm like her body's real arm and not like the more familiar Ghostrider weapons pod, she extended the remote gripper, still clinging to the McEverett Pack.

A sharp crack sounded close beside her, and duralloy bearings and shifting clouds of monofilament wire sang through the air, clattering off her armor like hail. The crawler's skirts were protected by auto-triggered frag launchers and *sempu*, deadly against infantry, but of little effect against a warstrider. Stepping through the hail, she swung the McEverett Pack, lobbing it underhanded onto the track in the space between two massive wheels.

Monofilament wire from the *sempu* blast tangled her duralloy armor, peeling off flakes of metal, binding her gripper hand to the pack. Panic gibbered, not far beneath her surface control. As the crawler continued forward, the McEverett Pack began slipping beneath one wheel, tugging her irresistibly forward.

With an almost explosive, coded thought, she jettisoned the arm. Her Ghostrider took a staggering step backward, suddenly freed. Then she pivoted and ducked, knowing that at any instant the detonator's pressure trigger would—

*WHAM!*

The blast picked the LaG-42 Ghostrider up off its feet, depositing it in a clattering, tumbling tangle of legs and hull extensions ten meters away. The fireball arced into the sky, blinding, dazzling in its intensity, and one of the house-sized wheels bounced and rolled past Katya's vision like a rim-bent child's hoop.

"Chet! Are you okay?"

No answer . . . not even a feed link through the strider's inboard ICS. Either Martin was off-line, or he was dead.

There was nothing to be done about it now. Raising the Ghostrider unsteadily to its feet, she turned, scanning the crawler. One hundred kilos of C-30 downloaded nearly a billion joules of energy in an instant, approximating the sheer destructive power of five hundred 100-MW lasers discharging at once. Katya saw chunks of duralloy spinning away through the smoke. The armor skirt had peeled up and away as though gashed by a giant's talon, and the port-forward tread had disintegrated into hurtling slabs of jagged metal.

The crawler, Katya saw, was no longer moving, no longer firing back. Either its crew was dead, or they'd been knocked off-line. The siege crawler had been reduced now to an inert, smoking mountain of duralloy.

Fifty meters away, one of the ascraft was landing, balancing to earth on shrill-whistling plasma jets. Katya tagged it with a comm laser.

"That," she said over the link, "was definitely in the proverbial nick of time!"

"Not really," Dev's voice replied. "We should have been here three hours ago."

Katya's heart leaped. It was him! It *was*!

"We landed at Stone Mountain first," Dev continued. "About three hours ago. I met General Sinclair at the field apron, and he told me where you were, what you were doing. Our ascraft are brand-new. They had mounts, but no weapons. We had the maintenance crews at the Mountain install the lasers and power packs and, well, here we are."

"Another five minutes and you would've been too late," Katya told him. "That's still pretty goking good timing!"

"Can that thing you're wearing still move?"

Katya turned sensors on her own hull. Most of her nanoflage had been stripped off right down to flame-scorched bare metal. Her left weapons pod was missing, as were half a dozen scanners and instrumentation pods. She estimated her input feeds were down by at least forty percent.

But a level one diagnostic showed that the battered machine could still stride. "Just watch me!"

"Come on, then. We'll give you and your people a lift back to Stone Mountain."

"On our way!"

# Chapter 18

*There is a great deal of talk about loyalty from the bottom to the top. Loyalty from the top down is even more necessary and much less prevalent.*

—*War As I Knew It*
General George S. Patton, Jr.
C.E. 1947

There was no sign of what was left of that unexpected infantry support team, but all four surviving warstriders boarded the grounded Typhoon, slotting into external rider slots in its belly, tucked away beneath the anhedral slant of its stubby wings. Eight minutes later, they were descending toward Stone Mountain Field, a stretch of camouflaged fabricrete apron surrounded by towering, feather-topped trees.

Katya's first need was to find out what had happened to Martin. The external controls to his module were dead, so a maintenance tech used a locking tool to crank it open manually.

The young pilot blinked up at her from his coffin, then shook his head. "Don't know what happened, Colonel. I got booted off-line and couldn't get back on."

"That's okay, Chet," she told him, relief turning her weak. "You stuck with me, didn't you?"

He grinned. "Not that I had much choice!" He was going to be okay.

"Hello, stranger."

Katya turned. Dev was there, tall and haggard-looking and grinning broadly. She fell into his arms, surprised by her own response ... as was he. They kissed.

"That's a nice welcome," he said, his eyes laughing. "I'm glad to see you too. You look *wonderful*!"

Her jacker's bodysuit had molded itself to her torso like a second skin, plastered down by sweat. Her hair was dripping and smelled like the fur of a wet, long-haired cat. She felt dirty ... no, *filthy*, and could smell her own stink clinging to her like a program-active nano-D cloud. She was in desperate need of a long shower and at least twenty hours of sleep.

And this guy thought she looked good?

A nearby entrance, concealed beneath armor, earth, and nanoflaged sheets of plastic, led through massive blast doors into the mountain's interior.

Sinclair was waiting for them in a small, bare-walled conference room, part of the complex of underground vaults known to the striderjacks as "the Bunker."

"We were watching your performance through drone sensors," Sinclair said as Katya took her place next to Dev at the long, synthwood table. Other officers were present as well: Generals Smith, Kruger, and Grier, as well as some members of their staffs.

"Colonel, that was a magnificent performance!" Smith enthused. "Congratulations!"

"It was Dev here who pulled it off, sir," she said. Enthusiasm bubbled, barely suppressed. *She was alive . . . and so was he!* "He pinned enough of the brute's PDLs that I was able to get a charge placed."

"Well, you did everything you said you'd do," Sinclair told her. "Preliminary reports have the rest of the Impie striders in full retreat. This'll hold them up for another day or two at least. We all owe you, owe you both a tremendous debt."

She looked at Dev. "Did you bring reinforcements from Athena? How many?"

He shook his head. "Sorry, Katya. I've already gone over this with these gentlemen. When I heard that a Ryu-class was going to get here before me, I sent the fleet elsewhere. To bring it back here would have been suicide."

"Surely it would be better to try!" A cooler rationality reasserted itself then, smoothing over the warm flush of victory, and survival. "Okay. No reinforcements. At least we have a breather, now. But I'm not sure it helps us much. Even if they only brought one crawler, it won't be long before their strider force wears us down. And we have no place else to go."

"But we do," Sinclair said gently. "Katya, it's time to carry out the rest of the plan. We've got to leave, for Herakles."

She stared at Sinclair for a moment, uncomprehending. Tired to the point where she could scarcely stand, with the pulse of combat still thrilling at her temples, the general's words didn't at first make sense. Leave? Now?

After she and the people with her had suffered so much, had invested so much in defending this place?

"Most of the delegates slipped out just ahead of the invasion," Sinclair explained to Dev. "They should be nearly at Mu Herculis by now. They took Fred with them."

"How many more do you want to get out?" Dev asked.

Sinclair glanced around the room at the others. "Senior staff," he said. "Myself . . . though I hate like hell abandoning ship in the middle of this."

"You *have* to go, sir," General Kruger said. Unlike Smith, Grier, or Sinclair, he was unshaven and his uniform blotched with dirt and sweat. The militia general had been in the field almost continuously since the invasion had begun. "We'll keep fighting the bastards here. They'll have to level every damned mountain in the Outback to root every last one of us out."

Katya felt cold. The exultation of victory had soured. "That's . . . it then? We're just leaving?"

"We have no choice, Katya," Sinclair said. "Now, people, I can't stress enough the need for complete secrecy. We will be limited as to how many people we can take out. Captain Cameron has only a single ship. This evacuation will be restricted to only absolutely essential personnel—"

"Excuse me, General," Katya said. "But what about the Rangers?"

"We're going to be too tight for space," Dev pointed out.

"We can bring out a few of your best people," Sinclair added. "We'll need them for the nucleus of a new 1st Confederation Rangers, on Herakles."

"You'll have a couple hundred troops to work with," Dev said, grinning. "Remember, I stole half of your Rangers for the Athena raid."

"That's not the point! I can't just abandon my people here!" Emotions seethed as rigidly held self-control cracked. She could feel the tears on her cheeks, the stinging in her eyes, but she didn't care. "My . . . my place is here! I can't go with you!"

"I'm sorry, Colonel," Sinclair said gently. "But you must. That's an order. You and Captain Cameron are the only two people who've had more than cursory contact with the Naga so far. And we're counting on you to establish contact with the Heraklean Naga. *Everything* depends on that. Do you understand?"

She looked at Dev, who stared back at her with a hard, level gaze. "Linked," she said. "But it's one goking hell of a way to run a war."

Hours later, she entered the encampment set aside for the genies, nearly ten kilometers down the slope from the landing field. It was almost full dark, though Columbia shed a blanket of cold, silver light across forest and looming mountain face. The sky was empty, and there was no threat on the southeastern horizon save the pale skyglow of Jefferson.

It was almost possible to forget that there was a war.

"Wait for me," she told the jacker of the magflitter that had brought her here, then opened the bubble top and stepped off into the brisk evening air. Squaring her shoulders, she got her bearings, then strode toward the main gate.

She was dreading this encounter.

A young soldier in armor stopped her and demanded her palmed ID before admitting her to the camp. The site itself was little more than a clearing lined with hastily erected plasform barracks half-buried in dirt and roofed over by meter upon meter of nanoflage sheeting. There were no open lights, no fires. The building she was looking for was at the end of what might generously have been termed a street.

The camp's official name was Bravo-three-seven, though the troops quartered there had taken to calling it Camp Baka . . . Camp Fool. Most of them were local militia, though this one round-roofed building housed the Port Jefferson Scouts. A guard—a human—admitted her past the guard station at the front door.

With the front door sealed off by a blanket hanging from the ceiling, there was light inside . . . and music. She was embraced by both as she stepped into the warmth of the barracks.

*. . and Nagai had withdrawn.*
*But Morgan called us to his side, Hegemon infantry.*
*And let us choose to stand and die, or choose instead*
*    to flee.*

The words and rhythm of "The Ballad of Morgan's Hold" pounded at her. Inside the curtain was a typical military barracks, lined with bunk beds and lockers and occupied by perhaps fifty people. Katya was surprised at the number. Only eighteen genies were carried on the Scouts' muster list at the moment, and so far as she knew no more were due to join the tiny genie outfit.

Then she realized that most of the people in the room were full humans.

One of the humans was jacked into a mentar, which he held in his lap, eyes closed as his thoughts shaped the chords falling from it in rippling, pattering trills. The rest were singing along.

*We disobeyed our orders when they said to sound*
*    retreat.*
*And Morgan laughed and said "My God, we'll see*
*    who's the elite!"*
*For fighting steel had broken faith, the samurai had*
*    fled.*
*But Morgan's men defied Nagai, they stood and*
*    fought and bled.*

Coincidence—and biting irony—bemused her. "The Ballad of Morgan's Hold" was an infantryman's song from long before the rebellion, one commemorating a heroic last stand on, of all places, Herakles. A handful of troops, of *crunchies*, under the command of Captain David Morgan, had held off wave after wave of Xenophobe attacks after the *Taisa* Nagai had ordered the defenders to evacuate the planet. Their stand had allowed untold numbers of civilians to evacuate up the Heraklean sky-el.

*Warstriders did not make that stand, it was the infan-*
    *try*
*Who stood and fought and died and paid the price of*
    *mutiny.*
*We took our stand on Argos Hill, four hundred fight-*
    *ing men.*
*And when the smoke had cleared away, sixteen walked*
    *down again.*

So caught up in the song were most of the men and
women in that room that Katya had not been immediately noticed.

"Attention!" someone shouted suddenly, and the
words and music dwindled away. With a clatter of
motion, people started coming to their feet.

"Carry on," Katya said. "I didn't mean to interrupt."

It had taken her a moment to realize just what it
was that was bothering her about the sight. It was the
intermingling of genies and full humans, something
she'd not seen since bringing Tharby and those first
few genies to Stone Mountain. Especially after that one
rape incident, there'd been so much prejudice among
the humans she'd thought they would never accept the
gene-tailored workers.

Then she realized something else. Of the humans
present, none had more than Level 1 hardware—palm
circuitry and a single T-socket behind one ear. Some of
the humans, judging from the length and style of their
hair, didn't even have that much.

Nulls. Katya had rarely had much to do with Nulls,
a growing lower class unable to interact in economic
or long-range AI transactions. There'd always been a
certain small percentage of humans who couldn't accept
the nano-grown cerebral implants or skin circuitry, and
there were more who refused the cybernetic enhance-
ments on religious, philosophical, or political grounds.

Frequently unemployable save in menial jobs, they were largely invisible to society as a whole. The military used them in nontechnical slots, as leg infantry, and for lifting, loading, storing, carrying . . .

The sorts of jobs genies were frequently employed in.

Nulls frequently felt the same sort of gulf between themselves and socket-equipped citizenry. Perhaps they felt closer to the genies, who were also Nulls, than they did to technically augmented full humans.

With a small, inner start, Katya realized that the entire group was watching her, waiting for her to speak. Within the stratified rigidity the Confederation was inheriting from the Hegemony Guard, officers did not casually drop in on their troops; striderjacks did not associate with crunchies.

Maybe that was a large part of what was wrong.

She noticed Tharby, sitting on the floor next to the mentarist. She'd learned from others already that it was Tharby and four other genies who'd taken down the Tachi at Anversen; she'd intended to seek him out, to commend him for what he'd done, to thank him . . . and to tell him she was leaving. With the entire room watching her, that seemed to be the cowardly way out.

"Excuse the interruption," she told them all. "I just came by to say . . . to say that I'm being ordered out. I'm sorry I can't take you with me. And I—I'm sorry I can't stay here, with you."

"Where you off to, sir?" Tharby asked. During the past few days, the genie's use of military courtesy had improved. His language had improved as well, becoming smoother, more . . . human.

She shook her head. Many of the soldiers here might well find themselves under Imperial interrogation soon. "Another star system. That's all I can tell you."

"Why we not go?" a big worker genie in the back called. "We fight Impies good!"

"Yeah! *Gok* 'em!" another chorused, and then the barracks walls were ringing with answering shouts and catcalls.

When the room was silent again, or nearly so, Katya tried her best to answer. "There's only room for a few, and that's saved for the people the topjacks say have to go. And . . . and they need good people to keep fighting the Impies here."

"Ha!" a full human said. "Well, it figures, don't it, tokes?"

"Like always," a *ningyo* said nearby. Cradling a Pk-55 fléchette rifle, she looked sleekly dangerous.

*Tokes.* The human soldier had called the genies tokes . . . *guys.* Or maybe he'd been referring to everyone in the room. Same thing. He was including the genies as part of his circle of comrades.

Then Katya understood what it was she was feeling here. The Nihongo word was *yujo,* which meant camaraderie, but which for soldiers throughout the Hegemony had taken on the special meaning of the warrior's bond, that special relationship shared with men and women who'd faced privation, loss, and death at your side.

The genies had proven themselves in battle. They'd been accepted.

"We have good friends here, Colonel," Tharby said, almost as though he'd just read her thoughts. "We will stay and fight the Impies. Thank you, for everything . . . and good luck."

"Thank you, Tharby." She had to fight back her tears. "And good luck . . . to all of you."

Turning, she pushed through the curtain, then stopped. She could not resist a parting lesson for her students. "You know, Tharby, what you did today was incredibly brave. It was also incredibly stupid. Lots of warstriders have antipersonnel charges or *sempu* blasters to kill people who try the sort of thing you did."

The genie grinned at her, golden eyes laughing. "Stupider than finding a place for *us* with full humans? I don't think so!"

"Good-bye, Tharby."

Turning, she fled into the night.

A burst of laughter and good-natured gibes followed her. Seconds later, they struck up the final verse of the song. Outside, she could no longer hear the words, but she already knew them by heart.

*At golden Tenno Kyuden they cannot begin to see*
*That honor's price is paid in full while glory can be*
*    free.*
*So give a cheer for Morgan's crew, the God-damned*
*    infantry,*
*The men who fought the Xenophobes, the grunts like*
*    you and me.*

Katya had never felt so torn. Duty required that she follow orders. Her *yujo*-bond and the responsibility she felt for those in her command demanded she stay. Besides, this was her world, her home. Could she simply turn her back on it all?

Yet Dev was going to Herakles. And Travis Sinclair. Damn! Simplest was to accept the bonds of military discipline. She'd been ordered to go; she would go.

But *gok* it was hard. . . .

*Chujo* Tetsu Kawashima pulled himself hand over hand into *Donryu*'s bridge space, positioned himself within the embrace of an empty control linkage module, and strapped himself in. Food and waste feedlines snapped home in his shipsuit connectors, and a pair of large plugs jacked home into the T-sockets behind his ears. His palm touched the interface, and his surroundings vanished, replaced by the squadron's Combat Coordination Center.

The room was a fiction, a virtual reality construct designed as an electronic working space for Kawashima's battle staff. For convenience and for decorum's sake, there was the illusion of gravity, though there were no chairs since ViRpersonas did not grow tired. A well in the center of the deck projected a three-dimensional view of New America and the space surrounding it. Golden points of light swarmed about the planet, each accompanied by a block of data giving ID, mission, and vector.

As Kawashima materialized next to the display, the other officers—there were twenty in all—faced him and, as one, bowed. The voice of *Shosho* Fusae Eto insinuated itself into his mind, speaking for the entire team. "*Konichiwa, Chujosan.*"

"*Konichiwa,*" Kawashima said, returning the salutes with a measured, courteous bow of his own. "Carry on, please."

In fact, there'd been no distraction from necessary duties, and no need to tell them to go back to work, since the linked minds of the battle staff continued to process information, whatever their virtual reality personas appeared to be doing.

The personas of his officers appeared relaxed, attentive to their duties, but he could feel the undercurrent of tension. No one, he knew, cared to risk the *chujo*'s wrath by mentioning what had happened.

It would have been easier, Kawashima thought glumly, if his orders permitted him simply to reduce the surface of New America to radioactive glass and slag. Such wholesale destruction was certainly within his power . . . but it would also be counterproductive. The discontent and outright anger such an act would provoke would undoubtedly do more harm than good. Fear, by itself, was never as useful a tool of government as were good public relations . . . an arcane science he'd learned about in his studies of Western history.

But his own job would be *so* much simpler if he'd been permitted to make an example of this world.

Bad enough had been the news that the Kyodaina had been destroyed, the Imperial thrust up Gaither Valley to the rebels' Stone Mountain base stopped cold. Less than thirty hours later, one of Ohka Squadron's destroyers, after rendezvousing with several ascraft from the surface, had broken orbit and accelerated toward the fringes of the system. Kawashima's subordinates thought nothing of the event at the time; ships were always coming and going, traveling to or from Imperial bases for maintenance or servicing, returning to Earth with field reports, or arriving at New America with reinforcements, orders, and news.

This particular destroyer, the *Arasi*, had only been in orbit around New America for a few days. According to its log, which had been routinely downloaded into the squadron's HQ data base, *Arasi* had been stationed in the Chi Draconis system—at Eridu—but had received special orders from Earth to transport several teams of *Kurogun* to New America's surface.

*Kurogun.* The word shocked in its sudden coldness. The "Black Forces" were the Imperial military's covert special operations unit. Swift, deadly, and secretive, with advanced training in *Kokorodo* and in numerous martial arts traditions, they carried the reputation of modern-day Ninja. No wonder no one in Kawashima's command had brought the matter to his attention. The *Kurogun* were never discussed, and it was widely assumed that the less one knew about them, their missions, or their whereabouts, the better for all concerned.

In any case, *Arasi* possessed all appropriate codes and clearances; its captain, *Taisa* Ihara, had exchanged greetings via laser ViRcom link with the commanding officers of several Imperial picket vessels, and nothing had appeared out of the ordinary. When the *Arasi* accelerated clear of New American orbit, no one had even bothered to alert Kawashima to the fact; Ohka's commanding admiral, after all, had more important things to occupy his thoughts than the movements of individual ships.

That had been four standard days ago. Today, early that morning by *Donryu*'s shipboard clocks, another vessel had arrived in-system. She was *Nagara*, a Sendai-class light cruiser under the command of *Taisa* Kakeui Matsushida. Thirty-five days earlier, Matsushida had left the Chi Draconis system, also under routine orders from Earth to report to Kawashima at 26 Draconis.

When *Nagara*'s log was downloaded to the HQ data base, however, *Donryu*'s command AI had sounded an alert. There was a discrepancy. According to *Nagara*'s records, the fleet it had left behind at Eridu had included the Amatukaze-class destroyer *Arasi*, and that had been a full five days *after* the *Arasi* had claimed to have received its "special orders" from Earth and left for New America.

The entry was specific and detailed. According to *Nagara*'s records, the pacification of Eridu had already begun. *Arasi* was taking part in the operation, bombarding key cities and facilities from orbit in support of the marine landings there. In fact, Captain Ihara was listed as receiving a special commendation from Admiral Takemura for his part in breaking up a concentration of rebel warstriders seeking to escape from the enemy capital at Babel.

The commendation was dated two days after *Arasi* was supposed to have left the Eridu system.

There was no doubt that *Nagara* was the ship she claimed to be; Matsushida had been a senior *chu-i* under Kawashima's command aboard the old *Aoba*, and he knew the man well. *Arasi* was the imposter; without question, her captain had been a rebel masquerading over the ViRcommunications channels as Ihara.

Which meant that the people the Empire was most interested in seizing on New America, Travis Sinclair and the Confederation delegates and the leadership of the Confederation's army, had all almost certainly fled. The enemy destroyer—she must have been the old *Tokitukaze*, reported lost at Eridu, he realized—had slipped into the very midst of Ohka Squadron, taking advantage of the inevitable confusion and bureaucratic blind spots that hampered any ponderously large military formation to conduct an evacuation right under the collective noses of the fleet.

"Please excuse me, *Chujosan*," *Taisa* Eto, his chief of staff said, giving a rigidly precise and formal bow. "*Shosa* Yoshitomi has submitted another request for reinforcements before mounting his next attack on the rebel base. He insists on speaking personally to you. . . ."

Kawashima felt his face clouding, saw Eto's face go carefully and emotionlessly blank as he braced himself for the storm. With an effort of will, Kawashima controlled his thunderclap of anger.

"Very well, Etosan. I will speak with him. We will discuss carefully and in detail the necessity of carrying out one's orders with the men and matériel at hand."

"*Hai, Chujosan!*"

The bird might have flown from its New American cage, but Kawashima was still determined to take that cage apart, bar by bar. The ruin might well offer some clue as to where the bird had fled.

# Chapter 19

*Needless to say, the development of cephlink tech-
nology, as with all technology, carries with it a
terrible potential for abuse.*

—*Man and His Works*
Karl Gunther Fielding
C.E. 2448

Over a week after the escape of the rebel destroyer,
*Chujo* Kawashima had left his accustomed surroundings
and cephlink simulacra aboard the *Donryu* for the direct
experience of a reality of a different kind. It was a
moonless night at Port Jefferson, and the grounded
Imperial transports bulked huge and shadow-edged
beneath the glare of glowglobes and the harsh illumination of a hovering, aerostat mirror reflecting the
output from an array of mobile spotlights set up on
the field. Technicians and maintenance workers were
everywhere, readying ships, servicing heavy equipment,
and swarming about the hulking, motionless forms

of black-armored warstriders, prepping them for new missions.

Accompanied by his coterie of staff officers and assistants, Kawashima strode rapidly from the lowered ramp of his personal aerospace shuttle. Soldiers along the way offered stiffly formal rifle salutes, while others stopped what they were doing and bowed. Neither slowing his stride nor acknowledging the salutes, Kawashima crossed the open field swiftly and entered a low, heavily guarded building with bunker-thick walls. A young marine *chu-i* met him at the door, bowing low.

"*Konichiwa, Chujosama.*"

"*Konichiwa.* I need to see them. Now."

"*Hai, Chujosama!*"

Once, this had been a storage warehouse at the edge of Port Jefferson's primary launch field, which accounted for the massive construction. Since the Imperials had taken the spaceport, however, it had been pressed into service as a command bunker, and the jackstraw tangle of sensor instrumentation and communications lasers still cluttered the roof.

And now that both Jefferson and Stone Mountain had fallen, it was being used as a holding place for special prisoners.

The final battle on the slopes of Stone Mountain had been savage, the casualties to Yoshitomi's marines staggering. The rebels had fought like fanatics, taking on Imperial warstriders in close-assault charges with explosive packs and homemade bombs. Kawashima had never heard of such insane tactics—rebel troopers had actually swarmed onto the feet of warstriders, jamming packs of explosive into their ankle joints. *Ankle-biting,* the ground commanders were calling it, a tactic that had claimed at least nine marine warstriders.

Finally, however, just two days ago, an Imperial assault team had at last reached the main blast doors leading to the Stone Mountain labyrinth, but only after a prolonged laser bombardment from orbit had finally broken the rebel static defenses. A one-kiloton nuclear charge had breached the door; another had been used to clear part of the mountain's interior. The rebels would not be using Stone Mountain as a military headquarters ever again.

After that, the rebels had begun surrendering.

Almost certainly, the majority of the rebel troops had fled deeper into the wilderness, the . . . what was it New Americans called it? The Outback, yes. The Imperial garrison here would face stiff guerrilla resistance from those survivors for years to come, but that was not his problem; guerrillas would not be able to carry out an interstellar campaign or incite revolt on other worlds of the Shichiju, which was Kawashima's primary concern.

But if many rebels had escaped, thousands had surrendered or been gathered up by far-ranging patrols of warstriders and infantry. Camps had been set up outside Jefferson, and a small army of Imperial Intelligence personnel were interviewing the POWs now.

Most would eventually be set free. The soldiers of every army in history were, at heart, much the same— ordinary people doing what they thought right, and only too willing to go home and pick up their lives when the fighting was done. Some, those with strong beliefs about the rebellion and about independence, might be released after having a *kokennin* implanted in their cephlink hardware, or else they would be shot. It was unlikely that their number was greater than five percent of the whole.

There were a few prisoners, however, of special interest to the Imperium, and these, at Kawashima's orders, were being held in the warehouse at Port Jefferson. There were some eighty of them assembled in the bare-walled emptiness of the building's main room. Most wore military fatigues, though some were in the rags of what once had been civilian clothing. They sat quietly as the *chu-i* ushered Kawashima into the building, each in a near-identical posture to all the rest, arms folded on knees, eyes staring vacantly into space. Each had a small, gray-white apparatus embracing the back of his head from ear to ear, from which tiny constellations of green and amber lights glowed. The *kanrinin*—the word meant *controller*—jacked into a person's T-sockets and overrode his or her voluntary neural input.

Of course, the *kanrinin* could only be used on people with temporal sockets. "Where are they?" he asked the *chu-i* who'd admitted him. The lieutenant bowed and led the way.

The big, central storage room was lined with smaller rooms, which might once have been offices or storage areas for special materials. Some had been appropriated for Imperial use. Others were now holding cells for prisoners who could not take the *kanrinin*. At the far end of the building, one such room was under heavy guard, the door sealed shut but phased to transparency.

Many of the prisoners taken at Stone Mountain had been Nulls, men and women unable or unwilling to take the cephlink hardware. Such people were of little importance and less threat; most had already been released.

But *these* . . .

They were genies, two males—a worker and a techie—and a breathtakingly beautiful *ningyo*. The males paced the narrow confines of their cell; the female sat, cross-legged, in a corner. Their fatigues were torn and caked with dust, and the techie had his left arm tucked into his blouse, using it as an improvised sling.

"They surrendered?" Kawashima asked his guide. "I heard the creatures preferred to die rather than give up."

"You heard correctly, *Chujosan*. All three were discovered unconscious inside a room under Stone Mountain. A wall collapsed, trapping them. The marine captain in charge was going to kill them but decided that their unusual behavior warranted special attention."

"Exactly so," Kawashima said, studying the prisoners with interest. Unlike full humans, even Nulls, genies were usually killed out of hand when taken unless they could be put immediately to work. These, however, were extraordinary. Throughout the battle there'd been numerous reports of genies, of *genies*, attacking Imperial troops and even warstriders with hand weapons and explosives. Astonishing. "Creatures bred and conditioned for docility and obedience are unlikely warriors, *neh*? We must learn what happened to alter their personalities so."

"*Hai, Chujosan.*"

"Get me the name and unit of the captain who brought them in. He will be rewarded. And take special care that these three are not injured in any way."

"Of course, sir."

"That includes the *ningyo*. She is not to be used by your men."

"Uh, yes, sir." The lieutenant looked somewhat less certain.

"I charge you with the responsibility for keeping them all safe and unharmed. They are prisoners of singular importance. They will be transported at once to Earth for closer study."

"*Hai, Chujosan.* It will be as you command."

Munimori, that fat pig, would be especially interested in these three, Kawashima thought. He would, no doubt, take a personal hand in their interrogation and retraining. Especially the female, knowing his tastes in genie entertainment.

The injured techie was glaring at him through the transparency with narrowed, golden eyes, as though reading his thoughts. The other two ignored him. Abruptly, Kawashima turned away. "Take me to a room where I can talk to that special prisoner you told me about."

"This way, please, *Chujosan.*"

The room chosen for him was identical to the one holding the captured genies, save that it had been provided with a desk and chair. The desk had the standard electronics built into it, complete with interface screen, network links, and 3-D projector.

The prisoner brought to him minutes later was human, wearing the tatters of civilian clothing and a *kanrinin* locked about the back of his head. He was short and chubby and black-haired, with dark eyes now gone vacant and a soft and pampered body running to fat. His guard guided him easily, with a hand lightly touching his elbow.

"That will be all," Kawashima told the guard. "Wait outside."

"*Hai, Chujosan!*"

Kawashima touched the desk's interface, downloading a command. The pattern of lights on the prisoner's *kanrinin* shifted, and his eyes focused suddenly.

"I am *Chujo* Kawashima, the admiral commanding the Imperial squadron. You, I gather, were one of the traitor Sinclair's senior aides."

"Uh . . . yessir. Pol Danver . . ."

"I know your name. I know a great deal about you." Indeed, he'd downloaded Danver's entire personal file before he'd left the *Donryu*. "What I want you to tell me, immediately and without any attempt at deception, is where your Travis Sinclair has gone."

Danver licked his lips, a quick, nervous flick of the tongue. "Sir, I, I mean, I don't know. I swear, he didn't tell me. . . ."

Kawashima kept his left hand splayed on the slick, black surface of the desk's interface. Danver's eyes were riveted on that hand, his fists clenched tight at his sides. The *kanrinin* could render a man instantly pliable, instantly docile. It could also transmit exquisite pain through direct neural stimulation.

"Technology invokes truly godlike power," Kawashima said, his voice light and conversational. His splayed hand did not move. "With a thought, I could plunge you into a lake of fire. I could reward you with an orgasm unlike any you have ever experienced. I could kill you, simply by commanding your heart to stop."

"Sir . . . please, *please!* . . . I'd tell you if I could! I swear! I never liked Sinclair. Never! I only worked for him because I had to."

That was certainly true. Danver's psychological profile suggested that he was a small and bitter man who sought power in the intrigues of petty office politics. Sinclair had a reputation for advancing personnel by merit rather than for seniority's sake, and Danver had almost certainly felt slighted by the rebel politician-general more than once.

"Perhaps, then, you could tell me about some of Sinclair's people. When he disappeared, a number of others vanished with him. Staff personnel. Senior military officers. Delegates to this so-called Congress of yours." Kawashima allowed himself to show a thin smile. "I notice that when they made their escape, they left you behind to face my marines."

"Yeah, you got that right. Uh, sir." Craftiness flickered behind the dark eyes. "Actually, Admiral-*san*, they were going to take me too. They didn't say where, but I was, well, I was pretty well placed, y'know? I was General Sinclair's chief aide."

"Go on."

"But I'm a realist. I knew this revolution could never amount to anything, except pain and suffering and death for millions of people. So I volunteered to stay behind. I, well, I figured I could surrender, see? Maybe help you to, to end this thing."

"I see." The man's ingratiating tone grated on Kawashima's nerves, but he nodded and smiled. "Believe me, Danver-*san*, you have made the correct choice. However, to prove your good faith, you must provide me with useful information. Otherwise . . ." He let his gaze drop to his motionless hand.

"Uh, yeah. I mean, yessir. Believe me, I want to help! Uh . . . look. Maybe you didn't know. Sinclair's definitely left New America. His people're claiming that he's hiding out in the Outback, but that ain't true. Some of his people managed to sneak him and maybe two hundred of the government's chief people off-planet."

"Indeed?" Kawashima had already surmised as much, of course, but the fact that Danver had told him as much suggested that the man genuinely wanted to cooperate. "Who helped him?"

"Uh . . . his name's Dev Cameron. He's, I don't know. Used to be a strider, though lately he's been jacking starships. He's the guy that captured one of your ships at Eridu. He's kind of a bigwig in Sinclair's organization, y'know? Young guy, twenty-eight, twenty-nine standard, maybe, but Sinclair's made him a navy captain and gave him command of a raiding force to go hit your shipyard at Athena."

Kawashima kept his face expressionless. Word of the raid at Daikoku had arrived weeks ago, but no one in Imperial Military Intelligence knew where the raiders had come from. Danver might prove to be a valuable source of information after all.

"And where did this Cameron take Sinclair and the others?"

Danver's tongue flicked across fleshy lips. "I don't know. I'm sorry, but . . . but I really don't know."

"Come now. You can't expect me to believe that. They must intend to set up the rebel government in some other system. Surely they would arrange for private communications channels elsewhere, through trusted staff aides, for instance."

Danver shook his head. "No! No, sir, they didn't tell me!"

"Think, Danver-*san*. You must know something, must have seen something." His hand remained on the interface, a menacing presence.

"Wait! There, there's one thing. Maybe. I, I didn't know much about, didn't think much about it, but there's one thing."

"Yes?"

"The Xeno . . ."

"A Xenophobe? What Xenophobe?"

"There's this crazy idea, see? The scientist-types've been kicking it around for a long time. You see, they made contact with a Xeno on Eridu. Talked to it, even. Then they got it to pinch off a piece of itself. The idea is that, since this piece of a Xeno knows about us, about Man, I mean, and knows how to communicate with us, they can introduce it to a wild Xeno on some other planet."

"A calling card," Kawashima said thoughtfully.

"Uh, sorry? What's that?"

"An old and long-extinct form of social propriety. Please, continue."

"I don't know a whole lot else. They brought the tame Xeno with them from Eridu. Kept it in a vault underground in Jefferson. I saw it there several times."

"Did you . . . talk to it?"

"Me? Jeez, no. Wouldn't catch me touching that slimy thing."

"What happened to it?"

"They moved it, I think, just about when your squadron entered the system. Again, I wasn't in on that part of it, but there was talk about sending it somewhere else aboard a liner the government had bought."

Kawashima sat behind the desk for a long moment, thunderstruck. This was an intelligence coup of the very highest order. Danver had just delivered two vital pieces of information. The first was the simple knowledge of how the rebels planned to communicate with wild Xenos, something that had eluded Imperial and Hegemony researchers ever since the Alyan Expedition. Up until now, communicating with a Xeno had required a DalRiss comel . . . and the nerve to confront a wild

Xeno in its underground lair. But it sounded as though the rebels had hit upon another way, one simpler, safer, and more certain. Kawashima had downloaded enough about Xenophobe biology to guess that the method might well work.

And even more important, Danver had just unknowingly shown Kawashima how to find the escaped renegades.

His palm still on the interface, Kawashima directed a thought to the desk's electronics. Danver stiffened, a look of intense fear flashing suddenly in his eyes as he felt the *kanrinin* switch operational modes. Then his eyes went blank, his knees buckled, and he dropped to the floor, his back and hips arching and jerking spasmodically. Danver's mouth gaped, fishlike, as he thrashed about, his entire body infused with overwhelming, uncontrollable, fiercely intense pleasure.

"Ah! . . . ah! . . . *AH! AH! AH!*" His cries brought the guard back into the room, but Kawashima dismissed the soldier with a careless wave. He remained unmoving for several minutes more, before sending another command through the interface. Danver shuddered, then went limp. For a long moment, there was no sound in the room save the wet rasps of the prisoner's breathing.

"I believe in immediately rewarding those who loyally serve me," Kawashima said at last. "You have been of enormous help to me. That was your reward."

"Oh . . . wow." Shakily, Danver sat up, but he was too weak to stand. A dark stain had appeared above the crotch of his trousers, which he clumsily tried to cover. "I . . . oh, wow . . ."

It was another five minutes before Danver could speak coherently. The impulse Kawashima had just sent through his pleasure center carried far more kick than any normal orgasm.

"The guard will see to it that you get a fresh change of clothing," Kawashima told the man as he slowly and shakily rose to his feet. "Tell me, Danver-*san*. Would you consent to receiving a *kokennin*?"

Danver blinked at him, as though trying to understand the words. A thin strand of drool hung from his lower lip. He tried to wipe it away and failed.

Where the *kanrinin* was an external device, a jack-in electronics module to control a prisoner, the *kokennin* was internal and far more subtle. The word was Nihongo for *guardian*, and for good reason. Grown, like a cephlink, by programmed nano injected into the bloodstream, the *kokennin* assembled itself as an addition to the link hardware in and around the sulci of the brain, tapping directly into the subject's personal RAM and providing an easy means of monitoring his movements, his actions, and his contacts. Though it could not transmit private thoughts—sadly, *that* technology was yet far from perfect—it also provided an easy and reliable means of learning whether or not the subject was telling the truth.

"I, uh, sure," Danver said. "Sure. Why not?"

"If you voluntarily accept a *kokennin*, I can offer you a position on my own staff. You could be of considerable use to me."

"Hey, that's great. Uh . . . does that mean that you, I mean, uh, if I work for you, do you think I could have, uh, have another shot of what you just gave me?" There was hunger in his eyes.

"Certainly. If you provide additional useful information or insight into the plans and thoughts of the rebels. I must caution you that such, um, experiences must be carefully rationed. There are many people, weak-willed and vulnerable, who become addicted to pleasure center stimulation."

"Yeah." He licked his lips. "I can see why. But you won't have to worry about me. I can handle it, no problem."

"I know you can," Kawashima lied. Eventually, probably, the man would become hopelessly addicted to PCS and would have to be disposed of. He directed a thought through the interface, and the guard appeared again. "Take this man to a room of his own. Provide him with a clean uniform, food, and whatever else he needs. Dismissed."

Kawashima was honestly not sure what else Danver could offer him but was willing to keep him on against the chance that he would, indeed, prove useful again. Besides, Kawashima felt a certain amount of gratitude. Through his cooperation, two invaluable pieces of data had been obtained.

In particular, he'd just narrowed Sinclair's possible hiding places from unknown hundreds to just five . . . the worlds where wild Xenophobes were known to exist.

*An-Nur II:* called Fardus—Paradise—a hellish place of desert sands and sterile rock, and the first world where Man had confronted Xenophobe.

*Sandoval:* thin-aired, barren, and frigid, a mining colony destroyed thirty-five years ago.

*Herakles:* partially terraformed world of vast oceans and rugged mountains, site of Colonel Nagai's disgrace.

*Loki:* chill and desert world of 36 Ophiuchi C, where the Hegemony had won its first clear victory against the Xeno foe. It was thought that all of the Xenos on Loki had been killed two years ago using ground-penetrating nuclear devices, but it was certainly possible that some lived there still. A world was an enormous place.

*Lung Chi:* the Manchurian-colonized world overrun in 2538, grave for five thousand betrayed Imperial Marines.

Kawashima did not count the sixth Shichiju world where Xenophobes were known. Eridu, after all, was where peaceful contact had already been made with the things, and, in any case, Sinclair and the others would not be likely to flee back to the world from which they'd just escaped. Nor did he count the Alyan worlds. They were far, far beyond the Shichiju's borders, there were

Imperial ships stationed there, and the alien DalRiss were a constant uncertainty.

His eyes narrowed at a new thought. Cameron . . . Cameron . . . wasn't that the name of the *gaijin* admiral who had destroyed Lung Chi's sky-el? Interfacing with the planet's Imperial link network, Kawashima downloaded several thousand bytes of data.

Yes . . . as with Herakles, at Lung Chi there'd also been the threat of Xenos coming up the space elevator, and Admiral Michal Cameron had sent a missile into the structure. Broken far above the surface, the sky-el had been subjected to far greater stresses than the one over Herakles and been shattered, with terrible loss of life. Worse, a million citizens and five thousand Imperial Marines had been trapped on the planet's surface. Cameron had been court-martialed and later had committed suicide.

He'd had two sons. One was Devis Cameron, a former Hegemony officer and winner of the Imperial Star, but now defected to the rebel forces.

Kawashima thought he knew where Devis Cameron had fled to.

Or . . . possibly not. Young Cameron might intentionally avoid a world which bore family connections . . . and might therefore allow him to be traced.

No matter. With New America nearly secure, Kawashima could afford to check all of the possibilities. He would dispatch flotillas of ships to each of the five systems, with orders to check the Xeno-occupied worlds carefully for any trace of rebel presence.

In fact, Loki was unlikely on several counts. The Hegemony maintained an important base in orbit and, in any case, there probably weren't any Xenos left to contact there. It would be possible to hide a rebel government within Loki's cities, certainly, but difficult to carry on business as usual with the Hegemony watching. Kawashima would dispatch only one ship there, with orders to inquire of the Lokan governor about possible rebel activity.

Sandoval, too, was unlikely, as was An-Nur II. A rebel government-in-exile would need supplies, food, air, water, or the means to manufacture them. Refugees on either of those two worlds would be so busy surviving they would have no time to plot rebellion. One small warship or two to each of those systems would be enough to scan them for signs of fusion-generated power.

Which left Lung Chi and Herakles. Those two he would check carefully with large squadrons . . . *especially* Lung Chi.

Smiling, he began composing the orders that would set Ohka Squadron in motion.

# Chapter 20

*The first encounter with Xenophobes was on An-Nur II, an Islamic colony orbiting the K5 star DM+2° 4706. A desert world, incompletely terraformed, the planet possessed but five major centers of human population, all existing under sealed domes, when the Xenophobes emerged from the ground in C.E. 2498 and attacked, apparently without provocation. The second incursion— alerting the Hegemony that this was an interstellar threat—was in 2508 at Sandoval, a mining colony on the tide-locked world of Ross 906 I.*

*But the first world with a large population and a viable environment to be attacked by the Xenophobes was Herakles. . . .*

—*A History of the Xenophobe Wars*
Constantine Li Xu
C.E. 2543

For some billions of years before the coming of Man, Herakles—Mu Herculis III—had remained a typical prebiotic planet, a place of liquid water oceans beneath stormy and opaque skies of carbon dioxide. Such worlds were common; life, requiring such factors as tides—in order to create the gentle pools where life might arise—and a precise balance between an environment too hostile and one too mild, was comparatively rare.

Just over thirty light-years from Sol, the Mu Herc system had been surveyed by the Imperial *Sekkodan*, the Scout Service, in the early 2200s. Like 26 Draconis, it was a trinary system, with a young, hot G5 IV star circled at a distance by a close-paired doublet of M4 red dwarfs. The subgiant primary was twice as massive, three times more luminous, than Sol; at 4.1 AUs remove, the world dubbed Herakles had been hot, cloud-shrouded and poisonous, with temperatures well above fifty Celsius.

Hegemonic terraformers had begun building the first chain of atmosphere generators in 2238. These mountain-sized nanofactories gulped down the native air and broke it into forms more useful to the newcomers—nitrogen, oxygen, and water—with vast reserves of carbon converted to diamond carballoy for the ongoing construction of the new colony's sky-el. As the skies cleared, the world became cooler . . . and cooler. Now, temperatures in the equatorial temperate zone rarely rose above twenty-five Celsius, and the mid-latitudes endured long and bitterly cold winters during the world's nearly six-year-long orbit.

With the sky-el in place in 2305, the world's colonization had begun in earnest. From a planetary engineer's point of view, the sky-el was little more than an immense suspension bridge, balanced in the sky above Herakles's equator, its center of mass positioned at synchorbit so that the entire, forty-thousand-kilometer-long structure orbited the world in precisely one local day, so that it remained forever suspended above the same point on the equator. The colony's capital of Argos had grown up at the sky-el's towerdown. In the early 2300s it was no more than a collection of diacarb domes above Stamphalos Bay, on the southern shores of the Augean Peninsula. Two centuries later, the city domes had been opened to a blue-gold and friendly sky, black volcanic rock and sand had been nanotechnically crumbled to soil, and genetically tailored life—carpet grass and forests, insects and small mammals, all the myriad intricacies in a newborn planetary ecology— was engulfing a world reborn in green. Half a million colonists lived on Herakles, and the Hegemony Emigration Service estimated that by 2600 a million people a year would be riding the sky-el down from Herakles Synchorbital to Argos after their month-long passage aboard crowded Koshu-Maru transports. The colonization of terraformed worlds would never catch up with the relentless pace of Earth's still-burgeoning population, but such worlds as Herakles offered new starts for those daring enough—or desperate enough— to quit the security of the seething hive cities of Man's birthworld for the poverty—and freedom—of life on the Frontier.

Those estimates had never been realized. In 2515, Xenophobes had emerged from underground, destroying the settlements of Tiryns and Hylas some eight hundred kilometers north of Argos. The Xenos had not been well understood at the time; it was thought they were part of an invasion force, landed by a fleet of starships somehow rendered invisible to the Hegemony's orbital detectors. The true nature of the threat, that Xeno travel and combat modes were fragments of a titanic, amorphous, single organism dwelling within the interstices of layered rock far beneath the surface, a creature that *had* been living there for some unknown thousands or millions of years, had not been uncovered until the Alyan Expedition of 2541. While the Imperial Navy concentrated on guarding the approaches to the planet from orbit, a single Imperial Marine battalion and two companies of the 62nd Hegemony Infantry had attempted to protect the capital at Argos.

Ultimately, as "The Ballad of Morgan's Hold" recorded, the attempt had failed. Herakles was evacuated, the last of the colony's defenders dead or escaped up the sky-el to synchorbit. In the twenty-eight years since the planet had been abandoned, no human had set foot on the former colony world; Herakles was once again a dead world, save for the Xenophobe victor.

The passage from 26 Draconis to Mu Herculis took forty days. Twice, en route, the fields bearing *Eagle*'s frail hull down that long, glowing corridor of otherness that was the godsea failed, dropping them abruptly once again into fourspace. Each time, the repairs grew trickier, more delicate, and more clever. Soon, Dev thought glumly, the battered vessel would be held together by little more than spit and good wishes, and only a miracle would serve to boost her straining fusion plants to producing output enough to achieve the mass implosion that generated paired singularities.

By the time *Eagle* approached the Mu Herculis system, the people aboard little resembled high-ranking military officers and VIPs. A starship's single most pressing problem within the K-T plenum was getting rid of excess heat, and despite every effort of the vessel's hard-pressed air-conditioning and cooling systems, the temperatures in her crowded passageways hovered near fifty Celsius, and the passengers, stripped to bare skin or to an absolute minimum of clothing, lolled on the dripping mattresses that took up every square meter of free deck space, soaked in sweat.

Captain Anders had extended the destroyer's habitat modules and spun the ship, creating a half G of artificial gravity as one token of comfort for the passengers. There was water enough for all, fortunately, and more could be manufactured easily enough through molecular factories programmed to recycle urine and wash water, and to add to the stores as needed by separating oxygen from carbon dioxide and mixing it with hydrogen drawn from one of the reaction mass tanks. Of more critical concern was food. *Eagle* had originally departed for Athena with a crew of 318 and food stores enough to last them five months. Her voyage to the Daikoku shipyards and back had lasted a bit more than two of those months, and now she was making another voyage of forty days' duration with two-thirds more people crammed aboard, and no promise of fresh supplies once they finally reached Mu Herculis. Dev had ordered that everyone go on half rations, including the nutrient feeds to linked personnel, in order to extend their food supplies for as long as possible.

Dev could not feel the heat when he was linked, nor was he aware of hunger, since the link module short-circuited all purely physical sensations of discomfort. He was riding the jacks as *Eagle* dropped out of the K-T plenum, emerging on the fringes of the Mu Herculis system. A full shift of one hundred starship crewmen were jacked in and ready. No one knew what to expect.

It had been some seventy-eight days since Dev had ordered Captain Curtis to bring the Confederation squadron here from Athena. With a voyage of just under nine and a half light-years from Athena to Mu Herculis, Curtis and the others should have arrived in-system over two months ago, the *Transluxus* and the other ships from New America shortly after.

Were the Imperials truly gone from Mu Herc, or had they left sentries on guard? It was possible that *Eagle* would emerge in the system, only to find the fleet from Athena destroyed or scattered, the *Transluxus* and her passengers captured two months before. There was no way of knowing until *Eagle* emerged in normal space.

Then, moments after the godsea had given way to the velvet black of space and the brilliant, gold-gleaming radiance of Mu Herc A, Dev heard the mournful flutter of a comm beacon, the signal feeding through *Eagle*'s scanner suite. The code it carried was that agreed upon with Curtis and the others at Athena, meaning that all was well, that the Imperium was not in residence here.

"Pass the word," Dev announced over the link intercom as he heard the signal. "We're home."

Linked, he couldn't hear the cheers, or his passengers' sobs of relief.

Days later, *Eagle* slipped into orbit around Herakles, taking up position alongside *Transluxus* and the other New American ships. Direct laser communications with *Tarazed* confirmed what the automatic beacon had already revealed, that there was no Imperial presence in this system, not even so much as an AI-manned watch satellite. From orbit, Herakles was a glorious sight, vast, violet oceans rimmed with gold, with swirls of cloud gloriously reflecting the rich, warm light of the sun. A Typhoon took Dev, Katya, and Sinclair down to a landing zone already staked out on the crest of Mount Athos. The senior squadron officers were waiting for them as they debarked.

"Welcome to Herakles, General!" Captain Jase Curtis exclaimed, advancing on them. "I gather you brought half the Confederation army with you."

"Well, not quite half," Sinclair admitted, grinning. "It just seemed like that crammed in cheek by jowl aboard that damned destroyer. How've you folks been getting on with Congress?"

"Oh, the politicians?" Commander Ann Petruccio said, grinning. "We shot them the first day. . . ."

"Don't listen to her, General," Captain Strong said, laughing. "We didn't want to bring them down until we knew where we stood with the local Xeno. We have them more or less happily roosting in the el."

"Right," Curtis said. "We wave at them each time they pass over."

As with most established colony worlds in the Shichiju, a sky-el space elevator had extended from the planet's equator to synchorbit and beyond, a titanic, spun-diacarb filament tens of meters thick and over thirty thousand kilometers tall. Argos, the capital, had grown up around the towerdown. In 2515, as Xeno combat modules swarmed up into the capital from underground, a five-hundred-megaton fusion device had vaporized Argos. Burned off at its planetary end, the sky-el had been launched free, its delicately engineered balance between world and orbit broken.

The entire, forty-thousand-kilometer length of the space elevator, all but the lower reaches of the structure that had been vaporized in the Argos blast, had been flung by its own orbital tension into a higher, slower orbit. Spinning now ponderously end for end, the sky-el still circled Herakles in a broad, elliptical orbit, though expert AI calculations indicated that the orbit was not permanent and would decay within a century or two. Each return to perigee sent one end of the enormous structure dipping briefly into Herakles's atmosphere, and though it had considerable mass—and therefore, inertia—each passage slowed it marginally, gradually hastening the day when it would impact, with spectacular and pyrotechnic fury, on the planet's surface.

"The Imperials maintained an outpost here for a good fifteen years after the evacuation," Curtis explained, "and they used the free sky-el as their base. I put some of my people aboard as soon as we made orbit. Herakles Synchorbital suffered some damage when the elevator broke free, but it's still airtight. There's a large habitat at the half-G level, plenty of office space, power from a small fusion plant. The AI is working. Weapons systems're shut down, but those can be brought on-line with some work."

"How about deep space scans?" Dev asked. "Communications, that sort of thing?"

"No scans. The synchorbital's sensors weren't equipped to handle a spin like that, though we might be able to cobble something together after a while. I have most of my engineering people at work now setting up grav detectors. Communications are no problem."

"And your planet-side base?"

Curtis pointed to a cluster of survival domes among the rocks and crags farther up the mountain slope. "That's it. Dome sweet dome. We're keeping things small . . . again until we know whether or not the Xeno's going to try to eat us. We're getting all we need from the sky-el, actually. There's still quite a bit of food up there—mostly stabilized nanoform—so we have plenty to eat. And the nano programmers are working. We'll be able to grow most of what we need."

"We'll have to keep using the synchorbital as our space station," Sinclair pointed out. "At least until we can arrange for something better. And I suggest we get people to working on the orbital lasers right away. We're going to need them, sooner or later."

"How long do you think we have, General?" Petruccio wanted to know.

"I wish I could tell you that, Commander. I really do. It depends on how bright our friend Kawashima is . . . and while I was on New America, he struck me as very bright indeed.

"We have one advantage working for us," Sinclair continued. "If we can get our orbital detectors set up and working, we'll have advance warning if the Imperials arrive. With a star as massive as Mu Herculis A, they won't be dropping into fourspace closer than a couple of astronomical units. As at New America, we'll have plenty of time to reboard our ships and haul Gs for deep space."

A starship's drive drew energy from K-T space by utilizing large quantities of energy from the ship's fusion plant and converting it to mass in the time-honored give-and-take equivalency of $E=mc^2$. That mass manifested itself as twin microsingularities, a pair of neutron-sized black holes circling one another in mutual and precisely tuned harmonic resonance. That resonance served as a kind of dual gateway, a channel for the incredible energies freely available beyond the K-T barrier, and a hyperdimensional path for the starship itself as it plunged into the faster-than-light realm of the godsea.

The microsingularities, of course, generated intense gravitational fields, though these were so tiny that their effects were not felt more than a very few meters beyond the drive containment fields. By the same token, however, the precisely tuned balance between the two singularities was extremely sensitive to the curvature of local space. Summoning those twin, captive demons too deeply with the gravity well of world or sun invited disaster. The energy channeling through from the godsea might be closed off as the black holes evaporated, but it was also possible for the energy flow to cascade wildly, generating an unstoppable avalanche of power.

"And the Naga?" Dev asked. "Have you seen anything of it?"

"In two months," Petruccio said with a shrug, "there hasn't been one damned sign of the Xenos. Not a planetary Naga. Not a traveler. Not a combat module. Not a wisp of nano-D or a positive DSA. Nothing. It's as though they got tired of waiting and left."

Dev glanced at the CO of the *Vindemiatrix*. She was a tall woman, with a shipjacker's brush-cut hair and a full, almost stocky figure beneath her freshly nano-grown fatigues. "Oh, it's still here," Dev said. "You can be sure of that."

"Unless Morgan's people killed it with their bomb," Curtis said.

"Unlikely," Katya put in, "given how big a planetary Naga is." She looked around, wonder alight in her eyes. "Is this really the site of Morgan's Hold?"

"That it is," Curtis told her. "It's listed as Mount Athos on the charts and navsims." He pointed. "We even found some of the 62nd's old equipment over there. Rusted-out combat rifles, armor, field gear, that sort of thing." He laughed. "No warstriders, of course."

The others laughed as well. That was part of the legend of Morgan's Hold, that infantry had fought Xenos when the warstriders had abandoned them. There *were* warstriders in the indicated direction, a Manta, a Fastrider, and a couple of Ghostriders, but those were manned and operative, standing guard over the makeshift landing area. The field area was busy, as ground personnel unloaded the newly grounded aerospace craft.

"And off that way," Curtis continued, "that's the Augean Peninsula, or where it was, anyway. As you can see, it's mostly underwater now."

Dev turned on the hilltop, taking his bearings. That stretch of sundance-glittering ocean was where Argos had stood. Once, the vertical tower of the sky-el must have gleamed golden in the sun right *there*. And the Xenos, when they came, would have swarmed up the slope from *that* direction, from the north. . . .

Every ground trooper and striderjack in the Shichiju knew the story of Morgan's Hold. The story had already gone down in legend with other hopeless last stands, with the Alamo, Roarke's Drift, and Kavalerovo. Garrisoned by one Imperial Marine battalion and two companies of the 62nd Hegemony Infantry—troops dispatched more to keep the peace among the panicky civilians than to attempt to protect them from the still mysterious threat—the planet had been virtually defenseless.

It had become more defenseless still when the Imperial troops, commanded by one Colonel Nagai, had decided to withdraw in the face of swarming hordes of Xeno snakes. He'd ordered Captain David Morgan of the 62nd to withdraw as well, but Morgan and 387 volunteers—most of the strength of his force—had refused. Argos had a civilian population of nearly eight hundred thousand, and that number had nearly doubled over the past weeks as outlying settlements had been overrun by the insatiable hordes of snake-like, deadly Xenophobes. His Hegemon infantry was all that stood between the advancing Xenos and the Argos Sky-el.

Chance and geography had favored the defense. Xenophobes, for reasons unknown, avoided seawater, and Argos was located on an equatorial peninsula jutting southwest into the Alcmenan Sea. Astride the narrow isthmus northward was Mount Athos, at thirteen hundred meters one of Herakles's more mediocre peaks, but ideally positioned for defending the single land approach to the capital.

The troops had held Mount Athos through wave after wave of Xenophobe assault, fighting them with hand weapons, with semiportable lasers and cannons dismounted from vehicles, with jury-rigged bombs and crudely programmed nano-D. They'd held out for nearly two weeks, during which time most of the planet's civilian population escaped up the sky-el to the gathering fleet of transports mustered there from across the Shichiju. The severely wounded in Morgan's band were evacuated with the civilians; the lightly wounded hung on, scavenging the battlefield for ammunition and partially charged laser power packs. In the end, sixteen unwounded members of the unit abandoned their positions on Mount Athos and escaped up the sky-el. Numerous Xenos had already broken past Mount Athos or tunneled up inside the city from below and were beginning to digest the city's structures, but Morgan's men had staved off the inevitable collapse long enough for the evacuation to be completed.

David Morgan himself had not lived to see the victory. On the third day he'd tried to drag a fallen comrade from beneath an advancing Xenophobe Mamba, been hit himself, and been crushed to death.

The stand, called Morgan's Hold, had been enshrined in song and story and ViRdrama throughout the Frontier, despite the Empire's efforts to suppress it. Nagai's abrupt decision to evacuate did not reflect well on Imperial honor and martial prowess when contrasted with the determination of the Heglegger troops, and more than one Hegemony soldier had been cashiered or worse for singing "The Ballad of Morgan's Hold," or even for having the words and music downloaded into his personal RAM. The song had become something of a cry of defiance by Frontier rebels against the Imperial tyranny.

Song and legend, too, remained part of the ongoing rivalry between foot soldiers and warstriders; Nagai's marines had been elite striderjacks, and their combat machines had been top-of-the-line Daimyos and Samurais. Reportedly, not one warstrider had been lost in the defense of Argos, and at the time it had been widely reported that leg infantry—leggers—simply could not stand up to Xeno snakes.

Morgan's people had given the lie to *that* idea.

The very shape of the planet's geography had been altered by the aftermath of the battle. One hour after the last human had left Herakles, a five-hundred-megaton bomb provided by Nagai's marines had been detonated in the sky-el, just above Argos. The fireball had eradicated the city and scooped out a vast, shallow crater into which the sea had poured, an avenging, white-foam flood. Thundering, rising clouds of steam had blotted out half the hemisphere for months afterward. From space, the Augean Peninsula now looked as though a gigantic bite had been taken out of it, and the new, inland sea created by the city's immolation was still radioactive.

Dev shivered, the reaction partly due to the thought of Argos's destruction, but partly too from the cold. He palmed the control patch of his bodysuit and wished up its internal heat.

He was thinking about the huge, pyramidal atmosphere nanoconverters . . . one of which Dev could see from here, a smooth-sided, triangular mountain against the northern horizon. The air tasted hard and thin, with a metallic bite to it. The oxygen percentage stood now at about twelve percent, with a partial pressure of .108 atm., low, but breathable. The Heraklean terraforming project had not been entirely complete when the Xenos had appeared, and the atmosphere generators had been shut down twenty-eight years before.

By making the air breathable, those artificial mountains had also rendered the climate cooler. Temperatures had been dropping steadily on Herakles for two centuries and might drop farther still if the converters weren't soon brought back on-line. If the Xeno hadn't destroyed them—and apparently it hadn't—they would one day make the world's air thicker and warmer as well.

"So where is the local Xeno?" Petruccio asked, shaking Dev from his thoughts. "We keep expecting to see him any day."

Dev looked around. The landscape in every direction was barren—the rock seared naked where the white flame that had destroyed Argos had lightly brushed across it. In the distance, though, Dev thought he could make out flecks of green and the gray and brown of endless rock.

"Underground, certainly," he said.

"And that's where we'll have to go to find it," Sinclair added. "We'll have survey teams out looking for cavern entrances or old snake pits as soon as we can organize them. Then we bring Fred down and let him earn his passage."

"Actually," Dev said, "I wonder if that'll be necessary. Looking for holes, I mean." He was staring once again at the triangular regularity of the atmosphere nanogenerator looming above the northern horizon. "If the Naga here is playing true to form, there's another way to reach him. A faster way."

He began describing his idea to the others.

*We see, of course, not with our eyes, but with our brain—same for hearing, touch, smell, and taste— and our conversations with others are carried out entirely inside our heads. External physical sensation is gathered by the visual, auditory, tactile, or other sensory nerves, and not until it is relayed to the brain is it interpreted as light and dark, as hard or soft, as lover's face or clenched fist, as smell of genegineered froses or taste of vinegar. Indeed, we live out our lives in magnificent isolation, a universe within our skulls, with but the slenderest and most deceivable of feeds bringing us fresh data about the outside world.*

—*The Rise of Technic Man*
Fujiwara Naramoro
C.E. 2535

They stood on the mountaintop beneath a sky gone black, vast and thick-strewn with diamond stars. Dev had asked Katya after a communal dinner in the main hab dome whether she would like to take a walk.

Dev knew that something had been troubling Katya since before their precipitous departure from New America, and he was pretty sure he knew what it was. Still, throughout the long passage between the stars, they'd had no chance to discuss it. *Eagle* had been crowded with passengers for which she'd not been equipped. He'd wanted to share some linked downtime with Katya, just to talk, but feared the suggestion would be taken as an invitation to ViRsex and nothing more. Strangely, he found himself shy around Katya now . . . but her evident distress made him want to reach out and take her in his arms.

Her willingness to walk with him delighted, as the night of this world entranced. Westward, zodiacal light mounted toward heaven, a diffuse and pale gold pillar just bright enough to banish the dimmest stars. Thirty light-years from Sol, the constellations were already strange, though northward the familiar hourglass of Orion was visible, only slightly distorted and with a distance-dimmed Sirius now shifted by perspective closer to far Rigel. Sol lay in that direction, Dev knew, but was lost here below the horizon.

Bright in the night was Zeta Herculis, a golden spark to the southwest. A subgiant like Mu Herc, six times more luminous than vanished Sol, Zeta was less than nine lights distant and nearly as brilliant here as was Sirius from Earth.

Between east and zenith, a gold thread stretched taut among the stars. Herakles's space elevator, cast adrift among so many stars, looked like a straight-line scratch against ebon black and was so large and so far that its orbital motion, like a natural satellite's, could not be distinguished by the naked eye. Clustered at its hub were swarming yet motionless stars, sunlight reflections from the ships of the tiny Confederation fleet.

Among the largest and grandest of all man's technological works, the broken sky-el seemed nearly lost among so much immensity.

"It's so vast," Katya said, awe behind the words as she stared into the heavens. "I don't know how the Naga can comprehend such emptiness, how they can *endure* it, it's so different from what they know."

"It is that," Dev agreed. "Especially when they never, like we do, just lie back and look up and wonder. What gets me is the idea of their actually bridging such gulfs."

"Hurling bits of themselves at the stars. The energies involved must be . . . staggering."

"Nothing less. You know, on the way here, I ran some calculations, based on what we know, what we *think* we know, from our Xeno links. Assuming one-ton projectiles—"

"Why?"

He shrugged. "A guess, frankly. The actual payload, the seed from which they populate a new planet, is probably all nano and no more massive than my fist. But the pod that carries it must sense other stars, must pick out worlds of proper temperature and magnetic field and, oh, whatever else is important to such a being. And it tacks and steers, somehow, on the Galaxy's magnetic field. Anyway, the world-Naga must pack one hell of a punch behind those pods when it launches them. Like a magnetic railgun, it must shoot the things skyward with tremendous speed. Not just vee-sub-ee for the planet, but escape velocity for the entire star system. Otherwise the pod would fall short and just orbit in the dark between the stars forever."

Katya shivered and drew closer. "That can't be a natural adaptation. It seems to be part of the Naga's life cycle now, the way it extends itself from world to world, but it couldn't have been so always."

"Sure. Picked up along the way, how many billions of

years ago? From the little I've seen, felt rather, the technology was absorbed from some unlucky, spacefaring culture assimilated early on, maybe from the same source as they acquired their nanotechnic parasites."

"Parasites?"

"Symbionts, then. Of course, once you get down to nanotech scales, words like 'organic' and 'artificial' start to lose their meaning."

"They do, don't they?" Katya said. "Still, reaching for the stars was never part of their original, their organic evolution. That had to have come later."

"And why not? The same could be said of us, now that we're free of Earth."

"Free?"

He grinned. "Thus speaks the New American revolutionary. Free physically, Kat, if not yet in spirit. That will come. We're already too different in culture, in ways of thought, for the Empire to hold onto us much longer."

"And we have the Galaxy as inheritance now."

"Shared with folk like the Naga and the DalRiss, yes. Both are so different, from each other and from us. I wonder how different the others we'll meet out there one day might seem?"

"We share starfaring, the three of us."

"Yeah, only the Xenos do it without even knowing there are such things out there as stars. I wonder how many of those pods are adrift out there, falling forever between the worlds because they didn't happen to be pointed in the right direction?"

Katya shivered again and he put his arm around her, drawing her close. She'd come out into the night without her accustomed bodysuit, clad only in the white bootslacks and pale blue vest she'd worn to dinner. The vest was open in front, secured only by a silver cord just above her breasts and sheer enough that even in this dim light Dev could make out the oval duskiness of her nipples showing underneath. Though the material contained the same microcircuitry for thermal control as did Dev's bodysuit, the costume exposed a fair amount of skin and the Heraklean night was distinctly chilly.

"You want to go back inside?"

"No. I want . . . want to linger here. To enjoy Starrise. And you."

An hour passed, the heavens wheeling slowly. West, the zodiacal light was fading. East, however, the sky glowed red and pale gray through a band of clouds hugging the horizon, as though with the light of approaching dawn. Minutes passed in long silence, the east growing slowly lighter. Then the clouds vanished and the false dawn was revealed for what it was. Bright, brighter by far than Zeta Herculis, the dazzling star cleared the eastern horizon and touched mountain peaks with blue and silver.

From Mu Herculis, Vega lay but three and a half light-years distant, a diamond-hard, blue-white beacon outshining everything in the sky, bright enough to read by, bright enough to cast distinct shadows on the ground and drown the night's other stars in glorious luminosity.

But Katya was looking north, toward the dimly seen bulk of the atmosphere generator.

"Dev . . ."

"Don't, Katya." He knew what she was thinking, what she was about to say. "Let's just say it's orders—"

"Orders!" Her anger flared, and he felt her tense beneath his arm. "How much death have orders caused already?"

"All right. Duty, then."

"That's worse. *I* could be the one going down into the Xeno's lair tomorrow, as well as you."

"Could be, but I'd rather that it was me and Vic. You had the last go-round, on Eridu, and it nearly killed you."

"I remember. How could I forget? But Dev . . . Love . . . I don't want to lose you. Not now. I feel like you're all I have left."

The words were at once joy and sadness. She loved him! As he, with newfound certainty, loved her. And yet . . .

"One of us has to go," he said reasonably. "We've had the most experience with the Xenos, you and I, and we can't both go, not when we might . . . uh, might have to make a second try."

She turned suddenly inside the reach of his arm, putting her own arms around him, embracing him tightly. *Bright, Cameron,* he thought to himself savagely as he hugged her back. *Real bright. Just the right thing to say!*

After a time, she pulled back. Her wet face glistened in the luminous diamond glare of Vega.

"It doesn't matter which of us goes, does it?" she asked. "Let me."

"You still have trouble with enclosed places, Katya." He said it bluntly, saw the pain at the truth in her eyes. "General Sinclair knows that too. He probably thought it would go better if the first person to make contact didn't have . . . other things on her mind."

"Maybe. I'm beginning to think Travis Sinclair is a cold, hard man. An AI programmed for political philosophy and military tactics."

"Because he didn't let you stay behind on New America? You can do a hell of a lot more good here. Besides, wouldn't you rather be here with me?"

The attempted lightness fell flat. "I don't know what I want, Dev. Not anymore. I used to think the rebellion was everything, that it was my reason for being alive. Maybe it still would be, if I wasn't always seeing people I cared for being sent off to face Imperials or Xenos or God knows what while I'm ordered to safety. I used to think I was doing something, that I was making a difference, somehow. Now I'm beginning to think the Nagas have the right idea. Everything is Self and not-Self, Here or not-Here. What you are and where you are're all that matter, and nothing else and nobody else in the universe is worth a two-byte download."

"Delete that," Dev said. "You've got bad data there. Besides, I always had the feeling that the Nagas were missing some of the subtleties of life."

"What . . . do you mean?"

"Have you noticed, when you're linked with one, how ordinary rock takes on a complexity you never noticed before?"

"Yes. . . ."

"It's all Rock and not-Rock, sure, but the rock takes on a, I don't know, a *flavor* you never noticed before. It seems to be tied in with the direction and intensity of the local magnetic field, the temperature, the actual chemical composition of the rock, lots of things I can't even put names to."

"The Nagas have senses we can't even understand," Katya said. "It only makes sense they'd be aware of things that we're not."

"Exactly. But the same is true, the other way around. A Naga misses an awful lot that might seem obvious to us." He drew closer, tipping her head back with a finger beneath her chin. "Things like this."

A long time later, they broke the kiss. "Still want to think like a Naga?"

"Mmm. No. I never did, not really. That was just . . . me. I tend to charge off sometimes before that little DATA TRANSFER COMPLETE sign winks on. God, Dev, you be careful down there tomorrow, okay?"

"I will. Remember, each time we've run into wild Xenos in the past, they haven't reacted much to our presence, have let us get right up next to them, in fact. I'm not even sure they're aware of us at all, save maybe as some sort of natural phenomena, moving rocks, or something. Certainly, they don't have the same sense of personal space we do, or the flight-or-fight-if-you're-too-close response of most Earth-born critters. Their evolution must never have included things like a nasty predator sneaking up too close, or an unpleasant neighbor who might whack you over the head with a club and drop you in the stewpot."

"Nagas don't have a head to whack."

"True enough. And it'd take a damned big pot to hold one. But you get the idea."

Katya was silent for a long time after that. "Dev?" she asked finally.

"Yeah?"

"What good's it going to do, anyway?"

"What?"

"Talking with the Nagas."

"You mean besides convincing them not to eat us? To leave our cities and stuff alone?"

"Well, that much is obvious." Despite her mood, she smiled. "But Sinclair is fixed on this idea of his for enlisting the Nagas, the DalRiss too, for that matter, as allies. I've spent a lot of the past few weeks wondering just what good such allies would do. Dev, the Nagas don't even understand the concept 'enemy.' For all that they've pushed us off one world after another over the past forty-some years, they don't understand the idea of 'war.' Hell, Fred just barely understands the idea of multiple individuals—that's what we want him to communicate to the Heraklean Naga, after all—and I think the idea of one individual killing another must be as alien to it as, as, I don't know. As a Naga's ideas about the shape of the universe are to us."

Dev thought about the question for a long moment before answering. "I could download to you the usual platitudes about synergy between alien cultures," he said after a while. "You've heard that sort of thing from Sinclair often enough. Diversity is good precisely because two cultures have different ways of thinking. Together they come up with things undreamed of by either."

"Sure, but we're not talking about a culture here, Dev. We're talking about a lump of black, sentient tissue mixed with God knows how many trillions of nanotech constructs that lives in the dark, eats rock, and thinks about stuff that no human could even imagine. Where's the synergy going to come from in that? Humans from different cultures *are* still human, after all. They have something in common. They talk and sing and make love and want good things for their children. They look at the sky and wonder. The Nagas are just too different."

"Hmm, maybe. Still, I have the gut feeling that no matter how alien the beasty is, putting us and it together is going to be like tuning in the microsingularities in a starship QPT. You're going to get one hell of a lot of energy out of the system that just wasn't there before. More than you'd expect from something so tiny."

Dev wondered if he'd chosen the right simile. In a starship's QPT, the resonance between two neutron-sized black holes yielded tremendous energy, true . . . energy enough to vaporize the largest starship and everything within several thousand kilometers if it avalanched.

What energies might the pairing of Xeno and human liberate . . . and would they be any easier to control?

Katya stirred, restless. "How . . . far down do you think you'll have to go tomorrow?"

"Wish I knew. Depends on the Naga, doesn't it?" He could feel her trembling.

"Here . . ." Reaching out, he took her left hand in his, the circuitries embedded in the heels of their palms touching. They kissed again, the tingle of their shared sensations racing up their arms and melding them more closely as one.

Dev had heard that some within the *Shakai*—that blend of culture, lifestyle, and class that encompassed the upper strata of Japanese society—had circuit implants grown in lips, genitals, and other erogenous zones in order to boost physical sensation. He'd always scorned such peripherals. They were hardly needed, and any increase in sensation was most likely psychosomatic in any case. Neural implant circuitry was not primarily designed to enhance sensation, but to carry data to and from the cephlink. Psychosomatically enhanced or not, the kiss went on for a long, long time and continued after Dev broke contact with her palm to let both hands stray beneath her opened vest.

"I want you," she whispered. "Let's go back."

"There's nothing but the ViRcom modules," Dev replied. "We might try linking through a two-slotter warstrider. . . ."

"No. Not ViRsex. I want reality. I want *you*."

Dev blinked. Most couples with full-link capabilities preferred virtual sex when they could arrange it. Despite occasional claims to the contrary, there was absolutely no way to distinguish sensations generated within the brain from those generated without, and there was the advantage of being able to create any desired romantic backdrop, drawn from memory or from purest fantasy. Dev knew of people, men and women both, who claimed never to engage in animal grapplesex, as they called it, at all. Children were more safely conceived in clinics, and ViRsex was cleaner, more comfortable, and less prone to stress, and in general more "real" than the real thing.

Dev wasn't sure he agreed with that philosophy. He'd engaged in both types of play, finding advantages and delights in both. He'd never engaged in real sex with Katya, however, and the intensity of her need surprised him.

"It, uh, it might be hard finding privacy."

"We'll find it. Please, Dev. Tonight I don't want to feel you against me, *in* me, through some God-damned machine."

And later, lying together in the narrow and frankly uncomfortable cot in her quarters back in the hab dome, Dev had to admit that he agreed completely.

There was a psychological technique made possible by cephlinks and personal analogues, a way of literally talking to one's self. The Japanese called it *jigano hanashi-ai*, the "ego-discussion." On the Frontier it was known as "jigging." A person could literally call up fragments of his own personality to discuss problems. Dev's included analogues he thought of as The Tactician, that cold and analytical part of himself that planned and executed battles; The Warrior, a frightening incarnation exuding the confidence of technomegalomania; The Kid, who was Dev at seventeen. There were others.

Dev rarely indulged in jigging. He'd long ago found that he didn't like these alter egos, to the point that he'd begun to think that he honestly didn't like himself. Possibly, that was a bit of psychological foreshortening, caused by the fact that his ego fragments were just that, fragments of himself, and not himself as a whole.

ViRsex, he found, spoke only to that ego fragment of himself he called The Lover, the part of himself concerned almost entirely with Katya as a sexual partner.

But this . . . *this* . . .

He snuggled closer to her, arms enfolding her tightly. *This* touched every part of his being, body, mind and soul, in ways he'd never imagined possible.

It . . . no, *she* . . . made him whole.

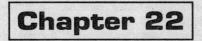

# Chapter 22

*A single Xenophobe "cell"—more properly known as a "paracell" or "supracell" to distinguish it from the microscopic cells of Earth-based life— masses approximately one to two kilograms and is capable of a slow, sluglike motility. Possessing little intelligence of its own beyond a certain innate homeotropism, it has been likened to an individual human neuron.*

*Xenophobe intelligence is, in fact, a function of the number and interconnectedness of a variable but large number of these paracells. Xenophobe travellers, consisting of several thousand paracells and massing three to five tons, may possess an intelligence roughly analogous to that of a human. A planetary Xenophobe, composed of as many as $10^{17}$ supracells, may possess an intelligence utterly beyond the human ken.*

> *Obviously, the nature of that intelligence is radically different from ours.*
>
>          —*The Xenophobe Wars*
>            Dr. Francine Torrey
>             C.E. 2543

The passageway seemed to stretch on ahead forever, smooth-walled, sloping downward at nearly a ten-degree angle. Dev was in the lead, encased in a one-man RLN-90 Scoutstrider, taking each step carefully as though in anticipation of deadfalls or pits. Walls, floors, and ceiling were smoothly rounded, the one blending into the next without visible seam or joint. It was like walking down a long, straight pipeline hewn through smooth rock; the tube's lumen was only three meters, so Dev had to keep his warstrider folded in on itself, legs sharply angled to keep his dorsal sensors and weapons packs from scraping along the ceiling. An array of four spotlights mounted on the forward hull of his strider cast a brilliant white light into the tunnel's depths ahead, though so far, for thousands of meters, there'd been nothing whatsoever to see.

Eighty meters to his rear came a second walker, a smaller, sleeker LaG-17 Fastrider jacked by Vic Hagan. His machine was towing a maglifter pallet in its wake, with Fred's travel pod strapped to its bed.

"According to your sonar we ought to be getting close." Hagan's voice sounded in Dev's link. Though they were in separate machines, the sensory data from Dev's strider was being relayed to Vic for analysis. This allowed Dev to remain alert with the Scoutstrider's weapons, just as though the two of them were jacked in side by side in a two-slotter combat machine. "Another five klicks or so."

"Affirmative," Dev replied. The same data was accessible within his virtual imagery, but he scarcely glanced at it. "I'll be glad when we hit bottom. I feel like I'm crawling around in somebody's large intestine."

"I'm linked with you there."

"Katya?" Dev called. "Are you still with us?"

"We're here, Dev." Her voice was hard and tight and edged with a crackling burr of static. The two striders had been leaving a trail of communications relays as they descended, but so much rock still swallowed both radio and laser carriers, and so many communications links amplified inefficiencies. No one knew how long the two striders descending into Herakles's bowels would remain in contact with their fellows on the surface.

Surely it was his imagination, but Dev could almost sense the weight of the artificial mountain pressing down on him from above. That mountain, and the other atmosphere generation plants, had been grown by programmed nano that had excavated thousands of tunnels like this one deep into the crust of the planet, transporting the rock up to the surface literally molecule by molecule, where it was rearranged into the unyielding fabricrete and duralloy and ferrocarb of the mountain itself, and its internal mechanisms. Those empty tunnels had been left behind, becoming part of the atmospheric nanogenerator's circulation system and a means of storing pure gases—oxygen or nitrogen—until enough had been accumulated that they could be released in the proper ratios.

And now, those seemingly endless nano-drilled tunnels had a new use.

*There was Rock . . . and not-Rock, Self and not-Self, a universe described in the dualistic is/is-not of an evolution shaped by absolutes. The dichotomy of being was simple and self-evident. Physical form could be described as Rock, infinite in extent, near infinite in its subtle variability and composition and chemistries at both super- and submolecular levels. Not-Rock was all else, the channels and chambers and node-enclosures of thin, near-vacuum that housed and enclosed and sheltered Self.*

*Mental form—awareness, consciousness, ego, thought, volition, action—was Self, though here the simplistic dualism of being and not-being, of yes and no, grew rapidly more complex. Once, perhaps, though the memories were hazy now with the endless march of intervening events, Self had simply been Self, but even Self could change. Indeed, Self measured the difference between Self and Rock not only in its capacity to sense, store data, and reason, but in its capacity for change, deliberate or otherwise. It had learned, incalculable numbers of events past, how to pinch off a minute fraction of its own being, tiny localizations of purpose and will distinct from Self, a thinking and sensing awareness that was not Self, but >>self<<.*

*The discovery of >>self<< was arguably the most important step in the evolution of Self, a means to reach out into the surrounding darkness and warmth of Mother Rock and gather experience, memories, even samples of the Rock beyond the Here of Self. A >>self<< would set forth, sundered from Self, keening the sharp pains of loneliness and loss. No longer Self, its experience of the universe was not immediately accessible, could not be accessible until the >>self<< returned to Self, was reabsorbed into a larger being and a more complete awareness and its memories commingled with the whole. The philosophical implications were staggering. Could there actually be experience—events, awareness, change, the stuff of memories—taking place in the universe beyond the grasp of Self?*

*Astonishing as the implications were, experience with countless billions of >>selves<< had proven this to be the case. There was Being outside of Self and more to the universe than an infinite sea of Rock. There was Here—where Self was—and there was not-Here. Events could transpire within a seemingly infinite not-Here, a process that defied all that Self had thought it knew and understood.*

*Self had still been grappling with the concept when it had encountered the Burning.*

From what Dev and Katya been able to learn from the planetary Nagas on the DalRiss homeworld of Alya B-V and on Eridu, Nagas began as small nodes of interconnected supracells deep within a planet's crust, planted there by the arrival of a Naga reproductive pod riding the world's magnetic fields down from space. With millions of nanotechnic organelles existing in symbiosis with each supracell's organic components, the creatures were able to hollow out pockets and passageways within solid rock, in much the same way as the terraformers had programmed the nano that had delved these tunnels beneath the atmosphere generators.

The devoured rock became raw material for new supracells, organic and inorganic components alike drawn from the world's inner treasure troves of silicon, oxygen, carbon, iron, nickel, and every other common element. The building blocks of a world, after all, and the building blocks for a living creature were all much the same, differing only in their ratios and in the manner of their arrangement.

For perhaps hundreds of millions of years, the Naga nodes tunneled and reproduced. Thermovores, they made use of the planet's internal heat, utilizing the energy to metabolize the rock literally molecule by molecule. Pockets or veins of pure metal ores or other substances were best, requiring less energy to extract them.

Eventually, the Nagas occupied much of the planetary crust, from just beneath the surface to that depth where heat and pressure exceeded their tolerance levels. Possessing numerous senses understood dimly by humans, if at all, they were able to detect large concentrations of pure substances at considerable distances, even through solid rock. To a Naga node, a human city, even a single warstrider, represented an incredible bounty of pure metals, polymers, and ceramics, of pure diamond woven into thin, readily accessible sheets, of vast numbers of nanotechnic machines the size of single, large molecules ready for assimilation and reprogramming. As the first Naga scouts neared the surface of a world occupied by humans, they were drawn to these concentrations of raw materials. Unaware that the delicate carbon-based life-forms in their way were anything other than some strangely patterned natural phenomena, the scouts began to feed. . . .

Which, of course, had been interpreted by humans as an attack by monstrous, alien, and utterly incomprehensible foes.

On Alya B-V, the DalRiss had been forced to evacuate their own birthworld as the Nagas emerged everywhere, transforming cities, the surface of entire continents into nightmare fantasies shaped by alien notions of line and form and function. In time, countless separate nodes had united, until every supracell on and in the world was interlinked, neurons of a single, vast brain of incomprehensible scope. At that point, the organism changed, its drives shifting from those of the restless, acquisitive phase to the sessile—and reproductive—contemplative form.

So much was known about the Naga, communicated by the now "tame" organism inhabiting Eridu through the intermediate agency of a living DalRiss comel. So much more was mystery still. What triggered the transition from the acquisitive to the contemplative phases? How long did it take? Xenophobe notions of time bore no relationship at all to those of humans; indeed, time seemed to mean little to organisms that possessed memories—and oddly packaged and disordered memories at that—stretching back for hundreds of millions or even billions of years and embracing long chains of successive worlds.

The question had taken on a fairly pressing, new importance on Mu Herculis. Twenty-eight years ago, the first Xenophobe scouts had emerged from underground and begun devouring human settlements. Three decades was the flicker of an eye compared to the time spans enjoyed by the Nagas, but when the organisms began breaking through to the, to them, alien surface of a world, that seemed to be a sign that the transformation was close at hand. When Dev had settled on Mu Herculis III as the place to conduct this communications experiment, he'd based the choice at least in part on the hope that the Heraklean Naga had settled down, beginning the change from the acquisitive to the contemplative phase. The Naga he'd communicated with on Alya B-V had been contemplative; the one on Eridu that Katya had encountered had still been acquisitive, but on the verge of making the change, with most of its nodes already interconnected with one another and its group intelligence already of a fantastically high order.

But in twenty-eight years, the Naga occupying the Heraklean crust had not shown itself since the day Argos had vanished in a sea of nuclear fire. A careful, almost kilometer by kilometer search of the planetary surface from orbit had shown no trace of the organism.

It was entirely possible that the thing was dead. Not likely, certainly, given that an organism that occupied much of a planet's crust massed as much as a fair-sized moon, but it was possible. If the Xenophobes attacking the Heraklean colony had been a single, relatively young node that had been located by chance near Argos, then the entire node could have been destroyed by the nuclear blast that had so altered the shape of the Augean Peninsula.

But Dev didn't think that likely. A planet is so vast a place, the coincidence of Man and Xenophobe both beginning their colonizations from the same point and at very nearly the same time was too great to consider seriously.

And yet . . . where was the Heraklean Naga now? Automated probes—AI landers bearing sensitive instruments capable of tracking a Xeno's DSA, the Deep

Seismic Anomaly associated with its movements far underground—had set down by the hundreds on every continent and major island on the planet. In two months they'd heard nothing save for the purely natural groanings and rumblings of a living planet's internal workings.

And so, Dev and Vic had decided that they would have to continue the search in a more direct fashion. The empty tunnels beneath an atmospheric nanogenerator penetrated the planet's crust to a depth of one or two kilometers in places, far enough down that the temperature reached seventy degrees or more, rising twenty-five degrees Celsius for every kilometer's drop in depth.

Surely the Nagas, with their singleminded hunger for pure metals and manufactured composites would have sought out the artificial mountains of the atmosphere plants, at least so far as to explore them. The mountain pressing down on Dev now was Heraklean Atmospheric Nanoprocessing Facility One, the closest of all of the planet's terraforming plants to the place where Argos had stood. The Xenos must have penetrated the place, at least as far as these tunnels.

Dev could imagine no other way of reaching the Naga than to penetrate the tunnels' lower reaches. The only problem he could see was one that had been haunting him for some time now.

Assuming there *were* still living Nagas within Herakles, their lack of activity was atypical . . . and therefore potentially dangerous. Quite possibly the planet's inhabitants were being quiet because they didn't care to receive visitors.

*Self was well aware of the not-Selves approaching from the place-of-Burning. It still had trouble accepting the distinctly alien idea of a not-Self that seemed to exhibit the volition, the sense of purpose that ought to be Self's alone. It could best accept the not-Selves'* *existence by thinking of them as a kind of >>selves<<, as disembodied parts of Self momentarily sundered from the whole. This explained the purposefulness of their advance as well as the tastes of pure metal and functioning submicroscopic units, of tightly channeled electrical and magnetic fields, of other-than-natural heat radiation that they bore on and within their curiously formed beings.*

*How, though, could there be >>selves<< that had not arisen by the direct volition and action of Self? That was a question unanswered, and possibly unanswerable.*

*Normally, of course, it would have been simple enough to absorb them into the whole, assimilating their memories of events from beyond Here and Self, but the memory of the Burning, and the driving need for survival that was indelibly printed within every one of Self's composite units, made it hesitate.*

*It could not face the agonizing pain and loss of Burning again.*

"Dev?"

"Yeah, Vic."

"My sonar is picking up something funny up ahead. I think the main tunnel dead-ends . . . but the returns are, I don't know. Soft."

"Yeah, I read the same. It might be what we're looking for."

For the last several kilometers, he'd been aware that the tunnel they were traversing had changed in character. It continued to descend at a ten-degree slope, and the lumen had neither narrowed nor enlarged. Still, human-programmed mining nano tended to leave a smooth and crisply defined, neatly geometrical surface, one given a denser composition than normal rock in order to support the tunnel roof. The tunnel walls now were slightly irregular, with a surface that appeared to have been altered by restructuring native rock into a slightly translucent, crystalline structure, obviously for the same reason.

This section of the tunnel had been eaten out not by human agencies, but by Nagas.

"Maybe we should just unwrap Fred and send him ahead, huh?"

Dev had been considering that for some minutes now. The trouble was that there was no way of predicting what Fred would do once he was released. Better to make sure they were face-to-face—if you could even use such anthropocentric imagery here—with the Naga.

"Let's wait," he told Hagan. "We haven't been attacked yet. Let's see if we can get closer."

"You're the boss. I make the range to be a little less than a kilometer, now."

"Let's just hope the tunnel doesn't tighten up," Dev replied. "I'm beginning to wonder if we'll even be able to turn around in here."

"Yeah. Anything bad happens, we're going to have to back up real, real fast."

*Change, or rather, the capacity to experience change, defined Self, separating it from unchanging Rock.*

*Or, to be more specific still, the capability to deliberately inflict as well as to contemplate change was what separated Self from its surroundings. Rock could change, becoming not-Rock, but that was a direct result of Self's volition. Self absorbed rock, changing its components at need to generate additional Self. Rock did not, could not, change of its own accord.*

*Change, as directed by Self, was all that made existence worthwhile. Consider the boredom of an infinite and infinitely unchanging universe!*

*Once, then, Self had gloried in change. Since the Burning, however, the need for change had itself changed. The Burning had brought pain, loneliness, loss ... and an abiding fear, almost as though Self itself had been pinched off to become a sharply limited and delimited* >>*self*<<. *These sensations and the associat-ed memories were now part of Self's universe, and they shaped its perceptions of all that lay beyond the truncat-ed and flame-seared boundary between Self and not-Self.*

*Immediately before the Burning, Self had become aware—through the agency of numerous* >>*selves*<<— *of the bizarrely alien not-Selves and not-*>>*selves*<< *that were now approaching Here. Incompletely under-stood, these alien not-Selves had once been understood as a special category of Rock, something natural and preexistent, but which sometimes seemingly acted with volition. Self had sought them out, partly curious, though mostly their apparent relationship with vast troves of unimaginably pure and very special and useful subsets of Rock was what had intrigued.*

*Intriguing, too, had been the number of* >>*selves*<< *that never returned for reabsorption after being dis-patched to sample these alien* >>*selves*<<. *Why? This growing uncertainty about the nature of the alien* >>*selves*<< *had been in the forefront of Self's introspective awareness when the Burning had flamed across being, vaporizing untold trillions of Self's com-posite units. Perhaps as much as a tenth of Self's substance had ceased to be, had become not-Self and, in the becoming, had transmitted sensory images that could still, upon reflection, make Self's being shudder in remembered agony.*

*How to avoid a repeat of the Burning now dominated Self's awareness. As the alien* >>*selves*<< *neared Here, Self could conceive of only two alternatives. It could retreat, as it had in the aftermath of the Burning, finding shelter in deeper and more secure embraces of Mother Rock. Comfortable as that thought was, it offered few advantages, for the not-*>>*selves*<< *were clearly capable of following Self wherever it might go.*

*Which left, of course, only a single, viable alternative, risky as that might be. . . .*

# Chapter 23

*Our modern perspective reveals that the Xeno-
phobe Wars were, in fact, a terrible accident, one
brought about by the fact that neither side in the
conflict had any clear idea about the true nature
of the enemy. Humans perceived only the Xeno
travellers and combat mode fighters, alien mon-
strosities obeying alien imperatives and wreaking
utter devastation wherever they appeared. The
Xenophobes, we now understand, perceived us
as part of the background, if at all, as a kind
of natural phenomenon that could be dangerous
and which had to be assimilated, neutralized, or
adapted to.*

—*The Xenophobe Wars*
Dr. Francine Torrey
C.E. 2543

"Vic!" Dev snapped, every sense almost painfully taut.
"Do you see it? Do you *see* it?"

"Affirmative." Hagan's view forward from his own

warstrider was blocked by the hull of Dev's machine, but he was getting a visual feed from Dev's RLN-90. "My God, there's a lot of it, isn't there?"

"The tip of the iceberg," Dev replied, wonderingly. "Worse. If this thing was a human, we'd be a couple of bacteria staring at the very end of its little toe."

The tunnel they'd been descending debouched on a vast cavern; so sudden had been its appearance that Dev had nearly plunged forward off the tunnel's edge and into that vault of primal blackness. The spotlights on Dev's Scoutstrider filled much of that cavern without illuminating it, for the far walls and the unseen floor of the pit were filled with a glistening, opalescent black substance in constant, queasy motion. Too lumpy to be oil or some similar liquid, the light-drinking surface was wetly uneven, composed of thousands of closely packed Naga supracells that slid over and around one another with the slick, mucoid lubrication of certain Terran gastropods. Each was connected to its neighbors by innumerable tendrils, like the axons and dendrites of human nerve cells, save that these were in direct contact with one another.

Too, these were moving, unlike nerve tissue. Dev had the impression that he was staring down into a living sea, one with currents and waves, but ponderously slow.

That sea of iridescent blackness was aware of him, he knew, not through sight or hearing, but through dozens of stranger, more subtle senses that probed and tasted rock and magnetic fields and the sizzling flow of electrical currents. The mass below Dev's warstrider was heaving itself up out of the pit, an ocean of black tar given mobility and will, extending a multiton pseudopod toward the opening in which Dev's Scoutstrider perched.

"Back!" Dev called, and he reversed his strider's movement, shuffling the RLN-90's half-folded legs back in the cramped space of the tunnel. "Get back, quick!"

Dev had managed to scuttle back perhaps ten meters from the tunnel mouth when the pseudopod plunged through the entrance, swallowing the glare from the RLN-90's spotlights, pushing forward like a thick, black paste ejected through a narrow opening by tremendous pressure. It hit his Scoutstrider with jarring force, toppling him sideways into the wall of the tunnel, then sweeping him along like a toy caught in a flood. The rush, the sudden impact were so abrupt that Dev didn't have time to fire his weapons. He was still trying to keep his warstrider upright when his link with the machine's AI flared static white in his mind, then winked out into blank.

"Vic!" Dev screamed. "Vic! Cut Fred loose!" If they could release the Eriduan Naga fragment . . .

And then Dev was awake and in his own body, locked inside the padded, coffin-sized crevice of his strider's link slot. Power was gone . . . as were his control systems. The Scoutstrider was an inert, string-cut puppet of dead metal, and Dev was trapped inside.

Vic Hagan backpedaled furiously as the nightmare, gelatinous wall of blackness exploded toward him through the tunnel opening. His data feed from Dev's Scoutstrider was lost in a flutter of static. He'd heard only a sharp-screamed "*Vic!*" from Dev, the name cut off short.

He'd positioned himself a good eighty meters behind Dev's strider, since he'd been linked to the view fed to him from the other machine. When the feed vanished, Vic could see the top half of Dev's RLN-90 starkly pinned by the lights of his Fastrider, its legs awash in the tarry ooze. The LaG-17 mounted two fifty-megawatt lasers, one to either side of its stubby prow like the mandibles of some spindle-legged insect. He triggered both lasers together, sending a double pulse of laser energy into the black sea advancing toward him up the tunnel, trying to sear the thing as close to Dev's RLN-90 as he could without risking hitting the other machine.

Nothing. The moving blackness drank the coherent light scarcely a ripple. Vic fired again . . . and again. A flash of silver rippled across the surface of the gelatinous mass, then vanished so swiftly he wasn't even certain he'd really seen it.

He took three more steps backward as the Naga mass advanced, colliding with the maglifter pallet where it hovered behind his strider. Sensors transmitted the shock of contact, the metallic brush and scrape as his left leg ground against Fred's travel pod. His full attention focused on the advancing Naga, Vic overrode the sensor data and pushed, still backing up the tunnel.

Balanced on tightly focused fields that rode the planet's own magnetic field, the maglifter pallet yawed to its side as the Fastrider forced itself past, slammed into the tunnel wall, then crashed to the floor. Vic squeezed past it, willing the Fastrider's legs to move faster, panic rattling at brain and heart as the night black horror kept rolling toward him.

His lights caught a piece of Dev's warstrider still afloat on the tide . . . a leg, Vic thought. Then he saw another piece, the right arm still bearing its hundred-megawatt laser, ripped from the RLN's hull in a careless display of raw power. He couldn't see the hull. The black mass reached Fred's pod where it lay now, dented and torn, on the floor of the tunnel and washed over it like an ocean breaker. The wrecked maglifter was swallowed an instant later.

Weapons were useless. Vic concentrated all of his energy on movement, backing up the tunnel with all of the speed he could muster. The Fastrider's legs scissored almost to a blur, duralloy-flanged feet striking sparks against the smooth floor of the tunnel, one outflung arm clanging against the wall in a desperate bid to urge the machine backward yet a bit faster.

The black tide kept coming. He wasn't going to make it. . . .

Dev thought he was facedown, though in the disorienting blackness of his strider slot, it was difficult to tell for sure. It felt as though the Naga had engulfed his Scoutstrider and was bearing it along within its mass, a tiny morsel, swallowed whole. A grinding, shrieking clash of tearing metal howled inside the narrow confines of the compartment, conjuring images of his warstrider's dismemberment . . . or worse, of the life-support hull cracking and the black ooze pouring in.

Never had Dev felt a terror this dark, this penetrating, and he had to battle with all of his swiftly tattering strength to keep from howling aloud and pounding on the sides of the strider slot with his fists. Instead, moving by instinct and by touch, he struggled to reach the storage compartment built into the side of the slot.

It opened when the panel read the data feed from his left palm. Urgently, wrestling to maintain some small bubble of sanity and rationality within a rising sea of panic, he thrust his left arm into the compartment, striking cool, dry softness within. He felt it envelop his arm, from fingertips to elbow, felt the touch grow cold.

The comel, manufactured yet alive, biological construct of the alien DalRiss, clung to his arm like a living glove. Dev's only hope of survival now, he knew with grim certainty, was to talk to the thing that had swallowed his Scoutstrider like a casually tossed peanut. Katya had survived being swallowed by one of these things. He could, too, *if* he could talk to it before it killed him.

As his outraged sense of balance told him his warstrider's hull was rolling to an upright position, his right hand hit the emergency manual release for the strider slot's hatch. With a hiss of equalizing pressures, the seal on the RLN's environmental pod broke. The hatch slid aside, revealing a blackness that was, if anything, more absolute than the black inside the slot.

Dev gasped. The air outside the Scoutstrider was breathable but blistering hot, stinking of sulfur and fuming, unnamed vapors driven from slow-cooking rocks. He took another breath, fighting the urge to gasp. The air here, if anything, was more oxygen-poor than that on the surface; desperately, he fumbled for the slot compartment that held a survival mask and bottled oxygen.

The warstrider hull slammed again against unyielding rock, flinging Dev against the side of his slot with brutal force. Metal screamed, then groaned and creaked with the growing urgency of a living creature at the edge of an agonizingly prolonged death. The RLN's torso, half-submerged and stripped of legs and arms and its usual clusters of antenna and sensory pods, was *folding* under the caress of incredible pressures exerted by the black sea.

Dizzy, blind, disoriented, Dev couldn't find the mask's compartment. Gulping at the air now, straining to find substance there to keep him conscious, he sat upright in the slot. All he needed to do was touch one of the Naga's interconnected supracells. . . .

His head banged rock half a meter above the warstrider's hull, and Dev saw a momentary explosion of green-and-purple light. Raising his left hand, he felt the rough drag of rock past the comel-encased tips of his fingers. The RLN's hull was moving, and quickly, born on the Naga's thick embrace through the tunnel.

But which way? Up the tunnel, in pursuit of Vic? Or back the other way, toward that reeking, briefly glimpsed pit? Keeping his head low this time, he struggled into a partly upright position, groping into absolute blackness with his comel-clad hand, trying to touch some part of the unseen mass that carried the wreckage of his strider, boatlike on gelatinous waves. He could feel the hull tipping again as it rolled over, spilling him toward the surface that carried it. Dev thrust his arm out farther, seeking contact. Where was the Naga's surface? Where? . . .

Pressures unbearable snapped the Scoutstrider's hull and the sides of the slot closed around his waist like the jaws of a trap. Dev screamed, the sound shrilling and echoing through the blackness. Agony tore at his lower back and legs . . . then vanished as he felt his spine snap.

A jolt, and he was free of the wreckage, but his back was broken and shock had left him dazed and incoherent. Strange thoughts flooded his brain but he could not order them, could not begin to understand them as anything beyond scraps of nightmare hallucination. Then, with a sudden, light-headed sense of falling, he was hurled through the opening of the tunnel and into the black and empty space of the great cavern. *I'm going to die.* The thought, as he recognized it as coming from some part of himself, was actually welcome, a peace that stilled the terror that threatened to rob him of his last shreds of human reason.

Seconds later, he struck the surface of the Naga. That surface was yielding, almost liquid, but Dev struck it after falling nearly fifty meters, and he hit with killing, bone-splintering force.

On the surface, Katya had broken the seal on her LaG-42 Ghostrider and was sitting up in the open hatch, keeping her left hand against the slot's palm interface so that she could stay linked with the communications net. Her full linkage had been broken, however. Impulsively, she wanted to experience her surroundings with her own senses, to *see* the mountain-high bulk of the atmosphere generator with her own eyes.

"Hey, Colonel?" The voice in her mind was that of her Number Two, Sublieutenant Tomid Lanager. "Don't you think you oughta button up?"

Another child, like Ken Maubry, now dead, like Chet Martin, abandoned with the other Rangers still on New America. Katya felt so very old.

"Negative," she snapped back, her mental voice harsh and biting. "Maintain your watch."

"Uh, yessir."

A half dozen other warstriders stood nearby, silently waiting. There were some people on foot, too, a platoon of armored infantry and a handful of senior officers, come to watch the great experiment. Among them was Travis Sinclair.

*That's the man who sent Dev down into the hole*, she thought, and she was surprised by her bitterness. She'd admired Sinclair, even loved him, in a hero-struck way. Now she saw him as another damned politician, a man so caught up in the jacker's rush of playing god that he didn't see the people around him as people. Perhaps he had once . . . but no more. This damned revolution of his seemed programmed for nothing but to devour children, and in the end no one would be better off for their sacrifice.

What had happened to her people—full humans and genies—back on New America?

A burst of static hissed against the background of her thoughts, then cleared. Vic's voice sounded, frantic with fear and speed. " . . . Hagan, do you read me? This is Hagan, does anyone copy?"

"We're here, Vic," Katya sent back. Fear clutched at her throat. "What's your situation?"

"I'm . . . I'm coming out. Katya, I'm sorry. Dev is lost. Dead. He must be dead."

The words left her numb, though somehow, she'd known them even before Vic had spoken. "What . . . what happened?"

"I don't know. We'd just reached the point where we could see the Naga—"

"You *did* see it, then?" Sinclair's voice cut in. Katya could see him holding a palm comm link with a cord jacked into his left T-socket. "The Naga? . . ."

"I saw it, yeah." Hagan's voice was dry. "It just . . . attacked. No reason that I could see. It just rose up and blasted into the tunnel and smashed Dev's Scoutstrider to bits."

"What about the Eriduan Naga?" Sinclair asked.

"I don't know. The thing got Fred, too. Just kind of washed over the pod and swallowed it. I didn't see any change in the thing's behavior. It just kept coming!"

"It's okay, Vic." Katya had to work hard to keep her mental voice steady. "It's okay. Are you clear now?"

"Yeah. I think so. It chased me maybe a kilometer up the tunnel, then quit. I don't see any sign of it now."

"Maybe that was the change we were looking for," Sinclair suggested. "The Eriduan fragment communicated—"

"I don't think so, General," Hagan interrupted. "Like I said, it just kept coming. Like it was mad, or something." There was a long pause. "Okay, maybe it did change its mind and turn back. But there hasn't been any attempt to communicate. And I don't . . . I don't think I can go back down there. . . ."

Katya heard the agony in Hagan's voice, the unsteadiness, the indecisiveness. The man was on the raw edge of collapse, and when she closed her eyes and tried to imagine him far below the world's surface, alone, surrounded by unyielding night, she could easily understand. "Vic, you can't do anything else. Get the hell out of there." The words burned in her mind.

"But if the Naga tries to communicate—" Sinclair began.

"Dammit, there's nothing more he can do! There's nothing more *any* of us can do!"

"Maybe one of us could go down and look for Dev," Lee Chung volunteered. "I'll go."

"You'd be wasting your time, Lee," Hagan said. "Katya. Don't let him come. I tell you, I saw the thing tearing his warstrider to pieces! I don't see how he could have survived. Oh, damn it, Katya. I'm sorry. I'm sorry. . . ."

"It wasn't your fault, Vic." Tears were stinging her eyes, blurring her vision. "He might . . . Dev might still make it."

The thought was not wholly irrational. Katya remembered well her own contact with a Naga, far, far below the humid, poisonous surface of Eridu. Somehow, the Naga she'd contacted—she found herself thinking of it as Fred's parent—had analyzed her body chemistry, then manipulated it to keep her alive, even when her survival mask's oxygen had given out. She remembered little of that encounter still, save for the first terrifying moments of it, closeted away in blackness absolute, with the weight of a world pressing down unseen above her head.

It was hard to tell, sometimes, what was memory of actual events, and what was remembered nightmare. She shuddered, pushing back unwelcome images of being buried alive.

Could the Naga hidden somewhere below the atmosphere plant keep Dev alive? She didn't have enough information to formulate an answer. The Naga was capable of it, certainly, as the Naga on Eridu had proved with her. But if Dev had already been dead when it engulfed him, even a Naga's near-miraculous mastery of chemistry would not have saved him. Xenophobes possessed remarkable powers of mind and of manipulation almost at the atomic level, but they were not gods.

No miracle of mere chemistry or of nanotechnics would call back the dead.

And if the thing had been trying to kill the human trespassers in its tunnel, it would have no reason to preserve his life.

She wanted to believe Dev still lived, however, and she clung to that slender thread, clutching against her awareness like a talisman.

"Vic?" Sinclair said. How she hated that voice now! "Can you patch a feed to us of what you saw?"

"Y-yeah. Stand by."

Dreading the images as she was, Katya nonetheless lay back down in her slot and jacked home her C- and T-sockets. Full linkage with Hagan's Fastrider resumed as he sent recorded images of what he'd seen in the tunnel. Briefly, horribly, Katya relived the nightmare darkness and close-pressing walls, saw the black tide surge forward, saw Dev's Scoutstrider hit, jarred backward, then swept under by the flood. She saw Vic's last glimpse of the RLN-90, the severed, metal limbs swallowed by the onrushing wave.

She was trembling as she broke linkage, and again unbuttoned the Ghostrider's hull and sat up, blinking back tears in the pale gold sunlight.

She didn't want to accept what she'd just seen.

Hours later, Vic's Fastrider appeared at the nearest entrance to the man-made mountain. The LaG-17 looked none the worse for its experience in the bowels of the planet, but it walked with what might be described as a beaten, even a despondent slouch of alloy legs and drooping hull. In all that time, there'd been no further word from underground, and Katya's desperate hope that Dev might still be alive was relentlessly unraveling.

"You all head on back to base," Katya told the others. "I'm going to stay here."

"Katya . . ." Vic began.

"Damn it, Vic! Get out of here!"

"Let's go, people," Sinclair said. "Katya and Lanager will keep watch here, just . . . just in case Dev makes it out."

He didn't sound as though he believed it.

Katya knew she didn't. Somehow, though, she still couldn't make herself believe that he was really gone.

The other warstriders filed away, leaving the Ghostrider in motionless, silent mourning outside the man-made mountain.

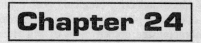

# Chapter 24

*If humans are master technicians, the beings known as Xenophobes are master chemists, possessing, apparently, a number of inward-turned senses that can analyze individual molecules in great detail. It is quite likely that they grow and program their own nano, and that much of their consciousness centers around, not their surroundings, but their own, inner workings.*

*It has been suggested that this peculiar evolution arose to keep creatures sane that, though possessing super-genius minds, remain locked away for eons in the black bowels of their unchanging caverns.*

—*Reflections on Intelligence*
Jame Carlyle
C.E. 2543

Three days later, the Imperial squadron dropped out of K-T space on the fringes of the Mu Herculis system.

Two Kako-class cruisers, *Haguro* and *Kinugasa*. Four light cruisers, *Nagara, Mogami, Suzuya*, and the newly grown and assembled *Zintu*. Four destroyers, including the Amatukaze-class *Urakaze*, "the Wind in the Bay." A dozen lesser craft, corvettes and light-hulled frigates.

And leading them all was Kawashima's flagship, the massive, kilometer-long dragonship *Donryu*.

Kawashima was linked into *Donryu*'s AI network, with schematics of the system unfolding with a computer's speed and crisp precision before his inner eye. Green diamonds glowed against the backdrop of stars, one embracing the golden glare of Mu Herculis A and almost lost in its light, a second surrounding the dim, red speck that was the system's red dwarf pair, and a third tagging a single, brilliant white star shining just to one side of the primary. The graphic diamonds marked nearby sources of neutrinos; the stars produced neutrinos naturally, as part of the nuclear processes burning in their cores; the white "star," however, was not a star, but a planet. A quick check of *Donryu*'s data base called up long scrolls of data on the Mu Herculis system. The world was Mu Herculis A III, and both the planet's surface and nearby space should be dead, with all fusion plants shut down years ago. The neutrinos marking the planet indicated that someone was using fusion plants there, that they'd either fired up the big power system aboard the orbiting fragment of the sky-el, or they were generating power aboard orbiting spacecraft and with smaller plants on the ground.

Kawashima had guessed right.

Certain at first that Cameron must have gone to Lung Chi, he'd changed his mind after reflecting further. The young rebel Cameron, after all, knew as well as did Kawashima that the Imperium had full access to the histories of both him and his father. Cameron would guess, surely, that any deliberate search for him must include the Lung Chi system, even if the searchers were unaware that he had with him a fragment of tame Xenophobe and hoped to use it to make contact with the strange beings.

Dev Cameron's record, or such of it as he had access to through *Donryu*'s data base, indicated that he had a talent for doing the unexpected. If he thought the Empire might search for him at Lung Chi, he would go to Mu Herculis instead.

Or not. The damned *gaijin* rebel was capable of carrying the they-know-that-I-know game back through any number of regressions. But Kawashima's gut instinct insisted that Cameron had brought the refugees from New America *here*, to a Xeno-dead system that no one had even thought about for twenty years. Just in case he'd guessed wrong, Kawashima had sent the remainder of Ohka Squadron—minus the destroyers he'd left at New America and the smaller craft sent to check Loki, An-Nur II, and Sandoval—to Lung Chi.

But the rebels, Kawashima had been certain throughout the month-long voyage from 26 Draconis, would be *here*.

*Donryu*'s AI swiftly sorted through the flood of data swept up by the flagship's scanners, analyzing it and feeding the conclusions through to her masters. The neutrinos were from a number of sources, all closely clustered together either in low orbit or on the Heraklean surface itself. The orbital sources were consistent with the neutrino signature of ten to fifteen shipboard fusion plants set to low output, plus numerous smaller ones . . . a picture wholly consistent with the number of ships stolen from the Imperial shipyard at Daikoku and the raiders that had taken them. The ground sources were smaller and much more tightly grouped, fusorpacks aboard warstriders or other large vehicles, most likely, and possibly base or shipboard fusion plants as well.

He'd found the rebels.

"Captain Obayashi," he called, rasping out the order over the ship's link network.

"*Hai, Chujosan!*" Gonichi Obayashi was *Donryu*'s commanding officer, Kawashima's flag captain in the parlance of an earlier, seafaring age. An efficient, tight-discipline officer with an impressive record, he'd commanded a cruiser during the Alyan Expedition and received command of *Donryu* as reward.

"We will implement the Noguchi option. Please make all necessary preparations."

"Ah." He could almost hear the reordering of Obayashi's thoughts. "Sir. So bold a maneuver could have unfortunate—"

"Please implement the Noguchi option, Obayashisan." He edged the polite phrasing with duralloy. "Indulge me."

There was the slightest of hesitations. "*Hai.* It will take a few moments for the program to run."

"Notify me when you are ready to engage. And pass the order to the other vessels in the squadron. When we move, we will move together."

Noguchi was the name of a mathematics wizard— some called him the modern Einstein—who lived and worked at Tsukinoshi, on Earth's moon. The Noguchi Equations were a complex set of variable field matrices that allowed shipboard AIs to better calculate the effects of local space curvature on orbiting singularities and to adjust the singularity harmonic tuning more precisely. In effect, they permitted warships to leave and enter K-T space far more deeply within the complex gravity wells of an inner planetary system than had ever been possible before.

Starship captains, a notoriously conservative lot, still resisted taking their huge and expensive charges under K-T drive closer than one or two astronomical units to a star; nor were the Noguchi Equations foolproof. Several vessels had been lost while experimenting with the new programs, and complex multiple star systems such as

26 Draconis increased the chance of disaster to near certainty.

Mu Herculis, however, was a simpler system; the B and C stellar components were small and far away, and Herakles, unlike New America, had no moon.

And if Kawashima took Ohka Squadron into the inner system in the normal way, it would be several days before they reached Herakles and entered planetary orbit. The rebels—he checked his inner timekeeping sense, then cross-checked it with the navsim feed—would know the Imperials had arrived in another three hundred minutes. By the time the Imperials reached the planet, the rebels would be packed up and gone, accelerating toward the far side of the Mu Herculis system at 4 Gs or better.

If he could jump closer *now*, however, before his own ship's neutrinos crawling planetward at light speed warned the rebels of the squadron's arrival, they would achieve complete and devastating surprise.

Such surprise was worth the risk. Kawashima *wanted* these people, wanted to end this ragtag revolution once and for all. Embers might smolder still on New America and Eridu, but with the leaders dead or mind-strung puppets, there would be no Confederation, no rebellion.

Within his link, he felt the flow of orders between ships, the data feeds, the terse acknowledgments. The special inner system control programs were running on all ships.

"Ohka Squadron, attention to orders!" he called, rapping out the command with brisk and military efficiency. He named four of the smaller ships in his group. "*Motiduki, Oboro, Amagiri, Tomoduru.* You will maintain course and speed through fourspace. Seek to cut off stragglers or damaged vessels that escape our net." As the acknowledgments flashed back from the frigates, he addressed the rest of his ships. "The rest of you, come with me. We will appear out of nowhere and confound these rebels who scorn the name and honor of our Emperor. *Dai Nihon! Banzai! Banzai!*"

The cheering echoes of the replies across the squadron's link net were still ringing within Kawashima's mind as he gave the mental order. As one, eleven Imperial capital ships and eight frigates and corvettes vanished from normal space.

*"RED ALERT! RED ALERT! ALL HANDS TO BATTLE STATIONS! . . ."*

The link-downloaded call jolted Katya, dragging her up from dark and smothering musings. She'd been off duty and had taken the time to wander a little way from the Mount Athos base, finding a rocky crag overlooking the sweep of what once had been the Augean Peninsula.

It had been three days. Dev must really be dead.

She pulled out a communicator and snicked the jack home in her right T-socket. "COM Control!" she snapped. "This is Alessandro! What is it?"

"Colonel, it's an Imperial fleet! We read nineteen targets, closing fast!"

"What range?"

"About eight hundred thousand kilometers—"

"What? How the hell did they get that close? Was somebody asleep on the jack?"

"Negative, negative, Colonel! They just, just appeared! Dropped out of K-T space a few moments ago! I saw them emerge on the broad-scan radar!"

"*Kuso!* I'll be right there!"

Katya sprinted back up the slope to the rebel base, which by unspoken popular assent had become known as Morgan's Hold. It was a long run, but she was in good shape and the nano meteffectors in her bloodstream were designed to enhance her physical performance on demand. She reached the fabricrete dome housing the base command center out of breath, with heart pounding, but on the way up she'd been able to tap a direct feed of data from the base, relayed down from orbit from the *Tarazed*. Eleven capital ships, including a Ryu-class, almost certainly the *Donryu*. Eight lesser craft. How in all the bleak hells of Buddha had the Impie bastards managed to figure out so quickly where the rebels had gone? And how had they managed to fine-tune their drives so precisely that they could emerge from the K-T plenum practically next door to Herakles?

"What's the status on our ships?" she shouted as she burst into the command center. It was a utilitarian control room, a bit cramped, lined with link couches and centered on a holoprojector that was currently showing a view of Herakles from space. The long, ruler-straight thread of the cast-off space elevator hung to one side. Nearby, a cluster of gold pinpoints hovered in space— the Confederation fleet. Outward, at the very edge of the projection field, a cluster of red lights gleamed balefully.

The Imperials were shockingly close.

"Almost to full-power and ready to break orbit," Sinclair told her. She was vaguely aware of a half dozen other senior military officers there in the control room with him, Grier and Darwin Smith among them, but their ashen faces were fixed on the projection. She doubted that they even knew she was there. The couches were occupied, for the most part, by younger men and women, coordinating the communications and battle control for fleet and ground forces.

"We weren't expecting them so soon," Sinclair said.

It took a moment for Katya to realize he was speaking to her. "Well, it was bound to happen sooner or later," she replied. "They must be on the jack over there, though, to have figured it out this fast."

"We're pretty well goked," he said, the crudity shocking on his lips. "Our ground forces are deployed around Mount Athos, but we don't have any place else even surveyed except for the atmosphere plant. Our space squadron isn't going to get clear in time. That damned Ryu is going to have them for breakfast."

She looked at Sinclair, caught by the pain in his voice. He was, she decided, a man forced to make a desperate choice, who'd just seen the result of that decision and knew he'd failed completely in his purpose. She could feel her anger and resentment of him, of his ordering Dev into that tunnel, evaporating.

*I never did get the hang of ordering my people into certain death*, she thought. *Maybe that's something no commander ever gets used to.*

"If our fleet can get away," she said gently, "then maybe we can disperse into the Outback. We can wait them out."

Sinclair looked at her, one eyebrow climbing. "This isn't New America, Katya. There's not much to eat out there but what we can nanogrow for ourselves. And there's no cover. They'll land their assault forces and hunt us down."

"We could try the tunnel system under the air generator," she suggested. "It's a labyrinth down there. We could set up traps, ambushes. If they ever managed to find us they'd be sorry they did."

Sinclair nodded. "Maybe. Maybe so. But we'll be a hell of a lot worse off than we would have been back on New America, you know. The rebellion . . ."

"Right now we have to worry about survival, General. The politics will come later. If we make it."

Reluctantly, he nodded.

On the holoprojection, the Imperial ships were moving closer with terrifying speed.

*Self continued to savor this bizarrely constructed and articulated not-Self form, cast so precipitously onto the fringe of Here. The . . . form was not Self, nor was it >>self<<, and the mysteries of its existence piled one upon the other in jumbled confusion.*

*It knew, now, that the form was called a human, that it was at least as intelligent as most >>selves<< and possibly more so, but that its memories and thinking processes were ordered quite differently from the Boolean is/is-not categorization of Self.*

*When the not-Self had first hurtled into the not-Rock niche within Mother Rock, Self had been ready to devour it, to absorb its mineral wealth, to leach out everything of value and distribute its very molecules throughout the whole that was Self. Curiosity had stayed that first impulse, however. The not-Self was harmless now, skinned of its shell of remarkably pure and intricately worked metals and artificial materials. It was vulnerable, easily manipulated, easily controlled and explored.*

*Self would have been able to understand nothing had it not been for the >>self<< discovered within the not-Rock passage. Assimilated into Self now, its memories circulating within the Whole, that alien >>self<< bore images, thoughts, and wonders incomprehensible.*

*So much that was new to think about!*

*Self's first action had been to probe the human, savoring it chemically. Among the data stored within the alien >>self<< were memories of another encounter with a human in that other, distant Here. Had that been the same human as this? It was hard to tell, but it seemed unlikely. The remembered tastes of that human were quite different from these, more alkaline, with a different balance of certain metabolic chemistries. Still, the two were similar enough for gross explorations. . . .*

*That remembered human had been acquired on the surface of the Void and carried deep into Mother Rock. There, that other Self—such a strange thought, that, another Self—had entered the human . . . this way. . . .*

*Smells and flavors—the closest human approximations to senses for which there were no names— assailed Self. The human tasted of hydrocarbons and salts, of metals and wonderfully complex carbon chains,* of a fine covering of artificial substances layered over most of its form. One appendage was sheathed in something else . . . hydrocarbons and long-chain polymers, substantially different in certain key ways from the rest of the not-Self, almost as though it were an entirely different creature.

No! It was a different creature, in symbiosis with the first! It called itself a comel and served as a bridge for thought and memory. A comel had been on the remembered human as well. How strange . . . and how wonderful!

Curiosity had burned, bright as a hot volcanic vent, drawing Self on. For Self, each new discovery was an Event, marking the passage of time. Thousands . . . no, tens of thousands of Events passed in flickering succession, discovery following discovery in bewildering array.

Shortly after the human had arrived, Self had learned that it was broken. It functioned still, after a fashion, and in a low-metabolic, energy-conserving state . . . but that curious chain of interlocking calcium nodules that stiffened the creature's main, central segment had clearly been broken, interfering with the transmission of neural impulses throughout its central nervous system. Other calcium structures had broken as well; Self compared the structures of his not-Self and the remembered one. This should be arranged that way . . . and this part should be like this. . . .

Countless gross differences between the human in memory and the reality Here were incomprehensible. The organs for the elimination of liquid waste, for example, were bizarrely different in this specimen than from those remembered by the alien >>self<<, and there were other differences, of chemistries, of fuzzy growths on the thing's surface, of layered deposits of fat. Self decided that these gross differences were natural and should be left alone; their organization and complex *functionality suggested evolutionary design rather than damage.*

*But on a finer level, the two organisms were identical, and . . . if the >>self's<< memories were any guide, this human's systems were rapidly failing. Self had begun experimenting, adding certain hastily constructed molecules a few at a time, and tasting the results.*

*Yes . . . that was the way. A touch here, a few molecules of a slightly altered hydrocarbon chain added there . . .*

*More time passed, Event piling upon Event.*

*Contact with the human was actually dangerous for Self. The creature possessed within its being a complex and interwoven network of tubules for circulating liquid throughout its body mass; the liquid within those tubules was an electrolytic solution almost identical in nature to the great, electrolyte-laden reservoirs of liquid water that overlaid some parts of the Rock along its interface with the Void. Contact tended to disrupt the electrical activity within Self's being, causing a sharp and unpleasant sensation that could be called pain.*

*Self had shut down certain of its own, internal receptors that were registering pain . . . and it had learned how to toughen the permeable membranes covering those portions of itself flowing through the minute pores of the human's outer integument. The deeper it probed, the more fascinated it became.*

*And as it explored, Self feasted on new memories, and on their meaning. With the alien >>self's<< memories for a guide, Self probed deeper, exploring the fantastically complex branchings of nerves . . . of ganglia . . . of firing dendrites . . . acetylcholine triggering chemical signals and sweeping waves of polarization . . .*

*To repair the damage in the broken part required the growth of new nerve tissue, duplicating it molecule by molecule, weaving new with old . . .*

*And then Self reached the top of the human's central nervous system, and stopped, astounded. Self thought, felt, remembered, acted with all of its body mass, but the human's separate body parts were specialized to an unimaginable degree.*

*Self had never imagined anything so complex or so mysterious as a human brain. . . .*

# Chapter 25

*If we think a Naga is strange, think how strange we look to the Naga. Look, it sees the universe inside-out from the way we do, like a bubble of vacuum inside an ocean of solid rock. It's so self-centered it thinks that it's the only intelligence in the universe, that Here is the only place in the universe, and that there are two and only two ways of cataloguing every fact in the universe. Then it blunders into us and finds out differently.*

*I think the poor thing really does very well in adapting to the strange and the unexpected. We could probably learn a thing or two from that.*

—*Scientific Methods*
ViRtransmission interview
with Jame Carlyle
C.E. 2543

Awareness . . . dim and pain-racked. Dev struggled up through layers of smothering darkness, trying to reach light . . . and failing. It was so dark . . . dark and stiflingly hot, and his back was broken, and he remembered feeling his back snapping and his body pinwheeling into darkness and falling and falling . . .

*Wonder . . .*

*Not-Rock thinks . . . it feels . . . bafflement . . . it actually senses its surroundings, but in a manner different from Self. It cannot sense this . . . or this . . . or this . . . yet it is aware.*

*What would Self be like if it had first come to being in the Void, an alien otherness of inexplicable phenomena and strange radiations. Might Self have been shaped differently by different conditions, shaped, possibly, like this tiny not-Self? . . .*

*That might-have-been was a new idea, an Event worthy of careful study. . . .*

Dev felt heavy, and the thoughts churning through his mind bore the alien, strange-tasting sensations of a dream. Consciousness faded into the black. . . .

*Encountering that alien >>self<< had been more shocking, more destructive of Self's certainty of its identity and place within the universe than had been the discovery that it shared a universe with humans. That >>self<< had not been generated by Self . . . but by another Self, a revelation of intricate complexity and unexpected wonder in a once-comprehensible universe that had left Self literally dazed.*

*Another Self? One might as well speak of another Universe, for the two were, if not synonymous, then closely paired. Self bore memories within its innermost being of previous Selves grown sated and complete, distant Selves launching countless pods of Will-be-Self into the not-Rock Void at the Universe's center. There were other Selves, certainly; there must be to explain the unremembered voyage across the Void to this part of the Universe of Rock.*

*But such . . . beings were far removed indeed from Here, unreachable by any means, separated by the Void itself and by uncountable numbers of Events. Here, unheralded, was proof of the physical existence of other Selves within a reachable portion of the Universe.*

*Self had contemplated the possibility of one day meeting other Selves. It imagined that such a meeting must be inevitable, though it had never imagined that such a meeting might happen Here. In its inverted cosmology, the Universe was infinite Rock centered—though such a word could scarcely be applied to infinity—upon an immense Void of not-Rock. For a given Self, the Cycles ran ever toward completion, encompassing billions of Events; ultimately there came the final Event, when Self had reached the inner surface of the Void and undergone the Change, when clouds of Will-be-Selves were hurled into the Void on internally generated pulses of intense magnetic energy. The Will-be-Selves arced across the Void, ultimately landing on some other part of the Void's surface.*

*Self had glimpsed that surface, and the Void beyond, though the Change was still many thousands of Events in the future. Still, it had imagined itself close to the final Event . . . close enough to taste, in fact, until the Burning had seared through Being, truncating Self and cauterizing untold aspects of being and memory and experience.*

*The memory caused Self to tremble slightly. The human rocked on the yielding surface, half-submerged in the whole.*

*For Self, the Burning was inextricably linked to these . . . humans, for it had first tasted them when its >>selves<< had first emerged on the surface of the Void. Humans, or things like them, had exterminated uncounted thousands of >>selves<< sent to probe and acquire those tantalizing concentrations of alien metals* *and materials sensed as delicious disruptions of Rock's inner magnetic fields, clinging to the edge of the Void. Humans had been present on the surface of the Void until just before the Burning.*

*It was natural to assume that the humans had somehow caused the Burning.*

*Almost, Self again closed its grip on the human, intending to dissociate the thing's molecules one from the other and absorb its substance.*

*But some of the new memories stopped it, made it pause and consider.*

*The new memories were from the alien >>self<<, and they continued speaking of another Here, another Self . . . and of humans much like this one. There were other memories as well . . . of shadowy glimpses of the Void, of myriad aspects of the Universe that were neither not-Rock nor Rock, or rather, perhaps they were very special subsets of Rock, solid and unyielding, yet with a variety of structure astonishing to a mind that had marked the passage of billions of separate Events, great and little, within the black warmth of Mother Rock.*

*Probing deeper, Self studied the memories brought by the alien >>self<<. There was so much that was strange there, things perplexing, things bewildering.*

*Most of all, there was wonder, for it seemed that the Universe still held myriad surprises far beyond what was Here and comfortably familiar.*

*Dev knew the Empire as enemy. The Empire had sundered his family, ordering his father to divorce his mother in order to take a socially acceptable wife with the promotion that elevated him to an Imperial command. That command had led to disgrace, to court-martial, to suicide. Dev's mother lived still, but with psychoreconstruction she had become a stranger, withdrawn and uncommunicative. And Dev's brother . . . where was Greg now?*

*Dev had been forced to find a new family. . . .*

\*     \*     \*

*Family? What is family? Impression of a gathering of >>selves<<, but more distinct, more ... independent. Not echoes of Self, but Selves in their own right.*

*Astonishing.*

*Fight the Empire. Not for revenge, though that was motivation enough at first. But because it is wrong. Because it stifles individuality, human purpose, the God-given right to try and fail and learn and try again.*

*Because it batters down the barriers that separate men from machines.*

*Because it tries to impose one way of being, one way of thinking on cultures as diverse as North Americans and Cantonese, as Japanese and Juanyekundan, as Latino and North Hindi.*

*Because it is inefficient, creating pain as it sacrifices individuality for conformity.*

*Because the proper place for government is not inside a man's heart or head.*

*Government. Conformity. Individuality. Bizarre thoughts, alien and incomprehensible.*

*Yet Self could feel and savor the flow of thoughts with a precise clarity now. The comel the human had been wearing on its ... arm ... had been absorbed, its patterns analyzed, its purpose clear. What the comel had been designed to do, bridging the gulf between thinking beings, Self could do now.*

*But with thought itself made perfectly and mutually intelligible, how does the One communicate with another that cannot taste the same aspects of the surrounding Universe ... or if it tastes them, tastes them as differently as Rock differs from not-Rock?*

*What happens if neural stimulation is applied ... here?*

\* \* \*

Dev awoke suddenly, fully alert . . . though he couldn't immediately tell if his eyes were open for the darkness pressing in about him was absolute. He felt as though he were lying on a waterbed, though the gentle undulations beneath his back did not seem to correspond with his movements.

His back . . .

He remembered those last few moments of terror, and he remembered the distinct whiplash of pain followed by empty nothingness in his lower body as he'd felt his spine snap. A good team of somatic engineers could graft him back together again, of course . . . but there were no somatic engineers here.

Fearfully, bracing himself against the worst, he tried to wiggle his toes. . . .

. . . and felt them move!

The relief as he realized that he could still feel his legs was indescribable, a flood of warm joy that lasted until he remembered that amputees could often sense ghost limbs where their real limbs once had been. Was that what he was feeling?

Anxiously, he slid an arm down, felt his touched leg . . . and reveled in the sensation of his fingers sliding over his thigh. There was no pain, just a curiously heavy feeling on his chest as he tried to rise, as though several kilos of wet clay were lying there.

There *was* something on his chest! He could feel it there, soft beneath his fingers. What? . . .

All of his memories up to the instant when he'd fallen into the pit were accessible to him. He was in that cavern still . . . must be lying in or on the mass of the Xenophobe.

Panic rippled through his being . . . instantly suppressed. He was still alive and apparently unhurt. He could sense the close, sulfurous heat of the place but was having no trouble breathing.

And he could remember now the strangest dreams. . . .

* * *

*The complexity of Dev Cameron conscious was delightfully more intricate than the merely chemical complexity of Dev Cameron's unconscious body. The thoughts flickering through his brain were wonderfully patterned, a rush and flow and ebb of neural currents, triggered from the very top of the brain, then flashing out across the surface of the cerebral cortex, sensed as a wave of interlocking sensory imagery.*

*Self sensed . . . strangeness . . . there were multiple personalities here within the single being that called itself Dev Cameron, multiple Selves within one being, but so completely interconnected and integrated as to make it impossible to distinguish where one left off and another began. There was a Dev Cameron that was determined to fight for something it called freedom against an oppressor it called the Empire; there was another Dev Cameron, rigid and precise and logical; still another hungered for—that was the only possible translation—another human called Katya Alessandro.*

*Currents within currents, thoughts beneath thoughts. This complex being was at once One and Many.*

*Dev Cameron's upper brain was physically divided in two, with each half regulating and manipulating different types of information in different ways. Strange, too, was the fine network of incredibly pure metals that overlaid and interpenetrated various parts of the brain, and the ceramic and alloy devices implanted in head and hand and interwoven with the nervous system in a manner that was clearly derived from nanotechnology. At first, Self thought that this network was natural, but closer examination revealed that it was something added to the organism from without. Curious. Humans did not carry their own, inborn nanotechnology with them but had been forced to develop it on their own as a kind of externally applied prosthesis.*

*They'd done a fair job, on the whole. Still, some things could use improvement. If there were more connections between the left and right sides of the brain, for example . . .*

*Like this . . .*

Dev was uncomfortably aware that his thoughts were far too clear, too precise, too . . . creative. He had never felt this way, and the heady, almost dizzying sensation, as though his own mind was racing ahead at breakneck speed, was frightening at first.

And the . . . *ideas*. Sudden. Brilliant. Inspired. Was he hallucinating?

Perhaps he was insane. He'd once heard schizophrenia described as an inability to control the leap and flow of thoughts.

Yet if this was insanity, it was a pleasantly creative one. The sensation was like the exhilaration he felt when he was in full linkage, commanding the raw power of a warstrider with his body, of a high-grade AI linked to his mind. But he wasn't linked . . .

Or was he?

He was linked with . . . *something*.

Turning inward, he perceived the Naga, and in a flash of inspiration perceived just what the Naga had done to him. With the ease of imagination, but with a clarity that he knew represented reality, he saw in his mind's eye the network of connections, no more than a few molecules thick, that crisscrossed throughout his body, threading especially along his central nervous system and concentrated within his brain.

Threads of Naga-growth exploded in a fuzzy mass from his face and his chest; the heavy weight on his chest was a specially grown Naga supracell, the source of the alien growth which consisted almost entirely of nanotechnic organelles strung together as connecting fibers.

Dev was reminded forcibly of some kind of fungus, of countless branching hyphae feeding on his substance . . . but before some deep and primitive part of his awareness could react to such a horrifying thought, inspiration provided realization and complete understanding. He was part of the Naga, as the Naga was part of him.

And there was nothing to fear, for the Naga only wanted to . . . *know*.

As he did.

*A universe of wonder, seen inside out. Rock as . . . minute globules, adrift in an infinite sea of not-Rock. Radiation . . . the wavelengths growing progressively shorter from the familiar, comfortable warmth of heat and the longer, slippery questings of radio. Revelation! The electromagnetic spectrum extended far beyond the known!*

*Was it possible to sense these radiations? Humans did, apparently. Many of their memories contained far more detail than could be expected from thermal imaging. Patterning the organ to detect those radiations was relatively simple. More difficult by far was the reordering of the means of perceiving the images.*

*Vision, after all, took place not in the eyes, but in the brain.*

Dev could see.

It was not the same as seeing with his own eyes, but he knew at once what was happening. Linked to a warstrider, he often shifted to infrared viewing, and what he was seeing now was like IR imaging, ragged patterns perceived as red and yellow and green that shaped form and substance in patterns that were nearly abstract.

His sharpened mind took the patterns and enhanced them, finding sense and order. He was, as he'd deduced, in a vast, underground chamber, lying on a sea of Naga supracells that extended in every direction and up the sides of the surrounding rock walls. The specialized supracell on his chest was linked to the whole by thousands of connectors ranging in size from the diameter of Dev's little finger to threads so thin they were . . . *sensed*, somehow, but not seen.

The actual sight of that thin fuzz of tendrils growing between the supracell and his own body jarred Dev unexpectedly, even though he'd already sensed its presence with another, newer part of his mind. The reaction, sharp and involuntary, sickened . . . and he was surprised to feel that sickening rippling out through the mass of organic tissue around him.

*\*I did not intend to cause distress.*

*\*\*No problem. I . . . we . . . are not fully integrated.*

*\*Yet.*

*\*\*Yet.*

*\*The association can be terminated at any time. The changes wrought within your/my body need not be permanent. They were necessary, first, to save your/my life, second to learn about your/my functioning.*

*\*\*Understanding. Acceptance.*

Dev recognized the shock of unpleasant realization that had been triggered by the infrared image of the supracell and its extrusions into his own body. There was within most humans a queasy mistrust of organisms that fed—as parasites or as saprophytes—on other organisms. Bacteria. Fungi and molds. Parasitic worms and insects.

But when the relationship between two species was mutually beneficial, it was true symbiosis.

Symbiosis, Dev realized with an unaccustomed burst of mental clarity, was the natural way of most organisms with which he was familiar. The mitochondria within his body's cells had begun eons ago as viral or bacterial symbionts within larger cell hosts and had become so completely integrated into the system that they were now cellular organelles vital to the cell's conversion of food to energy. On a far larger and more distinct scale were the bacteria within the human gut, without which humans would be unable to digest their food. . . .

What Dev was experiencing now was a symbiosis less complete than the one, more complete than the other, and differing from both in the fact that both the participants could voluntarily dissociate from one another . . . and in that dissociation would not cause their deaths.

And the possibilities of this new association were intriguing. Dev could already perceive how greatly his senses had been extended simply by increasing the efficiency of certain interacting portions of his cerebral cortex; sight, hearing, smell, taste, feeling all were dramatically heightened . . . and they were controllable, to the point that too much input could be dialed down as easily as the texture or intensity of a ViRdrama could be adjusted for the linker's comfort. And there were other senses, as well. He could *feel* radio now, in the pulse and tingle of long wavelengths issuing from the creature around him, as easily as he could feel its heat, and both wavelengths carried far more information to him than the simple sensation of temperature had borne before. His hearing was incredibly sharp; the sounds of supracells gliding over one another on a rock wall some twenty meters away were instantly pinpointed, immediately identified . . . and they brought with them a crude picture of their cause. He could shut his eyes and image his surroundings—softer and with less clarity than through his eyes—through his ears.

Was this, Dev wondered, what a dolphin "saw" with its natural sonar in Earth's ocean depths?

And the new connections between the two sides of his brain offered undreamed of potential. His intelligence, he was sure, had expanded to the point where a direct correlation with his former cognitive abilities was meaningless. He could process information faster and more efficiently; his memory worked as accurately as his implanted RAM but on a far vaster, more complete, and more accessible level; and his spontaneous creativity—

his ability to gain insights, intuition, hunches drawn from scanty or incomplete data—had grown to the point where it was almost a new sense in its own right.

The Naga supracell appeared to be dwindling. Actually, it was sinking, molecule by molecule, through the pores in his bodysuit and his skin, its mass rapidly trickling into the network of fine threads already growing throughout his body, or to pools of Naga-cellular material forming within empty spaces in abdomen and chest. The fuzz of molecular connections between himself and the Naga proper grew thicker.

Dev flexed his awareness, reaching out, savoring input from his own senses . . . and from those eldritch senses of his symbiont companion. He could sense, somehow, the entirety of the Naga, huge within its vast network of underground chambers, could read its history, could receive impressions from as far away as . . .

Then Dev drew back, shuddering, suddenly afraid. Even a super genius, it seemed, could be a bit slow to perceive the obvious.

Not until this moment had he realized that he was no longer at all even remotely human.

# Chapter 26

*What does it mean to be human? A particular genotype to be sure . . . but beyond outward form is there some abiding characteristic of thought or being that distinguishes what is human from what is not? Genies possess much within their genotype that is undeniably human; most possess ninety-nine percent or more of the original human genome, yet they are legally barred from a human's rights of property and self-government. Artificial intelligences possess nothing of the human genome, yet possess—some prefer the word "mimic"—certain human modes and processes of thought.*

*And a human possessing cephlink implants, with inwardly grown and artificial memory storage, with direct mental access to computer networks and AI control systems, with senses and a clarity of senses unknown to his ancestors . . . is*

*he less human than the naked child drawn
squalling and new from its mother's womb?*

—*Man and His Works*
Karl Gunther Fielding
C.E. 2488

"Here they come!"

Aerospace interceptors, sleek Se-280 Soratakas stooped out of the gold-blue sky. Missiles drew white, thread-thin scratches across the heavens before impacting in savage, earth-shaking detonations.

Katya pivoted her Ghostrider, tracking incoming targets. "Targeting!" she cried as red cursors locked on to one plunging Se-280, pinning it against the background of her awareness. The cursors flashed: target lock. Fire!

Laser energy dazzled as it reflected from the root of a wing . . . then flashed brilliantly as metallic vapor exploded outward. Slush hydrogen boiled into air . . . then ignited catastrophically. Fragments of metal and alloy composite rained down through the sky, trailing smoke, and a thunderclap rolled across the Heraklean valley.

"Good shot, Katya!" Vic Hagan called over the tactical link. "Now move it! There are too many of the bastards!"

"On my way!"

The assault pods were already touching down on the slopes of Mount Athos. The base at Morgan's Hold had been turned into a red-hot scar smoldering beneath a pillar of black smoke staining the afternoon sky. Everyone at the base had escaped, barely, by piling into every vehicle that could move. The convoy was heading north, now, a ragged line of magflitters and four-legged transport walkers, guarded to sides and rear by twenty of the warstriders that Dev had taken with him to Athena.

Those striders were all the rebels had to protect themselves with now. The fleet was already scattering as the

Imperial squadron moved into orbit. Two rebel ships had been destroyed before all radio communications had been lost in a firestorm of Imperial broad-spectrum jamming. Many of the Confederation government people were almost certainly still in the sky-el, trapped until a ship could be dispatched to rescue them.

There were no ships coming.

On the ground, the convoy had been attempting to reach the shelter of the air generation plant. They'd been only halfway there when the first Imperial interceptors had appeared overhead. A running battle had developed, the warstriders pausing only long enough to target and fire before continuing their northward trek. The rugged plain between Mount Athos and the generator plant was already littered with the funeral pyres of crashed and burning ascraft, which were not as robust as a typical warstrider and tended to disintegrate easily when tagged. Still, there were so many ascraft now, launched from the orbiting *Donryu*, that numbers were beginning to tell. Two warstriders had already been lost to laser and missile fire from the sky, and three more badly damaged.

"I've got one incoming at three-one-one," Sublieutenant Lanager called over the Ghostrider's ICS. "Elevation one-two. He's tracking on us."

"Got him, Tomid. Target lock! Fire!"

Laser light flared; the Se-280 wobbled, then pulled up, a thin streamer of smoke trailing from its port engine. The interceptors were harassing the column, trying to slow it enough so that the assault striders could sweep in and finish them off.

"General Sinclair!" Katya called over the tactical laser frequency. Sinclair was up ahead somewhere, riding in one of three KC-212 cargo transporters, four-legged, eighty-ton monsters more commonly called Rhinos. "General Sinclair, do you copy?"

"I'm here, Katya. Go ahead."

"General, I think the only way out of this is for me to take half of the warstriders and make a stand here.

The rest of the striders will escort you VIPs to the generator."

"Now see here, Colonel," General Smith cut in. "You're not in command here. . . ."

"I'm in command of the tactical element," she replied. "And you people aren't going to make it to the generator unless we manage to slow up the pursuit. Besides, we should take some of the heat from those interceptors off of the rest of you."

There was a long, heavy silence. "Colonel, I don't really see any alternative. However, I want you to delegate the authority. We need you now, more than ever."

To communicate with the Heraklean Naga, now that Dev was . . .

"Sorry, General. Can't do it." She'd already abandoned too many friends, too many comrades, for the sake of following orders.

"Colonel, that is not a request. That is an order. We cannot afford to lose you, our only expert on communication with the Naga."

"Katya, listen to him!" That was Vic Hagan. "Let me take the defense!"

"You stick with the transports, Vic. Get them to the generator."

"But—"

"THAT'S A GOKING ORDER!"

"Colonel, we can't let you do this . . ." That was Smith again.

"And you, General, will have a goking hard time stopping me!" Abruptly, she swung out of the line of march. "Yo! I need nine volunteers to kick some Imperial ass!"

"Here!"

"You got me!"

"Affirmative!"

"I'm with you, Katya!"

As the acknowledgments rolled in, Katya switched to ICS to speak with the young man slotted with her in the Ghostrider. "You can take off, if you want, Tomid. If you quick-step it, you can snag a ride on one of the magflitters. I was volunteering me, not you. I can handle this lummox on my own."

"That's a negative, Colonel," Lanager replied. "You think I could live with myself, leaving you slotted in here alone?"

Katya could find no answer for that. "Okay, Tomid. Thanks. But it's going to be a damned bumpy ride."

"That's why I came along, Colonel. Watch it! Incoming at two-five-niner, elevation one-five!"

An explosion hurled clumps of earth skyward, shaking the ground.

"Targeting! *Fire!*"

**\*\*I am afraid.*
*\*Why?*
**\*\*I am not . . .*
*\* . . . what I was.*
**\*\*I am no longer human.*
*\*I am no longer Self.*
*Loneliness . . . and curiosity. What am/are/I/we?*
**\*\*Let's go to the surface of the Void.*
*\*Why?*
**\*\*To . . . perceive. I sense vibrations there. Shocks transmitted . . .*
*\* . . . through the Rock. I sense . . .*
**\*\* . . . Events.*
*\* . . . Agreement. And the taste . . .*
**\*\* . . . of pure metals and churning . . .*
*\* . . . magnetic fields.*
**\*\*I feel them.*
*\*Curiosity. But the surface of the Void is a horrible, alien place, a gulf of not-Rock vaster and emptier than anything imaginable.*
**\*\*The surface of the Void is where I belong. Where humans belong. And the Empire has come. Do you sense their ships, beacons of mass and magnetism and flowing power suspended in the Void?*

*\*I/we sense them. But you/we are no ...*
*\*\*... longer human. Agreement. Sadness ... loss and loneliness. I need ...*
*\*... want ...*
*\*\*... to sense ...*
*\*... the surface ...*
*\*\*... Katya ...*
*\*\*... directly. Agreement. We go ...*
*\*\*How?*
*\*So. ...*

*Chujo* Kawashima's body was ensconced within his link slot aboard the *Donryu*, orbiting Herakles at synchorbit, thirty-two thousand kilometers up. His mind, however, was soaring with one of the Se-280s, linked to the aerospace craft's AI and primary sensor suite. The linkage gave him an excellent view of the overall landing area, and of the skirmish harrying the fleeing rebels on the ground.

The Sorataka banked left, wind shrieking as it was cleaved by the ascraft's stubby wings. "We have them running, *Chujosan*," the ascraft's pilot told him.

"Indeed. Order your squadron to press the attack. It looks as though they are deploying half of their warstriders along that ridge in order to give the others time to escape."

"Affirmative. Shall we attack the line, or the large transports?"

Kawashima considered. "The transports. If we can slow them before they reach the generator facility, we can trap them all. We will smash the defenders on the ridge from orbit, then move in with the assault striders."

"*Hai, Chujosan!* Downloading your command now. ..."

Dev emerged from an opening halfway up the side of the artificial mountain of the atmosphere generator.

Unlike the pyramids of ancient Egypt, this mountain's sides had not been covered with smooth, sloping sides, nor did they exhibit the stacked block architecture of the pyramids as they existed today. Instead, the surface was an open latticework of extruded iron and fabricrete plates and bars interlocking in a complex, three-dimensional array, providing support for the mountain's inner workings, and easy passage for the gases going in and out.

The wind on that slope of crisscrossing girders was stiff, but Dev scarcely noticed it. The Naga had encased him in a bulky but sleekly serpentine form as it had borne him up through the tunnel, but so complete was the linkage of natural and artificial senses that Dev did not feel as though he was in a Xenophobe snake; he *was* the snake, a coiling black sinuosity that issued from one of the mountain's numberless black passageways, emerging into the open air accompanied by an exploding cloud of nano. He savored the sheer power of his connection with the immense and far-flung brain.

No longer in direct physical touch with the Naga's supracells, the steady give-and-take of data continued through a newly forged radio link. Building the transmitters and receivers had been the work of a second or two, as nanotechnic fragments arranged themselves according to patterns provided by the absorbed but carefully recorded hull of Dev's warstrider.

As he emerged, radio noise assaulted him, a shrill keening of ear-rending harmonics and hissing white noise. Dev recognized the signal for what it was—Imperial jamming—and decreed a quieter atmosphere at radio wavelengths. The blast of radio noise generated within the vast and chthonic bulk of the Naga and directed with pinpoint accuracy toward each of the airborne transmitters blew circuits and burned out power couplings, then crackled along insufficiently shielded electronic circuits like the EMP from a nuclear detonation.

* * *

Kawashima was momentarily adrift in darkness. Then his vision cleared, and he was back within the virtual reality of *Donryu*'s combat coordination center. What had happened? His laser link with the interceptor squadron commander had been broken off abruptly.

It took a swift download from damage assessment to determine that a powerful electromagnetic pulse had, indeed, burned out perhaps sixty percent of all air-to-air and air-to-space communications. What was peculiar was the intense and highly directional nature of the pulse, aimed at individual aircraft, rather than broadcast over a large area.

What kind of new weapon did the rebels have down there?

No matter. Soon there would be nothing left on the surface of Herakles but his own troops and scattered, broken groups of rebels begging for permission to surrender.

"Weapons!" he barked. "Stand by to receive coordinates for surface bombardment!"

"What the hell is going on?" Katya had heard the blast of radio noise, and her sensors had detected the immense surge of an EMP . . . but one so tightly focused that its effects had barely brushed across her machine, or the other warstriders waiting on the ridge.

One Sorataka spun helplessly out of control and slammed into the ground. Others seemed to stumble in midair, struggled for a moment to regain control, then began pulling back. Clearly, they'd been caught by surprise . . . but by what?

Explosions jabbed and flashed across the ridgeline. The Imperial warstriders were moving up the ridge fast, at least thirty combat machines coming at a dead run and, a kilometer to the rear, a line of four-legged armored personnel walkers, each carrying a platoon of marine infantry. The Imperials were launching an all-out assault, striders and ground troops together.

Laser energy flared off Katya's hull and she dropped her machine into a partial crouch, returning fire. No time to think about mysterious radio bursts now. The rebel line of warstriders began firing, a ragged volley of laser and missile fire that slashed into the advancing Imperials.

The being that had once been Dev Cameron reared higher on its mountain ledge, scanning sky and horizon with a complex amalgam of senses—human sight and hearing, combined with eighteen external Naga senses ranging from the perception of magnetic fields to the rippling feel of flowing electrons to the dimly sensed mass of bulky objects bending space. He was sundered completely now from the main Naga body; the special supracell had enfolded itself totally into his body, and the molecular fuzz connecting him with the other supracells, the "whole," had dissipated. Within the shimmering black-to-silver-to-black again snake shape of his traveler, he looked completely human.

But the mind behind steel gray eyes was not. All that Dev Cameron had been was now a tiny part of what was there, perceiving, remembering, calculating, sensing, and above all *thinking* with a fiercely precise rationality that excluded sentiment and emotion. All that remained of emotion now was the shuddering thrill of power. Without even knowing his limits, without knowing if he even *had* limits, Dev knew now that he held powers literally godlike in scope. Through a broad-band radio receptor now embedded within his skull, he could hear the flood of voices over working radio circuits, could hear all of the separate channels at once, could separate each in his mind and understand what it was saying.

*More . . .*

Effortlessly, he reached out, following a particular thread of radio communication. In an instant, he was within an Imperial warstrider, an assault force Tachi, as it paced relentlessly after the fleeing rebel column. Dev perceived a strange kind of virtual reality, a narrow space that was not space centered within the Tachi's circuitry. He could sense the brooding presence of the strider's AI there, and the larger, slower, but more adaptive mind of the Tachi's human pilot.

Reprogramming the Tachi's onboard computer was simplicity itself. Change *here* ... and *here* ... push *there* ... Within two seconds, Dev's awareness had flicked to a second Tachi, as the pilot of the first tried frantically to restore power to weapons systems, power to the controls, power to any operations system until even his link net went down and he was left stranded and awake in the dark enclosure of his slot.

One after another, across the battlefield, the Tachis began to fail.

"Katya!" Vic called. "What the hell is going on?"

"I wish I knew, Vic. Something's taking them down ..."

"Yeah, but what?"

"I've got some odd scatter off some of the high-band radio," Torolf Bondevik put in. "Looks like high-speed data transmissions, but I can't read any of it."

"I see it. Damn! It almost looks ..."

"Looks like what, Katya?"

"A standard transmission algorithm, same as we use. But it's been speeded up ... looks like a download at something like ten to the fifth times normal speed."

"Impossible!"

"That's what I was about to say."

"We have the ridge targeted, *Chujosan*. Targeting something as small as individual warstriders at this range is impossible, but we should be able to destroy most or all with an area burst."

"Excellent. You may fire."

"*Hai, Chujosan!* Firing now. . . ."

A thunderclap assaulted Katya's ears, accompanied by the brightest, greenest light that she had ever seen. She was falling . . . falling . . . and then her Ghostrider struck the ground with a grinding crash. Her control circuits were gone . . . as was her link. She was awake, locked inside the padded confines of her slot.

She slapped the intercom 'face. "Tomid! Tom, can you hear me?"

No answer. She had to get out . . . and fast. She imagined that she smelled smoke. Pressing the hatch release bar, she gasped relief as the hatch blew clear, admitting a flood of golden light. Outside, the entire ridge had been transformed. Moments ago, it had been sere and rocky; now it was all flame-blackened dirt and loose rubble, all of it smoldering beneath a towering cloud of roiling smoke.

Dazed, she clambered from her strider, which was lying on its side, one leg gone, the other twisted back at a crazy angle. The hull had been scorch-blasted clean of nanoflage, and most of the exterior sensors and antennae had been stripped away. Either she'd just lived through a nuclear burst at close range . . . no. Holding up her left palm and moving her hand about, she could detect no radiation. The ridge must have been targeted for a high-wattage laser burst from space. Elsewhere, others of the warstriders on the ridge lay in junkheap piles. One was burning, half the hull melted away. Oh, God in heaven . . . that was Torolf's Scoutstrider. . . .

Tomid Lanager kicked out his own hatch cover and climbed out onto the smoking ground. The air was thick with the sharp stench of burnt plastic and lubricants.

"*Kuso,* Colonel . . ."

"Orbital lasers," she said. Suddenly, all the strength went from her body and she dropped to her knees. The ground through her skinsuit was still uncomfortably warm. "We never had a goking chance. . . ."

Many of the Tachi warstriders had been halted in their tracks, but others were swarming up onto the ridge now, closely followed by the lumbering, four-legged APWs. Imperial troops in black armor dashed down open ramps, gesturing with laser rifles. One rebel trooper brandished a handgun and was instantly cut down by an arc-brilliant flash from a plasma gun. The stink of burnt meat mingled with the odors of smoke and oil.

A pair of Imperial Marines advanced on Katya, lasers raised. Slowly, she raised her hands, palms out. There was nothing left in her for heroics.

"Up!" one snapped in harshly accented Inglic. "Both of you, hands up high!"

"Do as he says, Tomid."

"But Colonel—"

"Do it, damn it! I don't want you dead too!"

The marines gestured again. Grimly, Katya raised her hands.

# Chapter 27

*Throughout the length and depth of recorded history, Man worshipped a god created in his image. With genetic engineering, with implanted cephlink technology, with antisenescence drugs, meteffectors, and somatechnic reconstruction, with AIs and nanotechnology, Man at last began to remake his own image into that of God.*

> —*The Rise of Technic Man*
> Fujiwara Naramoro
> C.E. 2535

Not even godlike powers, evidently, could ensure success in battle where chance and coincidence and the randomness of chaos ruled supreme. As Dev had been shutting down the Imperial warstriders one by one, *Donryu* and two of her consorts at synchorbit had opened fire with their primary laser batteries. The flash and its accompanying thunderclap had stunned Dev momentarily, leaving him blind and dazed. As vision returned, he could see that the ridge where the ten rebel warstriders had stopped to make their stand had been gashed open and burned, the rebel striders scattered about in small and broken heaps.

Though kilometers away, he could enhance his vision, his brain filling in details lost to distance. Surviving striderjacks were climbing out of their disabled machines, as Imperial troops swept in to disarm them and take them captive. Most of the Imperial Tachis had moved off the ridge and were advancing again toward the fleeing rebel convoy.

*Kuso!* He could continue disabling the Tachis, but the Imperial ships were still parked in orbit thirty-two thousand kilometers overhead . . . and on the ridge, the marines had moved in and were stripping and searching the prisoners. Damn it, Katya could be one of those prisoners down there, and he could do nothing, *nothing!*

He couldn't touch the marines. Helpless, he watched, struggling to make his newly creative and intuitive brain come up with something. Perhaps . . .

The only ploy he could think of now was to hit the ships in orbit. Could he disable a starship the same way he'd knocked out the Imperial assault striders? It ought to be possible, if he could find a communications frequency and patch himself in. Vast power remained in reserve within the body of the Naga, which filled much of the generator mountain beneath his feet now, and extended far off beneath the crust and around the curve of the planet.

He reached out . . . searching for linkage with one of the Imperial vessels. . . .

Aboard *Mogami*, one of four Kako-class cruisers, computer systems began shutting down by themselves, one by one in rapid succession. The ship's AI began to describe what was happening . . . a virus program of some sort had insinuated itself into *Mogami*'s link network by piggybacking its way aboard on a communications carrier channel . . . and then the AI switched itself off, an electronic suicide.

*Taisa* Hijiri Ushiba was just groping his way up out of the embrace of his linkage slot after being unceremoniously booted off the link network when a bridge alarm began to shrill.

"*Taisasan!*" His second-in-command was floundering in midair, panic distorting his features. "*Taisasan!* The power tap!"

"I hear it, damn it!"

But how to respond with the computers shut down? Cold sweat broke out on Ushiba's face, spinning away in tiny, weightless, silver spheres as he shook his head. The alarm was the cascade alert, an indicator that the singularities were being called into existence within the ship's power tap chambers.

If *Mogami*'s computers were off-line, there was no way to tune the harmonic frequency of those spinning singularities. The micro black holes would go out of control. . . .

He had to reestablish control over the ship's primary power system. Thrusting himself back into the link couch, he brought his palm down on the interface. Possibly there was still a partial network. If he could access the right codes . . .

There! He was in! He sensed his chief engineering officer next to him within the virtual reality of the ship's network. In front of him, a computer graphic representing the otherworldly strangeness deep within the ship's power core glowed with ghostly light. Two dazzling pinpoints of stark and scintillating radiance circled one another so quickly that their image dissolved into a white ring of sparkling light. Energy, the heat and hard radiation of the core of a star was already starting to flood through the gap. . . .

"Can you scram the power tap, Engineer?"

"I'm trying, damn it, I'm trying! I don't even understand how it came—"

*"WATCH OUT!"*

Through his linkage, Ushiba saw the singularity pair going unstable. The image had been slowed somewhat to enable the human eye to perceive it, and therefore lagged behind reality. He never saw the final collapse, as one singularity evaporated in a blinding flash of raw energy.

The second micro black hole, slingshotted forward when its partner had vanished, tunneled through energy receptors and superconducting coils, through magnetic screens and plasma containment fields, through lead and iridium and polyceramic insulator shielding, a fast-moving, fiercely radiating pinpoint.

Traveling like a bullet, the singularity enthusiastically puckered the very shape of space around it as it plowed through electronic circuitry and bulkheads, air and human beings, steadily gaining mass as it devoured the heart of the *Mogami*. Hard radiation, gamma and X rays, flooded the inhabited portion of the ship as matter crowded down that hungry, molecule-sized gullet and vanished. It didn't have sufficient mass to swallow the entire ship, but between its radiation output and the gravitational tides wreaking havoc with her support struts and hull, the cruiser was doomed.

*Mogami*, her hull structure stressed far beyond her engineering specs, shrieked. . . .

*"Chujosan!"*

"I see it," Kawashima snapped back. "Order all ships to shut down communications instantly!"

"But—"

"Do it, then kill *Donryu*'s communications! They're infecting our AI programming!"

*"Hai, Chujosan!"*

*Mogami*, a six-hundred-meter-long, black-hulled cigar of duralloy armor and advanced nanotechnics, was *crumpling* before his virtual eyes, victim of a terrible engineering failure. An instant later, the rogue singularity emerged near the bow, a dazzling point of light hurtling out of orbit and into space.

Then the microsingularity evaporated in a burst of gamma rays and ultraviolet and visible light, a silent, dazzling explosion that washed across the hulls of every ship in the squadron, starkly illuminating them as though in the glare of an exploding sun.

"They're getting at our computers through the communications links, somehow," Kawashima said, more to himself than to his bewildered staff officers. "Helm! Power up! Take us out of orbit!"

They had to put some distance between this new rebel weapon and the squadron.

"*Chujosan!*" Eto, his chief of staff, called. "You're leaving the rest of the squadron?"

"When they see us leaving orbit, they will follow," Kawashima replied coldly. "If they do not, they will die."

"And our people on the ground?" The commanding officer of *Donryu*'s marine contingent was furious. "*Chujo!* You are abandoning them!"

"They'll have to look out for themselves," Kawashima said coldly. "Until we figure out a way to counter this . . . *thing.*"

"Engineering! Give us full thrust!"

"*Hai, Chujosan!*"

Dev could no longer reach the Imperial warships in synchorbit. *Mogami*'s destruction had left him triumphantly exultant at the length of his reach . . . and frustrated at having that reach cut short. The Nihonjin squadron commander had guessed too soon how Dev had been affecting his ship's computers and shut down all radio and laser-borne communication. True, he was now cut off from his forces on the ground, and his ships were cut off from one another, a mob rather than a fleet . . . but Dev had felt those ships right *here*, within the closing of his hand, to be crushed out of existence.

Reprogramming was too slow, and vulnerable to a simple closing of a physical circuit. There had to be another way . . . and fast! Fast! Turning his enhanced gaze skyward, he could see *Donryu* already accelerating out of orbit, big, slow and clumsy, balanced on a silent flare of star-hot plasma.

Think! If you've suddenly grown so creative . . . *think*!

Momentarily, he turned his gaze inward. The vast bulk of the Naga was spilling from the mountain like cold, black lava, emerging at last from the secret privacy of its hidden caverns. It drank in the sunlight. Crude, newly shaped eyeballs rippled and swelled and opened along its surface, surveying surroundings cold and alien.

Seeing was joy, a new Event.

*I/we see . . .

**You/we can generate powerful magnetic fields.

*Yes. For movement, for . . .

**. . . navigation, for . . .

*. . . for launching the Will-be-Selves into . . .

**. . . the Void, yes. That is what we will do.

*The Will-be-Selves are not . . .

**. . . ready, of course. I have other missiles.

*What?

**These. . . .

*Rock . . .

Kawashima turned his full attention to the virtual image of the planet, hanging now like a great blue-and-gold sphere astern of *Donryu*'s plasma flare. As that flare grew hotter, its radiation might well sweep across that part of the surface on the equator where rebels and Imperial Marines still struggled.

So long as the weapon that had reached out and crushed *Mogami* was destroyed as well, it didn't really matter. He would have liked to have taken Sinclair and the other Confederation leaders captive back to Earth, but the rebellion would be satisfactorily resolved if the leaders were killed, their fleet broken and scattered.

Something very strange was happening to the Heraklean surface.

The atmosphere just north of the Augean Peninsula had taken on a peculiar quality, glowing with an auroral light, sweeping around and around in a vortex of clouds that throbbed and pulsed with yellow lightnings.

*Buddha and all my ancestors . . . what is happening there?*

Lightning flared below, silent and vast. . . .

Katya was hurled to the ground by the shock wave, which left her gasping, her breath sucked from her lungs. God . . . what had she just seen? Shaking her head, trying to clear it, she looked up as the wind whipped and shrieked across her back.

Every man and woman on that ridgetop was down, Confederation prisoners and Imperial captors alike. There were no soldiers or prisoners any longer, only people struggling to survive in a wind gone mad. Beyond, kilometers beyond the ridgetop, the triangular shape of the atmosphere generator was wreathed in flickering, violet lightnings, as overhead, black clouds swirled about in a vast, dynamic whirlpool, the storm's eye centered above the apex of the pyramid.

The air crawled, against her skin, and her hair stood on end. The storm—such understatement in a word!—was causing frightful charges to build up in the atmosphere. Another flash of lightning, searingly brilliant, and she blinked hard against the green-and-purple afterimage. She *must* have imagined that; an instant before she'd gone blind, she'd thought she'd seen something peeling off the side of the mountain, then streaking skyward so fast that nothing could be seen but a bright, dazzlingly blue bolt of light.

Moments later, the sonic boom hit, but Katya never heard it.

She was already deaf as well as blind.

"Collision alert!"

"Point defense!"

"Too late!" *Donryu*'s weapons officer sounded as though he was about to lose all control. "Damn it, too *late!*"

"Point defense on automatic!" Kawashima snapped. "Analysis! What *was* that thing?"

"A rock, *Chujosan*," *Donryu*'s captain replied.

"Nonsense!" the Exec protested. "You don't throw rocks from the *bottom* of a gravity well!"

Kawashima was already replaying the image in his ViRsimulation, slowing down the speed by a factor of nearly a thousand. Gonichi Obayashi was right. It *had* been a rock . . . or, at least, a large mass of partly molten iron, scooped off the surface of the planet somehow and hurled into space. Its brief passage through atmosphere had heated it white-hot; its velocity as it passed *Donryu*, missing by a scant thousand kilometers, had been nearly one-tenth the speed of light.

Modern military literature contained many references to an old, old idea. In any war where one side controlled the high ground of space, bombardment of planet-bound forces became simplicity itself, so long as you didn't mind running the risk of altering the planet's climate. All you needed were a few small asteroids nudged into proper intercept orbits, or just a mass of nickel-iron large enough to survive the fiery plummet through atmosphere. A fair-sized asteroid had changed the face and the climate of Earth some sixty-five million years ago and driven the dinosaurs to extinction. Even a small asteroid dropped from orbit could annihilate a city.

But the advantage was supposed to be with the force in orbit. A planet was a damn poor place to throw rocks from ... about like standing at the bottom of a deep, dry well and chucking rocks at somebody looking down from above. The chucker was more likely to get one of his own missiles back in his face than he was to hit the target.

But the rebels had somehow found a way of accelerating several tons of iron to a velocity of thirty-thousand kilometers per second. There'd been no time to dodge, no time to do anything but automatically record the missile's passage.

*And, oh gods of my fathers, it's happening again! ...*

The lightnings gathered. The storm winds howled. Dev looked skyward, sharing his symbiont's newfound vision sense, relying on infrared and mass sense as the clouds swirled in.

\*\*You/we almost had him that time. You/we ...

\*... must adjust my/our aiming point to allow for ...

\*\*... the target's movement, exactly.

\*Ready.

\*\*Now!

A one-ton chunk of iron and fabricrete, part of the support structure of the man-made mountain itself, tore free as powerful magnetic fields focused along its length and pulled, accelerating it in the wink of an eye. Lightning forked overhead; with a thunderclap of raw sound, the jagged missile vanished in a bar of blue-white radiance.

Kawashima saw the second launch but had no time to analyze it, no time even to shout warning. Nine-tenths of a second after it left the planet's surface, the block of half-molten slag slammed into the heavy cruiser *Zintu*, in orbit some five thousand kilometers away. Traveling at thirty-thousand kilometers per second, the projectile was moving too fast for the staid, low-velocity Newtonian mechanics of $E=1/2mv^2$. The kinetic energy released on impact could only be calculated by the more familiar $E=mc^2$, an equation that yielded roughly $10^{19}$ joules.

Such numbers are meaningless; say, rather, that one thousand twenty-megaton nuclear warheads were detonated simultaneously. *Zintu* did not crumple or glow or burn. She was simply *gone* . . . and in her place stood a small and short-lived sun. Briefly, the Imperial fleet was bathed in the actinic glare that touched and dissolved those vessels nearest the ill-fated cruiser.

"We must get away!" Kawashima screamed into the link. "Engage the power tap!"

"*Chujosan!* No!" The ship's captain was so shocked he didn't even realize the magnitude of his rudeness. "This close to the planet—"

"Do it! Now!"

"It will take a few moments to run the Noguchi Equations. . . ."

Lightnings flashed across the planet's surface. Half a million kilometers away, the destroyer *Urakaze* exploded in a sudden gout of light, silent as death.

The next missile struck *Donryu*, driving right up her stern long before equations could be run or the microsingularities of her K-T drive summoned into existence. The discharge of $10^{19}$ joules of kinetic energy transformed the kilometer-long ship into star-hot plasma in an instant. . . .

*Again!*

Lightning flashed, the missile seared into the zenith. In Dev's own, inner eye, he towered above the planet's surface, riding astride the winds, hurling lightnings, directing the storm against the scattering invaders in the sky.

And they *were* scattering, fleeing into the depths of space. Dev focused his newfound power and hurled another missile through the protesting, cloven sky. Thunder cracked and rumbled, as the first rains began lashing out of the clouds. In space, another ship, a light cruiser, vanished, the sheer, raw energy of impact vaporizing her. He selected another target and fired. The mountain trembled with the launch. There were six enemy ships left . . . now four. . . .

*Is this what you/we call war?*

And then, the towering, larger-than-life feeling vanished. *My God, what am I doing? What have I become?*

**No. This is not war. It's slaughter. Useless slaughter.*

The magnetic charge he'd been focusing for yet another shot into a fleeing Imperial warship dissipated, unneeded. In space far above Herakles's equator, a cruiser caught at the fringe of a blast spun brokenly end over end, its control systems smashed by a glancing blow. The four surviving warships, under full thrust now, fled, seeking safety in the empty depths of space.

No more rocks pursued them.

# Chapter 28

*Reality . . . virtual reality. The two echo one another, mutually complementary, mutually supporting. Yet in the end it must be reality that lays the greater claim to our souls, for it is in our link with the universe as it is that we find the heart-quickening joy-flavor-terror-wonder that tells us we truly live.*

—*Intellectus*
Juan Delacruz
C.E. 2216

Katya rose from the ground as the mysterious storm wind died away. Sight and hearing had returned, though spots still danced before her eyes. Clouds still swirled across heaven, bringing with them sheets of rain, but the spectacular lightning storm was ended. She stood there, feeling the rain pelt her body and she felt . . . alive.

The rain lightened as quickly as it had come,

dissolving to mist sprinkling the steaming ground. An Imperial trooper in full armor stumbled toward her, weaponless, his helmet gone, his eyes wide with terror. She stepped into him with a slashing elbow thrust, snapping his head back and sending him to the ground.

A laser pistol rested in the holster at his hip. Drawing the gun, she advanced across the torn and scorched ground. Two more Imperials approached, saw her, and ran the other way. She let them run. The enemy was harmless now, demoralized by what had happened.

What had happened? She still wasn't sure. Other soldiers gathered in small and fearfully huddled groups atop the ridge. Katya noticed that some groups included both Confederation and Imperial troops. The events of the past few moments appeared to have obliterated those differences that had once divided them.

She was reminded of genie and human, singing together in the barracks at Stone Mountain.

A warstrider loomed against the smoky sky. It was a Ghostrider, and it bore on its prow the name *Victor*.

It was Vic Hagan's machine.

"Katya?"

"Vic!" She nearly fell into his arms as he dropped off the rungs set into the Ghostrider's leg.

"God, Katya! What happened here?"

She turned and stared up at the mountain of the atmosphere generator. It was silent now, still wreathed in clouds, but no longer spitting lightning. Parts of its regular surface looked uneven now, where huge chunks had been torn away.

"I'm not sure, Vic," she said. "But I'm hard-jacked certain that the Heraklean Naga had something to do with it, and if I'm right about that, then I'll bet Dev had something to do with it too."

"You mean . . . he's alive?"

"I think we'd better grab a magflitter and go find out."

"Where?"

She looked toward the atmosphere generator, wreathed now in muttering purple clouds. "There. Up there on the mountain."

Dev was deeply shaken. Arguing from a strictly military viewpoint, he decided that perhaps he should have tried to destroy all of the Imperial ships. He'd certainly been trying to do just that . . . and he could have succeeded had he tried.

On the other hand, he'd all but annihilated the Imperial squadron, destroying fifteen of the nineteen enemy ships. The survivors would return to Earth and other Imperial bases, bearing the story of a frightful, inexplicable, irresistible Confederation weapon, of white fire and destruction against which there was no possible defense.

For as long as this war continued, the Imperials would remember Herakles and wonder what weapon it was that the Confederation had used there. Hell, it was just possible, if there were any among their leaders who had a modicum of sense, that the bloody nose they'd received here this day would lead them to grant the Confederation independence without any further fighting.

Dev hoped so.

With a thought, he dissolved the side of the Naga traveler that had sheltered him through that artificial storm. The air was steaming wet, and still tasted of ozone and summer lightning. Stepping out onto the side of the mountain, he wavered a moment, then dropped to hands and knees. He felt so . . . weak. . . .

\*\**I/we must part company now.*

\**Why? Your enemy is crushed! And I/we have a new Universe to explore!*

\*\**I/we . . . I don't want to be a god. I can't be a god.*

\**What is a god?*

Dev couldn't answer. He was lying on his side now, unable to move. He didn't remember falling. Rain drizzled from a leaden sky.

*\*\*Please. Leave me.*

*\*Agreement/disappointment/sadness. It was good not to be lonely.*

*\*\*You won't be lonely. We'll still . . . talk. And I'll introduce you to others. But I don't think I can manage having you inside me like this. Not all the time.*

*\*Was there discomfort? Damage?*

*\*\*No. Temptation.*

*\*What is temptation? I don't understand.*

*\*\*Never mind. Can you leave me . . . as I was? Uh, you don't need to break the back again.*

*\*I would never do such a thing! You are Self!*

*\*\*I am . . . I want to be human.*

*\*You . . . love . . .*

*\*\* . . . Katya, yes.*

*\*Katya . . . loves you too. She told >>self<<. I do not . . .*

*\*\* . . . understand . . . no. But it is good . . .*

*\* . . . not to be lonely.*

A feeling like a ripple of warm silk passed along his chest. Dev opened his eyes, but the sight of the Naga supracell spilling out of his chest along thousands of hair-thin tendrils, slowly growing larger as it retreated from his body, was disconcerting. He kept his eyes closed until he felt his perceptions dwindling, felt the radio link with the Naga snap.

When he opened his eyes again, he was alone on the ledge.

When he tried turning his awareness inward, he found . . . nothing. Nothing! He could no longer examine himself internally. His entire being felt . . . *smaller*, and sharply limited. Only five senses!

Could he possibly go back to what he'd been?

It was a long time before he allowed himself to *feel* again, and then it was with the hesitant caution of a man who thinks he might be badly hurt, who fears the pain will come with his next wrong movement.

He suspected, though, that the parting Naga had left some changes intact. He retained a clarity of thought he'd not possessed before, a clarity undimmed even by the crushing exhaustion that pinned him now to the artificial mountain ledge.

The Naga was gone, withdrawn into its underground lairs. Dev felt a sadness, a loneliness unlike anything he'd known before, worse even than the day he'd lost his father.

Or possibly it was his father he was missing now; he'd never been able to mourn him, not really. Tears ran down Dev's face, mingling with the rainwater there. Tears of sadness for his father, and his mother too. Tears of happiness, too, for Katya . . . for he thought he could feel her approach.

Katya and Hagan arrived with a flitter moments later. "Dev!" She cried, vaulting from the vehicle and racing to his side. "Dev! You're alive!"

Vic helped him stand. "Thank God, Dev! I thought . . ."

Katya threw herself on him, hugging him close.

He clung to her, losing himself to her reassuring warmth. Somehow, he managed a ghost of a smile. The tears continued to flow. "I'm . . . human," he said.

# Epilogue

Tharby padded on bare feet across the richly carpeted floor, bearing a tray as he'd been trained. As he approached the Master's artroom, the door dissolved and Sonya walked out.

As was the rule in the Master's house, the *ningyo* was nude, while he wore only a white *fundoshi* wrapped about his loins. They were forbidden to speak to one another, but they made brief eye contact, and she gave him a curt nod.

These past few days, it had been necessary to be extremely careful around the Master. He spoke little, but from what the household servants had been able to piece together, the Empire had lost a battle, possibly a very important battle, at a far-off place called Herakles.

Tharby didn't know the significance of that battle, but he did know that if the Imperials were unhappy about it, then it was good.

Captured on New America, he, Yodi, and Sonya had been loaded aboard a transport and shipped to Earth, to Singapore Synchorbital where the ponderously fat man they knew as Master had ordered them interrogated, then retrained for his personal servant staff. The interrogation had been brutal and painful, but soon ended. Service to the Master was brutal and painful as well, and showed no sign of ever ending. Sometimes, Tharby nearly despaired.

Silently, he entered the artroom, which Sonya had just told him was clear. He paused a moment inside as the door rematerialized at his back. Inside, there was a tatami mat, a rack of swords, and the desperate, silent agony of the *inochi-zo*.

Tharby felt a powerful kinship with the twisted artform; they both were genies, though the living statue possessed far less of the human genome than did Tharby. Swiftly, he set the tray down, then approached the statue. Its pain-racked eyes followed him, pleading.

"I told you I would come," he told it. Reaching into his loincloth, he extracted a small bottle, unsealed the stopper, and poured the liquid contents into the soil from which the *inochi-zo* grew. The dark, human eyes blinked twice, then closed.

"Peace, little brother," Tharby told it. With luck, the Master would assume it had died of some unknown illness.

Someday, somehow, perhaps Tharby and the other servants could arrange the Master's death as well.

"The day is coming, little brother," he told the dying statue. "You will be avenged."

The genie turned, picked up the tray, and walked proudly from the room.

# AVONOVA PRESENTS
## AWARD-WINNING NOVELS
## FROM MASTERS OF SCIENCE FICTION

WULFSYARN
by Phillip Mann                     71717-4/ $4.99 US

MIRROR TO THE SKY
by Mark S. Geston                   71703-4/ $4.99 US/ $5.99 Can

THE DESTINY MAKERS
by George Turner                    71887-1/ $4.99 US/ $5.99 Can

A DEEPER SEA
by Alexander Jablokov               71709-3/ $4.99 US/ $5.99 Can

BEGGARS IN SPAIN
by Nancy Kress                      71877-4/ $4.99 US/ $5.99 Can

FLYING TO VALHALLA
by Charles Pellegrino               71881-2/ $4.99 US/ $5.99 Can

Buy these books at your local bookstore or use this coupon for ordering:

........................................................................................................................

Mail to: Avon Books, Dept BP, Box 767, Rte 2, Dresden, TN 38225                    C
Please send me the book(s) I have checked above.
❑ My check or money order— no cash or CODs please— for $_____is enclosed
(please add $1.50 to cover postage and handling for each book ordered— Canadian residents
add 7% GST).
❑ Charge my VISA/MC Acct#_____Exp Date_____
Minimum credit card order is two books or $6.00 (please add postage and handling charge of
$1.50 per book — Canadian residents add 7% GST).  For faster service, call
1-800-762-0779.  Residents of Tennessee, please call 1-800-633-1607.  Prices and numbers
are subject to change without notice.  Please allow six to eight weeks for delivery.

Name_____
Address_____
City_____State/Zip_____
Telephone No._____                          ASF 0494

# THE FANTASTIC ROBOT SERIES

## ISAAC ASIMOV'S

ROBOTS IN TIME

## by Hugo and Nebula Award
## Nominee
## William F. Wu

### PREDATOR
76510-1/ $4.99 US/ $5.99 Can

### MARAUDER
76511-X/ $4.99 US/ $5.99 Can

### WARRIOR
76512-8/ $4.99 US/ $5.99 Can

### DICTATOR
76514-4/ $4.99 US/ $5.99 Can

*Coming Soon*

### EMPEROR
76515-1/ $4.99 US/ $5.99 Can

Buy these books at your local bookstore or use this coupon for ordering:

Mail to: Avon Books, Dept BP, Box 767, Rte 2, Dresden, TN 38225          C
Please send me the book(s) I have checked above.
❑ My check or money order— no cash or CODs please— for $_____is enclosed
(please add $1.50 to cover postage and handling for each book ordered— Canadian residents
add 7% GST).
❑ Charge my VISA/MC Acct#_____Exp Date_____
Minimum credit card order is two books or $6.00 (please add postage and handling charge of
$1.50 per book — Canadian residents add 7% GST).  For faster service, call

Name_____
Address_____
City_____State/Zip_____
Telephone No._____          IAR 0694

# THE MAGICAL *XANTH* SERIES!

# PIERS ANTHONY

## QUESTION QUEST
75948-9/ $4.99 US/ $5.99 Can

## ISLE OF VIEW
75947-0/ $4.99 US/ $5.99 Can

## VALE OF THE VOLE
75287-5/ $4.95 US/ $5.95 Can

## HEAVEN CENT
75288-3/ $4.99 US/ $5.99 Can

## MAN FROM MUNDANIA
75289-1/ $4.95 US/ $5.95 Can

## THE COLOR OF HER PANTIES
75949-7/ $4.99 US/ $5.99 Can

Buy these books at your local bookstore or use this coupon for ordering:

Mail to: Avon Books, Dept BP, Box 767, Rte 2, Dresden, TN 38225          C
Please send me the book(s) I have checked above.
❑ My check or money order— no cash or CODs please— for $_____is enclosed
(please add $1.50 to cover postage and handling for each book ordered— Canadian residents
add 7% GST).
❑ Charge my VISA/MC Acct#_____Exp Date_____
Minimum credit card order is two books or $6.00 (please add postage and handling charge of
$1.50 per book — Canadian residents add 7% GST). For faster service, call
1-800-762-0779. Residents of Tennessee, please call 1-800-633-1607. Prices and numbers
are subject to change without notice. Please allow six to eight weeks for delivery.

Name_____
Address_____
City_____State/Zip_____
Telephone No._____          XAN 0593

## RETURN TO AMBER...
### THE ONE *REAL* WORLD, OF WHICH ALL OTHERS, INCLUDING EARTH, ARE BUT SHADOWS

## *The Classic Amber Series*

**NINE PRINCES IN AMBER**   01430-0/$3.99 US/$4.99 Can

**THE GUNS OF AVALON**   00083-0/$3.99 US/$4.99 Can

**SIGN OF THE UNICORN**   00031-9/$3.99 US/$4.99 Can

**THE HAND OF OBERON**   01664-8/$3.99 US/$4.99 Can

**THE COURTS OF CHAOS**   47175-2/$4.99 US/$5.99 Can

**BLOOD OF AMBER**   89636-2/$4.99 US/$5.99 Can

**TRUMPS OF DOOM**   89635-4/$4.99 US/$5.99 Can

**SIGN OF CHAOS**   89637-0/$4.99 US/$5.99 Can

**KNIGHT OF SHADOWS**   75501-7/$4.99 US/$5.99 Can

**PRINCE OF CHAOS**   75502-5/$4.99 US/$5.99 Can

Buy these books at your local bookstore or use this coupon for ordering:

Mail to: Avon Books, Dept BP, Box 767, Rte 2, Dresden, TN 38225          C
Please send me the book(s) I have checked above.
❑ My check or money order— no cash or CODs please— for $_____is enclosed
(please add $1.50 to cover postage and handling for each book ordered— Canadian residents
add 7% GST).
❑ Charge my VISA/MC Acct#_____Exp Date_____
Minimum credit card order is two books or $6.00 (please add postage and handling charge of
$1.50 per book — Canadian residents add 7% GST).  For faster service, call
1-800-762-0779.  Residents of Tennessee, please call 1-800-633-1607.  Prices and numbers
are subject to change without notice.  Please allow six to eight weeks for delivery.

Name_____
Address_____
City_____State/Zip_____
Telephone No._____          AMB 0694

THE CONTINUATION
OF THE FABULOUS
INCARNATIONS OF IMMORTALITY
SERIES

# PIERS ANTHONY

# FOR LOVE OF EVIL
75285-9/ $4.95 US/ $5.95 Can

# AND ETERNITY
75286-7/ $4.99 US/ $5.99 Can

Buy these books at your local bookstore or use this coupon for ordering:

Mail to: Avon Books, Dept BP, Box 767, Rte 2, Dresden, TN 38225          C
Please send me the book(s) I have checked above.
❏ My check or money order— no cash or CODs please— for $_____is enclosed
(please add $1.50 to cover postage and handling for each book ordered— Canadian residents
add 7% GST).
❏ Charge my VISA/MC Acct#_____Exp Date_____
Minimum credit card order is two books or $6.00 (please add postage and handling charge of
$1.50 per book — Canadian residents add 7% GST).   For faster service, call
1-800-762-0779.  Residents of Tennessee, please call 1-800-633-1607.  Prices and numbers
are subject to change without notice.  Please allow six to eight weeks for delivery.

Name_____
Address_____
City_____State/Zip_____
Telephone No._____                              IMM 0593

# THE GRANDEUR AND THE GLORY—
## THE LEGEND OF ROBIN HOOD CONTINUES...
### by PARKE GODWIN

### SHERWOOD
70995-3/ $5.50 US/ $6.50 Can
In a dark time, the cry for a champion resounds
throughout the land. The call is answered with
sword and bow by Edward Aelredson, the
courageous man called "Robin Hood."

### ROBIN AND THE KING
70996-1/ $5.50 US/ $6.50 Can
Once again grave injustice forces Edward
Aelredson to abandon his peaceful life to fight
for his people's freedom.

*And Don't Miss
Parke Godwin's
Other Exciting Fantasy*

### FIRELORD
77551-4/ $5.50 US/ $6.50 Can

Buy these books at your local bookstore or use this coupon for ordering:

Mail to: Avon Books, Dept BP, Box 767, Rte 2, Dresden, TN 38225                    C
Please send me the book(s) I have checked above.
❑ My check or money order— no cash or CODs please— for $_____is enclosed
(please add $1.50 to cover postage and handling for each book ordered— Canadian residents
add 7% GST).
❑ Charge my VISA/MC Acct#_____Exp Date_____
Minimum credit card order is two books or $6.00 (please add postage and handling charge of
$1.50 per book — Canadian residents add 7% GST).  For faster service, call
1-800-762-0779.  Residents of Tennessee, please call 1-800-633-1607.  Prices and numbers
are subject to change without notice.  Please allow six to eight weeks for delivery.

Name_____
Address_____
City_____State/Zip_____
Telephone No._____                         PG 0794